The Broken Hearts Club

Ethan Black

HEADLINE
FEATURE

First published in 1999
by HEADLINE BOOK PUBLISHING

First published in paperback in 1999
by HEADLINE BOOK PUBLISHING

A HEADLINE FEATURE paperback

10 9 8 7 6 5 4 3 2 1

ISBN 0 7472 6118 0

Typeset by Avon Dataset Ltd, Bidford-on-Avon, Warks

Printed and bound in Great Britain by
Mackays of Chatham plc, Chatham, Kent

HEADLINE BOOK PUBLISHING
A division of Hodder Headline PLC
338 Euston Road
London NW1 3BH

www.headline.co.uk
www.hodderheadline.com

For Esther,
who hates compliments.
Too bad.
A guy couldn't have a better agent.

A very special thanks to Kim Addonizio, for advice and use of lines from her superb poem 'Full Moon,' and to Ted Conover, Jeff Cooper, Phil Gerard, Bruce Weber, Ariel Reiss, Ken and Ann Smith, Steve Rabinowitz, Dan Katz, Ira Rosen and Phyllis McGrady, for recommending excellent source material, and most of all, to Wendy Roth.

ONE

'Grief? I'll tell you about grief,' says the man in the dark suit. 'And pain so bad you think you will die from it, so horrible you didn't imagine it could exist. Pain that hurts without visible wound. But it lashes you to a bed, it won't let you move, it reduces your imagination to an endless series of replaying images. You've all experienced it, or you wouldn't come here to tell your stories every week.'

The other three men acknowledge the truth of it by nodding, silently. They're at a small round table, in the private room, in the back of Mackey's Steak & Ale Tavern on Twelfth Avenue and Forty-fourth Street in New York. The plaster is peeling and the room smells of beer. There's a plank floor, and a draft from the tar-papered window. There's a pus-green glass fixture over the 40-watt bulb on the ceiling. Steam hisses in a pipe, somewhere behind the merry British coachmen driving horses, decorating watermarked wallpaper on the wall.

'It's the supreme grief inflicted by one sex upon another. It's the grief of a broken heart.'

'Amen to that, brother.'

'We should be grateful that our doctor got us together, chose us for this club. Men aren't supposed to feel like us, but we do. They're supposed to get over unhappy love affairs, but we can't. Maybe we're more sensitive than other people. Maybe there's something wrong with us. All I know is, after all this time, I wake in my bed, and the living room looks a thousand miles away. I can barely make my own breakfast, and I can't eat it if I do. I tell myself to go to work, but close my eyes instead, wanting the pain to stop. Wanting to be asleep.

'When I leave my apartment, every sensation I experience – sight, aroma, taste – reminds me of her. And when I make it back home at night, if I sleep at all, I have dreams. I can't stop.'

The man in the dark suit, a banker during the day, sips beer while the others nod in sympathy, in the brotherhood of pain. There are four steak dinners on the table, thick porterhouses with mashed potatoes, and long serrated knives on linen napkins. The meat is rare, and blood runs onto the china plates. The foam on the beer steins has shrunk to patches. There is a fifth seat for a member who has not shown up. The room is old and smells of mold and hundred-year-old wood. Of mice in the walls. Of sewage under the floor planks. The table is gouged with names of people who have eaten here before. Tiny Richie. Eddie the Squeeze. Edna loves Brian. Edna fucked Sam.

'I have horrible dreams,' whispers the Banker. He's looking at his psychologist, Ian Bainbridge, a stooped, gentle-looking man who urges him on, smiling, supporting. The Banker's neighbors and coworkers would never imagine he carries such agony inside. In public he's all smiles. He seems to love children. He invites women to the Hamptons for weekends. He gives away subscription theater tickets to the secretaries at the office, on nights when he has to work late. He owns a beautiful top floor co-op on Gramercy Park.

'What a catch,' the secretaries whisper as he walks down the hall, tall, handsome, patrician, rich.

I want to be like him, think the men.

'In the dream I had last night,' says the Banker, 'I went into her bedroom. We'd broken up weeks before, but I still had the key, and hoped to change her mind. She was asleep, under the covers, and the moonlight came in through lace curtains and fell on her bare shoulder, and she was so beautiful, so small and lovely, that my heart filled up. I went into the bathroom. I had to take a piss in the dream, I was a little nervous because I was afraid she might ask me to go away again. But in the bathroom the toilet began flooding and I saw that a skull was clogging it, rising, with the water, to the top.'

Overcome, the Banker cannot speak. He waves away help and dabs tears off his cheeks with a monogrammed handkerchief, an expensive Venetian brand bought at Barneys.

'If it hurts too much, you can go next week,' says the Psychologist, the one who never tells his stories, who simply listens each week.

'Thank you, but no. I think about her all the time, so I might as well go on. Just give me a second.' The Banker breathes slowly. In. Out. He continues, at length, 'She was a poet. She wrote verses. A banker and a poet is a good mix, I think. It gives balance to the world. I'd spend my days adding figures. She'd spend a week trying to come up with a single right word.'

The Banker smiles, drifting back. He speaks in a stiffer, more formal tone than the others. Perhaps it hides more pain. 'I was worldly, she ethereal. Niana was her name. Niana Embers. I asked her once, in bed, is that your real name, or one you made up?

'And she replied, gentlemen, a little dramatic in character, but it gave her fire, "I am a burning ember. I will burn you."'

The Banker's smile drops away. The skin stretches tight on his skull, showing the shape of it.

'And she did.'

'Start at the beginning. Tell us how you met her,' says the Mechanic, the youngest man present, sitting at his traditional seat, on the Banker's left.

'Yes. Of course. It was a set-up date. Can you believe it? A secretary in the bank, a married older woman, had a niece. . . . She saw me admiring the photo on her desk one day, and the secretary – she'd always liked me – said, "Do you want to meet her? She's single."'

'Well, I hate blind dates,' the Banker says. 'But I was thirty-one and nothing special had happened in my life in a long time. New York can be lonely, as you gentlemen know. You have activity every minute, but it doesn't bring joy. After a while it's mindless. Anesthetized time. You go to a restaurant. A party. I was lonely, and the photo – how can I say it? – seemed special to me. Some extra quality emanated from it. Most photos are only two dimensional, mere approximations of a surface appearance, but I felt, looking at this one, that her eyes, so bright and blue, so incredibly blue . . . and her hair, glossy and black, somehow blacker than regular black . . . I liked her lips . . . I felt as if – and I know this is impossible, but I'm just telling you how I felt – wherever she was in the city at that moment, she could feel me looking at her. I even felt embarrassed, the way you feel when someone catches you staring. And then I found out she was a poet, and I *knew* I really *was* seeing something special in that face. I believe a person can have premonitions about other people. Don't you agree it's possible, every once in a while, to presage some great event?'

The Mechanic says, 'What's "presage" mean?'

'To know that something is going to happen,' the Banker says, 'even though it didn't happen yet.'

'Yeah,' the Mechanic says thoughtfully, chewing. 'Presage. I presaged.'

'Tell us when it's your turn,' says the Psychologist, the guide.

The Banker, agitated, talks faster.

'Of course you presaged. Brains, human brains, doctors don't even know five percent what they're capable of. And I'm telling you I *knew*, looking at that picture, that when I met her it wasn't just going to be one blind date.'

'Fuckin' blind dates,' says the Mechanic.

The Literary Agent pipes in. 'I go on about one a week. You walk into the wine bar, the girl is pretty, you talk about your deals, you ask about her family, you make another date, maybe you have dinner, maybe you climb out a window to escape, like the story the Banker told us a few weeks ago, about the girl doing it to him.'

The Banker is growing irritated at being interrupted. No one dares interrupt him at the office. But he knows interruptions are permitted at the Broken Hearts Club. Anyone can contribute anytime. And the truth is, when the others tell their stories, he interrupts *them*.

'When I walked into the coffee shop, her back was turned, but I knew it was her,' the Banker says. 'She gave off a – well, a feminine emanation. A . . . a rightness. A beauty in the way she held herself. She was very small. Later, I would pick her up and carry her around my apartment. She would sit on the counter, in the kitchen, and she'd be telling me some story about a poem, or a reading she went to, or a fight she had with her mother, and I'd be overcome, gentlemen, with lust. I'd pick her up, by the waist, and she'd lock her legs – she worked out and she had strong legs – around me, and I'd just take her into the bedroom, or kitchen table, or couch on the balcony. She used to wear this silk robe, with orchids on it, a gold silk robe, and if it was open, even a little, and I saw her breasts . . . oh God, I miss her. I can't believe it ended.'

Tears stream down the Banker's face.

'Take your time,' says Dr Ian Bainbridge. He is studying these men, and their inability to recover from love, for a book he is writing. He writes articles on them, gives lectures on them. 'There's no rush. We have the room till eleven. It's only nine-thirty now.'

'We all have plenty of time now,' the Banker says bitterly, through his tears.

'The coffee shop,' the Psychologist says, kindly.

'The coffee shop. She smiled at me when I sat down, and I swear to you, I'd been with other women, lots of them, but that smile, when I saw it, it just went through me, and I felt like I was falling down a hole, a long hole, and more than that, I *wanted* to fall down it.'

The Banker laughs. He's quite good-looking, the Psychologist thinks, when he is not in distress; tallest of the four, with premature gray flecks in his thick blond hair and trimmed beard. He favors British-made, pinstriped suits. He also drinks the most of all of them. 'I told her, in the first second, I love you. We hadn't even had a cup of coffee yet. Believe me, such spontaneity is not my way. It's crazy. But she didn't think so. She put her hand on mine. Her skin was so smooth. And she wore rings, lots of them, on every finger. Silver ones, from those street artists in Greenwich Village,' the Banker says, drifting into memory again, unable to control himself. His eyes are getting wild. 'Later we'd spend Saturdays walking around the Village and I'd buy her jewelry.' He is speeding up again.

'Not expensive stuff. She liked silver. Bracelets or necklaces. Israeli or Egyptian. With bangles. Heavy links with coins on them. When we'd get home, she'd light candles, everywhere, scented candles, vanilla, spruce, cream, around the whole room, like a church of sex, gentlemen, the whole tiny apartment would get hotter, and in the light of those candles she'd undress. She wore thonged underwear, tight between her buttocks. I'd get so crazy. She loved that, how crazy I got. She'd climb onto her big bed like a little girl, and lean over and tuck her knees beneath her, and her ass would be up and she'd look back at me . . . coyly, you know? And she'd . . . do you mind hearing this?'

'That's what we're here for,' says the Literary Agent. 'We can say anything in here. We can think anything in here. Nothing is off-limits. We come here to say the things we can't say to anyone else.'

'Pain has no limits,' Dr Bainbridge says. 'Why should memory? Why should speech?'

'Yeah, no limits,' says the Mechanic. 'Her ass, you were saying . . .'

'We'd fuck all over the apartment,' the Banker says. His face is red now, and although it is winter, and the back room of Mackey's Steak & Ale is drafty, from a tar-papered window, the Banker's face has turned as red as if he has been lying in the sun for hours. A single bead of sweat trickles down the right side of his smooth, patrician forehead, out of his perfect hair, and into the trimmed Van Dyke beard. It drips onto his starched white shirt, beside the Yves Saint Laurent tie. At the New York Athletic Club, men think: I want to look as fit as he does, and as confident.

'She would do great things to my dick, gentlemen. She would sit on it, from the back sometimes, just ease onto me from the rear and ride it and buck and her hair would be flying. Or we'd go to the Hamptons and spread a blanket on the ground, outside, to hell if the neighbors saw us. We fucked in wicker chairs and we fucked on the rug and we never one time finished watching a movie we rented. We used to joke about it. I'd say, "Remember that scene in *The Picture of Dorian Gray*?" And she'd say, "Which one?" And I'd say, "When the girl takes off her halter top. When she reaches and unzips the guy and takes his dick out of his zipper. And leans down and makes him come by rubbing her breasts, both of them, against his dick, and it feels so good."

Which of course never happened in the real movie *Picture of Dorian Gray*.

'But it happened when we rented it. Oh God. I love her. 'I want to kill her.'

The Mechanic cuts into his steak, and the men watch the blood ooze onto the plate and stain the bright serrated restaurant knife. The Mechanic always eats the most, sometimes taking food off the plates of the others. He says, 'Get back to the coffee shop.'

'Right,' says the Banker. 'I told her I loved her and she didn't laugh! She covered my hand with hers. She nodded. She said, "People can know things right away." '

'Did she tell you she loved you too?' asks Dr Bainbridge, clinically, as if taking notes in his head. He is dressed like a farmer, in overalls and a flannel shirt, and is bald on top, with reddish, thinning hair sprouting on both sides of his bald pate. His avuncular look is accentuated by thick wire-rimmed glasses. It took him months to collect patients as extreme as these, to ask into the club.

'Later that night she did. We talked till the coffee shop closed. Two, two-thirty at night. Then we went to the all-night Polish soup kitchen, on Second Avenue, and ate a huge late night dinner. Potato soup and Romanian red wine and bread, black, thick, delicious. I never ate so good a meal. I was famished. And when I was finished, gentlemen, I was not sated. When I pulled out my wallet to pay, my hands were unsteady, and she saw it and entwined hers in mine. I'd heard love could be this immediate, this trouble-free. I'd read books in which love came to a person so fast, so powerfully. But I never dreamed it could happen to me. Love had always been hard for me. I admit it. I held back. And now, finally, it was happening.'

'The beginning's always great,' the Literary Agent says.

'We walked back to her place, a third floor rent-controlled walkup on Ninth Street. Junkies in the doorway. Some guy practicing a trumpet across the alley. I mean, four-thirty in the morning and the idiot's playing a trumpet. She must have had at least five big locks on that steel door. But inside, she'd really fixed it up,' the Banker says with admiration. 'There were ferns and special soaps in the bathroom, and beautiful books, old editions by Frost, and Keats. And antiques, British chests and a Mexican candelabra, really ornate stuff she got at junk shops. She had an eye, let me tell you.

'By that time we'd been talking all night, about everything. Poetry. Food. Her stupid cats that drove her crazy. She had these Siamese sisters. Anything. I . . . I still remember she talked about some book her mother would read to her when she was a kid. Dr Seuss.'

The Banker reaches for his beer, and drains the schooner as a knock comes at the door.

The men hear a waitress's voice, trying for gaiety, imparting only disinterest. 'You okay in there? Want anything else?'

'Everything's dandy!' the Banker replies in his business voice, jaunty, happy, the devil-may-care guy. 'Is that my favorite waitress out there? Is that Carrie?'

'It sure is.'

'You cute thing,' the Banker calls. 'If I wasn't involved with a girlfriend, I'd go for you in a minute!'

'Oh you,' the voice says, trying to be playful, which is better for tips, conveying only that sense of supreme boredom found in New York late at night, among the lonely. The footsteps go away.

The Banker looks around the table.

The effort at being civil has cost him. His voice sinks, grows tight with anguish. 'I don't want you to think it was only sex. The sex was great, unprecedented. God, when I came with her . . . But it was more than sex. It was the way she made my apartment richer, adding flowers, oranges in the bowl, a painting, a different kind of Australian wine. It was the way she took me to readings. It was the quiet stuff, sitting on the beach in East Hampton. Gentlemen, I even liked shopping with her. I was looking at her back rising and falling, in bed, at night. Hearing her breathing. She even snored and I liked it. It was incredible. It lasted three unbelievable months, and it ended horribly.'

'How?' says the Mechanic, finishing his steak. 'And by the way, you ain't gonna eat yours, can I have it?'

'You'll get a heart attack, with all the meat you eat,' the Psychologist observes.

'I don't have a heart anymore,' the Mechanic says. 'Greta broke it. How much more broken can it get?'

Guys aren't supposed to talk like this, the members of the Broken Hearts Club know. Guys are supposed to be stoic. To not cry. All their lives they've heard the slogans, watched the breast-beating. Love 'em and leave 'em. If it's not one girl, it's another. All their lives they've watched tough guys weathering breakups, leaving beautiful wives or girlfriends in movies, to fight wars, to join cattle drives, to train for submarine duty, to live alone in some cave. Real Men leave women without worrying about it. Real men are tough.

To the Broken Hearts Club, the walking wounded, these movie guys are as alien as a Martian. Guys, their fathers and mothers and buddies have told them, get over pain. Move past it.

Dr Bainbridge calls the men, in his articles, the Banker, the Mechanic, the Agent, and the Reluctant Patient, who still has not shown up. He says, 'It's 10:45. Fifteen minutes and we have to leave.'

'I'll finish fast, gentlemen,' the Banker says. 'My affair lasted three incredible months, and then one Sunday we were in East Hampton, at my house. We were listening to a Bach tape. It was morning. We were eating blueberry pancakes, and out of the blue,' the Banker chokes up, 'she says, "I think we have to slow down a little." '

The Mechanic groans.

'And I say, "What do you mean, slow down?" '

'And she says, "Well, I think you're getting a little too carried away about things. I need to go slower. It's this intimacy issue I have, I get nervous if I get close to someone too fast. It's not you, believe me. It's me." '

'I hate women,' the Mechanic says.

'You can't trust them,' the Literary Agent says.

'I go crazy. "Intimacy," I say. "*Intimacy*? What the hell have we been doing for three months if it isn't intimacy? And what do you mean, get close with "someone"? I'm not "someone." I'm me. What are you saying? What did I do? Tell me what I did and I'll stop it, I'll get better, I'll be a better person. Did I do something wrong?" '

The Banker screams out, in the cold little room, ' "What do you mean, go slower?" '

He's breathing hard now. His face is the color of the blood oozing from the half-eaten steak on the Literary Agent's plate. There's a spot of dribble on the left corner of his mouth. He is panicking as much now as he did back then.

'She says I'm overreacting. She says, "Why don't we take a few days off." '

'I'm sorry,' Bainbridge says, in his most supportive tone. He gets up, moves to his right, puts his arms around the Banker.

The Banker starts sobbing. His shoulders heave up and down, wrinkling the gray wool shoulders of his British pinstriped suit.

'I can't stand it. I can't stand it. I can't stand it,' he says.

The others wait for the storm to pass, and the waitress is at the door now, knocking. The Literary Agent yells back, 'Five minutes, okay? Lay off!'

'Oh God, I love her. I want her to die,' the Banker says.

'You don't mean that,' the Literary Agent says.

'I know. I don't. Not really. But sometimes,' the Banker

says, trying not to sob again, 'I can't help thinking about it. I never did anything bad to her. I was perfect for her. I loved her. I would do anything for her. I would kill for her. Niana,' the Banker moans, sinking into his seat.

'Niana.'

The waitress, at the door, calls out, 'Sorry, but the card game starts at eleven-ten!'

'Fuck the card game!' the Literary Agent calls. 'We'll leave you a big tip. Five minutes!'

'You can't stay longer every week!'

'Yeah, yeah, in a minute, okay?'

This time the footsteps are quick and angry, going away. The Literary Agent takes a fifty-dollar bill and leaves it on the table, for a tip. Bainbridge always pays for dinner, and drinks, lots of drinks. The Banker says, 'Didn't you ever think, at all, about killing them? All of them. The ones who did this to us?'

'No.'

'You must have.'

'I dreamt about it once,' the Literary Agent says. 'I woke up feeling terrible.'

'Tell us next week. Now we have to go or they won't let us come back, big tip or not,' says the Mechanic.

The men calm down. The Banker's story has touched all of them. They open the door. They do not speak as they make their way down the cramped, dark aisle of Mackey's Steak & Ale, past the men who turn to look, on stools. They've heard the yelling in back. Past Mackey, who stands behind the bar in a white apron, cleaning beer glasses. Past the young couples who come here after the theater, to eat hamburgers, to sit at the tables with their red and white tablecloths, and hold hands, and tell each other that they're in love, and marvel at their luck to find the one person in the world perfect for them.

'See you next Thursday!' Mackey calls out.

Another group of men, prosperous-looking, young, cigar-smoking dentists, bull their way toward the back room. Mackey takes a cut of the poker game every Thursday. They'll be in there until four.

Outside, it is snowing. Mackey's place lies across the West Side Highway from the Hudson River. The flakes are thick and there's a coating on the ground that makes the men's socks wet. The headlights of sporadic cabs barely penetrate the storm. A stiff wind clears a view momentarily for them, and they can see the black river, and the ghostlike glow from New Jersey across it, and then the curtain closes up again, and there's only the swoosh of tires, and the hiss of wind working its way around buildings, and a drone of an airplane too high up for them to see, taking off for Europe, or coming home.

The Mechanic and the Literary Agent leave quickly. Dr Bainbridge lingers, asks the Banker if he is all right. He seems worse than usual tonight.

'I got put on probation, at work.'

'I'm so sorry.'

'The bank's merging with another company. They're going to have to trim the staff. I'm under a little pressure, that's all. I'll be fine. I'll be fine.'

Bainbridge leaves.

And the Banker starts walking.

I don't want to go home, he thinks. If I go home, I won't sleep. If I go home, I'll turn on the television. I'll think about the way she used to cry out when we made love. Cry out in such happiness that she made me feel like the most powerful man in the world. Cry my name.

Oh God.

I'm not going home.

He decides to give in to a craving he saves for the worst, the absolute worst, nights. He decides to take the subway downtown and look up at her window. He has to be close to her. He won't *do* anything to her, won't contact her, he tells himself. He'll do what he always does. Come up her block quietly. Let his eyes rove up the red façade of her building, where she still lives. He'll hope the light is on in a window, and maybe that he'll see her silhouette. He'll pray, if he does see a silhouette, that it is her, alone, and not with a man.

The Banker walks faster, in the grip of his obsession. He heads east on Forty-fourth Street, through Hell's Kitchen, past the drugged-up prostitutes in doorways, in tight clothes, who call out, 'Hey, want a date?' He used them in the beginning, when Niana left him. He bought them and let them take him to hotel rooms and wash his dick and slip condoms on and call him honey, darling, baby, sweetie. The same words Niana had once said.

But the sex had been hollow, and left him feeling dirty inside. The sex hadn't touched him at all, except for a moment. A brief explosion of release in the genital region. A lessening of pressure in his groin. And a ballooning of the loneliness as he crept away, hating himself, slinking home, slinking to work the next day.

'Hey, honey, want a date?'

The Banker reaches Sixth Avenue, descends into the earth and takes the F train downtown, toward the East Village. His heart is pounding so hard. His mouth is dry. It's the way he used to feel when he was going to meet her. Against all his knowledge that this love affair is over, he is experiencing a horrible, rising hope. That a miracle will happen. That somehow she'll sense his presence on the street and look out, come down, seek him out, *feel* his emanations. That the sense he had of connection, when he first saw her photograph, still exists.

He can't help it. The private pain is starting up again, in his chest, the hollowness, as the train pulls into the Second Avenue station. He gets out. His heart is beating so violently that he has to lean against the dirty tiles of the wall, to calm down.

'You all right, mister?'

'Thank you, yes.'

He can't be seen like this. He has a position to maintain, a standard to uphold. He makes it up to the street. The storm is worse down here, the wind blowing like crazy, from the north, driving thick flakes lengthwise down Second Avenue. Faster than the cars. They drive into his face, stinging him, punishing him. They melt on his cheeks and mix with his tears.

It is impossible, he thinks, that she ever left me. It is inconceivable that something so good went bad so quickly. It has to be a mistake. It can't continue. God doesn't punish for no reason.

And then he thinks, if God's going to punish, I might as well do something to deserve the retribution I've been dealt.

His heart steadies somewhat as he rounds her corner. Even the junkies are inside tonight. The buildings look darker, closer together, and seem to lean in toward each other across the narrow street. The twenty-four-hour bodega is closed. The Korean grocery is open. He hides his head from a man washing flowers, even in a blizzard, and reaches the middle of the block. Only now does he dare let his eyes rise, to move across the buildings, three stories up. Dark window, lighted window, dark window, dark window.

Niana's window is lighted.

She has a sheer curtain.

Behind the curtain a lone silhouette moves.

You have to love me, the Banker thinks. You love me but you're afraid to admit it. You think of me too, don't you? How can something be so good between two people, and just stop? It's against nature. It's not right. You miss me, don't you? You're just too proud to call.

That's when the urge comes, stronger than it's ever been before. He fights it off, but when she moves away from the window, it grows so huge, he doesn't even realize he is moving until he reaches her steps.

I'll just stand here a moment and leave, he tells himself.

A moment later he thinks, I'll just try the door. It will be locked and that will be that. But the junkies have broken the lock again. They steal checks from the mailboxes. The Banker lets himself into the tiled foyer. A wave of nostalgia and pain comes, so acute that he backs against the wall and clutches his chest.

'I'll leave now,' he says out loud, voice tinny and funny in the foyer.

I'll go home this instant, before I do something I regret.

Outside, the storm thickens. All over the city people who have companions turn toward them in beds, hugging, kissing, holding each other while the wind hisses outside. All over the city the lonely feel more lonely. The storm is as violent as a broken heart.

The Banker turns to leave, and as he does, remembers, with a vivid flash of pain, what happened at the office this afternoon. He sees himself sitting at his desk, by his window. He sees the skyline of Manhattan, the mighty buildings tall against the gray of an incoming storm. He hears someone clearing his throat, in his mind, and watches the senior vice president walk toward his desk, the man's usual friendliness blunted and awkward. The Banker remembers the mundane chitchat because the vice president was too embarrassed to get right to the point.

You seem distracted. Your work's not as splendid as usual. You spent so much time analyzing the Blake Company Loan application that we lost it. I know you'll snap out of it, but I have to tell you, we've been ordered to trim some staff.

Buck up. I know you'll get back to normal before we start, er, dismissing people.

The Banker's vision clears and once again he is in the cramped little foyer. He sees his gloved index finger resting lightly against a bell. He hasn't pressed it. It's amusing to think how little pressure, at this point, would resume contact.

I won't ring it, he thinks.

He rings the bell.

TWO

Niana Embers, failed poet, failed romantic, a woman of passion, whose primary passion is fear, paces in her studio apartment at one A.M., regretting lost opportunities. She is forty years old now, a little chubbier in the face and hips, a little slower when she walks, a touch of gray in the curly black hair, but she knows she still has the power to draw men. She sees lust in their glances when she walks in the street. She's unsure whether it's her independence or the way they seem to know how much she loves sex, or the sense of her ultimate indifference that attracts them. But she's one of those women who will turn heads when she is sixty. She's one of those women who men will remember when they're old, rocking on porches, smiling as they look into the past.

Outside, the storm rattles her windows and drives thick flakes into the pane. The apartment is overheated, the walls stained from water that often drips down from the bathroom above. There's a typewriter on the folding table she uses as a writing desk. An onionskin sheet is in the typewriter. She is writing a poem.

Desire is a cold drink, that scalds the heart, she has written.

She could, if she wished, look around this room and remember all the lovers. The gym owner from around the corner, a friend now, who lets her use the StairMaster for free. The two Italian brothers, Tim and Frank, and the afternoons they used to enjoy here. The NYU professor. The Covington and Burling lawyer. The vice president of First Boston. The novelist. The unemployed butcher. The policeman who used to ring the bell when his shift was over, at five A.M.

The married ones. The ones who liked triangles. The ones who disappeared for weeks. The ones who told her they loved her as they went out the door.

And the Banker.

On the typewriter, she has written, *Somewhere women are standing at their windows like lit candles*.

Niana Embers is filled with sadness, filled with regret. She's unsure exactly when the sex became repetitive. Unsure of exactly when she realized she'd been running from people all these years, telling herself she was looking for something better, someone stronger, smarter, handsomer, wittier.

As the buzzer rings, startling her, she is thinking that she still loves her body, loves caring for it, working out, refusing liquor, paying a doctor to remove the broken veins surfacing in her legs. She's still proud of the washboard body, of the beautiful ass, of the way she can twist, in bed, and reach, and make a man happy.

But it's not enough anymore.

She makes no move to answer the buzzer.

After all, the outside door to the building is broken. Junkies wander in there all the time.

Niana Embers feels a tear forming. It's funny how you can block out thoughts of someone, and years go by, and suddenly the person is back in your brain. She laughs out loud at it. The Banker. The solemn, quiet, devoted banker. Of all the men in her life, she wonders, why come back to him?

The buzzer rings again, insistent.

She's in no mood for this tonight. She stomps to the door

and pushes the Talk button. 'If you don't get out of the hall,' she says, 'I'll call the police.'

She releases the button before hearing whatever the person downstairs has to say.

I'm sick of the junkies, of the neighborhood, of being alone at night.

Once, she liked to write at one A.M. because she felt the creative juices flowing. Now she works late because it is hard to sleep.

She reads, on the paper, *Moon, take them down.*

No one publishes her poetry. She works as a telephone marketer to raise the little money for rent. She eats cheap. She goes to old movies. She makes dinners with friends. But these days, for the first time, friends are not enough.

The buzzer rings.

'Christ!'

Niana Embers, real name Mary Jackson, flashes to the Banker. The puppylike love that shone in his eyes whenever they were together. The way the man had told her he loved her in the very first second. The way he'd bought her things, listened to every story. The way he'd never done anything, even for an instant, to make her annoyed.

But of course, in those days, love was annoying in itself.

I hurt him.

The buzzer rings.

I got freaked out and shut him out.

The buzzer keeps ringing.

She has a vision of the two of them, in an East Village cinema, at a film she'd taken him to. Three weeks into the affair, and he'd woken up sexually. He'd liked to put his hand between her legs as they watched the movie, some boring angst-ridden German film. Sad-eyed people smoking and complaining. Everything changes but the avant-garde.

He'd had smooth hands; that, she liked. He'd loved to run them all over her body, along her waist, down her bare arms, down her legs. He could do it for hours. He liked to suck at her, to use his tongue on her, and his finger at the same time.

He was a good lover. Not as good as some, but very good.

I'm getting wet. I'm dripping. I can't believe this.

The buzzer is screaming.

'Okay, asshole,' she says, jerking to her feet, storming to the intercom.

'Listen, I'm calling the cops in three – '

'Wait, wait,' the voice is saying. The voice says a name, the *Banker*'s name.

Niana Embers is stunned.

She says, disbelieving, 'You?'

'Yes.'

'Really?'

'It's me.'

'But what are you doing here?'

'I know it's late,' says the old voice, familiar and as incredible as a second chance. 'I was . . . walking by. I saw the light on. I'm sorry I bothered you. I can go.'

'No!' Niana is embarrassed by her own outburst. Coincidences don't happen like this. She suddenly feels fatter, older, silly, excited.

She tells the voice downstairs, 'Come on up.'

Her heart is pounding. She feels dizzy. In thirty seconds or so she will hear his footfalls coming up from the second landing, on the threadbare carpet that the landlord always promises to replace. She'll hear the banister creaking.

She rushes to the kitchen, as if she really has time to clean up, and shoves tonight's dirty dish, with its spaghetti residue, into the steel cabinet. She takes a bottle of Chianti from the cupboard. She puts it back.

She hears him coming now. A light, measured sound, and she remembers how he always walked with a stiff, almost aristocratic gait. She remembers her mother telling her, when she was a girl, in Indiana, 'Honey, everyone has an angel,

22

and the angels check in on you. The angels grant the next wish out of your mouth every now and then, but you never know when it will happen, so never wish for something you don't really want.'

He's outside her door. She feels him there, feels the masculine heat of him, out of the past.

Knock, knock.

'Oh, my God,' she says, opening up. 'It really is you.'

He looks different, older of course, but who doesn't? She doesn't care. He still has a smile to die for, she thinks, remembering the first time she saw it, in a coffee shop, on the night they met. The lovely smile. The voice shy, as if he too is not exactly sure why fate has put him at her door.

'You're not going to believe this, but I was just thinking of you,' she says.

'What were you thinking?' he says, standing there, an apparition.

'Never mind that,' she says, with the old coyness. 'Do you want some tea?'

Tea, she thinks. The most remarkable thing has just happened, and from the normalcy in my voice you'd think it happens every day. Do you want tea? Would you like to sit down? Tell me what you've been doing with yourself! I have Pepperidge Farm mint cookies. Do you still like mint?

As he enters, though, she detects more difference in him. He moves more slowly than he used to, and his shoulders are hunched a bit, as if he carries a weight. He's been hurt, she thinks with concern, thinking it has to be recent. She fusses with him. She brings the tea. They sit on the couch and talk, and it's like the old days. He tells her about the bank, and she tells him about the frustration of poetry. They talk about baseball, lasagna recipes, samba music, Superman comic books. After a while she sees with surprise that the clock says three-thirty A.M.

She thinks, I hope he wants to see me again. I hope this isn't just one visit and nothing more.

In the old days, she realizes, she would have reached out and taken his hand now. Squeezed it and caressed it and let him know she wanted him to stay. In the old days they would be in bed by now, heaving and grunting, licking, and whispering each other's name.

But she realizes now she wants more than that, even if it's just a dinner, or another talk, or an opportunity to maintain an illusion. She wants a chance at a future now more than a piece of a night. She doesn't trust herself to control her old bad habits if she asks him to stay here. She wants to be different, act different, allow herself to go slow and feel vulnerable rather than in control. She wants to forget loneliness, not accentuate it. She tells herself, like a girl, that maybe God will make something good come of tonight.

'I have to go to sleep,' she says, and instantly bites her lip. She didn't mean to sound like she was kicking him out, but she has little experience being vulnerable.

Seeing the pain in his face, she's about to correct herself, when he says, 'Why did you end things? Why did you hurt me like that?'

'Excuse me?'

'I think about you all the time,' he says, leaning toward her on the couch. 'At the bank. At night. I dream about you.'

'Oh, don't exaggerate.'

He doesn't seem to hear. He tells her he's seeing a psychologist, joined a men's group that the nice psychologist started: a club, he says, that meets on Thursdays, tonight in fact, in a bar. He tells her the group explores women like her.

'I thought psychologists weren't supposed to drink and socialize with their patients?' she says. 'And what do you mean, women like me?'

'Women who use men. Women who reject men. Women who hate men and don't appreciate love.'

He bursts out crying.

'Why did you hurt me so much?' he says.

She's starting to get frightened now, wondering if it was such a good idea to let him in. He's not the same person at all. There's this new anger in him. He's clenching and unclenching his fists, without seeming to realize it.

She thinks, No one stays the same.

Rising, as if this mundane signal would make him go away, she says, trying to soothe him, not wanting to see him anymore, wanting him only to leave her apartment, 'I didn't mean to hurt you. I thought you were a nice man.'

'A nice man?'

'You know what I mean.'

'A *nice* man? I loved you. I still love you. I'll always love you.'

'You better leave.'

But the crying grows worse. He completely loses control of himself. 'I don't understand it,' he says. 'I never did anything bad to you. I only loved you. Why did you make me go away?'

'Please,' she says.

'Please what?'

'Please stop.'

'But I love you,' he says, as if that will make everything better, make the world whole again, restore safety to the apartment, bring logic into their hearts.

An odd, glazed look has come into his eyes.

She says, 'Look, we can talk about this tomorrow if you want. We can meet at a coffee shop.'

'You don't mean that.'

'I do.'

'You just want me to go away again.'

'I don't really,' she says, gauging the distance to the phone, knowing she'd never make it. Thinking about the knives in the kitchen. The kitchen is closer than the phone, and she wouldn't waste time punching in 911.

'Really?' he says. 'You'll meet me tomorrow? You're not lying to me again? Really, we'll talk about it?'

'Of course,' she says, putting all her social skill, all her urban ability to lie, all her hope that she can trick him out of here, into her voice.

But it doesn't work. He sees through it. His face changes instantly into a mask of rage she has never seen on him before. On anyone before. It's like another person is coming out of him, a brutal person that doesn't even look like him. The transformation is instant. The mouth is twisted. The eyes have grown small. Sweat pours down his face.

She's up and running, for the kitchen. She hears his footsteps behind her as she reaches the counter and grabs for the wooden rack of knives. She half pulls a knife from its slot when she feels herself yanked backward.

She thinks, This isn't happening.

She thinks, My mother always told me not to let men into my apartment.

She feels his hand, that smooth hand that once caressed her, and made her feel like a woman, the hand that probed inside her, the fingers that touched and excited her, oddly familiar, close tightly over her mouth.

THREE

Voort opens his eyes and he's lying a foot from Camilla. Her shoulder rises and falls softly, above the Vermont-made quilt, and the winter light is gray and soothing in the room. He hears a plow scraping by outside. They're in the third-floor bedroom of Voort's Thirteenth Street town house, in his hundred-year-old feather bed. A four-million-dollar building belonging, according to the *Daily News*, to the richest cop in New York.

He's only known her four months, but he's deeply in love with Camilla. In fact, until he met her, he never truly understood the words 'in love.' At twenty-nine, Voort's a fine-looking man, tall, lean with wide shoulders, and eyes of Mediterranean blue. His ash-blond hair would be unruly if he did not keep it cut close to his face, although it twists over his shoulders in back. His round Dutch features give him, depending on his mood, a natural appearance of benevolence or intensity, both helpful in his work. He's had plenty of girlfriends, and liked them all. But never one who made him feel the way he feels now.

Until Camilla, he'd never known a woman he could watch, sleeping, and just the sight of her would make him happy. He never knew one he'd carry, in his head, when he walked into St Patrick's sometimes. 'God,' he'd say, praying, in wonder at the feeling in him, 'let me be good enough to make her truly happy. Make me be able to please her as much as she pleases me.'

Now Camilla rolls in sleep, in mild agitation. She talks in her sleep and growls, drifting out of REM, 'Asshole, get Turner on the line.'

Voort smiles. Camilla's a line producer at NBC, and she has the foul mouth for it. 'So you're the rich fuckin' cop,' she'd told him when they'd met at a Hudson River Project environmental fund-raiser six months ago. She'd had a dancer boyfriend on her arm at the time. Two months later, Voort had showed up at the boathouse, in Tribeca, where she raced kayaks, after his shift one night. He'd been thinking of her the whole time.

A week after that, she dropped the dancer.

Voort rises, careful not to wake her, and pads barefoot, on thick pile, down two flights to the kitchen. It's a Dutch kitchen, with wood plank floors and a gigantic oven and freezer. Peter Stuyvesant ate at this table. You could live in this house and have food to eat for a month without going out. Through the barred bay window he sees the snow tapering off, and white drifts half bury parked cars outside. Alternate side of the street parking would be suspended today. Schools would be out. Criminals would stay in. A nice slow day for the NYPD, he figures, turning on the coffee machine and NBC.

'In the news this morning, the entire town of Larkin, Oklahoma, was destroyed by tornadoes last night.'

Voort eyes the scenes of destruction and makes a note to find a charity, to send money. His wealth comes from inheritance. He lives day to day, on his detective's salary and excellent investments, but the two-hundred-year-old house and land it was built on were bequeathed from the Continental Congress to Voort's ancestor, Admiral Conrad

Voort, who blocked a British landing in Cape May in the Revolutionary War. The original land grant hangs, framed in the living room, on the brick wall near a fireplace designed to warm the whole massive downstairs.

Voort knew the words by heart by the time he was ten.

'For actions beyond the call of duty, and in lieu of payment, Admiral Voort and his descendants are hereby awarded, in perpetuity, lot 28 on the island of Manhattan, in the City of New York. The land or structure will never be taxed, by federal, state, or city authorities. Home and land may be handed from generation to generation. This edict will remain in effect until the last Voort dies, or sells the property, at which time all moneys from such transaction will remain in family hands, not to be subject to any tax levied by any US government authority, federal, state, or local. Thank you, Admiral Voort. Signed and witnessed.'

George Washington's signature is included below, along with that of Thomas Jefferson, Alexander Hamilton, John Adams. According to an auctioneer Voort knows at Christie's, just the piece of paper is worth a couple hundred thousand bucks. And the furniture – the original thick Dutch tables and bed, the Federalist living and dining room set, the Hudson River School oils in the bedroom – the man said, salivating, would go for six times that.

Voort hears the shower running upstairs. He and Camilla were at the downtown boathouse till two A.M. last night, by the West Side Highway, working on insulating the walls, winterizing the place. Camilla keeps her kayak there and works as a volunteer, taking water samples on the Hudson River Clean Water Project on summer nights.

He puts two steaming mugs and a ceramic coffeepot filled to the brim on a tray, and adds a china plate of mixed chocolate and plain biscottis. On his way upstairs he passes, on the wall, oil portraits of two hundred years of Voorts. The admiral's son, Pelham, is shown in his Police Commissioner of New

York uniform, in 1799, starting a two-century tradition of police service in the family.

Voort has read the old family albums since he was a boy. He knows his ancestors arrested the famed O'Brien band of Hudson River pirates in 1801, as they docked with loot stolen from John Astor's private yacht. He knows they hunted down killers in the conscription riots during the Civil War. He's read the newspaper headlines, in family albums, when a Voort helped Police Commissioner Teddy Roosevelt catch the Butcher Killer of Manhattan. He'd watched, as a child, while his uncle Felix Voort testified before Congress, on union busting, during a trial that sent half the teamsters' leadership to the pen.

'Well, look at this. It's the modern man. He cooks. He brings coffee. He brings sweets,' Camilla says, exiting the bathroom. She's got a blow dryer in one hand and a cellular phone in the other. She's already been talking to the office, he sees.

'You're not going to believe this. We want to do an hour on the tornado town, Larkin, Oklahoma, but the people there won't talk to our reporters. They say they're Baptists and they disapprove of the same-sex policy at the network. Jesus H. Christ.'

'What will you do?'

'I told the office to send down Harry Pierrepont. He covers religion, he can talk to those people. The town's totally wrecked. It would be a pretty good hour. Hey, is that chocolate biscotti?'

'It is.'

'That's what I like about your new special sex crimes unit. They teach you guys how to please the opposite sex.'

'It's pretty raw outside,' Voort says, getting hard, envisioning the boathouse last night. Naked, surrounded by space heaters, she'd straddled him in the supply closet.

She says, 'They're sending the car service. It'll be slow,

but they're operating. That's why we pay them a million bucks a ride.'

Voort bunches pillows on the bed and sips coffee as she falls back, eating and blowing her hair dry. Naked, she is the most beautiful thing he has ever seen. Her hair is long, white-blond and straight, between her shoulder blades and down to the rim of her ass, where her long legs begin. Her arms are long and slender. Her breasts are small and round, and she's tightly muscled everywhere, from long workouts in the gym. She can tighten her vagina during intercourse, sucking at his penis, making him feel as if she is pulling his whole body inside.

Camilla is a climber and biker. She swims five miles, two days a week. In spring and summers, after work, she kayaks the Hudson, twenty, thirty miles a trip on Sundays. Voort, a natural athlete, has taken quickly to the sport. Camilla's a good teacher. She was woman kayak champion at Queens College, where she went to school.

'What's Mr Dick doing?' she says.

'Thinking about you.'

'I noticed.'

'What's Miss Pussy doing?'

'She's wet.'

'And not from the shower, either,' Voort happily says.

'Lie back,' she says, ignoring her cellular phone, which has started to buzz loudly.

When she blows him sometimes, he thinks he'll pass out from pleasure. She's like a narcotic. She has fifty ways of doing it.

She starts by sucking at the very tip, hard, drawing it in and out quickly, almost violently. It makes his penis so hard he thinks it will crack into a hundred pieces. But just when he's about to come, she slows, and smiles up at him, coy, knowing that she's stopping it, knowing, from the rumbling in his balls, that he's on the verge of exploding into her mouth.

31

'Whoa there, Mr Dick.'

She goes back to the tip, then encircles the base of his penis with her thumb and index finger. In tandem, the hand and mouth glide, increasing the delicious pressure, more quickly now, nudging him toward climax, up and down.

His back arches. He spurts and feels as if all the liquid is rushing from his body. He feels as if the blood level in his brain has gone down.

He reaches for her.

She says, 'Not now. Later.'

Camilla rises and, as he watches, sated, begins dressing. No one looking at her quiet, elegant clothing would guess the sex animal who lives inside. Today she wears plain blue silk pants, very expensive, and matching business jacket, white knit sweater, and a single strand of gold that probably cost, easy, more than a month of his pay. Camilla has gone through many admirers. She also earns a big salary, and loves to shop.

But his reverie is interrupted as the bedside phone rings.

'Voort.'

'It's Mickie, Con Man. Sorry to interrupt you and the Valkyrie, but this is going to be bad.'

Voort, amazed, hears his partner heaving.

Mickie has been a detective for ten years. He says, recovering, 'I never seen anything like this.'

Voort writes down the address Mickie gives him, on the lower East Side, and then he joins Camilla, dressing. The producer and the detective. The professional voyeur and the professional participant. Both in a rush, both all business, putting on their tie and jacket and stockings and perfume. Voort takes pleasure from the domesticity of the scene.

'What else you have to do today besides cover the tornadoes?' he asks.

She stiffens. 'Nothing,' she lies.

She speeds up, back to him, pulling on her fur-lined boots.

Voort remembers it is Friday, the day she always acts distant and odd. He wonders what she does every Friday that's such a secret.

He remembers the dancer she'd been with the first night, at the Hudson River fund-raiser. A classic-looking guy, all jawbone and muscle. A Baryshnikov, Broadway kind of guy, the lead from the hit show *Hip Hop Meets Tap*, who'd gotten rave reviews in the *Times* and *New Yorker*, and who'd looked pissed as hell the second Camilla paid any attention to Voort.

He pushes the image away.

But going downstairs together, he has to admit that he senses dark waters inside her. Each week, as they grow more intimate, he knows, so does the moment when the dark thing will come out. She's great with sex, but more closed when it comes to talking. She's a demon in bed, but Voort senses there is something bad in her past.

He drains the last of the coffee and leaves the mug on the table by the front door, for the cleaning woman to clear away. With Camilla, he has the patience of a confident man. Patience, Voort believes, is the ultimate gift of love.

On the stoop outside, as if she senses his thoughts, she turns and gives him a long, hard hug. Her Lincoln Town Car idles in the half-plowed street, sending up exhaust smoke that half obscures the town houses and bare oaks opposite. A Sixth Precinct squad car pulls up behind it. Well well, Voort thinks. His 'n' hers pickup rides today.

One more downtown couple heading off to work.

'Tonight I don't think I'll see you,' she says slowly. 'I have to do something. But tomorrow I want to make dinner. I make a terrific carbonara. I'll do it all myself. Buy the food, get the wine, get dessert. You just keep from eating all day. I'll even clean up after. And I was thinking, next weekend, let's go out to Montauk. I know a hotel there. Efficiency apartments. In the winter, it's cozy.' She grins.

'You can't stay in the same two beds all the time.'

'Okay with me.'

'Voort, you're good to me. Don't think I take you for granted, ever, for a second. You're the best thing that ever happened to me.'

The big, tough TV producer.

Voort thinks, as they part: What are you hiding? Why is there a tear in your eye?

Voort makes it to the bathroom in the dead woman's apartment, kneels down and watches his breakfast come out; pieces of biscotti, almost undigested, and the dark cream color, in his bile, of the coffee. When there's nothing left he keeps heaving, aware of the smell coming from the living room. Mickie was right, he realizes. This murder is the worst I've ever seen.

He wipes his forehead with toilet paper and resists the impulse to wash his face, because that would involve touching the faucets, and the faucets might have the killer's fingerprints on them. The sink might have a small hair in it, or a piece of skin. Maybe the dead woman hurt her attacker and the man tried to clean up in this bathroom. Voort fumbles in his inside jacket pocket, finds a roll of Certs, and puts one in his mouth.

Back in the living room, detectives are dusting, cleaning, checking for fingerprints. The medical examiner kneels by the body, or rather, the biggest remaining chunk of it. The blood is everywhere, on the walls, table, smearing the kitchen cabinets. Whoever killed her dragged her, by her long hair, around the apartment. He stabbed her dozens of times. He tried to hack off pieces of her wrists.

Voort tries to still his heart. Falling in love with Camilla has somehow made him more sensitive, in general, to all situations. He knows he has to calm himself, to make himself more rational, or he may miss some important clue.

But what makes this murder worse, somehow, is the tiny apartment, the sense of care that clearly went into this place, the love so strong that even through the wreckage, he can feel how much this woman had turned a shitty little space into a home.

In New York, where square footage is dear, every once in a while he sees an apartment as lovingly put together as this one was. He sees a nest made by person with a small income, living in a cheap tenement, who year after year, from loneliness, or interior richness, built a life for themselves between four walls.

Voort takes in the fresh flowers, strewn everywhere now. The antique table, hacked and chipped, the Oriental carpet, a beauty, which had muffled the sound of the body being dragged around; Persian, floral, thick, crusted with sticky drying blood. There's the overturned Israeli copper water bottle, a decoration. There are the books, leather poetry volumes, hardbacks and not paperbacks, open like dead birds, some on the floor, some with pages ripped out. There's an old-fashioned record player, and hundreds of records. Always a sign of a music lover who lacks money, who poured love of sound into their plastic disks, and lacked funds to switch to CDs. The address book is fat and filled with names of people, women mostly. The phone bill in the smashed wicker basket shows she makes lots of local calls. This is a woman who has friends.

He's seen death many times, but since meeting Camilla, the tragedy of it seems worse to him. The loss of possibility, of a future. The loss of any chance for earthly love.

'You okay, Con Man?' Mickie says, having given him time to recover from the sight and stench of Niana Embers.

'Shit.'

'What's amazing is, for all the wreckage, the guy – I mean we're talking about someone hugely powerful here – the probable guy left no prints we can find yet. Nada. It's like he went crazy and cleaned up. We got a frontal shoe print in the blood by the foldout couch. Size nine and a half. That's it so far.'

'You talk to the neighbors?'

'Nobody heard anything. Nobody saw anything.'

'Find footprints outside, in the snow?'

'Yeah, only about twelve thousand of them, from the junkies on the block.'

'Who found the body?'

'The super. He's downstairs in his apartment, if you want to talk to him. A basket case.'

'Faking?'

'I don't think so.'

'What's he doing finding the body at five A.M.? Why was he in here at that hour?'

Mickie nods. They're in a corner together. Mickie's a short, powerful man in pleated Italian slacks and an expensive charcoal-colored Calvin Klein blazer. He's a married guy, lives on the Sound, in King's Point, and between him, his semi-famous surgeon wife, and his Chilean money fund investments, they make an income enabling him to indulge in his taste in clothes. The two detectives were teamed up because they are each wealthier than the police commissioner. Half the time fellow cops make fun of them. Half the time they try to borrow funds.

'I thought of that, Con Man,' Mickie says, looking up at the watermarked ceiling. 'But the apartment upstairs has a bad leak, busted toilet, and the water was dripping down all the way to 2C, beneath us. The super figured it was coming from here, not from the apartment above. He knocks. No answer. Ne knocks harder. The people downstairs are screaming at him, so he uses his key.'

'Two-C confirms it?'

'They were behind him in the hall, with their six-year-old. The doctor sedated the kid. Wanna talk to him?'

'Yes. We'll try the block too. Maybe someone saw something, looked out a window and got lucky.'

'The local precinct's doing it.'

'So will we. How about the Korean grocery? They're open all night.'

'I know, Con Man. She was forty years old. No husband. No kids. Never married. Worked as a telephone marketer. Wrote poems, but I gotta tell ya, I saw a couple. They're pretty bad.'

Voort glances across the wrecked studio apartment, past overturned ferns, and flowers, and soil and water and blood on the floor, to the smashed folding table and the typewriter upended, leaning against the emptied floor-to-ceiling bookshelves.

There's a lone sheet of white paper, half ripped, still caught in the rollers. He can see a splash of red on the torn sheet.

Voort is shaken suddenly by fear for Camilla. The city outside seems savage to him, and even though he knows she's at work, behind walls, surrounded by friends, he is scared for her. She's in no danger, he knows, but it occurs to him that something could happen to her. Voort can't stand the thought of it. It makes his heart constrict.

'Hey, Con Man. They found something!'

Mickie is across the room, with a patrolman – a Blue Guy, looking down at the overturned kitchen table. A heavy piece of woodwork, Italian baroque in style, a real solid antique.

'Look at this. It's fresh.'

Voort hadn't even realized his partner had left his side and joined the beckoning Blue Guy. It's like Mickie just appeared over there.

In the wood, someone has gouged initials.

'BHC,' Voort says, leaning down. The letters are jagged and as violent as the wreckage around them. The wood beneath them is pure white. There are still slivers of brown wood around the wound marks, because the letters are that fresh.

'The guy's initials?' says Mickie.

'That would be good.'

'BHC. What's BHC?'

'I hope we find out,' Voort says, envisioning a stranger, a man filled with violence, out there in the lessening storm somewhere, trudging through the snow, back to Voort, face hidden, a man carrying a violent secret in his heart.

Voort suddenly wants to call Camilla, hear her voice, her false toughness, her vibrant life force. He is filled with protectiveness for her.

But instead he says, 'I better check the body.'

Voort the professional protector makes his way to the lump of carved, dead flesh in the middle of the room.

FOUR

The Banker looks up now and finds that he has walked all the way to East Ninety-third Street. It's a lovely street of apartment houses and brownstones, dotted with small trees half bent from the weight of wet city snow. It's eight A.M. The plows haven't reached here. The lights are on in homes, and the streetlights blink off. The Banker turns west on the street, shuffling through the drifts on his way from Second Avenue toward Lexington.

He knows this block. He's been on this block many times. Another eighty or ninety feet, through one particularly high bank of snow, and he will reach the front stoop of the Psychologist's house.

A blast of snow hits him, and since he is already off balance, it almost topples him sideways. His pants are soaked and his shoes are worthless. His raincoat is buttoned wrong, and the blowing snow has smeared his usually perfectly knotted tie, and his shirt.

But there's no blood on his face, his hair. He cleaned it away at her apartment.

Oh God, the Banker is thinking. Let me wake up. Make it be that I'm asleep.

Another voice, the barest whisper inside him, says, *She deserved it.*

There's a sudden burst of opera singing from above, as someone opens and closes a living room window. There's the clatter of a cat trapped by snow in a garbage can, meowing and clawing at the aluminum. The Banker kicks over the can and a big, ungrateful calico bolts out, freezes, seeing the snow, and runs back in, trapped by fear on either end.

The Banker can barely see the tops of parked cars as he pushes his way up the steps to the glass double doors of Dr Bainbridge's brownstone. There's a sticker on the right pane that says HOLMES SECURITY. The rust-colored paint is peeling on the arched woodwork above the wolf's head knocker.

The Banker stands there, like the cat in the ash can, unable to move, trying to block out the horrible images.

Then he watches his bare, half-frozen index finger pressing down the tit-shaped buzzer, and the current seems to flow into the house and through his body at the same time, like a harbinger of his future, like the high-pitched vibration of a shuddering electric chair.

He is so caught up in his thoughts, he does not actually see the door open, but then Bainbridge is standing there, blinking through his wire rims.

'What's wrong?'

'I have to see you.'

'I have a patient coming.'

'Now. Please. Please.'

Bainbridge moves aside, and the Banker almost trips mounting the last step into the foyer. It's dark in here, and the house, even when he began coming as a patient, a year ago, was undergoing perpetual repair.

The Banker doesn't know if Dr Bainbridge is married. He doesn't know if he is involved with a woman. He has no idea if there is a feminine presence, right now, somewhere in this house. In fifty weeks of coming here, he has only seen the peeling foyer, the plaster marks by the French mirror, the double folding doors leading to the ground floor consultation room, and the room itself, with its matching leather reclining chairs, its writing desk and oval throw rug, its ugly green brocade curtains, which block even the view of whatever lies behind the house.

'I . . . saw her.'

'Niana?'

'I went there. I saw her. I hurt her.'

Behind the thick lenses of the wire rims, Dr Bainbridge's brown eyes grow wide with panic.

He asks, almost reluctantly, in a low, frightened voice, as if he does not want to cross a border of knowledge, as if he wants time to stop right now, 'What do you mean, "hurt"?'

'Is anyone here?'

'I have a patient coming.'

'*Now*,' the Banker says irritably. 'I mean is someone else in the house now?'

'No.'

The Psychologist seems oddly embarrassed by the admission, by the huge space fitting around only one soul.

'I'm cold,' the Banker says.

'You're soaking.'

'So cold.'

'Come in. Wait here,' Bainbridge says, even, in extreme concern, unwilling to let the Banker see what else lies in the house. 'I'll bring you warm clothes. You're about my size.'

The prober of people's secrets. The fierce guardian of his own.

Ten minutes later they occupy their traditional chairs in the consultation room, as if nothing has happened, as if this is simply one more visit in a long span of time. But they are dressed alike now, which strikes the Banker as funny. Normally he favors severe clothes, power clothes, crisp pin-striped suits and shirts with starched collars, silk ties with orderly patterns, cuff links that show customers that this is a man who takes extra care with himself.

But Dr Bainbridge is more casual, like a farmer, or an old hippie. He's gentler in appearance. He likes baggy jeans, French sweaters, denim jumpers, and sneakers or comfortable desert boots.

The Banker's in denim overalls now, with a mug of steaming chamomile tea on the table, by the ever-present tissue box. In the brief period of Bainbridge's absence, the Banker's sense of self-preservation has strengthened somewhat.

Now he says, almost coy, 'Doctor-patient privilege, right?'

'Excuse me?'

'What I tell you stays with us. You have to protect me.'

'What are you trying to say?'

'If you want to know, you have to swear,' the Banker says, thinking he sounds like an eight-year-old. 'It's between us,' he says, and adds, like a sweetener, like a promise both know will never be honored, 'Later, we can both decide what to do.'

'I promise.'

'I killed her.'

'Oh God,' Bainbridge says, burying his face in his hands, rocking a little. 'Oh no.'

But the Banker feels strangely better having said the words out loud. All night, into the morning, he'd been trying to block the truth of it, wandering, telling himself it didn't happen, feeling the awful power of a secret threatening to blow him apart. Now that he's said it, the pain goes down. It's still present, but it's better. The doctor's shoulders have sagged a bit, and the Banker sees where the weight went.

'I didn't mean to ring her bell, but then I saw myself doing it. I didn't mean to say anything when I heard her voice on the intercom, but then I heard myself answering back.'

'Oh God.'

'I went upstairs. She looked the same. I thought we were getting along fine, but then she asked me to go away again.'

'Maybe she's not dead. Maybe you just hurt her.'

The Banker looks at his doctor, and Bainbridge seems smaller and powerless and far away. Strength seems to be pouring from one man into the other.

'Believe me. She's dead.'

'I'll go to the police with you,' Bainbridge says.

'No.'

'You have to tell them.'

'I don't have to do anything except think about it. Her face, at the end, when she saw I was going to do it, when she understood how she had hurt me for so long . . .'

The Banker just trails off, remembering. He looks down at his hands. They seem the same to him as they did yesterday, but he knows they cannot be the same hands. Perhaps they are someone else's hands. Smooth and uncallused, from working with a pencil. Fingernails manicured. No marks, nothing at all to indicate that the hands had slashed anyone.

'What did you do with the knife?'

'I wiped it. I threw it down a sewer. I cleaned the blood off my skin.'

Bainbridge stands and walks towards his writing desk. There's a *Psychology Journal* on it, with the doctor's name on the cover, and the title of his article, 'Stalkers and Love. Why Certain People Cannot Tolerate Rejection.'

The Banker, alarmed, says, 'What are you doing?'

'Calling the police.'

'No!'

'We'll do it together. We'll find a lawyer. I'll be with you all the way.'

The Banker rises swiftly and closes the space between them, in his stockinged feet. The mug of tea splashes on the green and brown throw rug. At the desk, the Banker grabs the telephone receiver from Bainbridge's trembling hand. He hefts it like a club. The rage is back in him. For an instant he imagines the black receiver crashing down upon the Psychologist's skull. Smashing it like an egg. Would yellow yolk spill out on the desk, on the medical reports, on the air ticket for the doctor's Bahamas conference coming up?

A voice, electronic, disembodied, comes from the receiver.

'If you'd like to make a call, please hang up and try again. If you need help, hang up and dial your operator.'

The Banker replaces the phone in its cradle.

'You made me do it,' he says.

'This is crazy.'

'You started it,' the Banker says, realizing the truth of it, getting stronger by sharing responsibility, at least in his mind. 'The club. The Broken Hearts Club. What will happen to you if people find out you set it up? You got us drunk.'

Bainbridge says nothing.

'You culled us, the three of us, from all your patients. You looked for referrals, men who could not get over their broken hearts. You encouraged us to meet in a bar. You bought the alcohol, lots of it. You pushed us to talk about hate. I get it now! It's why you chose us. You were looking for people on the edge. Twisted people. *Looking* for people to write about. You want us to hurt them. It's what you wanted all along.'

'No!'

'Maybe,' the Banker says shrewdly, 'but what will the police believe? What will your peers believe? What will the papers say? TV reporters. Neighbors, big crowds of neighbors, at your door.'

Bainbridge walks slowly back to his chair. He falls into it.

'You'll be kicked out of the profession, at best. At worst, who knows? Who knows what I'll tell them? That we discussed it. That I talked to you about it. Maybe, yes, maybe even that I planned it with you. Maybe I'll lie to them. You'll go to prison too.'

'This isn't happening,' Bainbridge says.

On the mantel of the disused fireplace, which has been clogged with soot for the whole five years Bainbridge has lived here, the wooden clock chimes a quarter to nine. Fifteen minutes until his first paying patient. Lithographs hang on the walls, only slightly dispelling the tang of disrepair that permeates the whole house. There's a French café scene, merry and out of place, particularly at this moment, during this conversation. There's a trio of surgeons, a hundred years back, peering into the opened-up body of a patient. None of the doctors wear surgical masks. They will infect their own patients. A duo of flappers, hemlines tight, laugh and walk on the West Side promenade, by the Hudson River.

Bainbridge is either a man of varied tastes or is unsure which is most to his liking.

'That's better,' the Banker says, now that the threat has passed, now that Bainbridge is again sitting. 'You wanted me to hurt her.'

'That's not true.'

'You always talk about the hate. You like hearing it. You ought to see your face at those Thursday meetings, when someone gets carried away, one of us says, "I want to kill her." You wait for it. You feed on it. Maybe it's why you set up the club.'

'No.'

'Admit it. Maybe you never thought any of us would really do it. Maybe you never realized the power you had to trigger things in us. Always asking us how we feel, but can you say for sure, a hundred percent sure, you didn't like hearing it? Why spend the money, why take the time otherwise? Can you say, inside yourself, that you don't have a personal interest in the question? That you yourself don't have some kind of fucked-up pain, that you never imagined doing something like that yourself?'

'Imagining is one thing. Doing is another.'

'Can you tell me a hundred percent? That's all I want to know. Honest,' the Banker says, encouraged by what he sees on Bainbridge's face, guessing that he's touched upon some kind of at least partial truth here, feeling stronger after driving the doctor away from calling the police. 'You never, ever considered that one of us might hurt someone?'

Long silence.

'That's what I thought.'

'The funny thing,' the Banker says, 'is that I always thought it would be the Literary Agent to do violence. I mean,' he adds, pacing now, momentarily safe, pontificating, 'he was always the one closest to rage. Remember that time he broke the beer glass? Remember him waving the shards around? Remember he really got crazy, saying how he dreamt about slitting his old girlfriend's throat?'

Bainbridge, looking down, says nothing. He is so shocked that all will seems to have drained from him.

'You're quiet, gentle, and the Mechanic never knows how he feels. I'm usually so,' the Banker laughs, 'controlled. But the Agent, Eric Porter, is always *on the verge*. See what I mean?'

The doctor says nothing.

'And that guy who never shows up is probably the worst of all.'

The Banker pulls a couple of tissues from the box on the little wooden stand beside the patient's chair. He hands them to his doctor. Bainbridge's head is averted, but he dabs sweat off his forehead.

'It *is* why you picked us. I see that now. You collected three potential murderers who have the same problem you do. I can't believe I never saw that before.'

'Stop.'

'I'm going to stay here, with you, for a few days.'

'No,' Bainbridge says, startled, looking up.

'You said no one else lives with you. I don't think I left any clues at her apartment. The bank's closed anyway today, from the storm. I'll watch the TV and papers. In a week or so, if everything is okay, I'll go home again.'

'I won't let you stay here,' Bainbridge says without any

force in his voice. 'We'll call the police. Now.'

'We're bound together, all of us in the club. We've been pushing each other to do something like this, wanting one of us to do it. You know it.'

The clock is ringing nine o'clock. The front doorbell remains silent. Maybe, Bainbridge thinks, the patient will not come. I will call the other patients and tell them office hours are off today because of the storm.

'We can talk about it, work on it together. You can try to get me to turn myself in,' the Banker says, sure that he has won, making it easier for Bainbridge to give in, to fool himself one more time, to convince himself he might have some power in this situation. 'I'm willing to listen to you try to convince me. After all, you're my doctor.'

The Banker holds back a laugh. In an odd, powerful way, he feels free.

The doorbell rings, shrill, abrupt, insistent as only a psychologist's buzzer can be.

'The patient,' Bainbridge says.

'We're decided, then,' the Banker says.

'Only for a few days. And you promise we will talk about going to the police.'

'I promise,' the Banker says, touching the chest of the denim overalls he's wearing. He's never worn a pair of the things in his life.

Bainbridge rises in acquiescence, in dismissal, in a vain attempt to prepare for the next hour, listening to a patient's problems; love problems, work problems, he or she doesn't love me, my mother hated me, I think I'm homosexual, why can't I be happy, Doctor. Make me be happy, happy.

Happy.

The Banker thinks, climbing the stairs in the dark hallway, I feel safe here. I know I'm in control here, at least for the moment. Bainbridge has remained behind, in the consultation room, trying to collect himself and put on his professional mask. The bell rings again. The Banker imagines a man outside, like himself, a man in the grip of memory, or pain; of conditioning. Then the Banker realizes, surprised, that for the last few hours he has not missed Niana. It is the first night he has not felt like that in a very long time.

Upstairs, the house is even more unfinished than the part he's seen already. The hallways are dark and there are exposed wires, and plaster patches on the walls. The master bedroom has a mattress on the floor, half a bottle of wine, a book called *Grief, Violence and Recovery*. There are absolutely no decorations on the wall. A sheet covers the window, and when he pulls that aside, through locked bars, he looks down on a fire escape, a small alley, and a snow-blanketed private garden across that.

The Banker finds himself happy, at least for the moment, prowling in his psychologist's home. I'll have a whole hour to myself up here, he thinks. To open drawers. To look at his pictures. To see who he really is.

The doorbell, ringing, is abruptly cut off.

The Banker creeps back to the hall. He cannot see the person entering, because the stairs curl as they rise, but he hears the sharp staccato click of a woman's heels.

He hears a soft voice, a woman's. He cannot make out her words, though.

He hears Dr Bainbridge say, 'I know. I didn't hear the buzzer at first. I'm sorry, Camilla, come in.'

FIVE

The woman's sobs subside a little, her shoulders stop heaving and she says, through tears, 'Do you want cocoa? A sandwich? Do you want something to eat?'

Voort asks for juice, if she has it, because he sees she needs something to do. It's Saturday, a day and a half after the murder, and he's interviewing Niana Embers's best friend, Rachel Gold, in the twentieth-story condo she occupies with her husband and twin boys, on Central Park West.

He's been concerned all night about Camilla. He hasn't heard from her, and she always checks in, in the evening.

Rachel Gold says, 'Mary was mixed up but had a good heart. Mary always gave the twins presents. If she couldn't afford something, she'd knit a sweater, make a collage.'

Mary Jackson turns out to be Niana's real name. Mary Jackson was the farm girl who came to New York from Indiana.

Voort says, 'You're being helpful, Rachel. Anything you remember is good.'

'I was starting to think she was ready finally, for a relationship. It's not fair when a good person can't find love, don't you think? I told her, when you're ready, it'll happen. You won't be lonely anymore.'

Voort follows her into the kitchen, which gives him an opportunity to see more of the apartment, to study Rachel Gold as a suspect. Her feet are too small, he sees, to fit into a man's size nine and a half. She hasn't enough strength to open a jar of Calamata olives, compared to the power wielded by the murderer.

But of course, he tells himself, even a ten-year-old, at the proper moment, can be prodded, driven, hounded to wield enormous strength.

'Are you sure you won't have a sandwich?'

'Just juice. Cranberry's fine.'

Back in the living room, they cross a blood-red Persian carpet, with a floral motif in blues. 'It's the same kind Niana has,' Rachel says. 'My husband and I gave her one when we came back from Turkey. Excuse me while I check the twins.' She veers to the picture window, gazes down with concern at the white expanse of Central Park. She's worried about her sons. When murders happen, everyone is in danger. She looks helpless, trying to pick out two brown dots, trailing two sleds, in the wavy drifts below.

'I met her when I moved to New York, twelve years ago. We both grew up on farms, both wanted to be famous, to be big in New York.'

Rachel returns to the couch, sips her juice, but needs two hands to steady it, gives up and places the crystal tumbler on a ceramic coaster which rests on a coffee table of heavier glass. It all seems so breakable. 'We met at Tony Roma's, where we both worked as waitresses. We moved in together in a studio near Second Avenue, the apartment where she still lives. Oh God. I mean where she died.'

Rachel bursts out crying again. Voort looks away, honoring her grief, using the opportunity to appraise her in the mirror. She's a pleasant-faced woman, on the heavy side, and right now the friendliness in her features is mottled, ugly purple.

She wears a cream-colored turtleneck sweater, calf-length dress of wool tweed, which Camilla pointed out in a Sunday *Times* ad last week, and expensive high-heeled leather boots currently considered fashionable on Fifty-seventh Street. Her dark hair has strands of gray in it, and is held in a bun by a Tiffany silver clip.

The living room is so big Voort thinks it was once two rooms, or even two studio apartments. Huge Oriental carpets overlay each other at the edges. He faces Rachel across the coffee table on matching wing-backed couches of black leather, expensive models he has in his town-house den. There's ten-foot-high fireplace with a hand-carved mantel of entwined anacondas, bought in the Amazon, on vacation. He sees no books at all, real estate magazines in a wooden rack, and a black Sony TV, large as a small movie screen, occupying three-quarters of the far wall. There are absolutely no traffic noises, which means, twenty stories above Central Park West, that the panes are at the very least triple-strength glass.

Rachel asks, 'Did she suffer?'

'It was quick. Tell me more about when you lived together.' Voort wants her calmer before he gets to current questions. He needs her focused, needs a stranger's memory to do his job. His investigation is limited by her imperfection. His sheepskin coat lies beside him. He's dressed for raw weather in thick Italian cords and Eastern Mountain Raichle hiking boots. A red cashmere scarf drapes his powerful shoulders, a gift from Camilla, as was the double-pocketed, Prussian-blue, Maine-made flannel shirt.

Voort flashes to Camilla again. He's not heard from her since she left the town house yesterday. He's left messages on her machine, and being a phone junkie, she always checks it, and always calls back, even if she's in a rush, within a few hours.

Rachel Gold is saying, 'We were eighteen. We didn't eat a

lot. We didn't need a lot of clothes. We lived cheap. And we didn't have to be scared to have sex.'

'You mean, no AIDS.'

'Wild was normal. We used to double-date. I went for artistic types, writers, singers. Ha! I end up with a real estate mogul. She liked straighter guys. Brokers. Investment bankers. There was something steady in them she needed. She was needy and she didn't know it. You know the old Groucho line? I'd never belong to any club that would have me as a member? Well, if they started to like her, she'd be out the door.'

'Do you know if she had a boyfriend lately?'

Rachel Gold sighs, sits back but does not look comfortable. 'Who would have dreamed, at the age of forty, I'd still be talking about "boyfriends," ' she says. 'She went through them fast, and they always had money, but she didn't date them for money, just the stability the money gave them. In fact afterward, when she dumped them, she'd throw everything they gave her away – jewelry, letters, clothing. She'd make a total break. First go crazy over a guy. Live for the guy. Then, out of the blue, dump the guy. Get mad at him, erase all evidence of him. Toss a thousand-dollar necklace down the trash.

'I could never do it. I used to admire it, her power. Only later, when I grew up a bit, did I realize that she saw love as weakness, not strength.'

Suddenly Voort has the sense that she has switched subjects on him, stopped talking about Niana, started talking about Camilla. A vision of her lovely face comes to him, so powerful that he believes if he turns his head, Camilla will be sitting beside him, on this couch. He smells her. He pushes her away. He must concentrate if he is to find the killer of Niana Embers.

Rachel says, 'After a while it started to bother her, the way she acted. But by then she couldn't stop.'

Voort nods, and repeats, 'Couldn't stop.'

She's back at the window, searching down there for her sons. All this talk puts panic in the heart of a good mother. 'It's sad,' she says, facing away from him, as if the window is the glass of an aquarium, as if the life below is an exhibit. 'On the farm, when I grew up, there was so little to do it drove me crazy. But in New York it's easy to ignore your problems because there's so *much* to do. Always another man. A better man. A richer, handsomer, more talented man. Niana got into a way of acting. A pattern that passed time. Then one day she was older, years were gone, and there was no man, only the sad, sick shell of the idea that there might be something better. Am I making sense? She realized that she'd used her strength against herself. She'd given in to fear. And now I think she was finally ready to – it seems stupid to say it this way – grow up.'

She looks embarrassed. She feels she has talked too much, about things that are, at the moment, irrelevant. Voort finds himself liking her. 'Everything is helpful,' he says, and his kindness brings her back, away from the window, to the couch.

She seems to be aging by the minute. Voort sees the way she will look in five years, when she reaches half a century. The pleasantness will eclipse her femininity. The chubbiness will travel from her arms up her neck, droop her chin. She'll refuse plastic surgery. It will be a point of pride. She'll stay the farm girl, the overweight matronly wife of the real estate mogul, sending the boys off to Middlebury, Williams, Princeton, Yale.

'Mary Jackson,' Rachel says. 'Unhappy women change their names. Unhappy men never buy furniture. God. I sound like a shrink on the *Oprah Winfrey* show.'

He senses she needs to be guided in the conversation. 'Can you think of the names of anyone she had a fight with recently?'

'No.'

'The initials BHC. Do they mean anything to you? BHC?'

'No.'

'Someone who hated her. Someone who sued her. A neighbor. A pissed-off uncle. A kid on the block who would be grown-up now.'

'Sorry,' Rachel says, giving the same answer Voort and Mickie have received from Niana's neighbors, friends, farther back in Fort Wayne, Indiana. From her fellow telephone marketers. From the Korean shopkeeper on her block. From the old boyfriends they've tracked down so far. Everyone is sorry.

'Don't worry,' he says. 'Tell me about the last time you saw her.'

'It was two days ago. I'm a member at MOMA,' she says, 'the Museum of Modern Art. Whenever there's an opening, I take her. I buy lunch. It's my contribution to the arts. She has no money. She's a poet. A person can't help what they're passionate about, can they? A poet spends as much time on verse as a businessman spends on deals. I got lucky,' says Rachel Gold, glancing at a photo on the coffee table. It shows her in a ski outfit, with a handsome white-haired man. 'Michael earns enough money for a family twice this size. So,' she laughs, 'Niana's how I pay the world back. I take her for lunches. I buy her presents when we go on trips.'

'When you saw her two days ago, did she mention any men she was seeing?'

'There was someone who worked in a bank, I think, who she'd dated a couple times. It was petering out.'

'His name?'

She shrugs helplessly. She's starting to feel bad again. She's thinking: What if I forgot something important?

'Which bank?'

'Chase? Apple?' She looks helpless. 'Somewhere in the Village, that's all I remember.'

'Maybe her neighborhood branch. Did she meet the guy where she banks?'

'I . . . I think so. But do I think it because you suggested it, or because she said it? Oh, I want so badly to help.'

Voort wants the same thing, but he must not let impatience show. Soothe her. Make her feel good about herself. The bank, even if Voort can find it, will be closed until Monday. If the banker killed her, he'll be walking around all weekend, unless, of course, he'd already fled New York.

'Try to remember if she mentioned his name.'

'I'm just so sorry. We talked about a thousand things. Damn me,' she says violently. 'Rachel, think.'

'Could the name have started with a B? BHC?'

'I'm useless.'

He gets up and moves around the glass table, sensing her need for human contact. He puts his arm around her. She leans against him and he smells Shalimar perfume. He tells her, 'Believe me, getting a picture of a victim helps in ways you can't imagine. Everything is important. If you don't remember something, maybe it's because it's *not* important, and if it is, well, you'll just remember later. See what I mean?'

'You're kind.'

'I'll tell you what. We'll play a game, if you don't mind. Think back. Close your eyes. You're at the museum with Niana. Remember? What exhibit did you see?'

'Russian poster art from the Russian Revolution.'

'Did you enjoy the exhibit?'

'It was beautiful. The artists were brothers. On their posters, they came up with a new way of advertising films.'

'What way was that?'

'Juxtaposing images, from the films, I mean. They were the first ones to do it.'

'And did you eat lunch before, or after?'

'After,' she says, with an odd childish pride, glad to be led along.

'Good. Keep your eyes closed. You're in the members' dining room. I'm a member myself. It's pretty how the room overlooks the sculpture garden,' Voort says, flashing to a brunch he had with Camilla there, Sunday Jazz Brunch, two weeks ago. He tries to block out a sudden stab of worry for her.

She should have phoned back.

He tells himself he's just off balance because of the murder.

'Okay, you're eating lunch in the dining room now. What are you eating?'

'Tofu salad. Mary ordered some meat dish and a large salad. We split half a bottle of California white wine.'

Voort lets his hope balloon. Maybe she will remember something. 'What are you talking about?'

'What she always talks about. How there are no good single men in New York.' The black eyes open, flicker, even in a time of grief, to Voort's empty left ring finger, and he realizes that she's just checked to see, crazy as it is, if he might be able to date the friend who has died.

She had nothing to do with the murder, he now knows for sure.

Rachel says, 'I used to think like Mary, when I was single, that half the men running around were assholes. Now I think when a person is ready, that's what it takes, and they meet someone who loves them back.'

Rachel sits up higher.

'Clarence! That was his name. She *did* tell me. Clarence!'

Voort doesn't have to ask for the last name. He and Rachel stare at each other. They are both waiting to see if she will remember it, if she ever heard it at all.

Rachel closes her eyes and her mouth forms an O shape. She's trying to remember the way the last name began.

'Ogilvie!' she says triumphantly. 'Clarence Ogilvie. And she said he lives in Chelsea.'

Voort leans back and grins tiredly from the effort. Maybe

he's getting a break, a flash of luck. He gets a phone book in the kitchen. He finds four C. Ogilvies, and under them, in the whole island of Manhattan, only one Clarence. The address is on Sixteenth Street, near the Hudson.

Chelsea.

I better call Mickie, he thinks. On this, both of us should go.

Excited now, working with a lead, he punches in Mickie's sky page. While he waits for the return call, he asks Rachel the question with which he always ends interviews.

'Do you have anything you want to ask me?'

She looks surprised, then pleased, as most people do when presented with the opportunity. When communication is a two-way street, Voort has found, people feel gratified, connected. If they remember something important later, they are sure to call.

She says, 'You're the detective that big article was about in the *Daily News*, aren't you? The rich one.'

'That's me.'

'I read the city sued you to get the tax-exempt status lifted on your town house. They harassed you. They had a private investigator follow you. You sued and got a multi-million-dollar settlement, and then gave $200,000 to Belladona,' she says, naming the brand-new mayor, who, with Voort's help, just beat the old.

'That doesn't sound like a question,' Voort says.

'I have one, though,' Rachel says. 'You were checking me out the whole time you were here. You weren't just writing my words down in that little pad, were you? You were writing too much just to be putting down what I said.'

'If I was so good at it,' Voort grins, 'you wouldn't have noticed.'

'What do you think of me?' Rachel Gold asks.

He's surprised. He doesn't understand the request. She can see that, and she says, 'It will make me feel better. I want to know you're as smart as I hope you are. I want to see how your mind works. I want you to catch whomever did it. You won't offend me. You said I could ask anything. It's the only way I can think of to see how observant you are.'

He considers.

'Okay, but I'm guessing. You're on your second marriage and you're amazed how easy it is. Your husband wants you to hire a maid, but you won't. You do all the cleaning yourself, and the cooking. You moved into his apartment after you got married. He already lived here. And you're vegetarian, by the way, but he's not.'

She's staring at him.

Voort explains, 'All the photos of you two are recent, but the twins are older than the photos, and they look like you, so I'm guessing they're by a first marriage. When we shook hands I felt calluses that come from housework, yet the apartment is worth plenty, and the products in the kitchen are top stuff. So you're not cheap. Your husband clearly indulges you, if he's buying Persian carpet gifts, and in this income bracket that means someone else does the cleaning. He wants to hire a maid. You're the one who says no.

'Finally,' he says, glancing around the living room, 'the furniture's masculine. You didn't pick it out. You're the more prudent one. You're not used to having money. You chose not to change the furniture. It predates you. He lived here before. Oh yes. You made a face when you told me Niana ate "some meat dish." But there's a big turkey in the fridge, so it's for the rest of the family.'

Rachel Gold doesn't speak for a moment, then she looks sad. For months she will look like this when she thinks of Niana. 'I'm glad you're the one helping her,' she says. 'You understand love. You have a strong feminine side, Mr Voort.'

Voort says, shaking his head, 'Feminine?' He thinks about the compliment.

Filled with affection for women, he says, 'Stop taking credit for everything good.'

The Max Bar, where Mickie is supposed to meet Voort, is a trendy Chelsea gathering place attached to an art gallery. The gallery is closed, even on Saturday, because of the storm. The Bar is open, uncommonly empty, and Mickie's not back from Queens when Voort arrives.

It's a long, bright, narrow room with a step-up bar, art nouveau tables, and Japanese architectural drawings on the wall, from a Tokyo architect whose work has skyrocketed in value since he died of AIDS. Voort orders espresso from a pretty Latin bartender, with fingernails as long as lemon peels, and while she bends over the steaming machine, he finds the pay phone and calls Camilla's apartment again.

'Hi there. I'm not here now,' the voice says, shaking him with affection. 'Leave a message. 'Bye.'

When he gets back to his stool, the bartender wants to flirt, and when he mentions his 'girlfriend,' she looks disappointed, drifts back to the sink. There's one couple in a corner, nursing Irish coffees. There's a blast of cold air from the door, but Voort sees it's a woman coming in, not Mickie. The TV over the bar shows Larkin, Oklahoma, ravaged by tornadoes two nights ago.

'These are religious people, here in the heartland,' says the NBC correspondent with typical network superiority for anything between New York and Los Angeles. 'They hold nightly prayer meetings, and ask God for help.'

It's clear from the townspeople milling around the camera that the correspondent has been granted access. Once again, it seems, Camilla figured out a way to get what she wants.

Two cups later Voort feels the cold air from the front again, and this time it's Mickie. He's wearing a half-open blue cashmere coat from Barneys that cost a fortune, and a double-breasted Armani suit. He's got a Moscow-style fur hat on, dusted with cocaine-like snow.

'Always drink on the job. Especially our job,' Mickie says, ordering a manhattan. 'You know, a woman invented this drink,' he says. 'Winston Churchill's mother. A famous drinker. She put a cherry in with hard liquor.'

'It's not a real cherry,' Voort says. 'It's toxic.'

'What isn't these days?' says Mickie, eating it. 'The boyfriend in Flushing had an alibi. He was at a party till four that night, and he has plenty of witnesses. The expressway is crowded, and the subway smells like wool. Got the address? Maybe we'll get lucky.'

Voort throws six bucks on the polished mahogany bar, and the two richest cops in New York walk out onto the narrow street.

The weather's changed again, gone gray and raw, and there's a stiff west wind that brings the smell of brine from the Hudson. The snow on the ground is dirty. The swoosh of tires mixes with the scrape of shovels as doormen in brown uniforms clear walks, avoiding lawsuits against their co-op boards. Car owners dig out Chevys, with picks, spades, garden tools. They're afraid of cracking the windows. The city reeks of destruction. People walking dogs today don't bother to obey the law and clean up the shit staining the snow.

The cold wraps New Yorkers in cocoons of privacy. The cold isolates people padding past a few feet away.

'You seem quiet today, Con Man. Everything okay?'

'Yep.'

'At home?'

'Yep.'

'The Valkyrie?'

'Yep.'

'Lemme know if you wanna talk.'

Clarence Ogilvie's building turns out to be a renovated co-op near Tenth Avenue. The neighborhood's experiencing one of those rapid upswings that property owners pray for all over New York. Ten years ago junkies lived here, then artists, then gay guys. Now it's lawyers and Wall Street people. Soon it will graduate to Kennedys, Japanese, million-aire movie stars who spend three weeks a year in New York. The dogs will become purebreds. The delivery boys will come in cars instead of on bikes.

The lobby is massive, the wallpaper a Max Parrish copy. Nymphs lie by pools of springwater. Fruit trees bow with oranges, unnoticed by the sullen-faced occupants of the building shuffling past. There are mirrored pillars and a black marble floor and a doorman who acts stiff as a Hilton concierge spotting a bum in the lobby. Then he sees their badges and straightens slightly. They learn Ogilvie's apart-ment number and warn the man not to call up.

'So I unloaded the AT&T and moved into a Thai fund,' Mickie says. 'I'm telling you, Con Man. They devalued the currency. Southeast Asia's bottomed out and it's going to boom.'

There's music in the elevator, violas playing Chopin. The walls are burnished copper, so strangers riding with each other have no way of avoiding each other's trapped gaze.

Voort feels hope ticking inside him as they pad down the carpeted corridor of the eighth floor, soothing and gray as a psychiatric hospital. They knock hard, twice, at 8H. Both detectives are thinking, sick from the sight of the body yesterday: Let this be the guy.

No answer.

Then footsteps approach on the other side of the door.

'Police.'

An eye fills the eyehole. Mickie moves to the right, drops his hand in case Clarence Ogilive comes out shooting, or with a knife. Instead the door opens and they're looking into the face of a black man, about thirty-eight, half shaven, in brown horn-rimmed glasses and a gray sweat suit. The man has something in his right hand, between his fingers. Voort sees it is a single die. There's gambling in here.

'Yes?'

They identify themselves. Can they come in? They explain that they want to talk about Niana Embers.

The man frowns.

'Did something happen to her?'

Bingo!

'Do you mind,' Voort says, 'if we sit with you and talk?'

Now he is alert to voices from another part of the apartment, laughter, a television, the pop of a beer or soda can. Clarence Ogilvie looks afraid for an instant, then nods and leads them away from the voices, down a short corridor lined with color photos of women on a beach, and into a paneled den with a BarcaLounger, a matching brown leather couch, and lots of basketball trophies in a glass case.

'I won them at Columbia, before I got fat,' the banker says, trying for a light tone but failing. Then again, Voort asks himself, who gets happy when police show up?

Clarence Ogilvie sits in the BarcaLounger. He does not ask the detectives if they want coffee, or a drink, or food. He's blinking too much behind the glasses. He's rattled. He does not even suggest that they take a seat.

Mickie says, 'When did you see her last?'

'Tuesday. We had dinner. We'd dated a few times, but I told her I didn't think we should get together anymore.'

'You told *her*,' Voort says.

'It wasn't going anywhere. May I ask where you got my name?'

'How did she take it, when you dumped her?' Mickie asks, flipping on his reading glasses, taking out his pad.

Clarence Ogilvie flinches at the word 'dump.' He rubs his brow. He glances at the door, as if afraid whoever else is in the apartment might hear. He says, quietly, but with a deep voice, 'It wasn't serious between us. We just saw each other

62

three or four times. It hurt her a little, her ego, when I told her we should stop, but please, can't you tell me what this is about?'

'What were her exact words,' says Voort, acting kinder. 'Did she cry? Did you argue? Slow down. Tell us word by word.'

The man is growing panicked. 'What happened to her? I want to know!'

Mickie nods, understanding the question, but instead he says, 'Do you mind telling us where you were on Thursday night?'

'Thursday.' The banker breaks out sweating.

'Midnight to four.'

'That was the night of the storm,' Clarence Ogilvie says. His tone is dropping.

'You got it,' Mickie says. Now they're staring at each other, the fear in the room almost physical. An animal.

'Come with me,' Clarence Ogilvie says, and leads them out of the den, down a corridor, into a small living room looking out at a warehouse across the street. The warehouse is so close that the huge banner suspended from it seems only a few feet from Clarence Ogilvie's apartment. SOON TO BE CONDOS. CALL NILES REALTY.

But in the living room, on the rug, Voort sees a man and woman, and two children. The TV's on, showing a huge purple puppet, a man in a puppet costume, dancing and singing, 'All fall down!' The girl's in a pink pajama jumpsuit, with a kitty design on the chest. The boy's in pale blue, with a tiger.

The adults are clearly the parents of these kids, and all four of them look puzzled, between Clarence Ogilvie and the detectives. They've been playing Star Wars Monopoly. The pieces are all over the rug.

Voort realizes that the white die in Clarence's hand came from the Monopoly game.

It's not him, Voort thinks.

And now, as if picking up on the feeling, Clarence's voice gets stronger. He was thrown off balance by the detectives. But now he is not off balance. Now he is a man who has been wronged.

'This is my sister and brother-in-law, from Syracuse. They came in on Thursday night, before Kennedy Airport closed. We haven't left the apartment since Thursday at dinner-time. We've been playing this dumb game nonstop with the kids.'

Clarence Ogilvie comes close, puts his hands on his hips. For the first time, anger replaces fear on the banker's face.

Where the hell is Camilla? Voort thinks.

'You tell me now. What happened to Niana?' Clarence Ogilvie says. 'Or did you just figure the first black man you questioned, you'd accuse.'

SIX

'Anyway,' Voort tells Camilla hours later, 'everyone's coming up blank. No prints. No hairs. No clothing fibers. It's like the killer hired professional cleaners to come in after he was finished, like they removed any evidence having to do with him.'

'Just the BHC initials,' says Camilla, chopping garlic at the sink.

'And for all I know, *she* carved the letters in her own table. God knows why, but how can I be sure?'

The truth is, he doesn't want to be talking about a case now. It seems stupid talking about Niana Embers. It seems stupid to say anything else besides, Camilla, what's wrong?

She was in his kitchen when he got home, cooking with a vengeance, for her so-called 'Saturday night feast.' She'd bought groceries at Balducci's; stuffed peppers, stuffed mushrooms, fresh garlic, tomato, and basil angel-hair pasta, virgin olive oil, Holland tomatoes. There were two bottles of Oregon pinot noir, and hot bread from Frederico's. Smoked mozzarella and Calamata olives. Crisp Romaine lettuce. And some kind of sweet-smelling dessert, in a box, that he was not allowed to open.

'The way to reach a lover's heart is through his stomach,' she says.

The way to break a lover's heart is to stand at a chopping block and show him your back.

'I see you got your coverage of the tornado town,' Voort says.

He's eyeing her tight jeans, the way her ass moves beneath the denim, and her turquoise cashmere sweater, deliciously tight, defines her slim, lovely torso. She's got thick white socks on and no shoes, and her feet have lovely arches.

She says, as he hears a knife chopping steadily, 'We got 'em, but now the network's thinking of canceling the whole show.'

'Why?'

'They're assholes, that's why. We won three Emmys. Two Edward R. Murrows. And they put us up against *Medical Crew* and can't figure out why we lose ratings. They want to move me over to the *Today* show. Fuck the *Today* show. I'm not getting up at three A.M. anymore.'

Voort gets up, sips a little wine she's uncorked, moves close enough to smell the chopped garlic, and gently lays the round of his palm against the roll of her ass.

'Not now. Later,' she says, but softer.

'Now is later,' Voort replies.

'Naughty *boy*,' she says, letting him take the knife from her hand and lead her by the hand into the living room. Always ready, always a minute away from the world of the erotic. His heart is roaring. The button of her jeans slips loose beneath his thumb and forefinger. He can see, as he slides her jeans down, the tiny, orchid print on the thonged underwear beneath, and, as she arches her back to allow him to strip her, the incredibly lovely white twin moons of her unbelievable ass.

She drops back on the couch and extends her legs, one at a time, so he can pull the jeans off. They drop on the carpet. He works the underwear off too, down her long legs.

'Voort,' she says huskily. 'I'm so wet.'

Voort gets down on one knee. He can feel his dick, pumping against his jeans. He envisions the muscle bursting through the fabric. The light's already dim in the living room. She'd set the mood, with a half-dozen candles burning, and the window is uncovered, the view outside splendid, private. He sees the snow-covered branch of a maple tree.

Voort moves her knees apart, disbelieving at the loveliness of her pubic region. Her hair is white-blond, magically small, tightly curly, and he already sees a bead of wetness running down between the crack of her ass, onto his couch.

Her smell comes up, a bouquet of earthiness. Camilla, he thinks, rubbing his face against the skin of her thighs. He presses his teeth against the jutting sharpness of her hipbones, resisting the urge to bite hard, applying just enough pressure, with the tops of his incisors, that he hears her moan, and want more.

'Voort.'

He pushes the sweater up and runs his tongue along the belly muscles, into the suction cup of belly button, down to where hair meets skin, rimming the border of the pubic area. He places his mouth over her pussy, covering all of it. He breathes into her, slowly, so the warm air bathes her inside.

'I'm so wet.'

He sinks his tongue into her, first against the outsides, which increases her moaning. He probes deeper with the harder tip of his tongue, along the walls of her vulva, feeling the heat, feeling, as he moves around, the delight of reaching the little bud.

'Aaaaah.'

He pushes his tongue against the bud, then draws the length of it back and forth, slowly. He tries a rotating movement of his tongue, and is rewarded with more fitful breathing from above. Camilla is pushing back in pleasure, as if to escape him, as if to burrow into the soft pillows against her shoulder blades. As if she is so pleased she does not know which way to move. Into him or away from him.

Voort's chin is soaked with her. He dips down again, with his tongue, and at the same time takes his right index finger, inserts it inside her, and rubs the front of her bud with his tongue. He probes with his finger and finds the second pleasure spot in back.

Camilla gasps. She knows what he is doing, but still says, 'What are you doing to me?'

Now her thighs are trembling against his cheeks, and he alternates pressure, easy with the tongue, harder with the finger. Easy with the finger. Fast with the tongue. He reaches with his other hand, finds her nipple, squeezes.

'Christ, Voort. Oh, Voort,' she says. She repeats it. 'Oh, Voort. Voort.'

She's practically arched off the couch now, heels against the sides of the cushion, shoulders back against the pillows, ass and back defying gravity, in the air.

'I'm going to come,' she whispers as her trembling increases. 'I'm going to do it,' she says, and he readies for the explosion. When she bucks too hard, she could break his nose.

Voort pulls the finger out. She's primed now.

He withdraws his tongue. She's breathing hard. She has not come yet.

As gently as possible, Voort reaches with the very tip of his tongue, makes the barest, slightest contact, feeling the burning inside her. He doesn't move. Tongue against her, he stops.

She explodes, whimpering, jerking, bucking. Now he moves the tongue again, driving her more into herself, driving her deeper into pleasure, keeping the pressure up as she lurches left and right. He wraps his arms around her thighs to stay with her. His shirt is soaked by the juice of her. The explosion goes on and on.

When she's finished, he loosens his grip, a little, and her

eyes are squeezed shut, and there are aftershocks. 'Can you feel my legs shaking?' she says. Even then, she jerks one more time.

But Voort doesn't answer. Voort stands and pulls off his sweater and undershirt. He unbuttons his jeans. It's not just about sex. It's more than sex. It's something he's never had before. It's something he had no idea could exist.

Before he met Camilla, with other girlfriends, and there were always plenty of them, sex always stopped after climax. Sex was terrific, wonderful, it thrilled him, it relaxed him. It lasted hours sometimes. And after the acrobatics the climaxes came, the feeling of lovely humanity, and animalness, and for the moment, until next time, he would be through.

But with Camilla there's this extra quality, and now Voort stands before her naked. His penis stretches straight out. He bends over her. She touches him. It is excruciating pleasure. He guides himself in.

The moment he's penetrated her, she explodes again, fiercely, wrapping her legs around him, pulling him to her by the neck, groaning. Normally Voort can hold off awhile, gritting his teeth, going to the verge, halting and controlling it. But tonight she says, 'I want to come with you. Together.'

Voort frees himself of control, of boundary. He hears their cries of release mingling in the gigantic house.

Afterward they sprawl, half on the cushions, arms dangling. There's a sound of a siren outside somewhere, of an ambulance, Voort tells himself. Not police. There's the hissing of an expiring candle, and a puff of smoke accompanying it, and a soft bubbling from the kitchen, where she'd left her simmering Raphael sauce.

It is a perfect house for love, this house, because in the middle of the biggest city in the world, it provides absolute silence. It has allowed, for two centuries, Voorts to fully experience their loves, hates, their passions in private.

He'd grown up in this house. His grandfather had grown

up in this house. Sometimes he felt the ghosts of all the Voorts, making the air richer, making his roots deeper, tying him to this island, approving the man he had become.

'Do you remember when we met at the fund-raiser?' Camilla says.

'Is that where I met you? I forgot.'

'Very funny. Did you fall in love with me then?'

'Not then.'

'Did you think you would fall in love with me?'

'No. But what did I know?'

'Did you think we would go out?'

'You seemed occupied and happy,' Voort replies.

'Me too. But later I kept thinking about you. Do you know that night, in the ladies' room, women were taking bets on who would get you to bed?'

'Really?' Voort is flattered, he likes feeling attractive to women, but the truth is, Camilla's affections are the only ones he wants. That night seems a hundred years ago, during a time when he paid attention to other women. He remembers the brunette he had taken home from the fund-raiser, a beauty, an actress starring in the Broadway revival of *A Street-car Named Desire*.

'Did someone win the bet?'

'An actress.'

He'd grown tired of her quickly. Voort laughs.

'Do you remember when you showed up at the boathouse?' she says. 'It was two months after we met. I didn't even think you remembered me, and I was working on the east wall, painting it, it was raining outside and I turn around . . . I was a mess . . . my hair . . . overalls . . . and you're standing there, grinning.'

'I remembered you said you worked on the boathouse after you get off work, that is, if you ever get off work.'

'We went to Carmine's for dinner. You brought me back here for coffee. You put on music, beautiful Brazilian music,

70

and we just danced. You didn't try to sleep with me. You listened to everything I said. I'd never met someone who had that combination of attentiveness and patience. I didn't even know if you were attracted to me.'

'You don't have to sound so sad about it.'

'Yeah,' she says, but she looks sad anyway. 'You had two opposite sides, Voort. You were strong, and vulnerable. You're the only guy I've ever met like that.'

'There are plenty of us. Stop believing movies. Look at real guys.'

Camilla says, 'The sauce is burning.' She trembles, getting up. He thinks it's because she's still unsteady from sex, but then, as she pulls on her jeans, she starts to cry.

'I was going to tell you after dinner. I wanted dinner to be perfect, tonight to be perfect, or at least the beginning of it, before I told you.'

'Told me what?'

Camilla falls back on the couch. Another candle goes out, the big cinnamon one, which they bought in Stowe during their first weekend together, staying at the Gables Inn, hiking up Mount Mansfield, drinking wine at night, in the big canopy bed, as a fire snapped at the foot of the suite.

Now, without the candle, the light in the room dims and flickers, and the shadow of the tree outside, against the wall, twists like reaching fingers. Old, dried-out fingers.

'You won't like this, Voort,' Camilla says.

SEVEN

'It was my fault,' the Literary Agent, Eric Porter says, 'I admit it.' He's starting his story at the next meeting of the Broken Hearts Club. 'Karen and I had something special. I can't believe I took something so fine and wrecked it, threw it away.'

The men are in the back of Mackey's Steak & Ale again, with the porterhouses in front of them, and the beers, and the extra chair for the fifth man, who has still not shown up. A faint smell of sewage tinges the condensation smearing the steam pipe. Despite his painful words, Eric Porter is smiling. There is often a discrepancy between the look on his face and the words from his mouth.

'But why do I have to suffer so much, I ask you? Other people are as human as I am, as flawed, and they don't have to go through what I do.'

The men nod, urging him on, identifying with him. But the mood in the room is somehow different tonight. There is a less stable, wilder element. It is as if, collectively, they sense that the imbalance between the club and rest of the world has grown even greater than it was last week.

Porter seems angrier. The Mechanic is on his third beer already, although usually he does not drink. The Banker and

Dr Bainbridge walked in together, seemed to have actually traveled here together, which is odd, since they usually come from opposite ends of town.

'Karen Chambers,' says the Agent, standing in the place of honor, like a speaker at a luncheon, a literary lion, a political pundit, and, at the Broken Hearts Club, a man with a shattered heart. Physically, he is the strongest man in the group, blessed with a good physique, which he hardens by working out for hours each week. The loose-fitting clothes he favors accentuate the impression of prowess. His mustache is thick, and glossy as his artificial tan. His black hair is slicked back, showing a high forehead, in a style currently trendy on actors, designers, people who change appearance from year to year. Bright red suspenders bind his chest, beneath his pearl-gray Italian jacket, featured in GQ this month. Eric Porter has seen the new movies, sampled the current restaurants. At parties, he's in demand for his ability to gossip about which famous people are considered closet gays in the city. In business, he knows, to the decimal point, the royalties collected from the hit nonfiction work *Bloodthirsty*, now in its forty-first week on the best-seller list.

'Karen wasn't especially beautiful. But then again, I'm not exactly Tom Cruise,' he says. 'But I'm good in a relationship. I'm giving. Unlike our Banker,' he says, glancing left, at the man, 'I don't mind admitting that sex isn't the first thing on my mind. I'm trying to explain how I waited for her. Love is worth waiting for. We dated half a year before we reached the point where we were going to sleep together. And during that time, I was attentive. Believe me. I always brought her flowers and presents. I'd go to the doctor with her, if she was sick.

'And to show you the affection wasn't one-sided, believe me, if I was upset about a deal at the office, she was there for me too. She was a real friend. You hear me?'

'If it was so great,' the Banker challenges, a harsh, new

note in his voice this week, 'what went wrong?'

Eric Porter can't speak for a moment. His illusion is shaken.

'That's what I thought,' the Banker says. 'Things weren't as perfect as he says.'

'It *was* perfect,' Eric insists, clawing his way back, in memory, to a place that soothes him, to the point where history might have worked out differently, where dreams still had substance. But it's a visible effort. His face seems to break into pieces, each muscle struggling to maintain order, control.

'I have herpes,' he says shyly, reaches for his glass, says, bolder, 'You heard me. Herpes.' He drains the beer schooner. 'I've had it for ten years. I hate it. It makes me feel dirty. I got it from an NYU law student, after a one-night stand.'

'Karen gave you herpes?' the Mechanic asks, slightly bleary-eyed from his drinking.

'I'm not talking about *Karen*. I'm talking about before I *met* Karen. Don't you listen when other people talk?'

'Maybe it's you who doesn't explain things so well.'

'Let him talk,' Dr Bainbridge says, trying to assume his traditional role as guide, as mentor. He's using his calm, soothing 'doctor' voice, but it isn't working tonight. He seems less potent, less influential with the group. His eyes slide right, toward the Banker, Harris Tillman. A bubble of privacy has sprung up between them, which the others notice but do not remark upon. At the Broken Hearts Club, the story is the important thing.

'I'll try to be clearer,' Eric Porter says, removing his jacket. The suspenders seem redder, jollier, like Santa Claus with a broken heart. 'I didn't mean to snap. You guys are the best friends I have.

'Anyway, I don't even get outbreaks anymore, even though the disease stays in your body. But there was a three-year period when it would erupt maybe three times a year. Stress brought it on, and it would last a week, or ten days. The first sign is tingling. Then blisters. After a day or two, a scab covers it, and disappears half a week later. It never hurt. It tickled. But,' he says, drawing himself up proudly, 'it was always a point of honor with me to tell women I dated, up front, about the herpes. I have no use for people who spread diseases,' he says. His smile has grown much too broad now.

'So this will be a happy story,' Tillman mocks.

'What's the matter with you?'

'The same thing that's the matter with all of us, gentlemen. Our common affliction. A broken heart.'

'Millions of people,' Bainbridge says sympathetically, 'have herpes.'

'All I'm trying to say is she *knew* about the herpes. I told her on the first date, which is not easy to do. Believe me, my heart beat like crazy when I told her. I'd never been so nervous talking about it, but then again, from the first, I never liked someone as much as I liked her. I was terrified it would scare her off, but all she said was, "You have so many nice qualities, Eric. I can live with a couple of little sores that show up every few months." '

The Literary Agent's face goes white; his blood has drained from it. 'That's the kind of girl she was. Considerate. At first at least.' Grief overwhelms him now, bubbling up, and he claws at his face with manicured nails. They leave red slash marks, dissipating, red to pink, down his face.

'I hate her.'

'What *happened*?'

'After six months, we got to the point where we knew we'd sleep together. And I mean sleep, Harris, as in love-making. Not fucking, the word you use. Maybe I'm not sexed up as you, but I knew it would be special. The way she'd feel, and smell. She lived above a spice factory, she smelled from the mélange of spices. In the months leading up to it, I'd get dizzy with longing whenever I got a whiff of her, even in public. We'd be at a play, or museum, with a hundred people around, and that smell would come to me, and I swear, my knees would get weak.'

'I used to be like that with Greta,' the Mechanic says. 'Man, those lady smells.'

'It was love, not sex. It was real,' Eric insists. 'And I'm not going to dirty it by getting into every little sex detail. We were a perfect match, even our friends said so, even the hardass agents at our office, at IW and A, said so. We worked in the same profession, had the same interests. We loved Shea Stadium, the opera. We went to every movie screening in town.'

'She fucked around on you, right?' the Mechanic says, mournful. 'That's what Greta did. Fucked around on me.'

'Get to the herpes,' prods Tillman.

But a banging interrupts them, making Dr Bainbridge jump. The waitress's silhouette fills the translucent window in the door. 'Hey!' comes the cheery female voice. 'You need anything in there?'

Eric loses control. It's easier to be mad at help than the club members. 'What is it with you?' he shouts. 'Do you fucking wait for the most sensitive moment to come knocking? Do you listen to hear when people don't want to be interrupted, and then shove your stupid face at them?'

Silence. Then, 'Go to hell,' the hurt voice says, and the angry staccato march of heels retreats back toward the front room.

'Better apologize,' the Mechanic says, surprised at the outburst, and respectful of authority. The Mechanic always wants everyone to like him, all the time.

'Fuck her. I think she listens at the door sometimes,' Eric says.

'You better leave a big tip or maybe Mackey won't let us come back anymore.'

'Yeah, okay, a gigantic tip, okay? Do you mind if I finish

my story now?' Eric glares at each of them, daring them to interrupt. When they don't, he calms.

'That's better.' Except the door swings open now, without a knock, and Mackey himself, furious, stands there in the stained apron he never takes off. 'I don't need shit from you,' he says to all of them. 'Get out! Now!'

At once Eric is around the table, contrite, apologetic, palms out, actor extraordinaire.

'You're right, sir. I'm sorry. I had an unbelievably bad day at the office.' Eric digs in his back pocket for his wallet.

'Nobody curses out one of my waitresses,' Mackey says. 'The kid came back here to serve you, not to take shit.'

The agent gives Mackey two new one-hundred-dollar bills. 'One for you, one for her. But I want you to know,' Eric says, hanging his head, 'nothing excuses what I did. Money is nothing. How you treat people is the only important thing. I promise, I will never speak to her like that again. I mean it. I promise.'

'You better not.' Mackey, embarrassed at being bought off, leaves and shuts the door.

'Fat vulture,' Eric says, reaches over, drains his water glass.

'I was sure he was going to kick us out,' the Mechanic says.

'There's a lesson for you. Money talks. Bullshit walks,' Eric says. 'And if you don't mind, I'm up to the part, well, the weekend we knew we were going to sleep together. It had been building slowly, like I said, becoming friends first, getting that good understanding. That weekend, the twenty-first of August, we'd planned a trip, to New London, on the coast of Connecticut. Another agent had a beach house there. It was going to be empty. The agent was in Cannes. Karen stocked up on wine and cheese; Genoa salami, smoked turkey. I rented a convertible Mustang. I was so excited. It was so crucial that everything be perfect. I worried that something would go wrong. I was so distracted at the office, thinking about it, that, in a funny way, the trip, with so much hanging on it, became sort of stressful.'

'And stress brings on herpes,' Dr Bainbridge says.

Eric subsides. As he breathes, the red suspenders go up, go down. 'Yes. Suddenly, on the way up, in the car, at the very moment when I'm about to consummate our life, the stupid itching starts.'

'And you told her you had herpes,' the Mechanic guesses. 'And it screwed everything up.'

Eric Porter hangs his head. 'I made it worse,' he says. His voice cracks, and he sits, in misery, all the bluster out of him. 'Why did I do it?' he says. 'I never did it before that. Why did I do it then?'

'You didn't tell her?' the Banker says. 'Well well well.'

If Eric's will were strong enough, he would change history. If his angel granted him a wish, it would be for memory to dissipate into bad dream. 'Always before, with girls, I'd been scrupulous. If I felt even the slightest itch, even if it was nothing, I'd stop until I was sure I was safe to have sex. With Karen, I didn't want the herpes to be there so much I . . . I convinced myself . . . I told myself, on the highway, maybe it *wasn't* herpes. Maybe it was itching.'

Eric falls silent.

He says, in a deader voice, 'I didn't want to disappoint her. I didn't want to see her face the first time I was infected. I *did* check to see if I was infected, but I wasn't as scrupulous as I should have been.'

The men fall silent in the brotherhood of bondage. They all have turning points, in their stories, when events might have turned out a happier way. If regret is religion, the men are praying. If it is a replay of bad choices, they will remain locked, over and over, in their flawed pasts.

'The weekend started great,' Eric resumes. 'We *did* have sex, as good as I hoped. Sex on Friday, Saturday morning,

Saturday afternoon, Saturday night. Maybe I'm not as adventurous as you guys, in the sack, I mean, but plain old missionary position was heaven for me. I remember the spice smell when she put her arms around me. I remember that when we woke, in that giant bed, with the ocean breeze coming in, we'd slept all night completely entwined.

'By Sunday morning we were having such a good time, we were sad the weekend was ending. See how much we loved each other? We would be *with* each other on the drive back, and in the city all week, but still the idea of the weekend ending made us sad. So instead of getting in the car and just leaving, one last time we had sex.'

The Agent trails off, as his arms drop to his sides.

When he looks up, tears are coming.

'When we're finished, I'm lying there, looking out the window at the sky. It's so beautiful, and I've never had sex with someone I love so m-m-much,' he says, starting to stammer, which he hardly ever does, except in moments of horrible urgency. 'And then I hear her say, "What are these little s-s-sores, Eric?" '

'I'm sorry, brother,' Tillman says, the rage out of him for the moment. He feels terrible sympathy for his friend.

'The sores were there, all right, under my genital hair. I told myself it wasn't happening. She went crazy. Screaming that I betrayed her. Saying she never trusted anyone until me. I tried to explain, but I was in shock, everything had switched around so quickly, in less than one second. Whatever I said made it worse. "You mean you *felt* the itching," she screamed, "and you didn't tell me?" '

Eric Porter squeezes his palms against his ears, as if trying to drown out the high-pitched accusations always in there. 'I followed her around the house, to the porch, to the bedroom. I couldn't get through to her. I'd never felt so bad in my life. She made me put her on the train back to New York and drive back alone, in that stupid, cherry-red Mustang. I was caught in traffic for hours. She wouldn't let me up when I went to her apartment later. She wouldn't even look at me in the office, for w-w-weeks.'

'I'm really sorry.'

Eric is shaking. 'It's cold in here,' he says.

He adds, 'She never got herpes. And she never forgave me.'

'That's a terrible story,' Dr Bainbridge says, 'but I have to tell you, as a professional, if the bond between you was as strong as you say it was, the two of you could have gotten over this hump.'

'It was the end of everything.'

'Forgive me for not explaining myself,' Bainbridge persists. 'But from your description of how strong your bond was, I think the way she reacted, in the long run, shows that she had some issues of her own that had nothing to do with your disease.'

Eric's nose is running. He looks broken, eight years old. It's pathetic. 'I always wreck everything.'

'You hate her,' the Banker says.

'I loved her too.'

'Nobody has a right to hurt another person the way she hurt you.'

Bainbridge seems alarmed at the route the talk is taking. He starts to interrupt, but the Banker shoves his palm in the air, and Bainbridge shuts up.

'Did you ever think about hurting her?' the Banker asks, softly.

'Don't be silly.'

'But you did. You said you did, once before. So you've thought about it a little. Maybe holding something heavy in your hand, smashing it down, feeling it strike her bones.'

'Stop it.'

'Didn't you think it? Ever?'

'I would never hurt her.'

'Of course you wouldn't,' the Banker says. 'I'm talking about in your imagination. Nobody gets hurt in an imagination. Admit maybe one time you thought about it, maybe only for a second, maybe hurting her a tiny little bit.'

'Who wouldn't imagine it for the flash of a second?' Eric says. 'After what happened. Like there's a whisper inside me, saying, "Do it!" But it doesn't even last a whole second. Less than that.'

'I said stop it,' Dr Bainbridge commands, but his voice is devoid of power.

'What exactly *did* you imagine, when you imagined hurting her?' the Banker says. 'I mean, just for amusement.'

'I don't know. Hitting her. A slap, maybe. That's all. I'd never hit a woman anyway. I don't know if I've ever even hit a man. I never fought, when I was a kid. I was the peaceful type.'

'Just a little slap, eh?' the Banker says.

'What difference does it make?' Eric says. 'It's just imagination. In the real world, she's gone.'

'Absolutely right! But since we're talking about imagination, there's no harm in exploring it. Friend, this woman hurt you. Remember when you broke the bottle a few weeks ago? Remember you were waving the glass around? Is a "slap" all you were thinking about then? Or were you thinking about more than a slap?'

There's a scraping sound as the Mechanic pushes his chair back. He looks from the Banker to the Agent.

'You're making me nervous,' he says.

'I'm not talking to you,' the Banker says. He seems to have taken leadership from Bainbridge. '*Next* week it's your turn to tell your story,' he tells the Mechanic. 'Tonight it's Eric. Well,' he says, turning to Eric, prodding him. 'What *were* you thinking about when you waved the glass around that time? Tell your friends in the Broken Hearts Club.'

'Cutting her.'

82

'That's enough! Meeting's over,' Bainbridge says, and stands up.

The Mechanic also stands, looking grateful. But the Banker remains sitting, and Eric seems too dazed to move. The Banker waves his hand dismissively. 'You wanna leave, you two? Go ahead. It's 10:45. We have fifteen minutes left.'

He turns back to Eric, as if the others have departed already. He has a shiny, interested look in his face, like a biologist cutting apart a new kind of fish.

'What if you could hurt her and get away with it?' he says.

'That's disgusting.'

'Because you love her? Because you care for her? Because she's been so good and true to you, is that why?'

Eric Porter says, 'Leave me alone.'

'Or because,' the Banker says, 'you're afraid you'd get caught?'

'I'm leaving,' the Mechanic says, putting one arm into the sleeve of his grease-stained parka. 'I got a long ride home, to Washington Heights. What do you say we all get out of here, right now?'

'I'll go with you,' Eric Porter says, except his eyes are closed. The red suspenders rise and fall slowly.

The Mechanic says, 'Okay. Let's go!'

When Eric doesn't move, the Mechanic says, 'Then, good night.'

The Banker looks at Dr Bainbridge after the Mechanic leaves. His smile is too bright. 'We're only going to talk. I promise,' he says.

Bainbridge looks doubtful.

Tillman says, 'He's so upset, I can't just leave.'

'I'll stay too,' Bainbridge says, almost in a whisper.

'Excellent,' Tillman says. 'Maybe there's something you want to tell him too. Maybe you want to share with him what we've been doing this week.'

'What are you talking about?' the Agent, Eric Porter, asks,

but he's in so much pain he's barely paying attention.

Tillman prods Bainbridge, amused and strengthened by the fright in his face. 'Go ahead. Tell him.'

'My head hurts,' Bainbridge says.

'It's the liquor,' Tillman says. 'Drink too much alcohol and anything can happen. But our doctor knows that. He *buys* our liquor.'

Tillman's eyes are locked on Bainbridge's, over the Literary Agent's lowered head. And now that the threat hangs there, Tillman's smile turns sympathetic, as he knows, instinctively, when to offer the carrot, when to wield the stick.

'I've been thinking about what you wanted me to do,' he says – meaning, Bainbridge knows, turning himself in to the police. 'Maybe I'll do it. Tomorrow.'

'Really?'

'We'll only talk here. Eric and I.'

'Oh God,' Bainbridge says, desperate to believe, to feel like somehow he can make better, at least in part, what has gone wrong. There has to be a way. If only he can get Tillman to cooperate, to explain to the police.

'I'm thinking about doing it tomorrow,' Tillman repeats. 'You trust me. I trust you. I'm letting you go off by yourself, right?'

There's a long silent moment.

'Go home,' Tillman says with enormous sympathy and goodwill. 'Take something for that headache.'

Bainbridge doesn't move.

Tillman says, a little more irritated, 'Look, if you're not going to trust me, I won't be able to trust you.'

Bainbridge squeezes his temples.

'And you know what that means,' Tillman says. 'No go tomorrow. That's what.'

Bainbridge says, as if using all his remaining will to convince himself that Tillman is telling the truth, 'You're right. I need aspirin.'

After a moment he turns and leaves.

The Banker tells Eric Porter, 'I can't believe those guys,' as he rubs the man's shoulders, massages the hard lump of bunched muscle at the base of his neck. 'Leaving you alone at a time like this. Let's go somewhere else and talk about things. I'll buy you a drink, not beer, but hard liquor. Irish whiskey. It's so cold outside. We can talk about imagination more. I mean, men like us, all we have is imagination. Hate is all we have left.'

Two hours later the Banker, Harris Tillman, and the Agent, Eric Porter, leave Sardi's restaurant, the Broadway watering hole. They've had six Irish whiskeys between them, on top of the beer earlier in the night. New York has gone warm, even in January, the dead of winter. The weather seems schizophrenic this season. Freezing one moment. Broiling the next.

The plows have cleared the streets since last week, most of the snow has melted. The theatergoers went home hours ago. Broadway is left to the pimps, tourists, and neon Japanese product advertising signs.

They head to Eighth Avenue, where the Banker pays for subway tokens and they wait on the platform. The train hurtles from the tunnel, like a beast emerging from a lair. The white A on the front car, in its blue circle, identifies the route for late-night travelers heading south.

'If you take a cab, a driver remembers you. If you take a subway, no one remembers you,' the Banker says, steering his friend by the elbow into a crowded car.

'What difference does it make if someone remembers you?'

'You're right. No difference,' the Banker says, subject dropped.

The A train runs so seldom at this hour that when it comes, even at one A.M., it is filled with people. The light in the car is lonely. Steel wheels crack beneath the moving car, snapping like a breaking heart.

'I knew you'd know where she lives,' the Banker says shrewdly, confidentially. 'I could tell you'd gone there sometimes. And you say her husband's an airline pilot? Maybe he's away, I mean, not that we're going inside.'

'We're just going to look at it, right?'

'Exactly,' the Banker says, soothing his buddy. 'Do you think its possible, after all this time, that she regrets what she did to you?'

'No.'

'You say that because you don't want to get hurt again. But what if she's been wanting to tell you she's sorry? What if she's tried to find you? Wouldn't that be ironic? She's been wanting to talk to *you*, to tell you she made a mistake.'

'I'm drunk. You're confusing me.'

The train rumbles beneath the East River and eases out, on the other side, to the Brooklyn Heights stop at High Street. The men take the elevator to the surface. Brooklyn streets are emptier than Manhattan's, and this neighborhood is wealthy, with small tree-lined streets, gentrified. Eric Porter leads the way toward the East River, and her apartment house, which adjoins the sweep of the Brooklyn Promenade.

It's a Tudor-style building, and the block is charming. There are lots of trees, and the snow hasn't melted as much. It seems Christmassy, less stained by soot. The Banker slips the knife he stole from Mackey's from his coat pocket and drops it, and the linen napkin wrapping it, into the long pocket of Eric's Yves Saint Laurent coat.

He cautions, 'Don't hurt yourself.'

'I don't want that.'

'Right, I'll take it back.'

'You said we'd just *look* at the building.'

'Exactly,' the Banker says, putting away the knife. But he gives Eric something else, a folded paper napkin. 'I can see you're considering going up. Do me a favor. If you do talk to her, give her this for me.'

Eric, partly drunk, partly dazed, unfolds a cocktail napkin from Sardi's. He sees that the Banker has written BHC in blue ballpoint, on the front.

'The club's initials. It's just my way of going in with you, letting you know you have friends, you have backers. Don't think of yourself as alone anymore. Never again. You hear me? I mean, you want to talk to her. I know you do. Maybe you're afraid to, but it's just us here. Two friends who know each other's secrets. You want to, you're just afraid to. All those years, and wouldn't it be something if a single conversation could make you feel better?'

'Stop.'

'Don't mind me. I'm just babbling. Why wake *her* up, right? Why inconvenience *her*? *She's* the important one, not you, right? Isn't that what you're thinking?'

'My stomach hurts.'

Ten minutes later, surprised by his own boldness, Eric, minus the knife, is walking into the building. The marble lobby is empty, except for a doorman, a Hispanic on a folding chair, reading the late edition *Post* and the hockey box scores. A lone man who chooses to work at night. A brother, perhaps, Eric feels, filled with affection for the man. He too has suffered. Eric can tell.

Except the doorman is irritated. 'I no calling up there, sir. She's no expecting you. It's two A.M.'

'But it's important,' Eric says, 'to speak to her.'

'No!'

'You must call,' Eric says. Now that he is finally acting on his impulses, going up there has become incredibly urgent. He switches to his tough, professional voice. The voice of the upper class aimed down at the lower. A voice wealthy liberal New Yorkers pretend they never use. 'It's not your job to screen callers. It's your job to tell her I'm here. You'll be in trouble if you don't call. I'll make sure of that.'

The doorman scans his apartment list for the right number, wanting, at least, to wake only the proper person. He punches a code into the private intercom system. Eric hears Karen's receiver ringing, in her apartment. Tinny, and far away, but his heart is beating fast now.

He imagines a phone upstairs, waking her. He imagines her in a white nightgown, like she wore in Connecticut. He tells himself that perhaps he shouldn't have let the Banker talk him into this, but on the other hand he feels a kind of giddiness, as if by coming here, he has given himself a crazy second chance.

Anyway, the doorman's reached her.

'He ordered me to call you. I *know* what time it is,' the doorman is telling Karen, as Eric's heart balloons, and he fights off nausea. 'His name? It's Eric. Sir, what's your last name?' the doorman asks, angry at the position he has been put in, thinking this might kill next year's holiday tip.

'Porter.'

The doorman relays it. 'She no want to talk to you.'

'I just want to tell her how sorry I am.'

'Sir—'

'About the herpes, I have to explain to her—'

At the word 'herpes,' a flood of female voice pours from the receiver. Karen always cared too much about what other people thought. He knows she is thinking that this doorman, this paid stranger who talks to everyone in the building, this man who probably loves to gossip about residents, may hear the story of the herpes. So Karen agrees to talk to Eric on the phone.

'Please let me come up for a few minutes,' he says.

It's pathetic, this begging. It makes him angry. It's what he did in Connecticut, and for months afterward, to try to win her back. He never should have listened to Tillman and come here, humiliating himself. She refuses to let him up, and he's growing angry, but when he says the word 'herpes' again, she curses and says, 'Five minutes. That's all. And be quiet. The kids are asleep.'

Kids, he thinks. She could have had children with me. It could have been me helping them with their homework, paying their allowance, helping her feed them and diaper them, taking them fishing during summers, even yelling at them when they made mistakes.

Then he realizes that Karen *didn't* mention the airline pilot. Maybe they're divorced, or he's flying tonight, off on an airplane. Clearly he's not upstairs, or she would have said something about waking the husband up.

Eric begins to feel happy.

I'll have privacy with her again, for the first time since the horrible weekend in New London.

In the back of Eric's mind, he understands how insane his joy is, but that doesn't diminish it. He is happy. Actually happy. He is a lover, going to meet the loved.

He tells himself, in the rising elevator, that he will be polite, keep the joy to himself, and simply explain to her what happened back in Connecticut. Or maybe that's all water under the bridge now. Maybe they'll just chat about their lives, and the friendly talk will tell him he is forgiven now. He tells himself that all he really wants is for her to forgive him. After all, he knows she can never have him back, she has another life. He's a logical, thinking adult, he tells himself, and you cannot turn a clock back. He knows, because of that long-ago blunder, that things can never be the same again. He only wants his pain to stop.

Eric Porter wants to believe that a few words at two A.M. can fix a broken heart.

He straightens his tie in the elevator. I will be calm, he tells himself as the double doors slide open. But he finds he is trembling.

He turns to flee.

He turns back.

He advances down the empty hall, past locked doors, protecting the successful people, the ones with families.

He stops at 6J.

And now he realizes, all by itself, that his hand has gone down into the coat pocket, seeking the knife that the Banker put there. But of course it isn't there anymore. Of course he gave it back to the Banker. But the hand comes out with the Sardi's napkin, and the initials on it: BHC.

The Banker has waited outside, around the corner. 'Some things you gotta do alone,' he'd said. 'But I'm with you in spirit.'

Eric reaches to knock, but the door opens before he strikes it. She was waiting at the eyehole.

'Don't wake the kids,' she hisses. 'I told you a long time ago. Leave me alone!'

I wouldn't have used that knife anyway, he thinks. I don't even know why I looked for it.

She closes the door behind him, softly, after he walks in, and cautious, as she used to be, secures the lock.

EIGHT

Voort is nine years old the day his parents die. The worst morning of his life begins during a gorgeous July, cool and green in Central Park. It's a morning of excitement. A day of the Police Athletic League city softball championship. A morning when Voort, in his laundered 'Homicide Unit' team uniform, stands, heart pounding, in left field.

'Hit it to me!' he cries.

Tie game in the seventh, but his parents are not in the stands, among the screaming spectators. They have left him in the care of a police captain uncle, while they fly to Albany, for a fund-raiser to help, ironically, orphans of deceased police.

It would be nice if they were present, but growing up in a police family, Voort never questions the duty cops have toward deceased comrades. He does not question his parents' love for him. He knows, without a doubt, they would rather be here.

I can't wait to tell Dad about the game, tonight, at the barbecue on the roof, that they're throwing for the whole team.

He's filled with love for his dad, a respected homicide detective, a powerful man who takes the boy on cases and brings him after school to One Police Plaza, where Voort wanders halls, learns police work, makes friends with detectives, some of whom will work with him one day.

Now he one-hands a deep fly ball to end the inning. His teammates cheer, and as he runs toward the bench, he's thanking Dad for teaching him how to flip down his sunglasses in the outfield when a fly comes his way. Thanking him, with his turn at bat coming up, for teaching him how to raise his right foot before swinging at an incoming pitch.

I'll make you proud of me.

But as Voort enters the batting circle, he notices his uncle in conversation with a couple of detectives from One Police Plaza, in the stands. All three men head for Voort, who is warming up by swinging his extra heavy, extra powerful Louisville Slugger; who turns away to study the way the pitcher's arced balls cross the plate; to study, the way his father taught him, the gap in right-center field.

'Put down the bat,' his uncle says, face obscured by a glow of sunlight. Voort, squinting up, hears enormous pain in the words. It's a tone he's never heard from this generally cheery man. It fills him with dread, as if bad news is coming directly from heaven, irrevocable, from that far above.

A moment later Voort hears his own voice saying, as if it is coming from somewhere else, 'What do you mean, the plane went down?'

The funeral, two days later, is well-attended, by cops, the mayor, newspaper editors, representatives from city charities. The Voorts are well-liked, old line, exotic in the neighborhood. Everyone likes to be friends with a cop.

And later that day the boy, crying bitterly, wanders the house while the uncle and aunt wait downstairs with his packed suitcase. The family has decided to rent the place and invest the proceeds for Voort, who will receive them in installments when he turns college age.

They give him hours while he wanders through history.

He starts in the attic, with his father's old army clothes and his mother's prom dress, still crisply white, slim as her figure when she died. He goes into the master bedroom, where his parents read the *Times* on Sunday morning, his dad smoking his pipe, his mom her Virginia Slims.

His mother's dressing room is neat, with three dozen globe-shaped lights ringing her mirror, and a smell of French perfume he will remember forever, when he visits the cemetery on the anniversary of the crash.

Each step brings memories. He looks into the faces of the Voort portraits; the admiral, the beat cops, the commissioners, the uncles who rode police horses, drove police launches, snapped to attention in police honor guards when President Franklin D. Roosevelt visited New York.

Even in his grief, the connections, the history, the stories he knows, make him feel better.

Then, in his bedroom, the thing happens that changes the boy.

Voort is lying on his old Dutch bed, aching, looking out the window, thinking: Today is the worst day of my life. He can't understand how his parents could abandon him, even though, logically, he knows they have not chosen to leave.

As he lies there, suddenly, the room seems to grow peaceful. A warm, lovely feeling comes over him, a sense of supreme safety, honey running through his veins. It is the same feeling he gets when his dad tucks him in at night, when his mom brings him medicine when he has the flu.

But the feeling baffles him now. It comes from nowhere, and after a moment Voort understands and, amazed, sits up.

'Is that you?' he asks them in wonder, in the darkness.

The feeling vanishes as quickly as it comes. He bursts into tears, but he knows his parents have just visited. They've let him know, the only way they could, that they exist still, and so does their love. Voort is certain of this; he doesn't care if the presence was real or imagination. The comfort was so true and powerful that he knows, from now on, in a different way, he will still not be alone.

Events can hurt you, the boy decides, but not so bad if you fight back.

When Voort goes downstairs, he finds his uncle and aunt in the kitchen, going through bills, straightening up.

'I'm going to keep living here,' the boy says.

'That's impossible.'

'Nothing is impossible,' Voort says, 'if you know what you want.'

They reason with him. They are gentle with him. He will live with *them* from now on, go to school with his cousins, whom he loves. They will be a big family, solid, church-going, loving, supportive.

'No, move in with me,' Voort replies. 'The uncles can rotate. A couple months at a time.'

In the end the family gives in to his stubborn confidence. They love him, and the truth is they admire him for his unwavering point of view. To all Voorts, the house represents solidity, history, pride, even if at the moment it is personified by a skinny nine-year-old boy.

So his uncle comes to live with him awhile, then another uncle for months, and finally a Voort lawyer, a bachelor second cousin, gives up his co-op to occupy the second floor bedroom for the next nine years.

Voort enters his teenage years self-sufficient, outgoing, giving himself to friends, but always holding a piece back, a private piece, the part that had been wounded when his parents died. He is popular in school. He has athletic scholarship offers from Harvard, but he is a die-hard New Yorker, and chooses NYU. He has girlfriends, and other girls phone him all the time, getting crushes on him. Telling him I love you, I think of you, I masturbate over you, I want to marry you.

Voort has sex when he wants it. He has a full life. He considers himself a happy man.

Until today Voort thought he understood grief, had dealt with it. But now he sees that the loss of parents causes only one kind of broken heart.

He sits in a rear pew of St. Patrick's on a Friday, seven days after the murder of Niana Embers, and six after Camilla went back to her old lover. Mass ended an hour ago. German tourists are snapping pictures of the altar area in the nave, from the back of the cathedral, and a Japanese group is getting a guided tour near that. Voort lights candles, says a prayer for his family, his parents, for the city, its prosperity and safety. He puts a hundred-dollar bill in the charity box.

'God,' he prays, 'keep Camilla safe.'

Let her be happy and safe, he thinks. What a funny request. Not bring her back to me. Just keep her safe. He is protective always. She looked so unhappy, he thinks, so confused when she left a week ago.

I need time, Voort.

Take what you need.

He remembers her gathering her coat, remembers, after she left, going into the kitchen, stunned at the normalness of the place, that it was still the same, that the pot hadn't boiled over. That the floor was still shiny. That the drapes still covered the windows. That any kind of order still existed in his house.

I guess I'm not over Kenny yet. I guess I started up with you too quickly, Voort. I'll probably regret leaving. But I have to see him again and be sure.

Off across the left aisle, a priest he knows disappears into a confession box. Voort never offers confession. He comes to pray, not to confess.

Leaving the cathedral, he spots Mickie in back, leaning against a pillar. Mickie's wearing a double-breasted dark Savile Row suit, cream-colored, button-down shirt, emerald-green tie from Venice, and he's draped his double-breasted wool overcoat over his arm. Voort realizes he has not seen

Mickie in the last two days, as he wandered the city.

Mickie pushes off the pillar. 'Con Man, you called in sick? You hardly ever get sick, and it never stopped you from coming in before.'

'I caught the stomach flu that's going around.'

'I checked the house for you, your health club, the Greek breakfast place. I shoulda figured straight out, when something's bothering him, Con Man goes to mass.'

'You might try it sometime. It helps me think.'

'I go my way. God goes His. He let my first wife die screaming, of cancer. I try to be a good person. There are all kinds of trade-offs in the world.'

In the last week, neither detective has learned anything useful in the Niana Embers investigation. The dead ends were the excuse Voort gave himself for taking sick leave. Maybe a new way of seeing things will come to me, he'd thought, if I get away. And, at home, not sleeping, or walking the street at night, for hours, he'd kept returning in his mind to Niana's apartment. The shoe print in the blood-stain. The initials carved in the wood.

'Our boy did it again,' Mickie says, and Voort knows there's been another murder.

'I got the car outside,' Mickie says. 'It's in Brooklyn this time. They found the body a few hours ago. I'll tell you on the way.'

'Who was killed?'

'A woman. A married woman with three kids. Let's go. You don't look good, Con Man. Does your stomach flu have anything to do with what the Valkyrie does on Fridays?'

Voort halts on the wide, long steps outside the cathedral. Ten feet away a guide is telling a group of British tourists, 'Stay close with me when we get inside.'

'What do you know about Fridays?'

'Every Friday you're weird, so I figure Friday must be the day the shit hits the fan. That's why I'm a detective. I detect.'

A throbbing starts up in Voort's head as he gets into the car. He hears her say, *Don't call me. Don't try to see me. I'm not happy about this. I hope things will be all right after a while.*

A 'while,' Voort thinks.

How long is a while?

They take Fifth Avenue south, cut onto Broadway at Twenty-third, and head for the Brooklyn Bridge. The streets are filled with potholes, which this winter are particularly bad. Alternating freezing and thawing causes great damage in the world. The Con Edison crews are out, disappearing into manhole covers. Men in parkas and hard hats descend into the earth, through rising steam.

'Check out the folder on the seat,' Mickie says. 'But get ready. It's bad again.'

The grainy black and whites Voort takes from the envelope show an orgy of destruction. The dead woman's tweed skirt is up, the legs punctured as if a dozen men had attacked her, not one. The arms are fleshy, limp and so ravaged even a two-dimensional representation seems sticky with drying blood. Voort winces at the splashes on the walls, on the white tablecloth, on bed sheets. His heart breaks for whoever loved this woman. I've got to get myself under control, he thinks. I never had this strong a reaction to a case before.

'Mickie, how do you know our guy did it?'

'Picture number five.'

Voort finds the blowup of a napkin, and letters scrawled on it.

'BHC,' Mickie remarks, steering with one hand. 'He left it on the table, by the front door, like a calling card, neat as you please.'

'No fingerprints again?'

'Nah, this time was different. Like, when it came to afterward, another guy did it.' Mickie takes the bridge entrance, but due to perpetual construction, there's a traffic jam going to Brooklyn. The detectives get stuck behind an Entenmann's bakery truck. Voort reaches out the window, attaches the roof light to the car, and Mickie hits the siren. It does no good. No one moves out of the way, but the driver of the beat-up Ford on their right yells, 'Where the hell do you expect them to go? I got enough noise in my head now! Stop!'

Mickie says, 'This time he leaves prints, skin under her fingernails, witnesses, three of them. He even gave the doorman a name. And ready for this? He's carving her up; he wakes her kids, who come into the living room and see everything.'

'He kills the kids?' Voort says.

Mickie shakes his head in wonder, in bafflement over people, no matter how long you deal with them. 'It's nuts. It was like he was in a trance, they said. They said he got a weird look on his face and just said – ready for this? – "Go back to bed." '

Voort tries to understand it, but it is impossible. The killer is a stranger, as is the victim. Whatever happened between them, no one else will truly ever understand. The Chevy nudges out of the jam, siren screaming, and Mickie drives down Cadman Plaza, past the seat of Brooklyn borough government. Brooklyn Heights is an older and more casually elegant part of New York, with its quaint narrow streets, its writer residents, its pretty trees, its carriage houses and riverside Promenade. Lots of squad cars and an ambulance are pulled up outside the dead woman's apartment house. There's a van from Eyewitness News, and Voort recognizes a photographer from the *Post*.

'We're still not releasing the BHC initials,' Mickie says. 'Local precinct'll shut up about that too.'

In the apartment the body is gone; white tape crudely outlines its death spot. Voort checks the rooms, feeling the sense of utter violation. He sees lots of pottery knickknacks, some broken, some on their side. A little girl with a puppy. A Pope giving a blessing. He sees colorful modern paintings, the kids' stuffed animals. He finds no clues that the local crew and forensics missed.

As forensics keeps working in the apartment, Voort goes downstairs with Mickie, and without knocking they walk into the co-op office, where local detectives are interviewing the doorman who found the body.

'I try to tell the man not to go up,' the doorman is telling two veteran guys whom Voort recognizes. 'It's too late. But he say I lose my job if I don't call up.'

For such a wealthy building, the office is surprisingly seedy. It reminds Voort of an old saying he heard in NYU Philosophy class, which his professor called the 'Theory of the Commons.' That which is most common to all, the professor told him, receives the least care.

The desks are old, the paint peeling, the file cabinets more dented than the ones at the Harlem precinct. The doorman nurses a cold cup of instant coffee. The detectives act professional, but Voort senses the agitation in them. Something about the extreme violence upstairs has touched the core of the reason they became police. From the apartment upstairs he hears rock and roll music, Aerosmith. The Tudor-style lattice windows are open. The smell of snow and East River from outside is fresh and unseasonably warm. Voort sees buds on the trees out there. In a week, he knows, when the cold snaps back, they will die.

'But she told him to come up,' the precinct detective says to the doorman.

'He said something about giving her herpes. Then I think she got embarrassed. She was a private person. She did not want me to hear the rest.'

The detectives glance at each other. If the doorman is right, this news is significant, a possible way to track the suspect. Maybe the woman's doctor would have the name of the carrier. 'He gave her herpes? She's married, so she was having an affair with the guy?'

'I don't know. I never saw him before. He just told her he was sorry about the herpes. That's when she told him to give the phone to me. And when he came down, bloody, afterward,' the man shudders, 'I went up.'

'Where's her husband?' Voort asks, interrupting.

'Separated. He flies for American. But I think they were going to get back together.' The doorman looks at the cold coffee, and stretches. His shift ended many hours ago. 'Maybe she slept with this other man and he made her sick. And they had a fight.'

Voort confirms the description of the man, and the name, Eric Porter. He always double-checks information.

On the way back downtown, he and Mickie are excited. They have leads now, good ones, and forensics will run the fingerprints and DNA. They'll hit the phone books when they get back to the office, for Eric Porters. They'll find her friends and husband, and ask about Eric Porters. They'll check criminal records for Eric Porters. They'll show the sketch in bars and groceries. They'll check to see if Niana Embers knew Eric Porter, if there are photos, letters, addresses, clues. They'll distribute sketches to the Blue Guys, and after a few days, if nothing happens, to the press.

'That's makes two,' Mickie says, and suddenly the beast is in the car.

Will two victims become three? the detectives are thinking. Will three grow to five? Do they have a serial killer on their hands?

Camilla will be interested to hear about this, Voort thinks. Then he realizes, I won't be talking to her.

Voort, it's best that I stop now, before things deteriorate.

He'd told her, 'You have to do what you have to do.' But he'd thought, How do things deteriorate more than this?

They rocket off the bridge, reach One Police Plaza. They

give the name and description to the computer girls, give a sketch and a photo to the art department for distribution, then go back to their office and start with the phone directories. The best-case scenario would be only one or two Eric Porters in the book, in Manhattan, and they'd go to an apartment, and magically, justice would be perfect and the person listed would be the right one.

They're in a small, walled-in office, like other detectives in this new special unit, but inside they've paid for their own furniture. 'Why shouldn't we live like we can afford?' Mickie had said, and hired a decorator. The walls are painted a honey color. The couch is plush, expensive, Bloomingdale's, built to comfortably seat four. The desks are Shaker, picked out by Mickie's wife at a Berkshire auction. The file cabinets are mahogany. There are two new Sony TVs in the room, so they can watch four news shows simultaneously, splitting each screen in half. There's a small refrigerator. Other cops come in here sometimes, to rifle Cokes, OJ, iced tea.

The news is on now, CBS and NBC, and by five o'clock, when they've found forty-eight Eric Porters in the metropolitan area, news of the murder in Brooklyn gets its two minutes of fame on TV. Niana Embers got only a little publicity. A twelve-car auto pile-up had occupied the reporters that day. But today's a slow news day. Voort watches four blown-up photos of 'the victim, Karen Chambers,' appear on screen.

The sky's getting dark outside, winter dark. The lights are coming on at City Hall, two blocks off. Thousands of municipal employees stream from buildings in the area. The city, Mickie the Republican likes to say, employs as many people as a socialist government. Paychecks in hand, workers leave the Parks Department, Motor Vehicle Department, Fire Department, Human Services Department, Building Inspectors Department, Financial Services Department. New Yorkers are flush with cash for hot Friday nights of celebration, love, forgetfulness. Camilla is usually tired on Friday nights, after a week of battling executives at NBC.

But Voort's attention goes back to the screen as the Channel 4 newsman announces police have a suspect in the murder. 'Police seek a man named Eric Porter,' he says, causing Mickie to jerk from his chair.

'Shit!'

'Our News Channel Four correspondent managed to obtain a sketch of the man.'

'Fucking commissioner!' Mickie yells, slamming his hand against his desk as the magnified sketch goes out all over the city. The commissioner, it is well-known, cultivates relations with the press, and eyes the mayor's chair. Now NBC has robbed the commodity of time from the detectives. It's good for the city to see the sketch eventually, but not in the first few hours, when Eric Porter, unaware he has been identified, may be simply sitting at home, easy to reach.

Now he'll bolt. Now, in minutes, Voort knows, their phones will start ringing, as all callers are referred right here. I saw the sketch and that's my neighbor, callers will say. That's my brother-in-law. That's the guy I saw in Louie's Bar the other day, I swear it. That's the checkout man at the Fairway on Broadway and Seventy-fourth. I knew there was something weird about him, the way he looked at my legs.

In minutes Eric Porter, if he is guilty, may be throwing shirts in a bag, may be getting in a car, or on a bus, or train, heading out of the city. He'll buy different glasses, or a wig if he's smart. He'll grow facial hair. All because the commissioner released the photo too soon.

Voort and Mickie stare, helplessly, standing on taupe-colored pile, at the sketch that was supposed to be distributed to patrolmen. At the wide-apart eyes, the slicked-back hair, mustache, full lips, half parted, as if the man had just finished a beer.

'NBC,' Mickie says, 'makes me wish for a fascist

government. The kind that knows what to do with asshole reporters. Lock them in the clink.'

Sure enough, five seconds after the newsmen go on to the basketball scores, the phone starts ringing. Mickie flips his lucky half dollar into the air. 'Tails,' he says as it spins, gleaming.

'Con Man, you lose. Looks like you answer.'

Sure enough, when he picks up the phone, he hears a voice that is clearly not a police voice. It's too nervous.

'I asked to talk to someone about Karen Chambers,' the woman says, after giving her name, Jackie May. The voice is shaky, but there's authority in it. She tells Voort she's a literary agent. She just watched the news.

'One of our clients was interviewed on it, about his new book,' she says. 'Normally I don't watch TV in the office.'

'Yes?'

'Karen used to work here, and so did Eric Porter.'

Voort sits up. He wants the information to be true. He wants to be that lucky. He wants, for once, the very first call to be the one they're looking for. He says, guarded, 'You're sure?'

The voice is shocked, upset, but it conveys certainty. 'The company is IW and A, International Writers and Artists. I'll wait for you at the office. It's on Fifty-seventh between Fifth and Sixth. I can't believe she's dead.'

Voort hangs up, looks up the agency in the book and punches in the number of International Writers & Artists. He asks the IW&A secretary if he can speak with the agent who just supposedly phoned him. When the agent comes on the line, Voort says, 'Did you just call the police?'

'Very thorough. I'm impressed.'

Voort took the call, so Voort gets the visit. Mickie will stay in the office, answering calls, bugging the computer girls to get an answer on fingerprints from the FBI.

At this hour, traffic is bad, so Voort walks to the R train, going uptown, and it is in the R train that he spots Camilla, who rarely comes downtown, chatting with a redhead on the far side of the car. Her back faces Voort, so she does not see him. But the tall form, the expensive blue topcoat is Camilla, and he pushes toward her, heart beating, except when she turns to get off at Forty-second Street, he sees it is not her at all.

For the first time in his life, Voort thinks, just for a second, I wish I was someone else. I wish I didn't have to go through this.

The subway lets him off at Fifty-seventh and Seventh, one of the pockets of old New York, powerful New York. The boutiques are wealthy. Passers by dress better. It's a confident avenue, Fifty-seventh Street. People run the entertainment industry from Fifty-seventh Street. The agencies are here; literary, music, Broadway. People stride along this street, owners of their envied world. They don't merely walk.

Voort finds the copper-colored glass tower housing the literary agency. Following directions, he takes the elevator to the eleventh floor, where the receptionist bursts into tears when he identifies himself.

'Oh God. I knew Karen. She was the nicest woman in the world. Jackie said to send you right back. She's waiting in her office for you.'

As he threads the maze of cubicles, toward the big offices, it seems to him that this place is a world controlled by women. Women occupy all the offices he passes, women wearing headphone sets, connected to every publisher in town.

Jackie May is an executive vice president, a short woman in her late forties, petite with cropped black hair, a blue, tailored business suit, and, on her desk, lots of baseball trophies, snapshots of a cat, and a model sailboat. There's an autographed picture of Carl Yastremski. A baseball signed by Roger Clemens. A shot of the agent outside Boston's Fenway park.

Voort sits on a couch that gives him a view of Central Park to the north, over two blocks of rooftops. Floor-to-ceiling bookshelves are filled with volumes whose authors he recognizes. There must be millions of dollars a year of business on those shelves, he thinks.

'Eric Porter used to work here,' she says. 'He dated Karen, a few years ago.'

'He's still here?'

'He quit after they broke up. They were pretty close, and then something happened one weekend when they went away, but neither of them ever talked about it. She was private anyway, a little stiff and nervous. Closed. He was more emotional. He actually broke into sobs in the office one day. The day he quit.'

'Do you know where he lives?'

'I haven't been in contact with him, but I have records. Kyle!'

Instantly, a male secretary stands in the doorway, a tough-looking man with broad shoulders, cropped hair, and an earring. He holds a folder.

But the young man's voice is prep school, Ivy League. 'I hope you get the guy,' he says. 'His Social Security number is in there, and his old address.'

Voort feels more hope now, because to have a suspect's name is good, but to have the Social Security number is excellent. He excuses himself, calls Mickie and gives him the number. Voort goes back to Jackie May.

'Tell me about Eric. Do you know about his hobbies, family? Where is he from?

'It's funny. I checked all that while you were coming. He worked here four, five years ago. He was a little old for the job when he started, as an office boy, but that's the way people come in here. The good ones work their way up.

They answer phones, xerox manuscripts, tell the authors we're at lunch when we're really here, we just don't want to hear them complain.'

Voort smiles politely.

'Eric was diligent but unspectacular. He'd bring in an unsolicited manuscript, something that came in the slush pile, sometimes. Most of the stuff is terrible, but every once in while something marvelous arrives. But Eric's taste was bad. He was also a bit of an exaggerator; he had an inflated view of his own importance.

'Karen started the same time, but she had more friends, she traveled in artistic circles, knew some writers starting out, and brought in a couple of winners. You know the book, *Eyesore*?'

'Good book.'

'Karen brought it in. She became an assistant. He stayed in the mailroom. She became an agent. But I don't think that had anything to do with what went wrong between them. She quit a half year after he left, and moved to another agency.' Jackie frowns. 'The Hap Twitchell Agency. Maybe you should check with them. Eric mentioned moving to another agency too, but I don't know what happened to him.'

'Would you know who Karen's doctor was? Would you have any old medical insurance forms?'

'No.'

'Have you ever heard of the initials BHC? In relation to Karen?'

'That wasn't on the news. Is that the piece of evidence you're withholding?' she asks, and smiles when Voort looks uncomfortable. 'Half my clients write police procedurals,' she says. 'I read this stuff at home practically every night. And don't worry. I won't tell.'

'Did Eric have friends here?'

'He kept to himself. He was really in love with her. He

had pictures of her all over his cubicle. He took it terribly when things went wrong. By the way, that folder's already been copied. Take the whole thing. My home number's in it. I can't believe he still carried a torch for her. It's sick. Anything I can do, I want to help.'

'Can I talk to the people here who knew him?'

'I asked them to stay. They're in conference room two.'

Voort learns nothing new from the other agents, and as he heads back downtown, at eight P.M., he knows the computer girls are interfacing with the military, credit card companies, tax rolls, legal suits, motor vehicle bureaus. There will be an updated address for Eric Porter in there somewhere, matching the Social Security number. There will be a company that employs him, or a loan application, or a conviction for another crime.

We have him, even if he moved out of New York.

Mickie's waiting for Voort when he gets back to the office. The windows are dark in the Municipal Building across the plaza. The East River is a dark ribbon, flowing seaward on the other side. The bridge is lit, and brilliant, and, against sparks thrown up by welders on the lower deck, traffic flows freely both ways, for a change.

'I got wheat gourmet pizza. Olives and red peppers. And Jamaican ginger beer. Have a slice.'

'I'm not hungry.'

'Yeah, I noticed. You're shrinking. You look like you're wearing Lieutenant Fahey's shirts, not yours. Take a fucking slice, will you, and don't give me a problem. You want me to eat it all and get fat?'

Voort knows he should eat. He hasn't been eating. The pizza has no taste, and as he chews halfheartedly he spots the message from Camilla on his desk, by his phone.

I'll be coming for my things at the apartment tonight, Voort. Is it all right if I do this alone?

Mickie drinks a ginger beer, pretending not to watch him.

'Sorry.'

'Just tell me about Porter. We have his address?'

'Well, we ran the computers against him. Got his Visa card records, rent rolls. Taxes. Phone bill . . . Addresses? We got *two* addresses.' Mickie holds up a computer foldout, thick, filled with information. 'Yep, nothing like technology,' he says, but he looks disgusted.

'Then why haven't we picked him up?'

'Because according to this marvel of records,' Mickie says, dropping the sheets, 'he disappeared ten years ago. There's nothing after that, and I mean nothing. According to modern science, the envy of other police departments, the scourge of criminals everywhere, our killer died years ago, or vanished off the earth.'

NINE

Camilla Ryan, age twelve, stares at the evening news on television, at the dark-haired announcer, so handsome and sure of himself, and she waves impatiently to her parents and two older sisters, behind her at the kitchen table, in Queens, New York, to be quiet.

How can they talk during the show!

I want to be in television, Camilla thinks. Someday, I *will* work in television. I will write the news as it comes off the wires. I will tell the cameramen where to stand, to get a better shot. I will work in darkrooms, with tapes, and pictures, cutting them, molding them, finding out information before the rest of the world, deciding the best way to present it.

Dad laughs at her, 'Camilla, you'll go blind watching so much TV.'

She's a cheerleader-quality blonde with a ponytail down to her shoulder blades. She wears a white cotton halter top and matching culottes. A girl in tennis sneakers with her legs tucked beneath her, a Pepsi and ice beside her, untouched. There are so many things on that big Zenith screen to study. So many aspects that go into every second of marvelous TV. Timing. Angles. Personalities. Makeup.

Camilla says, 'I'm going to write Channel Four a letter, Ma, and ask for an intern job.'

Her family breaks out laughing at her delusions. The ground floor garden apartment is so small that the kitchen dining room is half in the living room. The place smells of canned tomato paste, and is filled with ceramic knickknacks her mom collects; glass shepherds, angels, beagles, girls with parasols and hoop dresses, photos of the family at Jones Beach, Coney Island, Cape May.

It's a Tuesday night, the beginning of her father's weekend as assistant buyer at Korvette's department store. Mom makes spaghetti every Tuesday, after getting off work at the beauty parlor.

Now Dad mops up sauce with Wonder Bread. 'Camilla, you're smart. Someday you'll be an executive secretary. Television? Whadda you think you are? A big star?'

The news goes off and she lets them turn the set off. They're filled with affection at Camilla's obsession, the way she does English homework watching Dan Rather on CBS. Does math during Gabe Pressman's commentary.

'Can we go on a tour of the studio, Dad?'

Her older sisters giggle. 'Forget TV. Go out with Danny Greene. He's handsome, with that black hair. He has a crush on you. He moons over you. He told us, in the school bus.'

They sing, 'Danny loves Camilla.'

Camilla eyes the dark screen. 'How do you think they get the timing so perfect, the way the voice-over and visual part are in perfect sync?'

'Danny and Camilla, sitting in a treeeeee . . .'

But a year later Danny has won her over, with phone calls, and movies, and quiet talks, and he brings her roses, a thirteen-year-old boy spending his allowance on flowers, and Camilla watches TV less.

In the evenings they walk the neighborhood, hand in hand, past the two-story garden apartments, with their air conditioners roaring, their owners sitting on stoops, resting from hard days working in gas stations, insurance offices, taxi-cabs, elevators.

The American Dream in Queens.

Even the name of the avenue nearby, lined with delis, candy stores, fruit stores, optometrists, means dreams. Utopia Parkway.

By high school they're a couple. By college she sees that her parents were right, and the world of Manhattan, and television, is far away. She spends every afternoon with Danny. His dad is dying of cancer and he needs her.

They enroll in Queens College together. He's swimming champion now, filled out, chest big, muscled, tanned in a way that makes other girls envy her.

'God, Camilla, he looks like Olympic swimmer Arnie Holtz! Right down to that adorable mustache. You're so lucky. I cream in my pants looking at him. You and your kayaks. Danny and his swimming. You'll live on a beach somewhere. It's so great!'

'Marry me,' Danny says one night. They're parked, by the Throgs Neck Bridge, in his father's Buick. They're looking over Little Neck Bay; the boats and shadowy marshes. where she likes to take her kayak on weekends, the twinkling lights outlining the curve of the span linking Queens and the Bronx.

She laughs. Kisses him. 'Are you kidding? We have years to decide.'

'I got into Buffalo Law School. Come with me.'

He's so handsome, and she loves kissing him. He's clean, and muscled everywhere, and he emits the faint smell of chlorine, a healthy, powerful smell. His hand travels down her thigh, slips under her sundress. The Beatles are singing, an oldie: a song about a girl who is 'just seventeen.'

Her parents and sisters have told her: He's your future. Stop dreaming about television, it's just a machine with wires in it. Danny loves you. You'll be safe with him. You'll have children. Some people never get the opportunity you have.

Yes, yes, I'll marry you.

Three years later she's in Buffalo, in January, during Danny's senior year in law school. He's lined up a job with a Washington, D.C., lobbying firm. Lobbying is easier than law, he tells her, and the hours are good. You make money, and go places, and have big expense accounts we can use.

'You want to be a lobbyist?' she says, disappointed.

'Only for good causes,' he adds quickly. 'Like the environment.'

She hates Buffalo, a shantytown with a city charter. A permanent snowstorm with buildings in it. A larger version of Queens, where things you see on television are so far away they might as well be on another planet, where she can't even kayak for seven months a year because it is so cold. She and Danny live in a one bedroom apartment and she works as an assistant in public relations for a local radio station.

Well, Washington will be fun, she thinks. It's not New York, but we'll have fun. I'll join a kayak club.

It's the semester before graduation, and she's taking a bus home, from working late. It pulls to her stop, across from a 7-Eleven. Danny needs their car, his dead father's Buick, to get to school. It's snowing, as always. Camilla slips on the ice, getting off the bus. Her P.R. releases go flying. She scrambles, gathering them, cursing Buffalo, and stumbles toward the apartment. At least it's his night to cook.

As she turns the key in the lock she hears the television inside. A woman's voice is crying, 'Danny! Do it harder!'

Then she hears Danny groaning, in the bedroom.

She has the most ridiculous thought, heading for the bedroom. It is, *Things like this happen on television.* Except then she's looking at the redheaded girl straddling Danny on the floor, on the green shag carpet by the carefully made-up bed, a wedding present from her parents. The girl's hair is bouncing, and her hands are reaching behind her to massage Danny's penis while he kneads her breasts. Danny's eyes rolling, white, come around in her direction, pupils focusing.

Camilla thinking, I don't feel a thing.

Danny says, 'Oh God.'

The redhead realizes Camilla's there now, and turns and actually gives her a look of triumph. The redhead, it turns out, had turned the clock in the room back, wanting Camilla to interrupt.

'You're wrong for him,' the girl says, a twenty-two-year-old, another law student, sitting on Danny, angry at Camilla, instead of the other way around, showing off a whipcord body, hands on bony hips, brazen, Miss America style.

'You better go,' Danny tells the girl, sounding more like a scared eleven-year-old than Olympic swimmer Arnie Holtz.

'Not now,' the redhead says, as if *she* is the wife, as if she has rights here, as if the furniture, dishes, memories are hers, not Camilla's. As if already Camilla is fading, like she never occupied this space at all.

'I'm Linda. Did he tell you about me?'

'No.'

'I didn't think so. He's such a liar. You have to be tough with him. You can't let Danny get away with things.'

'Jesus Christ!' Danny says, but he seems helpless.

Linda says, 'Did he tell you about Emily? Or Patricia? All these years. He didn't tell you about any of the women, did he?'

Danny's head is in his hands. He says, 'I love you, Camilla.'

Linda says, 'Sure you do, hon.'

Linda sits backward now, against their bed, their wedding bed, crosses her legs. Take a good look, she is saying, because this body is Danny's future. It was his past, when you didn't know about it. His present, when you are learning the truth, and his future. It is the body that will make him happy, or miserable, or disinterested, but it is the one he will know.

Take a good look.

'Who's Patricia?' Camilla says.

'Part of a parade,' Linda says. 'Well, he won't fool me. I'm like him. I know him.' She has a harsh laugh. 'We're two assholes, Danny and I.'

She gets up, gathers her clothes, taking her time. She dresses in front of Camilla.

After she leaves, the smell of sex and sweat remains, as does the impression of Linda's small, arched feet in the shag carpet.

Camilla says, 'Excuse me,' and walks to the bathroom, feeling stupid for being polite. In the bathroom, she throws up.

When she comes out, he's dressed, and crying.

'When my dad was sick,' he says, 'I promised him I would marry you. I . . . I never wanted to marry you. I liked sleeping with you. But he was dying. I couldn't break the promise. Do you understand?'

She's crying now too, as she walks out into the snow with a suitcase, and the keys to the Buick. Thinking that she's going to wake up any second, and it will be Sunday morning, and she and Danny will be in bed, reading the *Times*, eating cinnamon pastries, drinking coffee, making love.

Everyone I trusted told me he loved me. From now on, I can't trust them. I can't trust me. I can't trust anyone.

Camilla, in her dead father-in-law's Buick, drives back to New York on the snowy freeway, crosses the Triboro Bridge into Manhattan, avoiding Queens altogether, inserting herself into the anonymity, the activity, possibility, the womb of steel and brick and intellectual dialectics.

Danny lied to me for years, she thinks. He fooled me, every day, every second, every single second for *years*.

The pain is coming, finally. It is excruciating.

I will never, ever let anyone get close to me again.

'You're nice,' Camilla tells Dr Bainbridge now, nine years later, 'to let me come in the evening like this. I'm sure you have better things to do, whether or not I pay for it. You must hear the worst stories. It must make you depressed.'

'Don't worry,' Dr Bainbridge says. 'I can change my schedule one time, it's no big deal. You left Voort, and you're getting these disturbing hang-up phone calls. You need to talk.'

'I feel safe with you.'

She stretches her gorgeous, lanky body on the Norwegian leather 'stressless' chair, in the doctor's consultation room. Her arms are thrown back, over the top of the chair, wrists loose, silver bracelet dangling, breasts perked up, her long torso raised by the cushions, in the posture, Bainbridge thinks, of a naked beach beauty. He has a vision of Camilla lying on a terry-cloth towel, in the Caribbean somewhere. In the image, he's beside her. In the image, he touches her hip.

His breathing becomes ragged, but only he can hear it.

It's been a long time since I fell in love, he thinks.

'Do you really think Voort is making the calls?' she says doubtfully.

'They started when you left him. It *could* be a coincidence. Do you think so?'

After a moment she shakes her head wearily, and says, to herself as much as him, 'I know what you're thinking. I've only known him a few months, and that's the honeymoon period, when he's at his best. And I was wrong about my husband.'

She sighs. 'Maybe I just don't want to admit it might be him. I mean, I did call the phone company.'

'And they made a record of your incoming calls. Which came from a pay phone two blocks from his house.'

'I just don't understand how could it be him.'

'Um-hmmm.'

Bainbridge must concentrate if he is to appear concerned.

She changes the subject to the old boyfriend, Kenny, who she'll see in a few hours, after going to the gym tonight.

'I thought he was drop-dead handsome the first time I saw him, dancing in a show. He was incredible, with his shirt off, his muscles rippling. Dancers do things with their bodies that other people only dream about.' She smiles.

Her words make Bainbridge jealous. It's not professional, but these days, he realizes, he's become unprofessional about too many things.

I never should have started the club, collected those men together, bought them drinks, encouraged their hate.

Camilla scratches an itch on her forearm. Bainbridge envies even this touch to her skin. She is saying, 'Kenny never stopped calling me the whole time I was with Voort. He sent me roses at the office. He mailed romantic cards to my apartment. He left messages on my answering machine, telling me he loved me. He missed me. He wanted to spend his life with me.'

'How did you feel receiving these gifts?' Bainbridge asks, angry suddenly, thinking, Aren't you the lucky one? Two men want you. Nobody ever liked me that way. Is it my fault I'm shy? I have a lot to give, and nobody knows it.

Then he thinks, Christ, I'm starting to sound like my patients.

'Finally the messages got to me. But now I can't decide if I want to be with Kenny, or if I'm just scared of Voort. I mean, assuming he's not making the phone calls, just for now, I have no control around Voort. My feelings are so strong. . . . What are you doing? Did you hear something?' she asks, following his gaze to the door.

Ian Bainbridge jerks back. He'd thought he heard the Banker, Harris Tillman, come in a while ago, and just now he'd been sure there was a creak outside, the groan of a wooden plank with a man's weight on it, as if Tillman were there, listening.

'It's nothing,' he tells Camilla. 'I hired a carpenter to fix the banister. He has a day job and can only come at night. He has a key.'

'But he could hear us.'

'I was mistaken. Anyway, you were saying about Kenny and Voort?'

The parade of details starts again, as Bainbridge imagines the Banker outside, ear pressed to the wood, in that decrepit hall, grinning. Tillman's been eavesdropping and making fun of the patients this week, doing cruel imitations of them after they leave.

I will get him out of the house and I will call the police.

Camilla says, 'I get embarrassed talking about sex, but – '

'Don't be.'

'Well,' she says, the thought of sex bringing color to her face, 'with Kenny, when we used to do it, his body is magnificent. Hard and powerful. But with Kenny, all the time, I knew I was in control. With Voort, sometimes, I know this sounds crazy, but when I come, I forget where I am. Can you believe it? I almost blacked out once. It's terrifying.'

'When was the first time in your life you had that kind of feeling?' Bainbridge asks. 'Loss of control?'

He's furious at Kenny, at Voort, the rivals who have driven her to his consulting room. Each Friday, for weeks, she has tortured him with images of what he will never have.

She is saying, 'My father was . . .'

In fact, Bainbridge realizes, it was soon after Camilla became his patient that he put together the Broken Hearts Club, collected the group, telling himself it was 'research' into the psychology of men who have been rejected at love, who have rage about it, and think violent thoughts.

Camilla says, '. . . but I was never really aware of any problem about control.'

'Um-hmmmm,' he says, not listening, but he will play back the tape later.

Camilla shifts in the chair. 'I have good friends. I have a good life. I make good money. It took years to achieve it. It was probably just good sex with Voort, so why let it bother me? Why should I put up with something that rattles me so much?'

'Maybe you shouldn't.'

'That's why I left him, like you suggested.'

'You might consider staying away from Kenny too, while you and I figure things out.'

There's definitely a noise outside this time, a low snicker, and Bainbridge, mortified, watches Camilla, but she does not seem to have heard. She's too involved in her story. But she *must* hear the fingernail on the door, sliding softly.

'I told Kenny I'd meet him after I'm finished at jazzercize tonight. Only for dinner, I said. No fooling around. "Just because I left Voort doesn't mean you and I are back together." He said he understood, but believe me, it'll be a wrestling match after dessert.' She giggles.

Are you doing this to me on purpose, telling me these things to bother me? the doctor thinks, fighting off rage.

The clock tings on the end table, signaling the end of the session, plunging him into depression, her presence making his moods swing. When Camilla gets under his skin, even time annoys Dr Bainbridge. He can't stand that she's going to meet another man.

'Actually, my next patient canceled. So if there's something more you want to talk about,' he lies, feeling awkward, blushing, knowing Tillman is listening, telling himself he never should have brought the subject up, 'feel free to take a minute or two extra, before meeting your old beau.'

Not to mention that you told me he gets angry when you're late.

She laughs, standing, and her expression, on that incredibly gorgeous, blue-eyed face, is already receding from a look of honesty, from doctor-patient directness, to her urban mask, her tough TV producer veneer. But Bainbridge is not fooled. She's in love with Voort, but frightened enough of her own feelings that maybe he can keep her away from him.

Perhaps he should encourage immediate sex with the old boyfriend, knowing it could cause irreparable damage with Voort, and that she'll never really end up with the dancer, who presents no emotional challenge. The dancer is her puppy dog.

Voort is someone she cannot control.

Her finger brushes his wrist, thrilling him.

'You have the kindest manner. No wonder you were recommended so strongly by people at NBC.'

And when she smiles, he thinks, entranced, I've never dated a woman with a smile like that. Not as a teen. Not in college. Not in fifteen years of manhood. Women with smiles like that go for other people. Not me.

'Beau,' she says softly. 'There's a word I haven't heard in a while. A southern word. Hot nights. Bougainvillea flowers. My beau,' she says, testing the sound of it. 'I'm going to meet a beau. Doctor, I believe you are a romantic.'

Bainbridge hears a closet closing out there, hears Tillman hiding as he slides open the double doors to the foyer. She gathers her wool coat from the peg outside the office, and does not notice the fresh patch of snow melting just outside the room, which the Banker brought in. Bainbridge walks her out onto the front stoop, and is surprised, after concentrating on her, to see the city outside, completely normal.

'Good night, Dr Bainbridge.'

'See you Friday, Camilla.'

He thinks, I hate the three-day wait until I see her again.

As he reenters the house, a high, whiny voice, a man's imitation of a girl's voice, floats mockingly from the hall closet.

'Oh, Doctor,' Harris Tillman calls, 'I don't know what to

do about Kenny. Oh, Kenny, my darling, my love, my Keneeeee.'

The hated, taunting voice seems to strike him physically. Hearing it, he remembers the horrible news that only Camilla's presence, only her beauty, only the incredible spell she seems to put over him, had enabled him to push away for an hour.

'I saw the TV!' Bainbridge says.

'And?'

'You killed Karen Chambers!'

He is not grieving for Karen Chambers, he realizes, as much as for himself, for his own life, which is slipping away.

His headache floods back. He can't believe he forgot the awful news, and his predicament, even for even a moment.

'Who? Me?' The closet door opens. Tillman stands there, grinning, like a late night talk show host appearing before his audience. Like a jester with a painted grin on his face. It's a look of utter madness, with no redeeming social value at all.

Bainbridge says, 'You promised me you were just going to talk to him.'

'I didn't do anything. *He* did. And anyway, you're the one who's been working on Eric for months, Ian. Pushing him like you pushed me. That's the way the police will see it, and the board of psychologists. Hell, I just rode to Brooklyn with him. And by the way,' he adds, jerking his thumb at the well-worn wooden staircase, 'he's upstairs. Asleep.'

'No!'

'I took him to a motel first. He was crazy, ranting and crying. He wanted to give himself up.'

'And you talked him out of it.'

Tillman imitates Bainbridge. ' "Youuuu talked him out of it." Don't be snide with me. I've been living in your house over a week. You've had a hundred opportunities to call the police. Why haven't you?'

'You said you would think about turning yourself in.'

'You knew all along I wouldn't do that. Now you're an accessory to two murders. You and me and him.' Tillman's light green eyes roll up, toward the stairs. 'I read those articles of yours. What did you call us? "Three men inches away from institutionalization"?'

'What if someone saw you bring him here?'

'That's better. *That's* what you're really worried about. Your neighbors always see patients coming. Anyway, I put phony glasses on him. A wig. A hat. I had the cabbie drop us two blocks away. When I got him upstairs, I sedated him.'

'You got into my medicine?'

'Would you rather he started screaming when we had a patient here?' The Banker laughs. 'That would be great.'

When *we* had a patient here, Bainbridge thinks.

Upstairs, Bainbridge finds, Eric Porter is sleeping heavily, on the spare, single mattress in the otherwise bare and previously unused extra guest room. No sheet. No blankets in the overheated room. Just a man, unconscious, in a rumpled suit, suspenders, and stockinged feet.

Plaster bits, fallen off the ceiling, speckle his trousers. It is as if the house is deteriorating as fast as the Broken Hearts Club.

Tillman sniffs. 'We live in a dump. How can we live like this?'

'Go back to your own apartment.'

'Sour milk in the fridge. Roaches. Busted laundry machine. It's like a tenement. We ought to get some paint. Or maybe wallpaper. Wallpaper would do wonders in here for us.'

Us, Bainbridge thinks.

'Feel free to move out,' he says.

'Oh, you don't really want us to leave,' the answer comes. 'Be glad we're here. After all, if I get arrested, or Eric does, you go too.'

At the mention of other club members, Bainbridge

remembers the Mechanic, up in Washington Heights. 'Oh my God!' he says, panicked. 'I can't believe I forgot him. He must have seen the news too!'

'See what I mean? You're afraid he might tell, not the other way around. But you're too smart to have forgotten him.'

The doctor hangs his head. The room is spinning. There seems to be a tickling, disembodied sound in the air, from some gigantic invisible clock.

Tillman rubs Bainbridge's neck, with a powerful circular rhythm. 'What a knot. He won't tell anyone, certainly not the police. We can be sure of that.'

'You're a mind reader now?'

'A computer reader.'

'You broke into my files!' Bainbridge shrieks. Eric Porter remains asleep, drugged, breathing steadily.

Bainbridge charges through the dark, cramped hall, bumping into the wobbly banister. He knocks a pot holding a dead fern over. A roach is crawling on the baseboard. The pain in the Psychologist's temples is spreading into the back of his skull, down his left arm. He's created a monster, he sees. Tillman is worse than he ever thought a man would be. He's a demon. Unstoppable. Only now does the Psychologist see the difference between an intellectual exercise, the creating of his little club, and the consequences of playing God.

He hears music start up downstairs. Tillman has put a Bach sonata on the CD. The sound of violins fills the empty space between the uncovered floors, saggy steps, plaster-marked, exposed plumbing.

He broke into my *files*.

Bainbridge feels naked, dizzy. In his panic, the very walls seem to be undulating.

The office is the only room up here that's even halfway finished. It's in the old nursery. The peeling wallpaper depicts happy boys and girls, in bathing suits, on a beach, building sand castles with plastic shovels as soothing foam washes along the shore.

'You just relax. We're relaxed. Very relaxed,' says Tillman. He's leaning against the doorjamb, eating a bologna sandwich. 'We're out of mustard, by the way. Let's buy the spicy kind, okay?'

In the center of the room, facing into the house, is an old sea captain's desk, inherited from Bainbridge's mother. The Apple computer on the blotter is on. His mom's old gray file cabinets line a wall. Her oval, cotton, multicolored throw rug cushions her faded leather swivel chair. He inherited, along with his mother's money, the old stand-up radio, the lovingly brushed white Haitian cotton couch and matching sitting chair. The only photo in the room shows Bainbridge, age eight, in shorts and a T-shirt, on a backyard deck with his mother, in a suburb. She's cradling the boy in her lap. A shadow obscures the expression on her face.

On the blue computer screen, the file says, BROKEN HEARTS CLUB.

'It wasn't hard to figure out the password,' Tillman says, chewing. He's had no food since the Thursday porterhouse at Mackeys, and it seems hard to believe that was less than twenty-four hours ago.

'Bastard.'

'Me? I don't know, according to what you wrote about me, I thought I was . . . what's the word? Influenceable? Weak-willed? Isn't that the way you described me in your file? Filled with latent rage?'

'You had no right to look.'

'You never tried to cure me, to make me better. We were experiments. We were ways *you* could act out the way you hate the world. You were never, ever, our friend, so don't tell me what I have the right to do.'

'He'll call the police, the Mechanic.'

'I'm happy to hear you're finally admitting what you're really afraid of. Arthur? The referral who came to you because his old psychologist was afraid of him? Arthur, who attacked his old girlfriend? Who put her in the hospital? Who had the shit beaten out of him by detectives frustrated because she wouldn't press charges? And he never even went and filed a complaint about *them*?'

Tillman laughs. 'You're afraid *Arthur* is going to call the police? A man who can't even watch television, or read newspapers, because they give him ideas about hurting people? I read the referral report,' the Banker says, licking a spot of mustard off his thumb. ' "Despises authority. Walks the other way if he sees a police car coming. Dangerous personality change if he doesn't take his medication, which he forgets to do half the time. Walking time bomb. Perfect for the violence and rejection project." No, I don't think Arthur will go to the police.'

Bainbridge realizes that he hears moaning. The horrible sound is coming from himself. His heartbeat seems so loud he envisions passers by outside, in the street, able to hear the rhythmic pounding. His head is killing him. He grabs it, but the pain won't stop. Tillman just stands there, as if enjoying a Broadway show.

'Why don't we hold the next meeting of the club here,' Tillman says. 'It's not a good idea to go back to Mackey's.'

'No more meetings,' Bainbridge says.

'I think you know if we're to protect ourselves, there are one or two more things we have to do.'

'No.'

'Pretty woman, your patient,' the Banker adds. 'Beautiful, actually. I can see why you have a crush on her.'

'I don't.'

'Ha! I listen to you talk to patients all day. You don't change your schedule for *them*. You tell other patients, "It's a strict rule. I never change the schedule." '

'I told you not to listen at the door.'

'So I'll stop. Meanwhile, want me to follow her?'

Bainbridge is speechless.

'You know, give you a report on the man she meets. If they go to his apartment. If they're there all night.'

'Shut up!'

'Whatever you say,' the Banker says. The sickly green glow from Bainbridge's mother's old lamp shade seems to tinge Tillman's skin, give it a pale, unworldly hue. To the doctor, the man's features seem different; sharper, even though that's impossible. People's features don't change so fast. But the jawbone looks stronger, the handsome nose straighter, more powerful, like a Roman emperor's, a man unrestrained by Christian religion, by any notion of charity. A creature who makes human sacrifices to the deity he worships. Tillman even seems taller, as if, through symbiosis, he is absorbing the vestiges of will from the doctor he once went to, for help.

'I'm going out,' Tillman says. 'Didn't she say she was going to the gym first, for a couple of hours?'

Bainbridge screams, 'Leave her alone!'

'I promised, didn't I? I swear,' Tillman whispers, in a voice so soft Bainbridge can barely hear. A voice, even now, capable of being incredibly persuasive. 'I can't punish the one who hurts *you*, can I? Don't you want to know where she goes? I bet if there were a file on you in that computer, I bet it would say,' Tillman says shrewdly, ' "He wants to know where she goes, whether or not he admits it." '

'I don't.'

Tillman goes to the closet, ignoring the order to stop. He puts on his coat, muffler, his costume of urban prosperity, which makes women glance at him on the street. He puts on silver-colored earmuffs, of wolverine fur. It keeps his fine blond hair in place. He slips on fur-lined gray leather gloves.

'Go buy food,' he says, descending the hallway stairs,

while the Psychologist trails after him, begging. Don't go. We can work on the building, like you want. We can get new wallpaper. We can go shopping.

Tillman goes out the door.

Now Bainbridge stands alone in his hallway. He's in agony. What's happening is a nightmare. He tells himself it has to stop. He will stop it this very instant. He will not let Camilla get hurt.

Call the police.

He brushes sweat from his eyes, strides into the kitchen, reaches for the phone, ignoring the dishes in the sink and tilting bags filled with garbage. And his mother's old paintings of sunflowers, which she made herself. Some of the flowers have faces; sad, inquisitive faces. One sunflower is screaming. It has skinny little hands, and, as in an Edvard Munch painting, the palms press tight over the sunflower's ears.

On the counters are his mother's old crystal ashtrays, with cigarette residue in them, twenty-year-old tar and nicotine. The stain reminds him of her.

This is the first right thing I've done since I moved in here, he thinks, punching in 911.

'Police!'

The doctor hangs up quickly. He's realized, with their modern technology, the police might instantly know his telephone number.

I couldn't be anonymous if I call from here.

Bainbridge, soaked with sweat, thinks, I'm so mixed up.

Why *shouldn't* they know my number? he tells himself. In the end they're going to learn it anyway. But he finds himself dressing for bad weather, pulling on his old Confederate Army coat and rubber boots. This dressing, this preparation to call the police from a pay phone, gives him time to think.

Bainbridge goes out into the night, and passes up three public phones, getting farther away from his brownstone, until he is two blocks from his house, on Lexington Avenue.

Maybe I'm delaying because I don't really want to do this.

He finds a phone, but has forgotten to bring a quarter. He makes change in a newly opened Korean grocery.

I have to call. It's the right thing to do. Tillman is dangerous.

But the pay phone is occupied now, so he starts walking again, looking for another, past the well-lit stores, the pizza places and boutiques and shoemaker and pharmacy. Past people who will not have to go to jail tonight. People who have the luxury, a luxury he never appreciated before, the incredible safe luxury of being able to exist without fear of police.

I'll never get to walk on the street again if they arrest me. Never get to go into a restaurant again. Never have patients. Never take a vacation. Never be able to go to a movie on the spur of the moment, buy popcorn, choose the seat I want to sit in, watch the coming attractions, walk out if it stinks.

Bainbridge sees himself alone, on a single bed, a jail bed, between steel walls, shoulders slumped, an old man looking out of a tiny cell at eternity.

He's shaking now, from cold and fear. But he forces himself to keep going. The next phone is broken, vandals have cut the receiver off. The phone after that has the coin slot jammed by gum. But he finally finds another phone, and drops the quarter in, and as he does so, realizes, on a police emergency call, he never even had to pay in the first place.

He breaks out laughing. An old woman, walking a poodle, stops a few feet away and crosses the street to get away from him.

'Police emergency!'

He forces himself to speak. His voice is shaking. 'I have information that can help you solve two murders. Niana Embers, on the lower East Side, a week ago. And Karen Chambers, the woman in Brooklyn last night.'

'What is your name, sir?'

'I just want to give the information.'

'Is there an emergency right now, sir?' the voice asks.

Bainbridge envisions the Banker out on the street, walking behind Camilla.

'Not exactly at this moment. I'm talking about two murders!'

'I'm sorry, but this line is for immediate emergencies. If you have information about a murder,' the voice says, and, incredibly, tells him to call another number. He hangs up. He can't believe this. But he punches in the number, hearing the electronic beeping over the thunderous slamming of his heart.

'Please deposit twenty-five cents for three minutes,' a recorded voice says.

If you're calling about people who have already died, the phone company requires money.

This time a voice says, 'Hotline.' It's a polite voice, but not too excited. The doctor has a feeling the voice has been answering calls about murders for too many hours.

'I have information about the death of Niana Embers, and Karen Chambers.'

'Your name, sir?'

'The man who killed Niana Embers is a banker. His name is Harris Tillman. He works at the Apple Bank, on Fourth Street in Sheridan Square, in the Village. Did you get the name? Tillman.'

'May I ask *your* name, sir?'

'No.'

'May I ask how you know that this Mister, er, Tillman, is responsible?' And with a sinking feeling, Bainbridge realizes he is simply one more voice on a phone to this man. The officer on the hotline has probably been answering phone calls like this for two weeks now, has probably talked to hundreds of callers. Callers saying my grocery clerk did it. My subway driver looks like the sketch on TV. There are probably hundreds of names the police have to check out.

Bainbridge says, 'He stabbed her, and then he gouged out initials on the table. Initials. BHC.'

This time the voice changes radically, seems interested suddenly. Bainbridge realizes the initials were never mentioned in the newspaper, or on TV.

'Sir, I'm wondering if you would mind giving me your name.'

They'll arrest me in the end, the doctor thinks. Why not give them my name? They'll know it as soon as they arrest Tillman.

'Sir, okay then: If you won't tell me your name, can you tell me how you know this man, Mr Tillman?' The voice is gentle, as if afraid the doctor might hang up.

'He's a patient of mine,' Bainbridge manages to get out.

I'll never see Camilla again, he thinks, and feels his heart cracking.

'Ah, you're a doctor. Someone else would like to talk to you.'

I'll never see her again. Never feel her touch me again, the way her fingers brushed me as she left the house tonight. I'll never get to look at her, to tell her how much I could make her happy. And I could make her happy.

Another voice comes on the line.

'Hello? This is Detective Mickie Connor.'

Bainbridge hangs up.

He's shaking. He fears he can't breathe, even though he can see his breath rising. He stumbles back through the night, past knots of teenagers, private school kids, who beg him, 'Mister, can you buy us beer?' He sees his reflection in a window, a man wrapped against the cold, in an old hippie-style Confederate Army coat. A man pushing through air as if it is almost solid.

He needs to hear her voice. He can't wait three days. He needs it right now, this instant, this second.

The cab he flags drops him on Fourteenth Street, four blocks from Voort's house, at a pay phone he's never used before. He knows her number by heart. When her answering machine comes on, he feels weak with pleasure, listening to the voice, the smooth feminine quality in it, the promise of delight.

When the greeting stops, he lets his silence hang on the line, knowing that another machine in her apartment is recording the number he is calling from.

She will think Voort is doing it. She will stop thinking good things about Voort.

Tomorrow, he thinks, I'll call her from a pay phone near One Police Plaza.

Then he flags another cab, reaches his street, his stoop, his door, and when he gets inside he locks it, leans against it, breathing heavily, like an exhausted swimmer who has barely made it to shore.

What did I almost do to myself?

I'll convince Tillman to tell the truth, that he did it. And Tillman promised he would leave her alone. He promised.

A voice in his head, almost a whisper, says, go away. Change your name. Just leave, leave this place.

Bainbridge makes it upstairs, checks on Eric Porter, who is still sleeping, snoring soundly, in fact, lids twitching, deep in dream. Bainbridge hopes that the Agent, in his imagination, occupies a place where he does not have a broken heart.

Dr Bainbridge strips off his clothes. He falls onto his mattress and puts on an extra quilt, then another. The heavy weight substitutes for a human body. It's been years since he slept with a woman, since he felt a real human body next to him, instead of a clutched pillow, an extra blanket, a stuffed toy his mother gave him long ago.

He breaks into sobs. He is a man alone, in a dark room, weeping.

After a while he reaches down. He touches himself. Even the human feel of his own fingers is lonely.

He moves his hand up and down, slow, then faster.

He moans, unsure whether he's experiencing pain or pleasure.

'Camilla,' he whispers.

There is no one to hear her name but himself.

TEN

An hour later, when Camilla has still not come out of her health club, Harris Tillman strolls in and tells the desk attendant that he's just moved into the neighborhood and is considering joining.

'Can I go upstairs and look around?' he asks, smiling. 'Alone?'

'We're supposed to escort you.'

Tillman can be incredibly charming when it suits him. His smile broadens. The truth is, he explains, that he reacts negatively to high pressure sales tactics. He's ready to spend money here, and if he likes what he sees, two other friends, and their families, will join too.

From the gleam in the clerk's eye, he sees his guess was right. She gets a commission for each new member she signs up.

'Okay, you can go alone.' She winks. 'Our secret.'

She's attracted to him, he sees, and he lets her know, by the brush of hands, that he's grateful in a way that may mean a more social reward later. She's not bad-looking, in an athletic way, with her trim butt, tight belly muscles, her hair in a neat short cut, her artificially tanned calves disappearing into white athletic socks.

Upstairs it's a madhouse, noisy, as crowded as the rush hour train. People pedal bicycles that go nowhere, march on treadmills that go nowhere, climb stairs that rise nowhere, beneath gigantic suspended TV screens showing CNN, MTV, *Wheel of Fortune*, where someone has just won a power boat and, consequently, an audit by the IRS. It's a big glass room, a fish tank of humans, where the type-A clients are wrapped in colorful spandex, as they work off high calorie pasta lunches, admiring themselves in mirrors, always rushing, even when they do not move.

He catches sight of Camilla inside a smaller room, in the music exercise class, where rows of men and women plunge and flail to some bongo drum African juju beat. It's so loud, it makes the glass walls vibrate. The teacher keeps shouting, 'Go! Harder!'

Watching her, the banker has to admit that she's a fine-looking woman. Her long blond hair bounces, in a ponytail, against her beautiful ass.

But she's not his type. He prefers small, darker women. Women he towers over in the bedroom, who he can pick up and physically carry around. From his anonymous viewpoint by the Perrier machine and complimentary cheese, cracker, and grape tray, he is growing angry at Camilla's cheery energy. She wreaks havoc with men's lives, tortures the Psychologist with sex stories, and then, having received secular absolution, as if she's said her Hail Marys to Sigmund Freud, she glibly bounces off to exercise class.

Despite the fact that he teases Ian Bainbridge, Tillman feels sorry for him, sorry that he wastes his affections on a worthless recipient like Camilla, who doesn't have the capacity to appreciate them. As the music ends and class disperses, he hurries downstairs, takes a membership application from the hopeful clerk, goes outside and finds a bar doorway with a view of the club, and, feeling his rage build, waits.

She comes out fifteen minutes later, carrying a gym bag, and for a moment he fears she is going to hail a taxi, which would mean he'd have trouble following her. But she was just appreciating the bright, starry night. She turns left and hurries south along Madison Avenue, to her rendezvous with 'Kenny.'

Tillman, fifty feet back, keeps the distance constant.

He actually feels himself growing stronger, and relishes the surges of power, as if the Broken Hearts Club has reinvented him. He has to admit that the Psychologist, despite his crippling timidity, has helped him a lot.

Last night I helped Eric do what *he* had to do, to free himself. I like helping my friends.

His footsteps quicken, closing the distance. He and Camilla are the only people on this particular block, hurrying past a closed hair stylist, a grate over an electronics store, a pile of blue cellophane bags holding a mountain of garbage and recyclables. No one is looking down from the windows above. The two of them, man and woman, are utterly alone.

I am the strength of the Broken Hearts Club.

The giddy reverie lasts until Camilla makes a sharp left on Eighty-sixth Street and rushes toward a familiar restaurant, *Café Tonni*, announced by a black script on a yellow awning. The sight makes Tillman miss a step.

Because the Café Tonni is where he used to take Niana on spring nights, during their affair, after a movie at the Cineplex, or a play, or dance performance at Lincoln Center. The Banker freezes while Camilla hurries in the door, and a blast of canned saxophone jazz floats out into the night, to mix with the traffic noise and the diesel complaint of a passing bus.

The Banker suddenly can't breathe. He remembers sitting at a small table with Niana Embers, in back, near the lit fireplace. He remembers a half-filled bottle of Ruffino Chianti on the checkerboard table. He remembers Niana's ringed hand on his fingers, rubbing him. He remembers the way she liked to reach beneath the table, find his thigh, and caress.

All his strength goes out of him as he sags against the plate-glass window of an auto insurance store. What have I done? he thinks, in an agony of clarity. The images in his head have changed to Niana's apartment. He sees the blood-spattered body. He sees his hand, dragging her by the hair, her eyes rolling, her throat gurgling, as she tries to cry out, but she can't, because he's hurt her so badly he's stopped even sound.

'What have I done?' he whispers out loud.

He can't see. He panics. He's blind! He claws at his eyes. His vision clears.

It's a trick, a whisper inside says. This remorse. It's Niana, from beyond the grave, still trying to control you. They never stop, he thinks, feeling the anger flood into him again, like medicine, morphine for the soul, like a soothing lullaby in the fevered brain of the infant he is in his heart.

Harris Tillman understands the big picture now. It's so clear. He must always be vigilant. Even when they're dead, he sees, they try to reach back and control you, through your own thoughts.

In a fury, he closes the distance to the restaurant. By the time he pushes through the door, his power is restored.

The place is unchanged, one of those rare New York landmarks that doesn't alter itself seasonally. The restaurant has three levels, each separated by a single step, and none of which is visible at the moment from the pack of bodies. Fern bar in front. Dining area for snacks. Back room for dinners. Seven days a week the place is full.

He pushes his way past a trio of women by the bar, holding Broadway playbills, laughing, past a couple staring stonily at each other, in the sullen stage of fighting, past another couple kissing madly, oblivious to the rest of the world, locked in passion, the woman's hip pressed against the lip of the bar. He spots Camilla in the back, the very rear, at a table beside the one where he last ate here with Niana. She's holding hands with Kenny, the semi-famous dancer, whom Tillman recognizes from playbills glued on construction walls around town.

They look very much in love, a champagne bottle in a bucket at the side of the table, a waiter leaving, having just taken the food order. They're leaning toward each other. They're so locked into each other that the air between them probably seems like a barrier to them. Tillman notices other men in the room looking covetously at Camilla, and women glaring at her, giving her the supreme feminine compliment of wishing she would disappear.

He makes his way to the empty table directly behind her. When he scrapes his chair back, sitting down, he feels the fabric of his jacket brush against the coat she's suspended against the back of her chair.

He hears Kenny saying, 'I'm so happy you left him. We have time, love. You don't have to make any decisions tonight.'

And she says, 'I'm not promising anything.'

And he says, 'I'm not crowding you. You want space, you got space. Hell, take all of outer space, I'm so happy tonight.'

'Can I take your order, sir?'

Tillman asks the waitress for a Laphroaig, fifteen years old, please. It's Ian's drink. By ordering it, he acknowledges that he is on a mission for the man. He orders tomato bread and tortellini Alfredo. It occurs to him that this is the same meal he ate here when Niana was with him here last.

Behind him the dancer is saying, 'So my agent told me to keep working, even without a contract. "You're valuable to them, Kenny. Don't worry, coupla months with no contract," he says, "and they'll get cold feet and pay you what you want."'

Tillman sips his Laphroaig, feels the peaty flavor of it rise back up in his stomach, more like smoke than liquid. I am hearing the love song of modern romance, he thinks philosophically. Let me tell you about my contract, darling. Oh, beloved, those fuckhead producers owe me a raise.

And now he realizes Camilla has spun around, is staring at something, not him, thankfully, and Tillman dares to glance at her, and sees her face has gone white, she is trying to smile, but seems terrified. The dancer's face has flushed as they both eye a handsome blond man who, drink in hand, is weaving around tables, coming toward them.

'Hello, Voort,' Tillman hears the woman say.

Wow, *this* is interesting, Tillman thinks gleefully. Wait until I tell Ian. So this is the guy she loses control with. This is the guy she loves sex with. This is the man Ian hates. The trio behind him is so involved with each other, he is free to watch without being noticed. Voort seems more casually elegant than the dancer, in his turtleneck sweater, Italian cords, expensive but understated watch.

The dancer says, 'It's Murphy's law, that's all I can say. Little awkward, hey, running into you like this.'

'I pick one place you *never* go,' Camilla tells the blond man, 'so we won't bump into each other, and of course, that's what you do too.'

'How you feeling, Camilla?' Voort says.

'Fine.'

'You left your blue sweater in the upstairs closet.'

'Oh? I wondered where that was. Forget it. How are you doing, Voort? Are you okay?'

How the hell do you think he is? Tillman thinks, his sympathy going out to Voort, the guy being screwed over. Do you think he's dancing in the street? Do you think he's here celebrating freedom? Do you think he's able to just forget you, you bitch, the way you dumped him?

'I'm okay. You need anything?'

'She's good,' the dancer says, clearly needing to make sure

they both know he's still here, threatened by any contact between Voort and Camilla.

'I don't need anything,' Voort says.

'I'll, uh, call you sometime.'

'Well,' Voort says, and all the real communication lies in the silence that follows, which seems accentuated by the gay noise blasting all around them, the laughter from the bar, and the cheer of a crowd on TV, at Madison Square Garden as one of the Knicks sinks a shot. The collective happiness of people spending money, and getting value for it. The juxtaposition of the fun makes the pocket of silence behind Tillman seem louder to him than the thunder of a breaking heart.

Voort says, 'It just seemed odd not to come over, once we saw each other.'

'I'm glad you did,' she says.

'Here comes the food. It was nice chatting,' the dancer says.

Voort turns and leaves, and Tillman, watching the measured retreat, the back straight, understands what the effort is costing Voort. He loses interest in Camilla for the moment. He is now fascinated with Voort, and wants to see where he goes. He signals the waitress, acts embarrassed and apologetic as he tells her a 'family problem' came up, and he asks for his check.

'You mean, you're not going to eat anything?'

'I'm sorry. My beeper went off. It's . . . well,' Tillman says, looking like he might break into tears any minute, 'It's my sister. She's sick.'

The waitress squeezes his shoulder in sympathy. 'Sir, I'll just charge you half. You come back and visit us again when everything is all right. I hope your sister is okay.'

By the time Tillman gets outside, five minutes later, he's not sure which way Voort went, and he guesses south, because from what he overheard Camilla say in therapy, south is the direction of Voort's famed town house. Tillman hurries that way and, two blocks later, spots the man, trudging, a block ahead. Voort's so preoccupied, Tillman sees, that he has not even bothered to put on his gloves in the cold.

They move this way, the man and the shadow, through the night, linked, in Tillman's mind, by the pain of a broken heart. He can't help liking Voort a little now, even if Voort is Dr Bainbridge's rival. Tillman feels Voort shedding bits of pain, as if he is filled with so much of it that bits drop off as he passes, leaving a trail. As if hurt is a physical substance that can be shed like dirty residue, like dog shit, or garbage, or the mounds of city soot that doormen wash away.

In Midtown, Voort slows his pace. The pain is getting to him. He walks into a Chinese restaurant on Fifty-sixth and Madison, hangs up his coat on a rack, and heads for the bar. At eleven P.M. it's almost empty, as it serves a business crowd and the hotel crowd. Voort takes up a swivel stool at the fancy-looking bar.

'Yo, Voort,' says the black-jacketed Asian maître d', coming over. 'Meeting the lovely lady tonight?'

'She's working, Robert,' Voort replies. 'I think I'll just have a drink.'

'On us.'

'You know I can't do that.'

'I'm not offering it to you because you're a policeman. It's because of your stock tip. Brown 'n' Black went up thirty points and split three for one. I made eight thousand bucks. Accept my gratitude, Voort, not a bribe.'

'In that case, a double Maker's Mark.'

The bar is one of those great, soothingly lit bars, where the glasses are crystal clear and the mahogany is polished, as is the mirror running from wall to wall. All those bottles on the shelves, back-lit, seem calming, with their amber, emerald, druggishly black liquids. The ice is made from springwater. Tiny orbs of light glow on the silvery ceiling. The place is a planetarium of pinprick bulbs. Tillman slides into the vacant stool of soft burgundy leather, on Voort's left.

'Cold night,' Tillman says.

'Yep.'

'Laphroaig, fifteen years old,' Tillman tells the bartender. Voort's not looking back in the mirror. Voort is looking down at his drink, moving the swizzle stick against the clicking ice.

'Cheers,' Tillman says, taking a big swallow.

Voort nods, picks a cashew nut from a silver dish, pops it in his mouth and chews thoughtfully.

'Sir, I don't want to bother you, as I see you are having a private moment,' Tillman says, after figuring out the right approach. 'But I hope you won't mind talking to a stranger. Something bad happened to me tonight, and I guess, if it's all right with you, I want to talk about it with someone. Your bad luck, sir, but if you want,' Tillman says, sliding off his stool, 'I can move away.'

Voort is looking into his face now.

'I'm even embarrassed mentioning it,' Tillman says. 'It seems trivial. At my age, who would dream a woman could still break a man's heart.'

'I'm sorry,' Voort says, turning now, almost imperceptibly, toward Tillman, but enough so Tillman knows that Voort feels the kinship of the rejected and will not ask him to leave.

'If I'm bothering you . . .'

'No. Tell me. It's good to talk sometimes, especially to a stranger. You can say things you can't tell someone you know,' Voort says.

'Then you know how I feel.'

Tillman makes up a story about a woman he loves in his apartment building. They met in the laundry room, he tells Voort. She's a dance coach at Lincoln Center. They had a terrific time for the last seven months.

'Then, out of the blue, she tells me she's going back to her old boyfriend,' Tillman says.

'That's tough,' Voort says.

'I must say, sir, it can sting,' Tillman says.

'Buy you a drink,' Voort says, signaling the bartender for more anesthesia. But Voort doesn't volunteer any information about his own situation. Voort just says, 'I feel for you, buddy. I hope it gets better, that's all I can say.'

Tillman goes on, embellishing the story, but Voort's reticence annoys him. He knows damn well Voort's gone through the same experience. Why does he keep his own feelings in?

'Have you ever had anything like that happen to you?' Tillman asks. 'I mean, one minute things are terrific. The next . . .' he says, trailing off, as if he cannot believe what happened to him.

'Me?' Voort says, finishing his Maker's Mark. 'We're talking about you.'

'Actually,' Tillman confides, 'I even joined a group about it. Men like me. We meet once a week and tell stories of what happened to us.'

'You mean, just talk about it, with strangers?'

'They're not strangers. After a while,' Tillman says, 'they get to be pretty close friends.'

'Sounds weird to me,' Voort says. 'Bunch of guys in a circle. But everybody has their own way of doing things.'

'So nothing like this ever happened to you,' Tillman says.

'Nope.' Voort lifts his glass as if toasting women. 'I've been lucky in love. Even when things ended, while they lasted, I felt pretty damn alive.'

What do you mean, lucky? Tillman wants to scream. Lucky that someone told you to get out of their life forever? Lucky that someone deceived you, led you on, and then threw you off a cliff? Are you saying you're better than me? You're not, Mr Liar. You're not.

But he says, 'That's a terrific attitude. Thanks for listening. It's getting late.'

Tillman leaves Voort, walks to the coatrack, and, as no one is watching, steals one of Voort's gloves, which is sticking out of a pocket. He walks out of the bar, and when the cold winter air hits him, it fuels the fury inside.

But then he begins to pity Voort. He remembers, buttoning his coat as he walks, that right after Niana dumped him, *he* told himself the same kinds of lies that Voort does. He tried to convince himself he'd been lucky even for a little while, to have found real love. He made excuses for the woman who had deceived him, and he refused, until Dr Bainbridge helped him, to admit how furious he was.

Which brings him back to Camilla.

I can pay back Ian and even do a favor for poor Voort.

He knows Camilla's address in Tribeca, having looked it up in Ian's files.

A police cruiser goes by, its shadowy occupants scanning the street, windows, rooftops. Tillman nods at them, good citizen that he is, happy to see policemen as he walks to the subway, heading for the converted warehouse where Camilla lives. By the time he gets there, he has forgiven Voort, has decided he understands what Voort is going through. Hell, why should I expect that poor guy, in only a few days, to evolve to the point that's taken me years to reach?

He feels better now. The whispery voice inside reminds him, *You are the protector.* And Camilla's block is nothing special. It's treeless, the buildings mostly post-World War Two warehouses, with arched windows, ledges filled with flowerpots, and balconies at the corners.

She rents unit 2L, he remembers, avoiding permanency even in her living situation, subletting a co-op. The problem is, from the street, with all those windows up there, which apartment is hers?

As Tillman ponders the question, a man exits the building,

walking a Dalmatian, or rather, being pulled by it toward the nearest hydrant. The man's flannel bathrobe hangs down beneath his goose-down parka. His Irish shepherd's cap half covers one ear. The dog must have woken him, nuzzled his sleeping master when nature called.

Tillman says, 'Pardon me. Do you live here?'

'Whaddaya think, I'm paid to do this?' The good thing about New York is that at two-thirty A.M. people are still walking around, getting off work, going to friends' houses, leaving lovers. At two-thirty A.M. the kind of casual inquiry Tillman is making is normal enough, if politely asked.

Tillman smiles at the joke. 'I'm thinking of buying one of the units. Do you mind if I ask you, do you like the building?'

Now the man is looking at him as a possible neighbor, sizing him up. 'Sure.'

'Any problems with the co-op board?'

'They're anal retentive.' The man scratches his ear. 'They have no personal lives, so they take it out on other people. But I can live with them. They keep us solvent. They managed to pay for a new roof without raising the monthly charge.'

'Pets allowed, I see. I have a Labrador, myself.'

The man warms now. 'They're great guys. I just wish they didn't have to shit so much.'

'True friends,' Tillman says.

'Better than ex-wives.'

Tillman laughs. 'Don't start me on *that*,' he says. 'By the way, it's 2L I'm thinking of buying. Do you know which is the L line?'

The man gazes up at the building, bleary-eyed.

'Let's see . . . A to M is the front, so L will be the first one on the side, in the alley, the unit next to the fire escape. And 2L will be two stories up.'

'Thanks. Whoa,' Tillman says, watching the Dalmatian squat. 'He had to go, all right. What did you feed him tonight, a five-course dinner?'

The man laughs, and puts on a plastic glove, and gets a little yellow plastic shovel from a plastic bag.

He says, looking up as he picks it up, 'The things you do for a dog.'

Tillman walks around the block, counts two hundred, and sure enough, when he walks back, the man and the Dalmatian have gone back into the building.

It's 2:45, and now Kenny the dancer comes out of the building, coat open, grinning, on top of the world.

The dancer hails a cab.

Tillman walks into the alley, locates Camilla's second floor window beside the fire escape. The light is still on, and he sees that the window is open a crack.

Eyeing the distance between pavement and fire escape, Tillman addresses Camilla in his head: Maybe you needed fresh air while you fucked his brains out. Maybe you liked the breeze on your back while you straddled him, pumped against him, rode him and made him cry out in pleasure, the way Niana Embers did with me.

A short way down the alley, Tillman spots a trash Dumpster on wheels, and finds, when he tries to move it, that it's chained to the apartment house. Anything smaller than a car, in New York, must be shackled to something bigger if it is not to be stolen.

But the chain has a few feet of give on it.

He pushes the Dumpster. It squeaks and squeals, loud in the alley, but it moves, and, as a large rat flees from under it, he maneuvers it so the Dumpster is beneath the fire escape.

He scans the dark windows. No one is looking out at him.

By closing the Dumpster and climbing on top of it, Tillman finds that he can wrap the tips of his fingers around the bottom rung of the fire escape. He's not strong enough to pull himself up, though. He scans the wall of the building. There's a hole where a loose brick fell out. By wedging in his shoe, he can now fully grasp the bottom rung.

He pulls himself up. He's on the fire escape.

Excited, Tillman starts climbing toward her window. There's flickering light in there, the kind of glow that comes when a TV is on.

He can hear the words in the newscast now. A man is saying, '. . . monster storm which is now in Ohio, and which is heading east. Roads are closed. Power lines are down. Already, in Pennsylvania and New Jersey, people are stocking up on water, lanterns, toilet paper. This is the big one.'

I promised Ian I wouldn't hurt you.

But Ian doesn't know what you've been up to tonight.

Tillman tiptoes up the rungs of the fire escape.

He raises his head, slowly, to the crack of the window, but he makes a noise, and she whirls. He ducks, counts to ten, and looks up again.

Peekaboo, he thinks, seeing her naked back.

Quite intentionally, he drops Voort's glove on the fire escape. Only Voort's fingerprints will be on it.

I see you.

ELEVEN

Less than an hour later, Voort, drunk enough to do things he'd normally only think about, pushes his way into the Big Buddy Car Service on Twenty-first near Third, a plain, small office, nothing more than a street-level waiting room with a lone wooden bench, Formica floors, and a glass booth for the fleet operator.

I'm about to violate police orders, and I couldn't care less.

Ever since he left the Café Tonni, his rage has been building. He keeps seeing Camilla and the dancer at the back table, holding hands. He sees the bucket of champagne and the expression of delight on the dancer's face. He hears the sound of Camilla laughing.

Like I never existed. Like she can move from one man to another without a second thought.

I don't want to think like this, but I can't help wondering, has she been fucking this guy for months?

He thinks, She wouldn't do that. He thinks, hating the thought, Maybe I don't know her as well as I thought I did.

Maybe that's what she was doing on Fridays. Meeting him.

There are only two people in the car service office at this hour, Voort and the operator, a skinny, bald guy in a plaid flannel shirt, behind triple-strength bulletproof glass, the wall of choice for urban late night businesses. The operator is small, dark, mustached, smoking a filterless cigarette and talking on a radio to his drivers. Keeping tabs on them. Car 123 to Kennedy Airport. Car 901 to pick up an old lady going to Lenox Hospital. Hurry. Car 12 is stuck on the service road of the Long Island Expressway, behind a four-car pile-up, with a pissed-off broker in the backseat, coming home from a bachelor party to his even angrier wife.

'Police,' Voort says, banging on the operator's window, holding up the gold detective shield. The operator's eyes widen. Voort knows a frightened man when he sees one. Good.

'Yes, sir?'

'I'm a detective investigating a murder. One of your drivers had a pickup last Friday morning,' Voort says, repeating the date that the car picked up Camilla at his town house, and the hour, taking her to wherever she disappears to on Fridays.

Already, it seems like months ago.

Voort tells the operator the passenger was Camilla Ryan of NBC. He knows damn well that the dancer lives on Sixtyseventh, near Lincoln Center. He tells himself, If the car dropped her there, I'll kill them.

'Where'd that car take her?'

'The information is, uh, privileged, sir. We're not supposed to tell.'

Voort gives him the cop stare. 'I said, it's a murder investigation.'

'I could call my boss,' the operator suggests.

Voort shoves his face toward the pane. 'What's *your* name?' he demands, implying that the man is in trouble, raising his voice and watching the operator wince.

'Lou.'

'Lou what?'

The man whines, 'Whaddaya need to know my name for?'

Voort just looks at him.

'Actually,' Lou says, crumbling, 'I don't have to wake the boss. He's always saying I gotta have initiative. I'll look up the information for you in the logs. It'll take a minute.'

'Take all the time you need,' Voort says, stepping back, trying to keep the rage from his voice. *It's wrong to do this.*

But Voort's out of control. He tells himself, Fuck wrong. Fuck both of them. He has an image suddenly, of a vacation he took with Camilla. He sees them in Montreal, holding hands, walking on the cobblestone streets of the French Quarter. He sees them in the Jacuzzi of their suite, in the Auberge du Vieux Port, steam rising around her face, a bucket of iced champagne on the floor. He sees himself taking a single cube of ice from the bucket, thrusting it down into the hot water, sliding it, as it melts, down her thigh to her groin, against her pubic hair. She moans and throws her head back from the new sensation, the combined fierce cold and heat.

Camilla fills her mouth with champagne and leans forward. She takes his nipple in his mouth. He can feel the sizzling champagne against his nipple.

Even now, in the car service office, half drunk, he can remember the way their nerve endings seemed to explode with pleasure. The way, when they left the tub, they moved, kissing furiously, to the brass bed by the open window, with the street sounds from the French Quarter wafting up; pedestrians and cyclists and waiters, and Camilla crying out so loud, 'Voort, *Voort, I'm coming*!' that he heard applause from the café two stories below when they were done.

'Encore!' a woman shouted down there. Voort and Camilla burst into laughter, and in response, so did the unseen fans.

'Bravo!'

Ten minutes later there was a knock at their door. The owner of the hotel called, 'Excuse me, but the people in the café sent up wine for you. It is excellent French red wine!'

I want to eat everything, Voort, she told him. I want to

drink everything. I want you again already. I want you now.

The car service operator brings Voort back to the present. 'Sorry I don't have what you need yet. Another couple minutes. We have a big fleet of town cars. Have you ever used our cars, sir? You know, we do many jobs for NBC.'

'Just find out where Ms. Ryan went.'

Voort flashes back to the casino, in Montreal, the gigantic four-story playhouse for adults, where he and Camilla played blackjack for hours. Voort sees the croupier doubling their gigantic pile of chips.

'You two are ve-reee luck-eee! Blackjack a-gain!'

The operator breaks in again. 'Ah! Camilla Ryan! That car took her to East Ninety-third Street, between Third and Lex.'

He gives Voort the address.

Outside, the cold air sobers Voort enough to make him embarrassed by what he has done. But he can't stop. From a pay phone, he calls One Police Plaza, asks one of the young detectives on his staff, on the Niana Embers investigation, to get hold of a reverse phone directory, which gives names and phone numbers by address. He gives the kid the address on East Ninety-third and asks whose name the phone is listed under, at that address.

'Only one person, Voort. He must own the whole house. It's a doctor. Ian Bainbridge. That's the only name I have there.'

'A doctor?' Voort asks, surprised.

'That's what it says.'

Voort hangs up. His head hurts. He needs to sleep.

She went to a doctor?

Voort hopes she is not sick. Even furious, he cannot abide the thought of Camilla suffering.

Man, she's making me crazy.

Another flashback. Voort sees them leaving Montreal, in his Jaguar, roaring down Quebec Route 10 on their way to

Vermont. Camilla inserts a Bach tape into the stereo. The top is down. Her blond hair is streaming, and she's so tanned that the blond hairs on her arms sparkle.

'Voort, I think I'm falling in love with you,' she says. 'It's scary. Do you feel the same way?'

Bach plays, with his restrained power. Bach, always in absolute control.

'I'm not scared about it. I'm happy.'

Camilla, why would you lie about visiting a doctor? Voort thinks.

TWELVE

W e've got both entrances to the bank in sight.'
 At eight the next morning, in the car, Mickie's on the hand radio while Voort, nursing a hangover, eases the Chevy into a parking space on Jones Street, a block-long strip of West Village brownstones, small apartment houses, and trendy French-style cafés. The day is raw. An ice storm hit the city three hours ago, closing roads and causing accidents from Staten Island to the Bronx.

Ice dangles from the skinny bare trees, glues trash can lids shut, and glitters in black patches on Jones Street.

Mickie instructs the detectives who are waiting two blocks away, 'We want all the employees in first. We'll hit 'em before they open, ten before nine.'

He's in a camel's-hair coat, blue cashmere scarf, and Gucci shoes protected by old-fashioned rubbers. Voort's wearing his sheepskin coat and a pullover wool cap.

Mickie tells Voort, 'Which gives us fifty minutes. I'm not standing outside longer than I have to.'

He hands Voort, from a paper bag, a buttered kaiser roll, in waxed paper, and a medium-size black coffee in a blue cardboard cup with a Parthenon motif. He lifts a pocket-size tape recorder off the seat between them and switches it on.

'Tillman works at the Apple bank in the West Village,' says a frightened, middle-aged male voice on the tape.

Voort snorts with frustration. 'If he's so concerned, why not say his damn name?'

He's exhausted. When he got home last night, Mickie had left a message about the tipster, and Voort had taken a cab to the office, worked until four A.M. checking Harris Tillmans in the phone book, running the name through law enforcement computers, coming up with nothing except a sixty-four-year-old Harris Tillman in prison in Salem, Oregon, for grand auto theft.

He'd slept two hours, on the office couch, which was as comfortable as a feather bed, and increased his appreciation for Mickie's expensive taste in furniture. Mickie also kept a laundered Bennington handmade quilt in the office armoire, extra pillows, and Jamaican Blue Mountain coffee beans in the freezer.

Red-eyed, chewing without tasting now, he watches Jones Street residents easing from their brownstones, heading off to work, slipping on ice. A well-dressed man and woman gingerly descend their stoop, young brokers or lawyers, Voort imagines. Happy-looking, as their future seems secure at the moment. They hold hands.

The woman, from behind, resembles Camilla.

'The caller disappeared by the time the squad car reached the pay phone,' Mickie says.

On the tape, the voice says, 'I'm afraid he's going to hurt someone else.'

Spotting Camilla last night, in the Café Tonni, Voort had wished, for an instant, to disappear himself. But this morning what remains is cold anger. Seeing her old boy-friend holding hands with her had crystallized the unpleasant reality, and Voort prefers reality to wishful thinking any day.

And as for the doctor she visited, Ian Bainbridge, Voort

sees in the cold light of morning that it is Camilla's business. He will leave it alone.

'Time's up, Con Man. Move.'

They leave the car and walk west on Fourth Street, Voort's heart speeding at the prospect of an arrest, his anger blooming, focused on the killer, as he passes closed pubs and souvenir shops, and vendors cracking sidewalk ice with picks, breaking the glaze into shards as sharp as broken bottles, or throwing steaming water on it to melt it.

Other vendors unfold their wares of Chinese rabbit-fur hats, sunglasses, cheap leather gloves or scarves. Name a problem, they sell solutions. The vendors seem connected, by instant wire, to fate. If the oceans rise and New York is flooded one day, they'll produce at that moment rubber rafts and life jackets. Fishing line and hooks, to sell residents as they flee.

Voort sees, at the corner of Fourth and Christopher, that a woman detective is pretending to use a cash machine by the north entrance of the bank. A young male detective, a crutch beside him, sits bundled, on a stoop on the Fourth Street entrance, opposite the Seventh Avenue Gay Cruise Line billboard. He shakes a paper cup as he begs passersby for change.

'Five minutes,' Voort says into the radio. 'And nobody leaves the bank before we do.'

At eight-fifty, he strides to the Fourth Street entrance and raps sharply on the glass door. An elderly security guard inside points to his watch and mouths, 'Ten minutes!' Voort presses his gold shield against the glass, and the man rushes forward and unlocks the door, eagerly responding to Voort's higher authority.

Inside, the marble lobby is quiet, sunny, and smells of fresh coffee and cleaning fluid laid down last night. Tellers count cash behind thick bulletproof glass windows. A radio plays the Imus show. A technician closes up a newly repaired cash machine.

Voort notes that none of the clerks seem nervous, but then again, they do not know the police are here. He tells the guard, quietly, 'I'd like to speak with the manager.'

She turns out to be a petite, Pakistani woman named Shari, superbly poised and dressed in a tight business suit and high heels that match her close-cut, blue-black hair. Voort is surprised to find himself attracted to her. It's the first time in months he's noticed a woman other than Camilla.

'We'd like to talk to one of your employees. Harris Tillman,' he says as she touches his badge.

Her brows dip, making her look five years younger, maybe twenty-three, twenty-four. Not to mention she smells good, with a fragrance with which Voort is unfamiliar, but appreciative.

'But there's no Harris Tillman here.'

'Are you sure?'

She has a terrific smile, but the certainty in it only sinks Voort's already low spirits. 'I know my staff,' she says. 'Can you tell me what this is about?'

Mickie's glance at Voort clearly means, *That phone call was phony.*

Voort shakes his head: *The caller knew about BHC.*

He says, 'Can we talk in your office, Shari?'

Gracefully, she leads them off the main floor, past the tellers, who are whispering to each other, having noticed something going on of interest, past the customer service counter and, in the back room, into a mid-size glass cubicle with an olive-colored, floral-pattern couch and a gray steel desk, brightened by lots of fresh flowers. White roses. Pink tulips. Yellow gladiolas in vases. Potted ferns top her computer terminal, beside a family portrait taken at the Bronx Zoo. In front of 'Jungle World,' the husband's got his thick arm around Shari, and her slender ones wrap two young daughters. Voort is amazed that such a tiny woman is a mother. If he put both his hands around her waist, he thinks, his middle fingers would touch.

'Maybe we've come to the wrong branch,' Voort says. 'Would it be possible to find out if Mr Tillman works at another one?'

'Why not?' She crosses her lean legs, at the desk, lifts the phone with fluid, feminine movements. There's a compressed quality to her, an energy held back during professional hours. She's cool on the phone, making the inquiry at headquarters, and when she hangs up, she says, 'There's a Sylvia Tillman in Midtown. A Clara Tillman in Cobble Hill. But no Harris Tillman. Are you sure you have the right name?'

Mickie slumps against the windowsill. 'It's Tillman.'

Voort just asks, 'How long have you worked here?'

'Two years.'

'Is there anyone who's been here longer?'

She reaches with a long fingernail and presses an intercom button. 'Chuck, come to my office, will you?'

And to the detectives, 'Would you like a cup of coffee? We've got Kenyan Highland. I buy it on the street, in Astoria. It's so cheap, I think it's stolen.'

She makes a pun, grinning, 'It's "hot," officers.'

'No thanks,' Voort says.

'Yeah,' Mickie says as Chuck Niles waddles in. 'Coffee.'

Niles is a pear-shaped, unobtrusive man in his fifties, with thinning, sand-colored hair and watery brown eyes. He's wearing a sharply pressed starched shirt with red and white stripes. His tie clip shows the Panda-World Wildlife Fund insignia. His voice is gravelly, and Voort guesses he's a heavy smoker, an impression confirmed by a faint whiff of tobacco mixed with the smell of Old Spice. The handshake is powerful, doesn't go with the puffy, out-of-shape body, and the palms are thickly callused. Voort imagines the man on weekends, wielding a heavy shovel around his house.

Niles says, 'I got mugged in Little Neck last year and the cops caught the man within the hour. I don't care what people say. You guys have my gratitude. You do a fine job.'

'Mr Niles, we're looking for a man who may have worked here a few years ago. Harris Tillman.'

'Harris? No kidding! What did he do?'

Voort says, suppressing excitement, 'Would you know how to contact him?'

'He used to live in Gramercy Park, but we're talking, God, years ago. He was nice, generous, used to buy pizzas, Cokes, doughnuts for the office. Had a place in the Hamptons he rented with other people. A couple of the girls had crushes on him. But I always thought he had another side.'

'Why did you think that?'

Niles leans his fleshy hip against Shari's desk. 'He was too cheery. My wife told me, a long time ago, whenever someone acts one way in public – goes overboard, if you know what I mean – it'll turn out they have an opposite side. The quietest person will have the worst temper. The happiest person will suffer the worst depressions. My wife says the best thing about a person is also the worst thing, know what I mean?'

Mickie says, 'What was Mr Tillman's other side?'

'I saw it when he fell in love. The girl had a weird name . . . a poet, I think. He went into a funk when she dropped him. It was all he talked about. It was scary, he was so depressed.'

'Scary how?'

'Well, a couple of us worried he might hurt himself.'

'Did he see a psychiatrist?'

'I suggested it.'

'Did he have a family, do you know?'

'I don't.'

'Did anyone keep in touch with him after he left?'

'He disappeared. Someone went to check on him, see if he was all right. Actually, it was one of the tellers who had a crush on him. But he'd moved away, and left no forwarding address. Same with the phone number. Zippo.'

'I'm wondering if you have any idea what the initials

BHC might mean, in relation to Harris?'

'BHC?' Niles squints as he ponders, seems to be looking into the distance. For a moment he has forgotten anyone else is here.

'Nope. But,' he says, brightening, 'Harris is in one of the photos of the branch picnic, on the wall upstairs. They keep it up because it's the only time any of our teams ever won a championship. Want to see?'

The bank is open for business now, and as they go upstairs, Voort notices busy customer lines at the cash machines, at the tellers' windows.

Upstairs is the Foreign Exchange department. Niles walks them to a cluster of half a dozen eight-by-eleven fading photos of the bank softball team, on a wall by the busy traveler's checks counter. He picks out Tillman in the back row, but Tillman must have moved just as the picture was taken because Voort sees a frustratingly blurry smiling man on the tall side, with his arms around the players to his right and left.

'You can borrow the photo and make a copy,' Shari says.

'Any other pictures of him?'

'Not that I know.'

Voort slips out his penknife, with its magnifying glass, and tries to get a better view of the face. Blond hair falls over the forehead. There's a tan mark just below where the baseball cap would have been. Average shoulders. Lower half of the face obscured by a player in front. About six foot and an inch or so.

'The face isn't too clear,' says Shari, disappointed for Voort, 'is it?'

Everyone has the face of a killer, Voort knows, and the very same people have the face of a saint.

'It would be helpful if we could see any employment records on Tillman,' he says.

'For records that far back, you have to ask Midtown.

They'll want to know more of what this is about.'

'Mr Tillman has information that might be useful in solving a crime.'

She raises an eyebrow, and Voort sees himself in the black pools of her pupils, reflected. Her expression tells him that the explanation is not good enough.

'People might get hurt if we don't find him,' Voort adds.

They follow her back to her office, admiring her walk, the tight leg movements, the way the dress clings to her. Shari calls headquarters and argues with a middle-level manager for a while, then gets switched to the public relations department, personnel department, and finally the legal department. All the while, Voort is impressed with the urgency she puts into her voice, as if locating Tillman has become her cause too.

Shari tells the lawyer, 'Mr Hayakawa, I'm certain they're police. They showed me their badges . . . Yes, I called the precinct and confirmed it.'

She looks angry when Mr Hayakawa denies her request, and as she hands the phone to Voort, meaning, I did my best, her finger brushes the inside of his thumb.

Voort imagines Harris Tillman out there, a man walking, crazily walking. Building toward combustion. In the vision, the man wears the most anonymous clothes; a gray coat, and a wool cap like a workman, and rubber-soled boots against ice patches. No one pays the man any attention. The man is safe in a crowd, walking, moving to control his rage.

Voort realizes that in the image, Tillman is walking the same streets that he himself did last night.

But the lawyer's voice over the phone brings him back to the present. 'I'm sorry,' Hayakawa is saying, 'but I need a court order before I can release personnel records. It's not my decision. It's policy. The reason is, we're being sued now by a *convicted* felon, who had a clean record when he worked here, but was caught for something he did *after* he left, because we voluntarily gave his records to police. It's a privacy issue. So if you want better cooperation from companies, you should lobby the government to amend the privacy laws.'

'I'll phone my congressman,' Voort says, as Mickie snorts, although actually, being a big donor, Voort can reach his congressman anytime, and will definitely complain, as he has before, on law and order issues.

Meanwhile, Mickie mouths one word, 'Lawyers.' To cops, there's nothing worse than dealing with lawyers. They're trained pessimists. They never answer questions. They spend their lives, like cops, looking for something wrong.

In the end, because of the bank's rules, and the inaccessibility of the Assistant D.A. responsible for getting court orders for this case, Voort and Mickie have to waste crucial time going downtown, finding a judge they know, and getting the paperwork. It's mid-afternoon by the time they get it and travel to bank headquarters, wait for Hayakawa to get back from a late lunch meeting, and shove the damn court order in his face.

But Hayakawa's not a bad man, as it turns out. In fact, he's felt terrible about this morning's conversation. He's younger than his voice suggested earlier, boyish, in his mid-twenties, with a cowlick, and old-fashioned suspenders over his crisp white shirt, as he sits like a mob don in his huge leather chair. They're in a massive corner office looking down on Midtown, a gray unrelenting stretch of tar, ice, and concrete, in contrast to the blown-up African safari pictures adorning his wall beside a Yale Law School diploma.

'The problem's the precedent system,' Hayakawa lectures. 'Legal precedents get narrower. Ramifications wider. Congress ought to appoint a committee to recommend ways of putting our own laws in sync.'

Voort eyes a pride of lions under a tree. He sees a crocodile dragging a baby elephant into a black river. A leopard lies on a branch at sunset, as a group of khaki-clad tourists, the lawyer among them, sip sundowner drinks in a Land Rover, and watch, thrilled to be close to a predator.

'I got Tillman's records, hoping you'd show up. I'd feel terrible if someone got hurt because of the delay. Take the time you need. Use my office. I hope you understand the position I was in before,' Hayakawa says.

But Voort's getting excited again. Like the lions, he and Mickie are hunters. They have prey in sight. They have Tillman's file; a history, Social Security number, address of an apartment he still might live in, the ID number of an old bank account.

'No living relatives,' the employment application says.

Aloud, Voort reads Tillman's performance reports, which show deterioration.

From, ' "Never loses his temper. He'll go far." '

To, ' "Seems depressed." '

To, ' "Harris has been increasingly despondent since the souring of a personal relationship. His work has dropped off. He's lost us loans. Frankly, I was glad when he quit." '

By three o'clock, two-thirds of a day wasted because of the court order, they're back at One Police Plaza, waiting for the results of computer checks. It's snowing again outside, and the flakes are large, tinged brown, as if they have picked up soot while falling, as if making contact with earth in an undamaged condition is impossible in New York. The wind out there keeps changing direction. Snow smacks into the window, then blows the other way, at stalled traffic on the bridge.

'Sylvia thought you might want to come for dinner Friday,' Mickie says.

'I have plans.'

'Reading, alone, in you living room?'

'Mickie, I like my house, and sometimes it's not so bad to think things over by a fire for a bit. Anyway, one of the nephews has a birthday party.'

'What's wrong with Camilla, to walk out on you like that?'

'When I figure that out, I'll be glad she's gone,' Voort says as the phone rings.

Surprise, though. It's not the computer girls, but Shari from the bank. On the phone, she seems less professional, almost shy, saying she made inquiries about Harris Tillman, telling Voort things she's learned about the man this afternoon, but nothing important, things so trivial that Voort senses there is another reason for the call.

Sure enough she starts telling him about her two daughters, then says she's divorced, and only displays the photo of her husband on her desk to keep men away.

'The divorce was finalized six months ago.'

She says, 'I feel so silly. I've never called a man like this before.'

Voort feels the heat rise up in him, the itch in his groin, and the warm, fluid feeling when an attractive woman likes him. But he tells her, 'I'm still involved with someone, in a way.'

'A way?'

'I'm not over it.'

'Maybe you will be.'

Voort laughs. 'Well, I'd rather be over it, if I had a choice.'

'Would it be too forward to say I would like to see you if you start getting over it?'

'It would be something I appreciate hearing,' Voort replies.

Mickie grins when Voort hangs up. Outside, the snow is so thick it obscures all visibility. 'You know what they say, Con Man. The best thing when you lose one is to go find another.'

'The best way is to go through it, before you even look at another,' Voort says. 'You've been married so long you're as good on dating advice as a priest.'

'Burn it out, eh?'

'Napalm it.'

'Anybody home?' a woman's voice interrupts, from the doorway. 'You guys are in such a rush, gotta have your information now, and look at you, your feet on desks.'

It's Hazel from the computer room, holding a thick printout in her chubby hand. There's a number tattooed on her wrist from Auschwitz, the German concentration camp. Her family was not Jewish, but the Nazis had believed otherwise. She was eight, and an orphan, when American troops liberated the camp.

Hazel says, 'Your information, Sherlocks, on Tillman. I wanted to see your faces when you see it. You'll never guess, and I guarantee you're not going to believe.'

Mickie groans. 'Every time things look good, our guy throws us a curveball.'

'This a ten thousand-mile-an-hour fastball,' Hazel says, advancing on soft-soled orthopedic shoes into the office. 'This is Jerry Koosman and Sandy Koufax and all the fastest southpaws that ever took the mound rolled into one.'

Hazel lays the printout on Voort's desk. Hands on her wide hips, she surveys the cubicle.

'This isn't an office. It's a Bloomingdale's showroom. Rumor is you have champagne in the refrigerator.'

'Consider the contents of that refrigerator your personal, round-the-clock reward,' Voort says.

'I can be bought.'

The three of them cluster around the printout, scanning the pages. Voort hears Mickie gasp.

'This is unbelievable.'

'And it's no mistake,' Hazel says. 'I double-checked. I triple-checked. I had the other girls check.'

Mickie falls into the couch. 'Murder two is committed by Eric Porter, a guy whose Social Security number was used for five years. And now Harris Tillman's Social Security number was used only *four* years, and it stops, to the month, when Porter's starts.'

'Which means our guy switches identities,' says Hazel. 'And obviously now he's out there, walking around with a new one. How many other women has he hurt?'

'But *why* does he switch identities?' Mickie says. 'He didn't hurt anyone back then. He did it now.'

'Maybe he's been hurting people all along,' Hazel says. 'Maybe you just don't know about it.'

But Voort's frowning. 'He switches identities when he gets rejected,' he says. 'Both times, right after the end of a love affair, he disappears. It has to do with that,' he says. 'I have to tell you, from personal experience, when you go through something like that, you want to change. So maybe our guy is sick about it, psychotic about it. Normal people want to move away, get a new job, change their lives when their heart gets broken. Maybe he can't take it. He's murdering old girlfriends. Maybe with him, rejection is exaggerated, for some reason.'

'So what set him off now?'

'Who knows? I'm just talking. Maybe he really changes his whole life, except,' Voort says, 'there's something else going on here, that we're not seeing. I have the feeling we're dealing with one guy, the same horrible violence both times, the same BHC, but also like it's *not* one guy. It doesn't make sense yet, because of the different ways he did the two murders. He's scrupulous the first time. He couldn't care less the second.'

'Maybe he got carried away the second time. Maybe he was in a rush.'

'No,' Voort says, feeling the answer just out of reach. 'He wasn't in a rush. He saw the kids and just told them to go back to bed, remember? He spent time with the doorman.'

'Maybe he was in some kind of mood,' Hazel says.

'He was in a mood, all right,' Mickie says. 'Maybe it's

two guys working together. But that doesn't make sense either. Two guys sharing Social Security numbers? I never heard of that.'

Hazel snorts. She picked up Russian-Jewish intonations in the death camp. 'So if you never heard of it, it's impossible?'

Voort shakes his head, trying to reach for an answer. 'I'm saying there's an extra element here that I don't, for the life of me, understand.'

Out in the hallway, someone must have told a joke, because a huge chorus of laughter erupts, male, hysterical, echoing in the building. To Voort's ears, as he reads, in shock, it is as if Tillman himself is laughing at them.

'We better show this to the Chief of Detectives,' Mickie says. 'The commissioner will get into it. Hell, everyone's going to want a piece of Tillman now. Or whatever the hell he's calling himself.'

Hazel says. 'How many identities, in the end, are we talking about?'

Hazel pops open a Mountain Dew and drinks thirstily.

Outside, the heavy falling snow obscures pedestrians, cars, even footsteps.

Hazel wipes her hand with her mouth. She looks unhappy, gazing at the report.

'You're looking for one sick son of a bitch. A man who covers his tracks. I feel sorry for the next girl, whoever she is.'

'That caller said he was Tillman's doctor,' Mickie says. 'Are you thinking what I'm thinking? That the caller could be a shrink?'

Voort stands at the window, remembering the way he felt last night, in the Café Tonni, the way his heart ruptured at the sight of Camilla and her old boyfriend, the way he wanted to be somewhere else, to be anywhere or anyone else at that moment.

The way he'd wished he went to a shrink himself.

THIRTEEN

The five-year-old boy lies in bed, tears streaming down his face. One day he will become a psychologist, will publish articles about love and rejection, obsession and sex. He presses his palms against his ears, but can't block the screams out.

'You cheat on me!' his mother wails, downstairs. 'You fuck around! You were never loyal, ever since we got married!'

She's so loud the boy feels as if the sound pierces his bones, punctures cartilage and grinds through his eardrums into his bloodstream, traveling toward his heart.

There's a crash down there, something heavy falling.

The boy is shaking.

'Clara, you're sick!' his father yells. It's impossible for the boy to believe that his father, his quiet, considerate father, the corporate insurance salesman, the man who throws footballs to him on Sundays, reads biographies to him at bedtime, performs puppet shows for him, has turned into an animal down there. The fight moves, from the sound of breakage, from the dining room to the den, living room, foyer, as though, if the adults stopped even for an instant and tried to hold the violence in check, they would rip each other apart. Books would fly from the bookshelves, like in the monster movie on television last week. Glass coffee tables would shatter.

The boy curls, in his flannel pajamas, into a ball, and wishes he would float away, out the French window. He's an only child and his huge, expensive bedroom is on the second floor of the Westchester colonial. The full May moon is yellow, pus-colored against a sky of dark blue velvet, and it burns his face; it shines on his New York Mets banner, bat, model navy ships, Frisbee, stolen Stop sign, RCA color TV, glowing fish tanks, Persian cat, on the two-foot-tall 'Protector' marionette on a chair, the cartoon figure from TV brought to life as a puppet, a wooden man with a cloth cape and a black face mask, bulging muscles, and strings that his father makes dance at bedtime, making the boy laugh, making him fill with love and feel safe.

His father says, making the puppet's arms move, *I will protect you! No one will ever hurt you because I am your Personal Protector!!!*

The boy needs the Protector now, because downstairs his mother is screaming, 'Don't you walk out on me!'

And his father answers, 'Clara, the only way I'm stepping foot in this nuthouse again is if you see a psychiatrist! You make these accusations up!'

Crash.

'Clara, you are out of your mind!'

The boy wishes he could dissolve, like the TV boy in the science fiction movie last week, who lived on another planet. A happy place where kids played all day, floated in antigravity suits, ate alien candy, huge, gooey pieces of it, and had parents who loved them. He wishes the Protector Puppet would come to life and go downstairs, and shut them up.

And take him far away.

The boy hears closets slamming, stomping in the foyer. *Don't go, Daddy!* He envisions his father throwing clothes into his Samsonite. Two pearl-gray dress shirts, like he's going on a business trip. Two maroon ties. One V-necked beige sweater. One pair of gym shorts, never to be used.

His mother screams, 'Jack, don't leave meeeeee!'

The front door slams.

He feels like the pain inside will slice him in two. Out the window, the boy sees his father, two stories down, storming down the walk, past the tulip bed, the bonsai tree, toward the cream-colored Mercedes in the semi-circular driveway.

He pounds on the window. His father looks up, a man in a Burberry, with his suit bag over his shoulder. Like he's going to Chicago for a day, except it's the middle of the night. The eyes are obscured by the hat brim, but the hand comes up, gives a wave, a lie, a promise to return. The same casual wrist movement that brings delightful life to the Protector Puppet conveys a falsehood now. His father's mouth moves, but he's too embarrassed to shout his message, embarrassed neighbors will hear.

What is he saying? I'm sorry? I hate you?

'Daddy, I'll be good! Whatever I did wrong, I won't do it again.'

But the boy hears the rumble of the car engine. The Mercedes backs from the driveway. It accelerates down the block.

The boy is splitting in two. He wants to go with his father. No, he wants to stay here. He hears glass smashing downstairs, a rhythm of destruction. He shouts, trying to drown out his mother's screams. He remembers how, in kindergarten this week, his private school for extra-extra-special smart children, extra-genius imaginative kids, Miss Patricki told the class about something called mol-e-cules, particles so small that, bonded together, they make up all matter. Molecules are powerful, she said, but the boy knows the voice downstairs can shatter the basic building blocks of what is real.

'Lying bastard!' his mother screams.

It seems impossible, outside the window, that the suburb has remained peaceful. The lights are off in the other homes, where parents don't fight. The boy looks longingly at oaks lining the winding street, at split levels and colonials, the front yards big enough for extra houses, the lawns smooth as polished marble, the street lamps' electrical imitations of antique gas lamps. The autos, Volvos, Jaguars.

'I'll kill you!'

She's coming up the stairs.

Oh no. Not again. Not tonight. Not now. Something is building up in her, bad and getting worse by the second. He hates when she comes at night.

Please God, let the Protector Puppet come to life and stop her, stop the bad thing, the way the real Protector cartoon does on TV.

He pretends he is asleep, squeezes his eyes shut and wishes, as he does whenever fights break out, that he is the son of the psychologist in the Tudor mansion across the street, a thoughtful, easygoing, understanding man. A community leader who actually knocked on the door one night, during a fight, and offered to 'help' his parents.

Or he could go live with the banker, down the block, who he sees every morning, in his pressed overcoat, taking his daughters to the school bus. Unlike the psychologist, the banker always looks angry. Once the boy even saw the banker pick a boy up by his ears, when the boy was teasing one of the banker's two daughters. The banker scared the boy so much he never bothered the daughters again.

I'm not here. I'm somewhere else.

I'll run away. I'll knock on the door of the last house on the street, the one inherited by the mechanic. He told me he likes me. He can teach me about cars.

The mechanic. A good-natured, slightly confused twenty-year-old who'd inherited his $400,000 house and kept the neighbors pissed off, because he was always working on cars over there; revving engines, hoisting thirdhand Jaguars up on concrete blocks.

But in the real world there is no place for the boy to go. His door opens. She's framed in the hallway light, slumped and crooked, coming at him inside a wedge-shaped glow as yellow as disease. His mother's face is different than he has ever seen it, fierce, sad, lost in a way that reminds him of a wax Indian he saw in the Museum of Natural History last week.

'My boy. My little boy. You should be glad that asshole is gone. He fools around. He's a fraud.'

The boy thinks, 'fool around'? When he runs in the house sometimes, which he is not supposed to do, his mother yells, 'Don't fool around.'

The boy has a vision of his father, in another house, running and breaking furniture. He knows this is not what his mother means.

'Oh, my little boy. Except now you're my big boy. Come here. Let me hold you.'

His mother's arms come around him. He's trembling. He likes that she is here, but she is scaring him too.

'Darling.'

Her hands are on his shoulders. But they feel different, needy. Something is wrong with the way she is touching him.

His trembling becomes shaking, but that makes her hold him tighter, and she croons to him, she seems to be drawing into herself. And then a good thing happens. The boy stops feeling anything. He feels like he is going to sleep. He's peaceful. He's only vaguely aware of her hands reaching places on his body they have never touched before. He's floating. He's in the tree outside looking back in at a woman and her son. The woman is doing strange things to the son. It's quite pleasant. For an instant he is actually glad his father has gone.

171

At that second, the feeling stops.

His mother slaps him across the face, so sharply that the back of his head snaps back into the wall.

She hisses, 'I can't believe you did that to me! I can't believe you put my hand there!'

She hits him again. Harder. He's bawling, terrified.

'Don't you *ever* tell anyone you did that. If you do, the police will take you away. I'll make sure of that. They'll listen to me. They'll put you in jail. You'll never get out. You'll live in a cell, like an animal. Like your father!'

She storms from the room.

The boy follows her, begging, confused, knowing only that the thing he just did, the pleasure he got, was unforgivable.

'Mama, don't let them take me away!'

Two nights later his father returns to get his clothes, and move away permanently. There's another fight, and afterward his mother comes to the boy's room again, as if she has forgotten what happened earlier.

Sweet boy. Little man. The only one I can depend on. Lovely, loyal boy. The boy can't help it. The vague feeling comes over him. He floats outside again.

Afterward, she hits him again.

'Wear a shirt over that bruise in school tomorrow. Nobody better see it, or the police will take you away! You disgust me. Filthy boy!'

Now it is years later, at the last meeting of the Broken Hearts Club, and Arthur Davis, the Mechanic, says, 'Her name was Greta.' Ian Bainbridge, Harris Tillman, and Arthur sit at the gray Formica table in the doctor's kitchen, in his house on East Ninety-third Street.

There are two empty seats at the table. One for the man who never shows up. One for the Literary Agent, Eric Porter.

'Eric's not feeling well. He went upstairs,' Bainbridge says.

The room is a throwback, ugly forty years ago, when constructed, hideous now, with its peach-colored paint, smudged from decades of finger marks, grease, free-floating soot, crushed roaches, pencil lines on the wall where children were measured. The linoleum has yellowed. Holes mar the plaster-work from thumbtacks that once held calendars, from screws that fixed racks of copper pots. Steel cabinets in matching, faded peach show Scotch tape marks where old menus, homework, lists of phone numbers once adhered; the smudges, vestiges of long-gone occupants, more substantial than anything the current resident has supplied.

'She was a nurse. I met her in the emergency room at Mount Sinai.'

Arthur Davis, the youngest man in the group, wears jeans and denim shirts, and construction boots. His skin is so smooth he gives the impression of never having to shave. He's pale, from working inside all the time, and his hands are as callused as his face is smooth. He repairs expensive foreign cars – Jaguars, Mercedes, Jensens – and carries himself with a shyness that comes from dealing with customers who are better educated, richer, better traveled, better read, more confident.

'When is the other guy, the one who never comes, going to show up? And why are we meeting here, not Mackey's?' Arthur asks.

'Mackey told us not to come back after the argument last week.'

'And the fifth guy? Who is he anyway?'

'He'll come when he's ready,' Bainbridge says.

Bainbridge tries to listen but he is exhausted, more tired than he can remember ever having been before. He feels as if his body lacks substance and, letting go, he might float into the stratosphere, a burned-up cinder, a speck of used matter to decompose.

His head hurts. His vision is so blurry that it seems for an instant he is the only one in the room. But then it clears and he sees the Mechanic.

'She screwed around on me,' Arthur says.

Harris Tillman asks, 'Arthur, have you read the paper this week? Or followed the news on TV?'

'I never read the paper. Or watch the news.'

Harris smiles. 'You are a special person, Arthur. To cause you pain is an unforgivable sin.'

'Harris, please,' Bainbridge warns, knowing where Harris is heading, feeling the pressure building, the sense of malevolence in the room that is already out of control.

'Who asked you?' Harris replies.

Bainbridge sits back and starts eating. He's famished. Consumption is the only power he has left. He stuffs his takeout burger into his mouth, finishes his fries, and he's still hungry, as if he is absorbing protein for all of them, storing energy for what he knows will happen, what he tells himself must *not* happen, what he feels himself being swept into, out of control.

A voice in his head, the faintest whisper, almost not there at all, says, *You can't stop it. You know that Tillman will try to get him to kill her tonight.*

The boy is twelve now, shy and smart, and he keeps to himself in school, earns A's on tests, and the respect of teachers, who tell the other kids, 'Why can't you be nice like him?'

A good boy. A quiet boy, who asks girls on dates once in a while, but he's too unsure to be confident. He's drawn to girls, they're so soft and they smell good, and he likes the way their limbs disappear beneath the folds of their dresses. Their hair bounces beautifully when they run, and he knows what pleasure they are capable of giving, even in their little bodies, but he's not supposed to know, he only knows because he's a bad boy, a filthy boy, and he's terrified about how to treat girls, frightened he will do something wrong to them, too much, or too little, and they will slap him and the secret will come out.

And they will call the police.

One time he hears Rebecca Waite joking about him, in lunchroom, telling the other cheerleaders, 'He takes me to a movie, but he won't touch me. He follows me everywhere. If you leave him for a minute, he panics.'

He works summers doing yard work for the literary agent down the block, a friendly, insecure man who makes up for it by being a braggart, an exaggerator, talking about deals he's closed, famous writers he knows, the latest plays and books. The agent tends to be a follower, though, always doing whatever his bossy wife orders, or going along with the other men in the neighborhood; watching football, playing cards, drinking beer at the swimming pool.

Another neighbor, the young mechanic, teaches the boy about Fiats and Austin-Healeys; how to replace a broken rotor, or change a timing belt, oil a gearbox, adjust a clutch.

He has no friends his own age. The adults are his friends.

But none of them guesses the secret he shares with his mother. No one imagines that at night, sometimes, she comes to his room. It never happens when she has boyfriends. If she has a boyfriend, in fact, she barely talks to him, doesn't even look at him for long periods, just tells him what housework to do, in a monotone. Rake the leaves. Mop the basement. She leaves meals for him, with an excuse why she won't join him. I ate already. I have a stomach ache. I'm meeting a friend for dinner. I'm not hungry tonight.

Why should she eat with a dirty boy?

And when the boyfriends leave her, as they always do, after the screaming fights and accusations, she comes to his room, weeping, apologizing, and he is so happy when she pays attention to him, so hungry for it. Even if it is only for half an hour, he imagines that somehow, this time the bad things won't happen.

He tells himself things can never get better unless he gives them a chance. He can't just flee, like his father. All the relatives tell him, You take care of your mother. You have all the responsibility now.

'My boy,' she coos to him on these occasions. 'My little boy. You're the only one I can depend on. You're the only one who doesn't leave.

'I've been nasty, but that's ended. A mother and a son share a special bond. A secret bond. A bond no one ever knows about. A bond that only heaven sees.'

When this talk starts, and he gets afraid, the boy closes his eyes, feels her hands start to move on him, floats out the window, pretends he lives across the street, in the big Tudor with the psychologist. He pretends he is one of the psychologist's children. He sees the family playing Scrabble, by a fire, in the den, and they're laughing, the way he saw them do when he had dinner there once.

The psychologist is telling his children, the boy among them in his head, you are handsome, smart, talented, good at Scrabble. I love you. I cherish you.

The boy closes his eyes tighter.

Kill her, someone, anyone, he thinks. Help me. Mom, I wish you were dead. I wish a truck would hit you. I wish a tree would fall and crush your bones.

Oh God, I'm sorry I thought that, I didn't mean it. I love my mother. I'll make up for it. I'll be extra good to her. God, forgive me, please don't punish me.

She tells him, 'No woman will ever love you. Women will always leave you, and it will be because you are bad. No one will ever believe you if you tell them about me. You are dirty, and I hate you, and you don't deserve to live.'

One day when she comes to his room, when he is fifteen, he floats out the window as usual, when she reaches for him. Except this time when he comes back, she is holding her bloody nose.

'You hit me!' she screams. 'You hit your mother!'
'I didn't.' He has no recollection of it.
But she never comes to his room again.

Now, years later, Bainbridge is thinking, I hung up on the
police when I could have turned in Tillman. He's listening to
Arthur Davis continue his story, the tale of his broken heart.

'I was replacing the passenger window on a Jaguar one
night. Vandals had busted it. I cut my wrist on the glass. I
took a cab to the emergency room. You know how hospitals
are. You could be shot and they make you fill out forms. My
blood's all over the floor, but the clerk's just asking, "Do you
have Blue Cross?"

'Suddenly this nurse marches over and yells, "Get him
treated right away!" '

Tillman laughs derisively. 'She was just doing her job. She
probably didn't want the hospital to get sued.'

But Arthur is lost in the good part of his memory, the
uninterruptible part that caused him to lose his heart in the
first place, the unassailable core of the betrayal to come.

'I wasn't even attracted to her,' he says, looking down at
the scar on his left wrist, where the injury had been. 'She was
too heavy for me. And also, I'm shy. Not like you,' he tells
Tillman, who is nodding. 'I didn't think she was interested in
me. I thought she was just doing her job too at first. But she
stuck around, worked on my hand, and when I was ready to
leave, she told me she was getting off work. She asked me if
I want to take a walk, or get coffee.'

'She tricked you,' Harris Tillman says.

The doctor rises, his head hurting terribly, and makes his
way to the cabinet, for Advil, and cool water, as he hears the
Mechanic say:

'Mount Sinai's across from Central Park, and it was
summer, a nice night. She told me, after work each day, she
liked to stand under the trees across the street, cool out,

breathe in the leaves, get the medicine smells out of her system. So we went across Fifth Avenue and found a bench and talked, for hours.'

'Just talked,' Tillman says lewdly.

'I told you I was shy,' the Mechanic says. 'It was during the talk, when I found out she worked on cars, and that her dad was a mechanic, that I started to like her a little. And during the walk home, I noticed the way she smiled. It was beautiful. The color of her coat, green, went well with her face. She didn't seem heavy to me anymore. She looked pretty, and then later, more than pretty, if you know what I mean.'

'You fucked her when you got her home,' Tillman says, his eyes shiny.

'No, I never did that.'

'Never? How long did you see her?' Tillman asks, dumbfounded.

'Two months.'

'Then what the hell did you do for two months?'

'Well, she came to the garage, and helped me with the cars.'

'Wait a minute. You and she dressed in overalls and put the hoist up and looked at *cars*?' Tillman says.

'*Your* girl read poetry. Mine liked cars. You think poetry is great? Rhyming words?'

Dr Bainbridge says, gently, through the pounding, worsening headache, trying to defuse what he knows Tillman is trying to do, trying to get a little power back, 'If you never slept with her, Arthur, maybe you can't really say she screwed around on you.'

The Mechanic breaks out crying.

'She did!'

For a moment he cannot speak. He is overwhelmed. The muscles in his face have frozen, his eyes roll back, showing more white, and his fists, on the table, drain of color. The doctor notes the corded muscles in the man's hands, scarred and callused.

'You upset him,' Tillman tells Bainbridge.

'Like I said,' Arthur says hoarsely, 'for two months, three times a week, she came to the garage, at night, when the other mechanics, Pedro and Cassidy, were gone. She'd bring a bottle of wine sometimes, and we'd get a mushroom pizza. She'd put on overalls and we'd turn on a radio. Those luxury cars have terrific stereos. We'd work on the engines. Or spread a blanket in the backseat and eat picnics. Sandwiches and wine. Or sometimes she brought this hummus stuff, it's made from peas, she said, from Egypt or France, somewhere far away, and it was good, hummus.'

'In the *garage*?'

'Why not? It's clean and warm, and the cars smell of leather and polish, walnut, mahogany. My apartment is little. It doesn't have wood like that, and my building smells of cabbage and my chairs are lumpy and secondhand. It's not even as quiet where I live as the garage at night. My neighbors are always fighting. And Greta had two roommates. So where were we supposed to go?'

'I was just asking,' Tillman says.

'I'm sorry. I didn't mean to snap. It's not you I'm angry at.'

'We're brothers in pain,' Tillman says. 'Isn't it funny the way, as soon as *they* come into the conversation, they make friends fight?'

Ian Bainbridge groans, slumped at the table.

'Two months went by,' the Mechanic says. 'Harris, I admire the way you told your girlfriend, on the first night, that you were in love. I'm not like that, but I fell in love too. She was all I could think about. Sometimes I'd even go, late at night, to the Fifth Avenue entrance to the hospital, and stand in the shadows across the street, and wait until eleven, when she was finished, and I'd watch her come out and cross the street, sometimes alone, sometimes with a doctor getting off work.

'But I was too nervous to ask her on a real date. I was afraid, if I did, everything would change.'

'But you did ask her in the end.'

The Mechanic sinks into his seat. The memory has robbed strength from his legs. He looks at his uneaten takeout hamburger without really seeing it. He is seeing the past.

'I was so nervous. I'd bought tickets, good ones to Lincoln Center, the symphony. She'd told me how much she loved classical music. I didn't know about music, but she kept telling me how beautiful Bach was, so I got tickets for that. But I didn't tell her. I was going to surprise her. Second row. A sold-out performance. I rented a tuxedo. It seems silly, but—'

'Silly? It was a beautiful thing to do. She was leading you on,' Tillman says. 'Seeing you three times a week like that.'

'That's what the voice in my head tells me.'

Dr Bainbridge says, 'I don't feel well.'

'I asked her to go, that night,' the Mechanic says. 'I was so scared, the first half hour, working on a Jensen, that I could barely make out the words she was saying. She'd cut her hair, it was just above her shoulders and she smelled good, like she knew this was the night when something more would happen, I wasn't imagining it. We finished putting the hubcaps back on, when I blurted out the invitation, the concert, Saturday night, would she like to come?'

The Mechanic bursts out crying.

'Why don't we take a break,' the Psychologist says, squeezing his head with both hands.

'Oh, it's much too late for that,' Tillman says.

The boy is twenty-one now, a college junior at Northeastern, in Boston, on academic scholarship, when the phone call comes. He's been out of his mother's house since he was seventeen, living on his own, supporting himself as a mechanic. He has a few male friends. He's too shy to date. He's never met the lawyer who is calling, who shocks him, saying, 'I'm sorry to tell you your mother died. She was in Saks, buying a sweater, and the next thing, she had an aneurysm. Quick and painless. Sir, are you all right?'

He feels nothing at first. No pain. No anger. For so long, whenever she's come into his mind, he's blotted her out. He thanks the lawyer and says he will come to the funeral. He does not need money. He has his mechanic job.

The boy catches a plane and is one of only three people at her funeral, and the other two, a reverend and a lawyer, are paid to be there. The lawyer tells him, 'We never located your father. Apparently, when he left, he completely changed his identity. New credit cards. New Social Security card. There is no record of him anywhere, that I can find.'

'Maybe he died.'

'There's no record of a death certificate. I'm sorry to tell you this, son, but it looks like he wanted to have nothing to do with you. If a person wants to disappear, it's so easy, you wouldn't believe it. There are places down on the lower East Side, men who sell false identity papers, birth certificates, job recommendations, who even get you a new Social Security card. I know a guy who does it. He works for illegal immigrants. Instant citizen. Instant history. It costs a lot, but it works.'

That night the boy stays, sleepless, at a motel, watching the neon blink, watching the cars rush by, remembering the nights with her, her voice when she was screaming. He wishes he could forget.

But in his dreams she comes back, into his motel room, walking right through the locked door, unstoppable, dead and still coming, his father gone, unable to protect him, no one can protect him, and he can't move because he is five again, and she has many arms, like an octopus, hands that clutch and caress and hit him at the same time, while she screams that no one will ever listen to him, hear him, care for him, stay with him, love him.

He wakes drenched in sweat, showers, and arrives at the lawyer's in his only suit, hair combed, shoes shined. His mother liked when he dressed up, at least during the periods when she was speaking to him. It seems fitting to dress for her to say a last goodbye.

And the lawyer seems friendly enough, a little pompous but otherwise kind, until he opens the envelope, and reads.

' "I leave all my worldly possessions, my bank accounts, my Paine Webber account, my bonds which are worth plenty, the contents of my strongbox, everything that I own, to my only son . . ." '

The boy, surprised, breaks out crying. Considering her opinion of him, he never expected to get anything from her. Perhaps he was wrong about her, and she did love him.

' ". . . but don't imagine, son, that by doing my motherly duty, leaving these things to you, that I forgive you for the terrible things you did to me when I was alive . . ." '

The boy looks up, shocked. The lawyer is staring at him. The boy feels himself floating up, out of his body, toward the ceiling. He looks down at himself.

' "I would never accuse you to the police, because I am too loyal to do that, and the lawyer has been instructed to destroy this message so there will be no record of it. But you raped me—" '

It's too much. The boy comes back into his body.

'No!'

' "You abused me." '

'I didn't!' the boy cries, but he can see in the lawyer's eyes how the man does not believe him, how the man, like everyone else, people on the street, people at work, people forever, will regard him if they know.

' "You always had a filthy mind, and a filthy body. I pray to God that he forgives you." '

'She made up stories,' he tells the stony-faced lawyer, wishing he were anywhere else.

' "I hope you will be a better man than you have been so far. Otherwise you are doomed to hell. I hope you have learned that it is a sin to do the kinds of terrible things you did to your mother. I am glad to be leaving you, and the burden you represent. I am glad I won't have to see your face anymore, and feel your disgusting hands." '

The boy leaps to his feet. The lawyer will accuse him, half an hour later, of ripping the will from his hands. Of tearing it to shreds. Of throwing the bits away so they drift, spinning, to the carpet. Of screaming, in a voice that is not the boy's normal voice, in a voice that is deeper, as if it were another, meaner boy's voice, 'Lies!'

The boy will have no memory of the lawyer backed against the wall. What he will remember is the disgust on the lawyer's face, so palpable that it is as if his mother is still hitting him, driving him from the room, into the elevator and outside, and to the airport.

He feels as if she is beside him, in the plane. He feels the other people staring at him. They *are* staring at him. They know, somehow, what his mother said, even though it is impossible. They believe her.

The stewardess looked at me funny. She knows. Everyone knows.

He is so tired when he gets home, and his head is killing him. He can't stand it. He wishes he were dead. He wishes he were another person. He takes aspirins and, head throbbing, lies down as a voice in the room, soothing and light as a whisper, as tender as a thought, says, 'My dear, dear troubled boy. My poor child. I will take care of you, always.'

He looks around, but no one is there.

'Let me love you. Let me care for you. Let me do what has to be done.'

At length, the boy lapses into the deepest sleep of his life.

'So I finally build up the courage to ask Greta to go to the symphony, and she tells me she can't,' the Mechanic says, speeding up, as if he wants to get through the bad part. 'She tells me she's in love with someone else. A doctor. The man I saw her with, in Central Park, under the trees. She loves him. She's been trying to forget him, but she can't. She's saying, over and over, that she's sorry.'

Harris Tillman stands, looking enraged, towering over the slumped Mechanic. 'Then why was she spending time with you in the first place?' Tillman says.

'Because he was married,' the Mechanic says. 'He had a wife and kids and she wanted to forget him, she prayed that she'd forget him, but she couldn't.'

'She led you on,' the Banker says.

'She did, didn't she? She didn't tell me about him, and that was a kind of lie.'

'A big one.'

'All those months, and I never had a chance. She tricked me.'

'You were a distraction to her,' Tillman whispers.

'What's that?'

'A game. To keep herself busy while she waited for the great doctor. I bet during that same time, she had sex with *him*.'

'I don't want to think about it.'

'I bet all the time she was fixing cars with you, she was fantasizing about him, what he looked like with his clothes off, how he'd fuck her, on a table, on a floor, from behind, up the ass, in closets at the hospital, at hotel rooms that he paid for with his big salary, all those juices sopping, how they'd lie in bed laughing about his wife, fooling her, and laughing at you, the poor mechanic, who never had a chance, who was mooning around for her. I bet you were a big joke to them.'

'You don't know that,' Bainbridge says.

'You think she cared about you for one second? Forget it,' Tillman says.

Arthur Davis has a fork in his hand. Suddenly, he drives it at the table, with such a vicious movement that the prongs leave gouge marks in the wood. He hits the table in a slow, methodical, repetitive attack; drives the fork into the table. He sweeps his arm out, shoving food and glasses to the floor.

'I hate her. My mother—'

He stops.

'What about your mother?' Bainbridge asks.

'I didn't say anything about my mother,' Arthur says. 'Why'd you bring her up?'

'Because you *said*,' Bainbridge says, leaning forward, ' "My mother," and then you stopped.'

Arthur shakes his head, stares at the fork in his hand, as if becoming aware that it is there. He throws it on the floor and it clatters and slides on the yellowing linoleum, and hits the wall, bouncing back. The floor is a mess.

'I didn't say that.'

Tillman agrees. 'I didn't hear him say anything about his mother.'

The Banker massages the Mechanic's shoulders.

'Tense,' he says. 'Let me ask you something. You can't stop thinking about her. All this time.'

'Yes.'

'You wish you could stop, but she tortures you.'

'Yes.'

'You'd do anything to get her out of your mind.'

'She married that doctor. He left his wife. They live on East Eighty-fifth. They both work in that hospital, still.'

'They're happy because you suffered.'

'That's extreme, Harris,' the Psychologist argues. 'You're presenting this to him as if their entire bond is a joke they played on him.'

'She made him jealous by hanging out with you,' Tillman says, ignoring Bainbridge. 'She never had any intention of spending serious time with you. You were a toy for her. Maybe they still laugh at you. Maybe they lie around in bed, fucking, and when they're finished, he says, "Whatever happened to that pathetic mechanic?" And she says, "Who cares?"'

The Mechanic's eyes have gone glassy and his breathing has slowed. His shoulders rise and fall rhythmically. 'I hurt her once,' he whispers, looking ashamed and excited at the same time.

'I know. You told us. You waited for her on Fifth Avenue. You had a bat. You hit her. You put her in the hospital. She wouldn't press charges because of the doctor, not wanting to drag him into it.'

'But the police beat me up. They came back, when they were off duty. They got me outside the garage. They wore masks, but I recognized their voices. They told me, if I ever touched her again, they would kill me. I was afraid to complain. Oh God. It hurt.'

'Re-laxxx. That's better. Let me ask you something else, or would you rather I didn't? Maybe you're too upset to hear another question,' Tillman says, 'because if you are, just say so, and we'll stop for a while. Hey, you want a drink? Our mutual friend and benefactor and patron and shrink, Dr Bainbridge, has some excellent single malt around here. How about one little sip, to calm you down.'

'No more drinking,' the Psychologist says.

'What's single malt?' the Mechanic says.

'I'll get it,' the Banker says, and, at the cupboard, bringing out the Glenlivet and three glasses, he says, 'Maybe I should ask my question later, when you feel better.'

'I don't care what you do.'

'Then I'll ask.'

'I hate her,' the Mechanic says, voice low, primitive, coming from somewhere deep.

Bainbridge's headache is massive and blurs his vision. Once again, for an instant, it seems to him that he is alone in the room, and the other two men are not even there.

'Just as a matter of curiosity,' Tillman asks the Mechanic, 'how would you feel if you read in the paper that she had an accident? If you personally had nothing to do with it, but you found out she'd been hurt?'

'You mean like, she'd been punished,' the Mechanic whispers, brightening.

'Exactly. By a protector. God.'

'I'd like it, and I don't care who hears it!'

The Banker massages the Mechanic's shoulders. The clock over the sink says eleven-thirty, turning to eleven thirty-one. Outside the bars on the window, the night is clear, and cold.

Tillman says, 'I have an idea. Let's all take a walk over to Mount Sinai. I bet you could use the exercise. Didn't you say she gets off about midnight?'

'I'm going upstairs,' says the Psychologist. 'I need to sleep.'

'To sleep? Or to make a phone call? I don't think it's a good idea for you to leave us at the moment.' The Banker blocks the doorway. 'Take your nap when we get back. Get your coat, Arthur. Doc, get your coat.'

'I won't,' Bainbridge says.

Tillman pulls himself up. He is much stronger than the doctor, and towers over him. The threat of violence in the room is palpable.

Bainbridge cringes as Tillman pushes him against the wall. Sweat pours down the doctor's face.

'Now, Ian, when you started our nice club, you said it would be sort of group therapy. What kind of therapy would it be if our doctor wasn't present? And what kind of field trip would this be if it didn't include the founding member of the group?'

FOURTEEN

Mount Sinai Medical Center is a complex of eight buildings, towering, one after the other, block after block, in a mass between East Ninety-eighth and 102nd Streets, south of East Harlem. It is a vast city of medicine; X-ray and CAT Scan machines in the basements, muscular rehabilitation in one pavilion, pregnancies in another. Inside, glass walls, tinted brown against the sun, twenty stories high, seal walkways connecting buildings, atriums, plazas, balconies, as if Greater New York outside, with its nightclubs and politics and crime and businesses, is no more than a distraction when considered against microbes, against illness, against survival and death.

At eleven P.M., Greta Harden Berger, who has less than forty-five minutes to live, is finishing her rounds as chief nurse and employee of the year on the eleventh floor Oncology Unit in the complex's North Pavilion. She is a cheery woman, short, round, and much loved for her positive attitude, and she needs every iota of strength to get through a rough shift tonight.

She tells the Dominican boy in 1123, whose leg is about to be amputated because of bone cancer, 'Remember, Valdez, I've got tickets to Shea Stadium for June third. Tell your father he has to buy the beer.' To the once gorgeous fashion model in 1131, a bald twenty-two-year-old who looks like an old man now, whose face, which once sold jeans, perfumes, underwear, and shaving cream, now is a yellowed skull with skin stretched over it, she says, 'Tomorrow we try solid foods, Tina.'

To her favorite patient, the sixty-year-old Scarsdale divorcée in 1121, who woke this afternoon after stomach surgery, Greta says, massaging her wrist, ignoring the smell of shit-and-grass-colored bile running through plastic tubes in and out of the woman's body, 'I'm sorry, Jessie. You won't be able to eat anymore, ever. We'll feed you through the tube in your neck. Have you ever thought about checking into a hospice?'

The other nurses are slicing pieces of spice cake in the break room. It's an orderly's birthday party.

'Good night, Greta!'

'Hey, Greta, avoid the Madison Avenue entrance! They still haven't caught the mugger!'

She's wearing jeans, flat-heeled shoes, a plain white sweater, and a single strand of gold around her neck. She takes the blue cloth coat off a peg in the break room and, with a younger nurse who is also getting off, heads out of the octagon-shaped ward, into the atrium separating the North and South pavilions, and along a balcony hallway high above the ground floor, toward the elevators.

The other nurse is young and pretty, from Trinidad.

'Greta, you have seniority. Why do you choose to work such a late shift?'

'I don't mind. The other girls prefer days, and Jack usually is in surgery until ten or ten-thirty anyway.'

'Why work in Oncology? Why not kids, or pregnancies? I have trouble dealing with dying patients, and I'm only here three months.'

'My mother was a nurse, and she told me, "If you're lucky

enough to have love in your life, share it. If you share it, it makes you stronger. The stronger you are, the more you have to share." '

The elevator comes, humming, and they are the only two people in it, whisked down, the pneumatic doors hissing open to spill them into a huge triangular marble and steel atrium. Their heels echo. They are dwarfed by the scope of the massive architecture, as if the designer of this mini-city regarded its occupants as irrelevant and constructed a monument to its own timeless components – glass, steel, marble.

'Greta, why do you limp like that? Did you have an accident?'

Greta stops and frowns, remembering. It is a horrible memory, and just thinking of it makes her left hip, the damaged one, indeed, her whole left side begin to ache.

'I was attacked by an old boyfriend, years ago.'

'What did he do?'

'He had a bat. He was crazy. He was a shy man, and when I told him I'd met Jack and we were going to get married, he was fine at first. He said he understood. But then he started phoning all the time, and following me. It was terrible. And one night, when I thought he finally got used to it, he came at me outside. He broke my hip.'

'Oh God!'

'You never know about someone,' Greta says. 'He was actually a man who, at one point, I thought I might end up with. Jack was married when we met, and I felt guilty about it, but I was in love. I tried not to be. I tried to stop it. I tried to date other people. I thought he'd never leave his wife, and Arthur – the man who attacked me was named Arthur – was sweet, quiet. In the end he turned into a monster.'

'Does it still hurt?'

'Jack says I should have surgery on it, to correct the limp. But I hate the idea of being in a hospital.' She grins. 'Especially this one.'

The two nurses break out laughing, and their girlish delight echoes into the empty atrium, against the false potted palms and girders, the soot-brown glass and interior brick walls with windows, as if they look into real apartments, not confining hospital rooms.

'Yeah, who wants to stay here,' the nurse from Trinidad jokes as they start walking again.

Out on Fifth Avenue the evening is slightly warm, for winter, and humid, with a westerly breeze out of Central Park. Traffic is light, mostly cabs, and Central Park across the street is pretty, like a Currier & Ives print, the bare oaks and maples dusted with snow.

'This man who attacked you, he was a doctor like Jack?'

'A mechanic.'

A grin. 'You did pretty well for yourself in the marriage department.'

'I would have loved Jack no matter what he did.'

'Well, I go to Brooklyn. We can't all live in these Fifth Avenue duplexes like you, Greta.'

'Be careful walking to the train, especially on Madison.'

Greta watches the retreating back of the younger nurse until she rounds the corner and heads off for the Lexington Avenue line on Ninety-sixth Street. Her own apartment is two blocks north, overlooking the park, and Jack told her he's ordering takeout Thai tonight – crispy noodle, peanut beef, big fish – and he's rented a couple of comedy videos. Woody Allen. Jim Carrey. After a shift on the Oncology Unit, Greta loves to watch comedy videos, to calm down.

Greta strolls across Fifth Avenue to the park side, feeling her breathing slow, feeling herself relax, feeling the smells of alcohol and puke and dissipation diminish, against the sheer life force of the city. The snow in the park smells like basil. From here, the hospital opposite, with all its human struggle inside, seems like just one more apartment building, nothing more. The stars are out, and the moon clean in a three-quarter phase, turning the air crystalline, making taxi headlights stark moonbeams, giving the few clouds in the sky a silvery, benevolent air.

'Greta?'

She turns as the shadow of a man detaches itself from the larger shadow, the park shadow, by the rock wall boundary of the park, beneath a big oak. The man's shadow has something long and thin in his hands.

He knows my name, she thinks, so he must be one of the staff.

'Who—'

'It's Arthur. Remember? I was just walking around and I saw you. It's Arthur.'

She backs a step. She thinks, no no no no.

Her heart is thundering. She remembers, last time, years ago, but it seems like yesterday, that she turned to flee and he caught her. He was always faster, and now she limps, she is even slower than before.

She tells herself it is impossible he has come back, after all this time.

Oh my God. Oh sweet Jesus. He's got a golf club.

No one is on the street. She glances up, at the hospital, so far away, across Fifth Avenue, at the lone face of a patient, a boy, on the sixth floor, his forehead pressed against the glass. Greta knows, when you try to look out those sealed windows at night, all you see is a reflection of yourself.

Last time, she tried to run. She got two feet before the bat descended.

'How are you, Arthur?' Her voice, she is amazed to hear, sounds normal, soothing, as if she is on the ward, addressing a patient.

'This is an amazing coincidence,' he says, 'running into you.'

Coincidence? She wants to laugh with fear.

But she manages to say, 'How have you been? You look

terrific. Fit.' Although actually he's deteriorated, she thinks, since she last saw him. She barely recognizes him. He's really filled out, and he's older.

He doesn't answer.

She forces herself to sound chatty. 'I always tell myself I ought to work out, but my schedule is hell, you know, with all the cutbacks. I never get a chance to go to the gym anymore.'

Arthur looks over her left shoulder. He says, as to someone standing there, but she's heard no other person approach, 'I just want to talk to her for a minute! I haven't seen her in a long time.'

'Who are you talking to?' she says, glancing back. There is no one behind her.

Arthur says, as if answering a question from the unseen person, 'I *know* I should hurry. You don't have to talk to me like I'm a baby!'

'Arthur,' she says, feeling cold. 'There's nobody there!'

He just stands there, staring, and then an incredible thing happens. His eyes glaze and he slumps and straightens again. She is shocked by how much he seems to have become an entirely different person. It's more than a change in mood. Straightening, he has added inches to his height, and, with his shoulders thrown back, they seem wider. His features have realigned themselves, the mouth becoming harder, the lips thinner, haughty, the eyes small, angry, and fiercely intelligent lacking the docility that in the past usually marked Arthur.

'Arthur! What . . .'

He holds his head differently, lower, which increases the sense of power emanating from him. And when he speaks, she is terrified to hear a different voice coming out of him, a more cultured voice, deeper, disdainful, an upper-class voice aimed at the lower, a voice she would never associate with Arthur.

'You won't talk him out of it, Greta.'

'What do you mean, "him"?'

His new, more distant expression reminds her of the cancer researchers on the eleventh floor, to whom she occasionally brings biopsies, severed human flesh that, by the time they see it, represents only germs to them, inhuman microbes not a piece of a living, breathing patient.

Arthur says, 'It's about time you felt some of what Arthur feels. It's about time *you* tasted a little of Arthur's pain. Arthur's broken heart.'

'But you're Arthur!'

She takes a half step back, but Arthur moves with her, step for step, even walking differently now. His shy gait has become a confident step. Her instinct for survival tells her, through mounting panic, that further retreat will trigger something violent, will let loose the force that, at least for the moment, he is barely holding in check.

'Why don't we . . . talk a bit,' she says, trying for her nurse voice, her professional voice, the voice she needs when patients are screaming, dying, desperate to escape from their own sick bodies.

Arthur slumps again and slowly straightens. There is less intelligence in the face now. It is bland again, slightly confused again. The tight, patrician lines, softening, make the face more oval. It is the face of the Arthur she used to know. She never dreamed that a human being, simply by changing mood, could alter appearance to this degree.

'You broke my heart,' he says pitifully. 'Didn't she, Harris? She broke my heart.'

She wants to cry. This is not happening. I will wake up any second and I will be in bed, with Jack, at home.

Arthur says, 'She laughs at me. Both of them. They fuck and laugh at me. Like you said, Harris.'

'Don't hurt me,' Greta begs.

Greta backs another step, hears the snow crunch beneath

her, crushed. She's dizzy with fear. She manages to get out, 'I'm sorry if I ever caused you pain.'

He answers in the gruff voice. 'You made his whole life pain.'

The club is swishing. She knows she cannot outrun him She says, voice trembling, self-control deserting her, 'It's been so long, Arthur. You can't still be thinking about this.'

And instantly she knows, from the rage that leaps into his face, that she has said the worst possible thing.

'You see?' the newer voice says triumphantly. '*He's* tortured and *you* don't even think about it. To *you* it's just some lark that happened a long time ago. See, Arthur? You never meant anything to her.'

'That isn't true!'

The voice mimics her, cruelly. 'That isn't *true*. That isn't *true*. If Arthur was so fucking special, missy, what were the names of the two other mechanics at Arthur's garage?'

'I . . . I don't remember. What difference does it make?'

'What was the first thing you told Arthur when you met him, in the emergency room? I know. Do you?'

She is crying now. 'Don't hurt me,' she says.

'Greta. You think people like you can just go through life, hurting him, and you never have to pay?'

'What do you mean, "him"? *It's you!*'

Her logic, for an instant, seems to get through to him. He blinks, rapidly. His shoulders slump. For a moment he resembles the old Arthur again, the mechanic, the quiet man.

She allows herself to hope.

But then Arthur tilts his head back, cocks it as if listening to someone whispering to him. He nods to the invisible voice. He asks her, almost shyly, 'Greta, were you sleeping with that doctor at the same time you were going out with me?'

She lies. She puts all her ability to act, all her desire to live, into replying, 'No. I promise.'

The golf club is rising, a shadow on the snow, thin as a syringe, powerful as a bat, shiny as the moon.

'You lied, Greta. It's not right to lie.'

Oh God. This isn't happening.

She turns to run.

The moonlight is so bright, burning the snow over her shoulder. She seems to be moving through water, slowly, impossible to run.

She sees the shadow man, behind her, bring the golf club down.

She screams.

There is a crunching noise, and the scream stops.

Ten minutes later Dr Ian Bainbridge straightens up, beside a big willow tree, where he's been sick. The only sound in the park is his moaning. The snow is piled more deeply here than outside, on Fifth Avenue. It is lovely, undisturbed by footprints, undulating and almost fluorescent-blue beneath the bright shiny moon, stretching away, through copses of oak and maple, toward Sheep Meadow.

It is also stained by the remnants of his dinner, hamburgers and fries, Coke, and bile.

'Oh God. Oh God. Arthur really did it,' he says.

'And you stood there,' Tillman says. 'And watched.'

'You made me come.'

'That I did. It would have been painful for you to refuse. But in the eyes of the police, Doc, you're a full accessory now. *Three* murders.'

Bainbridge whispers, 'She didn't do anything to you.'

Tillman and the Mechanic, several feet off, stand over the nurse's body which Tillman has dragged deeper into the park and leaned against a tree.

'She looks asleep, if you don't pay attention to her head,' Tillman says.

The doctor says, 'What am I going to do?'

'I'll tell you, Ian. Whatever you do, it can't change what happened, so relax. You okay, Arthur?'

Arthur stares at the body.

'Arthur?'

'The golf club sounded funny when I hit her.'

'Yeah, well, wipe it. We found it on a garbage pile, so no one will trace it.'

Tillman throws it away. It sparkles, spinning, and falls into the snow.

He kneels at Greta's body and removes something from his breast pocket. It's a black Magic Marker, the Psychologist sees. Tillman bends over the calf of her jeans.

B, he writes. H . . .

'I'm going home now,' Arthur says simply, turns and starts walking out of the park. He calls, over his shoulder, ''Bye.'

Tillman says, finishing, 'That'll warn the others.'

'What others?'

'Anyone who hurts us,' Tillman replies. 'Anyone who messes around with us. Any of the women who screw us over, cheat on us, tell us to leave, think they're putting one over on us.'

The words penetrate Bainbridge's horror. He looks up. Tillman's face is all shiny, mad, Bainbridge thinks, and not sated. If anything, he looks hungry, excited.

'But there aren't any more women who hurt us.'

'Is that so?'

'Well, who's left?' Bainbridge leans over, heaves, but nothing comes out. His sickness brings a little tenderness into Tillman.

'There, there. Take it easy. I don't think we're finished, and you don't either. You're too smart for that. Doc, as a club, we need to have things in common, to share things. Not just thoughts. Actions. To bind us. You tried to call the cops once. Who's to say, if I leave you alone, if time goes by, if you think about it, you won't call again. Now you're scared, and I can control you. Maybe later you'll start to feel remorse, and I won't be around to stop it.

'You understand? I can't have you hurting *me* now, Doc, or Arthur, or Eric. I can't have the police showing up after *me*, just because *you* changed your mind about things.'

Bainbridge shouts, 'I won't change my mind!'

'It was never a club for the brokenhearted. It was the revenge club. The rage club, fucking the people who fucked us over club, and you're the charter member, our glorious Svengali benefactor, and now it's time for you to go through initiation too. Once you do, I'll feel safe. And you'll shut up about things. Maybe close your practice after that, leave New York, make a new identity. It's easy. There are people you can go to, on the lower East Side.'

'I can't think!'

'You started this club because you didn't want to be hurt again. And Camilla's had sex with that dancer. I followed her. I saw it.'

'You saw them go into her building, that's all.'

'Ha! The dog goes out to take a shit, and when she comes in, wagging her tail, you're not sure she did it because you didn't actually see it, huh?

'Ian, we're taking care of all the women who broke our hearts.'

'But Camilla didn't break my heart.'

Tillman grins. 'Hey, when you're right, you're right,' he concedes, breaking off a small branch from an evergreen hedgerow, gesturing Bainbridge to precede him out of the park, so he can wipe away the prints, the trail, the blood.

The doctor complies.

Tillman says, starting to brush away evidence, 'Let's give her the chance.'

FIFTEEN

It is eleven A.M. the next day, and the man who worships anonymity, who has made it a business, is frightened of one of his own clients. Seventy-seven-year-old Alexander Leibovitz, a magician, a conjuror of new identities, sips Mountain Dew from a cold bottle and puts the finishing touches on a new, bogus birth certificate, in his basement shop on Avenue A, on the lower East Side of Manhattan.

'Ian Bainbridge' should be here any moment.

In contrast to the tenement it occupies, Leibovitz's two-bedroom, rent-controlled apartment is redecorated in a hacienda style, with stucco arched walls, cedar floors, table and armoire of Mexican pine, Navajo throw rugs, and the finest collection of miniature flowering Chilean cactus in New York. A pleasantly humming machine in a corner blocks out street noise as it sprays the odor of desert sage.

The buzzer rings and Leibovitz's heart constricts. He is terrified of 'Bainbridge,' who has probably just entered the foyer outside.

Leibovitz totters on his hospital walker to the closed-circuit TV monitor. He's tall as a basketball center, pale as a cancer patient, steady as a diamond cutter, bald as a Buddhist monk. On the monitor, sure enough, 'Bainbridge' is standing stiffly by the mailboxes, looking up at the monitor, wearing a forest-green parka and jeans.

The face of the man in the foyer is the face on the picture of the Massachusetts driver's license, and on the new passport that waits on Leibovitz's desk.

'*Vay iz mir,*' mutters Leibovitz, who fled Romania for the U.S. in 1954, and who nicknames all his clients, since they all use false names anyway, 'Der Stick Man.'

Also on the desk behind Leibovitz is a Visa and American Express card in the name of Otis Becket, a forged Social Security card, and an Oxford Health Plan identity card.

The real Otis Becket died at three years old, in 1958, in Pittsfield, Massachusetts. He was run over by a car.

Wishing this meeting were already over, Leibovitz buzzes the Stick Man into the waiting room, which is sealed by two Medico locks from the inner apartment, where he lives, where he makes false IDs for the men and women who ring his buzzer at night, who wear sunglasses even when it rains, or arrive in cars with tinted windows. He thinks of them as Mr Big Boots, Mr Rastafarian, Miss Plaid, Mr Government Witness, Mrs AWOL Marine, Mr Delinquent Father, Mr Illegal Immigrant Number Two Thousand and Nine.

'Two more minutes,' he tells the Stick Man over the intercom, watching the odd, stiff stance, the way the head hangs to the left, the way the man never lifts his arms above his waist, the jerky, birdlike movements that have characterized this man each time he has visited, four times in all, over the last twenty years.

The client seats himself on a white wicker chair and reaches for a *National Geographic* magazine.

Leibovitz works faster, finishing the lamination on the passport photo. In his workroom are two computers on antique desks, hooked to birth and death records in forty-one states, Social Security records, military records, motor vehicle bureau records, marriages, divorces, voter registration lists, credit reports, and obituaries in towns from Bangor to San Diego. There are dyes and special papers and expensive inks and the laminating machine. There are cameras for passport photos, Green Cards for immigration cases. There's a printer where he can produce letterheads from two hundred businesses, for letters of recommendation to employers. There are, in a glass case, colored contact lenses and wigs which he sells at a big markup.

Leibovitz takes the pile of Otis Becket identity cards through the living room, toward the steel door closing off the waiting room. The walker makes progress excruciatingly slow. He unlocks the Medicos.

In the waiting room, the Stick Man jerks to his feet, expressionless.

Leibovitz says, with false cheeriness, 'How long has it been, nine years?'

The man merely examines the passport and credit cards. Every few years, when he shows up, his appearance is different, from wigs, clothing, hairstyle, colored contact lenses. But the movements never change.

Leibovitz says, 'Usually people come here once. But you. A three-year hiatus. Then five, four. Then nine as Dr Bainbridge.'

The Stick Man reaches into an inside pocket and Leibovitz feels his chest constrict. But the hand comes out with a white folded envelope.

'These IDs will fool people? Computers are better at tracking identities now.'

Leibovitz says proudly, 'You're right. Forging identities isn't as easy as it used to be. These days, everything is cross-checked by computer; at borders, by police, by corporations. You can't just hand them the document anymore. The document has to hold up against a check. So I find someone who really died, a long time ago, who would be your age now. I make sure his Social Security card wasn't canceled, which is easy to do, and I reissue a card by myself. I print up a phony birth certificate with real information on it, on a standard Massachusetts form in this case, and I use that to apply for a real passport, which I can obtain in forty-eight hours.

'With the passport and birth certificate, and counterfeit bank statements, I simply apply for credit cards, and as for the driver's license, let's say I have a friend in the motor vehicle bureau in Springfield. You have been cleanly inserted into computers in that state. That's one reason my fee has gone up. I share it. You are completely safe if authorities – landlords, credit companies, police, customs – cross-check your identity cards. Of course, if you commit a big crime and they really go into things, that I can't guarantee.'

'Four thousand, cash,' the Stick Man says, handing Leibovitz the envelope. He adds, almost to himself, 'Bainbridge asked me to join his club, but I never showed up. They kept a chair for me, in the restaurant. No way would I join that bunch.'

'That's nice,' says Leibovitz, who has no idea, who does not want to *have* any idea, what the man is talking about.

The Stick Man doesn't leave, though. He stands there. He has completely gone to seed, become pear-shaped, stooped and flabby, since the last time he was here. Leibovitz's throat goes dry. He has dealt, for five decades, with men running from police. Men who carry weapons. Men who employ other men to kill for them. And in all that time, it is the Stick Man who has frightened Leibovitz the most. There's less violence on the surface with him. But the twisted thing beneath seems, to Leibovitz, never to be far away, and to be more threatening because he has never been sure exactly what it is.

Now the Stick Man says, 'Don't you ever worry that one of your clients will hurt you? An old man, with a walker. Maybe they'll be afraid you'll tell on them.'

'Cameras record everyone who comes, and there are tapes, recorded here and, simultaneously, in another apartment. That's my insurance.'

The Stick Man seems to be deciding whether or not to believe Leibovitz.

'That's smart,' he says at length. 'I need one more thing. Maybe you know where I can buy it. A gun.'

Leibovitz shakes his head. 'I do papers only.'

'I don't believe that.'

'You never asked for a gun before, never needed one.'

'Circumstances change. Besides, it's just a precaution. I'm sure I'll never use it. It's for defense only.'

A hundred-dollar bill has materialized between his index and middle finger, crisp and new as a bogus identity.

The Stick Man says, 'The gun should be untraceable. I don't care about the caliber, except it shouldn't be too big. I don't want a bulge in my clothes.'

'I told you. No.'

'Two hundred.'

I will not deal with this person again.

Leibovitz says, 'It's not a question of money.'

'Everything is a question of money, not to mention that you're frightened of me.'

'I'm seventy-seven years old. At my age, you're scared of everyone.'

The Stick Man's hand seems to move by itself, snaking out, and the fingers grip Leibovitz's shoulder so hard that he twists, but cannot get away. The pain is getting worse. The Stick Man is as emotionless as a mechanical vise.

Leibovitz half falls, buckling against the remodeled stucco. From this angle he can see, over the Stick Man's shoulder and through the barred basement windows of his expensive apartment, a bit of scaffolding on the slate roof across the street, and the sky, which had gone dangerously gray-black, from an oncoming winter storm.

'Where did you say I could buy a gun?' the Stick Man says.

Leibovitz tells him.

At two o'clock on the same day, Mackey Kassulke, owner of Mackey's Tavern, where the Broken Hearts Club used to meet, strides across the cramped, low-ceilinged lobby of One Police Plaza, through a visitor's turnstile and up to a temporary reception desk manned by two Blue Guys who issue floor passes for nonpolice personnel needing to get upstairs. The Blue Guys are bored out of their minds after seven hours on duty, but since they never know when an important official will come in, they have to look alert.

Mackey waits on line, behind a *New York Times* photographer on his way to shoot the commissioner for the Sunday magazine. The headline on his folded-up paper reads, DEAD NURSE FOUND IN PARK MAKES THREE.

When Mackey's turn comes, he says, 'I own a restaurant by the West Side Highway. The guy you're looking for, the one who murdered the three girls, I think he's a customer.'

The Blue Guy appraises Mackey – the clean-shaven jaw, direct gaze, good posture, new tweed coat, quiet tone – and decides he's not dealing with a nut, even if Mackey is the eleventh person today to walk in off the street claiming to know the identity of the killer.

The Blue Guy says, 'There's a hot line, you know, to call.'

'I did. Two days ago.'

'So?'

'I never heard back,' Mackey says, sweating slightly in the overheated municipal building. 'The story's a bit nutty. I had a feeling I'd do better in person with this.'

'Sir, we process every call, but there are so many, sometimes it takes a few days to get to one.'

'Yeah, right, except I really think it's him. And now he did that girl in the park, so I figured I better come in person. But

206

you want me to leave? I'll leave. I came here special. Believe me, I got better things to do.'

The Blue Guy has specific instructions from Voort, from the task force heading the investigation. He is to use his judgment with visitors. He can turn them away or send them up. The Blue Guy calls upstairs, writes a floor pass, and directs Mackey to the ninth floor and a detective named Quinlan. Mackey squeezes into the elevator. He's never seen so many high-level cops in the same place. Half the older guys are wearing gold braids, medals, and decorations, like it's a parade in here, or a funeral.

Quinlan turns out to be a reed-thin black detective on a phone, in a squad room filled with detectives. He waves Mackey into a creaky wooden chair beside his Apple computer. Outside the big window, the sky, to the west, over Jersey, has gone purple as a bruise. Mackey's read, in the morning paper, that the incoming storm has paralyzed western New Jersey, closed schools, downed power lines, trapped old people in homes.

Quinlan is writing with his left hand, cradling the receiver on his shoulder and saying, 'Ma'am, I heard you. Your cousin Bradley always hated nurses. Right. About the initials. Bradley Horatio Cooper. BHC. But didn't you say he lives in Seattle?'

A couple more minutes and Quinlan hangs up.

'Want coffee?' he asks Mackey. 'I need it.'

Mackey says, 'I own a bar/restaurant by the West Side Highway. Couple months ago a man comes in, medium height, bald on top, white guy, educated, says he has a club, him and some other guys, and they want to rent the back room on Thursday nights.'

Quinlan leans forward. He's not taking notes. He's just listening. He cocks his head to the right when he listens, so Mackey figures he's a little hard of hearing in that ear.

Mackey says, 'It's going to sound nutty. But a guy who

kills women, hey, he's gonna be a nut, right? The first Thursday comes, he shows up alone, with a big paper bag; I can't see what's in it. He pays cash for the room. He orders four dinners. No one else ever comes. But the waitress hears him talking in there, like, to himself, in different voices.'

Quinlan says, 'One man.'

'I told you it would sound crazy.'

'Keep going.'

'Hell, he paid, right? For the room. For the dinners. What he does with them is his business. If he wants to sit there talking to himself, what do I care?'

Quinlan pulls out a yellow legal pad. He writes the word 'bar' on the pad and the word 'dinners.'

'Next week, same thing. One guy. The bag. The four dinners. This time the waitress hears him yelling in there, to himself, about some woman, who he hates, who left him. He's screaming, "I'll kill her." '

Quinlan says, 'What's the man's name?'

Mackey looks sheepish. 'Bill Smith, he said. But he paid by cash, in advance, and left a huge cash deposit against damage. Over a thousand. Anyway, the next week, the waitress goes into the room. The guy's dressed up in a black wig, hair slicked back, phony mustache. He even stands taller, he's talking in another voice. It freaked her out.'

'Why do you think he's the one who did the murders?'

'That's what I'm getting to. On the news, they showed that police sketch, and it was him, I tell you, when he was dressed up. And *then*, when they showed the other sketch, of that Banker, for the second murder, it could have *also* been him, a different time, when I went in the room. That's what the paper bag must hold, see? Wigs, phony beard. Four dinners. Four disguises.'

The detective says, 'The guy's been coming in like this for weeks? And you didn't think there's anything odd about it?'

'This is fucking New York,' Mackey snaps. 'Walk on the

street for twenty seconds if you want to see odd. I figured maybe he's an actor, a director, practicing parts, who the hell knows. Like when Whoopi Goldberg did the one-woman show on Broadway – which I saw by the way – don't you think when *she* was rehearsing, *she* put on wigs? She talked in different voices? Broadway's only five blocks from the restaurant. Those actors are all crazy. Maybe he's method acting, I figure. Or maybe if he tries to practice in his apartment, when he gets to the screaming parts, the neighbors complain. He had money. He was polite. He paid for the room. He tipped big. The point is, between me and the waitress, we saw him dressed up like both sketches on TV.'

'Do you have any idea where he lives, what he does for a living, anything else about him?'

'Nope.'

'Did he say what kind of club he had?'

'A men's club.' Mackey laughs. 'A one-man club.'

'And he comes every Thursday?'

'Actually, the last time we saw him was the night the woman in Brooklyn was murdered, and believe me, he was going nuts in that room, yelling he hates some woman, he wants to kill her. He scared the waitress.'

Quinlan leans back in his swivel chair. During pauses, since arriving here, Mackey's been hearing three or four other detectives in the room, on phones, and now he realizes from the snatches of conversation that they are calling doctors in the city. He hears one saying, in language that could only have been devised by a lawyer, 'I'm required by law to tell you this talk is being recorded, unless you object.'

Another says, 'We're trying to track down a burglar who's been hitting doctors' offices. So if the doc can spare a minute on the phone, it'll save us a trip over there.'

But this is a lie, Mackey realizes from comments the detectives make to each other. Apparently, the detectives are only interested in comparing the doctors' voices to a voice they have on tape, the voice of an anonymous tipster.

Mackey realizes the detectives have made up the burglar story so as not to scare away the tipster, who must be a doctor.

Of course, Mackey thinks, there are only about seventeen billion doctors in the city. Against three detectives making the calls.

Quinlan says wearily, 'He orders four *dinners* and you think he's an actor? Actors never have money. My brother-in-law is an actor. He mooches his meals at my house.'

'You going to bust my chops, or you going to use what I told you? Since when is it against the law to order dinners and pay for them? Fuck you. It's him.'

'Everyone says "It's him." '

They glare at each other. Honor being satisfied on both sides, Quinlan picks up the phone and calls the art department.

'Maybe you can help us come up with a sketch,' he tells Mackey. He adds, to himself, 'You, the guy in Brooklyn, the woman in Astoria . . . Boy, is Voort going to love the list today.'

Voort, meanwhile, upstairs, can't take his eyes off the photos of the dead girl. They're awful, covering the corkboard. Black and white, eight by eleven, they reduce the end of Greta Berger to two dimensions. Turn them sideways and the images disappear, as if they never existed. Turn them upside down and you see a plain white surface, as if a murder never occurred at all.

Voort looks over the nurse's smashed skull, the crimson-stained snow. The legs, tangled up in each other, as if, panicked, they came to life on their own as she fought to be the first one to get away from the attacker. The blowup of the upturned neck, white in the flash of the police photographer's camera, resembles a ski slope. The lone shoe in the snow, clothing freed from a body, reminds him of an art exhibit at MOMA he saw with Camilla last month. 'Landscapes and Clothes.'

The commissioner himself chewed me out this morning. 'How many deaths do we have to have before you get a lead, Detective'? he said.

'He killed her on Fifth Avenue,' Voort tells the detectives, the new shift coming in, the men and women assigned to work with him. 'He dragged her into the park. We found the golf club in the snow, twenty feet from the body. No prints. No footprints. But once again, initials. Check out this picture, here.'

He jabs his index finger against a blowup near the bottom of the corkboard. It's the calf of the dead woman's jeans, and the letters, in Magic Marker, BHC.

Voort's in the 'Situation Room,' a glassed-in conference area with a long pine table, plain metal folding chairs, and three corkboards standing on wooden legs, only two of them tacked over with photos. The third is covered by a street map of the upper East Side, with concentric circles, in black Magic Marker, ringing the corner from which the anonymous doctor phoned Mickie four days ago.

The circles represent areas police are concentrating on, phoning doctors.

'You don't look like you've slept,' one of the three incoming detectives says to Voort, reaching for a paper plate of stuffed mushrooms that Mickie the gourmet brought in.

'Slept? What's that mean?' Mickie says.

Voort's shaved, though, wearing cordovan loafers, thick gray Italian cords, and a wool sweater he picked up in Florence last year, forest-green with a crew neck.

Mickie's in a gray wool suit from Barneys and a freshly laundered white Donna Karan shirt with a wraparound collar. He looks like a film producer, like he could walk into the Paramount lot and walk out with a deal.

Voort sighs. 'Last night a kid gets home from clubbing about two A.M., totally wasted. He takes the family borzoi out for a walk. The borzoi gets off the leash, runs into the park. The kid follows the dog. The dog's at the body. Between the kid and the dog, the snow is messed up. The kid freaks out, runs out to Fifth, stops traffic. Soon we have a couple of cab drivers stomping around there too.'

Mickie adds, 'Don't forget the *Daily News* photographer.'

'Who could do that? We talked to the other nurses. First, there's a mugger been robbing people outside the hospital, but on the Madison Avenue side, not the Fifth Avenue side, and she wasn't robbed. Husband has an alibi. Turns out she was attacked, years ago, by an old boyfriend. It's our only lead, and it's old. A mechanic. We're checking him out, trying to find him. Arthur Davis.'

One of the older detectives perks up. 'I remember him.' The detective grins. 'Someone beat the shit out of him when she wouldn't press charges against him.'

One of the women detectives, a Bosnian who joined the force two years ago, speaks up. '*Someone*? You're such a dinosaur. Guys like you are why I left Bosnia.'

'I'm Tyrannosaurus Rex. And you want me on your side, believe me. Weird thing, though, when Davis was being, er, beaten up, he suddenly zones out. Starts talking in a different voice, deeper. His eyes get like, glassed up. A nutso switcheroo. He says he doesn't even know an Arthur Davis.'

'Where's Arthur Davis now?' the woman asks.

'We checked his old garage, where he worked years ago, got his employment records, Social Security number. Hazel's running him. Meanwhile, Mickie'll divide up who goes to the hospital, neighbors, patients. The mayor, the commissioner, Addonizio,' he says, naming the Chief of Detectives, 'wants the guy caught, fast.'

'Like we don't?'

The phone rings and Mickie reaches over the plastic bins

of pesto pasta salad he's ordered for the crew, and Saratoga springwater, picks it up, says, 'Yo,' then frowns.

'Con Man,' he says, handing the receiver to Voort. 'You'll want to take this in the office. I'll finish up here.'

'Hello?'

It's the Blue Guy at reception downstairs, telling him a woman is here to see him. Camilla Ryan.

The room is hot suddenly.

Voort says, 'Send her to my office.'

His heart goes berserk as he coolly replaces the receiver, tells the detectives, 'I'll be back,' and heads out of the Situation Room, hope blooming.

She dumped the dancer.

Of course, Voort reaches the office first, sits down, stands up, straightens papers, looks out the window, sits down again. Here she comes, he sees through the glass, a missile of love, incoming toward his heart, a tall beautiful blonde, in yellow today, lemon-yellow tight business jacket, lemon high heels and hip-tight matching skirt. Moving in past the police picnic signs and country-house-for-rent signs and union meeting signs and collection-for-injured-detective notices. She's carrying a leather snap-up folder, as if the two of them are about to hold a business meeting, as if she will pull out, when she enters, graphs and flow charts and angles of attack for her reporters, her cameramen, her television announcers.

The points of those high heels click closer, against the floor.

'Camilla.'

She slams the door behind her. The pane rattles. 'You bastard!'

This is not what he expected, the way she comes right up to him, blue eyes blazing, face flushed the color of lipstick, the dark blood color seeping down her neck along the lines of her veins.

'Asshole. You went to my *car service*? You told them you

were checking me out for a *murder investigation*? Didn't you think they'd call the network after you left, that they'd let us know someone is asking questions about us? A murder investigation? *How dare you check up on me!*'

'I was drunk.'

'You were *drunk*,' she repeats, as if he's just admitted intentionally transmitting syphilis, murdering an infant, stealing from a church collection plate.

'So now you know where I went on Fridays, Mr Big Fucking Detective. Are you satisfied?'

Camilla is shaking with rage. He has never seen her this angry. She's so close he can see the pores on her face. The smell of her perfume and sweat is tinged with a more acrid, bitter odor, which he realizes is fury.

'I might have felt guilty before, leaving you, but not now. First the phone calls,' she says. 'The hang-ups, which I didn't want to believe was you. And now this!'

'What phone calls?' Voort says.

'Don't even try it,' Camilla says. 'I traced the number. Voort, I thought you were smarter than that. You know I have caller ID, don't you? Maybe you don't. So why call me from a pay phone a block from your house, huh?'

'I *am* smarter than that. I *do* know you have caller ID. Why would I call?'

But she's too furious to hear, to appraise, or even think. She says, 'Or calling from right outside One Police Plaza. You think I'm stupid? You think I'm not going to guess,' she says, coming closer, voice building, skin redder, 'that it's you? Four hang-ups last night alone.'

'To tell you the truth, I don't think you're the one who should be accusing anyone of things.'

'What's that supposed to mean? Just what is that supposed to mean? Oh, Camilla,' she says, to herself, spinning away, not wanting to look at him, wanting to look at anything else, a window, a floor, an insect, at the dirty snow beginning to fall outside, 'you know how to pick 'em.' She laughs, an ugly, self-hating grunt.

'Camilla, listen to me. If someone's been calling you and hanging up, I want to find out who it is.'

'Sure you do. Or maybe you're going to tell me it's an accident. Or the phone lines are screwed up. And it started, by pure coincidence, the night I left you. Two hours after I go, I get the first call. I'm such an idiot. I always pick wrong. You looked so smooth, Voort, and confident. You seemed so normal, or maybe guys are all like you. Maybe it's a basic flaw. Maybe, after you get to know anyone, they turn out to be animals. My husband. You. Everyone betrays everyone in the end.'

He sees his reflection in the window and against the oncoming storm, reaching for her shoulder. In the reflection, she spins away before he can make contact. Her perfume is excruciatingly close. Her back heaves, but with passion, not weeping.

'One more phone call from you, and I'll go to the Chief of Detectives,' she says. 'I'll wreck your career. It's still between you and me, but that's ended now.'

Voort puts all his forcefulness, all his truthfulness and love and power into his voice. 'Camilla, look at me.'

She falters. She looks disdainfully, hatefully, at him, and the emotion drains a little, becomes, at least for a moment, doubt, vulnerability, fear, and she peers into his face. He puts all his will onto the surface. He tries to let her see inside him. For an instant, a fraction of time, he sees her straining, wanting to believe.

Camilla reaches into her handbag and pulls out a black leather glove, which he recognizes. It confuses him, this change of topic.

She says, softer, 'By the way, this was in my apartment. It's yours?'

'I wondered what happened to that,' Voort says.

Her expression locks up again, twists, and he has lost her, although he does not understand why. She says, 'It wasn't *in* my apartment. It was outside my bedroom window, on the fire escape, where you left it. If I hear from you again, if you call me, if I get a single fucking hang-up from you, from a phone anywhere, I'm going to the Chief of Detectives. You understand? Stay away from me. Don't call. Don't write. Don't even think about me, or I'll know, and I'll ruin you. It'll be the end of your fine two-hundred-year family history in the police. You make me sick.'

'The fire escape,' Voort says, reeling. Thinking, I'm sure I had both gloves last night.

He realizes that Mickie and another, older detective are in the corridor outside, knocking on the pane in the door.

'You fooled me,' she says. 'God, am I glad I listened to my doctor. I'm thankful I learned the truth about you now, not later. I can't believe,' she says, with withering disdain, 'that I ever liked you. That I let you touch me.'

He tries one last time. 'If someone's hanging up on you, whether or not you want to see me, you have to find out who it is.'

He watches her back, marching down the corridor toward the elevator.

Mickie and the old detective stand silently, watching with Voort. Mickie just shrugs. The other detective says, 'Man, I remember the way it was in Korea, when you fought the hordes off, and they finally ran away. Man, a relief.'

'You were on her fire escape?' Mickie says.

'Yeah, right, I was on her fire escape taking pictures of her naked. I was a skell watching her undress. What do you think?'

'Okay, sorry. Forget I said it. Freddie here may have a match on the doctor's voice,' Mickie says. 'He talked to a shrink on East Ninety-third, six blocks from the phone the tipster used.'

216

'Let's hear it.'

They close the door. The detective plays a tape of the doctor's voice, which starts off, 'Bainbridge here.'

Voort groans. 'Not Ian Bainbridge, Camilla's shrink. Give me a break.'

Bainbridge sounds uneasy on the tape, then nervous as he listens to the detective caller's lawyer-designed introduction. Bainbridge says, 'I'm sorry, but no one you describe showed up here, asking to be a patient.'

'Okay, play the other tape.'

Mickie switches on the original recording.

'I think it's a match,' Voort says after a moment. The other detectives nod. 'The voice. It's all wavery.'

Nobody says anything for a minute, but they all glance toward the elevator. Camilla's disappeared, but in a way, she's so forceful that it seems she's still standing there. Mickie says, delicately, 'Maybe I better be the one to talk to him.'

'Maybe I better hide in a basement and never do anything because she's pissed off,' Voort says. 'Maybe I should drop the case. Maybe I should crawl under a rock.'

'Thattaboy,' Mickie says.

Now Detective Quinlan comes into the office. The young guy has been working the tip line on the BHC case.

Quinlan holds a manila folder toward Voort.

'Today's hot tip list,' he says. 'Coupla doozies.'

Voort gets his jacket off the rack and puts the folder in the breast pocket without looking at it.

'Let's get the car,' he tells Mickie. 'I want to talk to Bainbridge. Now.'

SIXTEEN

The storm begins with hail. Silver-dollar-size missiles scream out of the west, from the Jersey side of the Hudson, in sheets, cracking windows, sending pedestrians fleeing into subways, stores, apartment houses, theaters.

It's only five P.M. but the sky is blacker than Voort has ever seen it during the daytime. The hail, hitting the Chevy, sounds like a machine gun going off next to their eardrums. It's pitted the right side of the windshield. Voort steers over a crunching mass of pellets coating the street. The furious assault seems as if it might rip through the roof, through fabric, flesh, to smash through the chassis onto the street.

'Officer down at Fifty-seventh and Sixth, from hail,' the radio says.

Mickie shouts over the storm, 'It's biblical!' By the time they skid through the intersection at Eighty-fifth and Third, the hail has turned to ice pellets, and the high staccato machine-gun noise is louder on the roof.

'Biblical? Change your mind about going to church?'

'Nah.'

The sky is purple, and the low, bruised cloud mass seems to undulate above wildly bouncing traffic lights, forming small nipples in the sky, as the hail becomes ice, a fine

219

glistening coat over curb-your-dog signs, sidewalks, asphalt, canopies protecting Korean groceries, which sag, rip, fall on crates of winter apples and squash.

'Ever seen anything like this?'

'Yeah, in a movie, with Charlton Heston. When the Egyptians wouldn't let the Hebrews go.'

Ahead, on Third and Ninetieth, cars tilt across their lanes, smoking hoods against caved-in doors, dented vans against grilles of delivery trucks. Voort hears sirens behind him, and more from the East River direction, except they don't seem to be moving, just wailing. He hears an ambulance siren, and a police siren. Now he hears the lower, deeper bellow of a fire truck siren.

Mickie says, opening the door, 'Do I see a *delivery kid* on a bike? Ouch! That looked painful.'

He and Mickie are out of the car, shielding their heads and trying to keep from slipping, heading for the most damaged cars, to help.

Voort rips open the front door of a caved-in Firebird. The dazed teenage driver is bleeding all over the steering wheel, to a tape blaring the British group Naked Birds, singing, 'Mister Fury.'

Voort says, easing the kid over broken glass on the bucket seat, 'Watch your hand, chief.'

The kid's crying. 'Dad'll kill me.'

Voort says wryly, 'Kill's a relative term. You're safe on that account. How about I talk to your dad myself, on the phone?'

He sighs. Looks like the visit to Bainbridge will wait a while.

'If you don't know how to drive,' Camilla snaps, from the backseat of the car service Town Car, 'How about I do it? You sit in back!'

'Ms. Ryan, it's slippery.'

'Haven't you ever driven in ice? You're supposed to be a professional!'

In the rearview mirror, the driver's eyes are fearful, as the Lincoln half crawls, half slides south on the West Side Highway. The heater is roaring. The driver's in a madras short-sleeve shirt, as if it is July, not January. He says, 'Ms. Ryan, I never saw snow until today. In Bombay, it doesn't snow.'

She realizes he fears he will lose his job. The car service fired the operator who gave Voort information the other night.

I shouldn't take it out on him, she thinks. I'm so pissed off. Maybe I ought to go see Bainbridge.

Camilla reaches, touches the man's bony shoulder. 'I'm sorry. I'm having a bad day and I didn't mean to use that tone. The boat-house is coming up on the right.'

I *can think there*.

The storm, here on the west shore of Manhattan, has turned to snow. The wall of ice has passed, and large wet flakes fall, obscuring vision, coating the Town Car's windshield, piling on the street, forming a mantle on the low rooftops of the repair shops and Travelers' Insurance building along the east side of the road.

On the river side is the bike path, white as a country lane, deserted at the moment. Ahead, a mile off, she should be seeing the lights of the World Trade Center tower, but nothing penetrates the wall of snow.

The wind sounds louder than the static on the radio.

'There! It's the entrance to the parking lot!'

The Town Car skids into the lot as the driver's eyes take in the concrete divider sliding past four inches from his window. When they stop, he breathes in relief. But he's puzzled.

'Ms. Ryan, you want to go here? There is nothing here.'

He turns, over the beaded seat cover. There's a card of a Hindu god, an elephant wearing clothing, on the dashboard,

221

and a folded newspaper in Hindi, and the radio is playing soft jazz, Wynton Marsalis, against the howl of wind.

'Excuse me, but you are not dressed for weather.'

'I only have a few feet to walk.'

After she gets out, the rear wheels skid, going nowhere, then they catch and the vehicle eases into southbound traffic, toward the Battery.

The snow feels good on her skin, cold and wet. But Camilla is exploding inside. Her head throbs with rage.

Voort's voice, in her head, says: 'I didn't make those calls to your house, Camilla.'

She answers out loud. 'Liar.'

Instantly, wet snow begins soaking into her stockings, melting against her wrists, where her gloves end, and inside her high-heeled shoes.

She won't cry, she tells herself. She will not cry. What's the point of crying, since he's out of her life anyway? She hates him. Once again, the man she chose turned out to be someone else, not who he pretended to be; to have a secret self, to be a trickster mouthing lies, a control freak hiding behind gifts and vacations and sex and words of phony love.

I left you for a good reason, Voort. I see that now. I sensed who you were all the time. I just didn't know it at the time.

In her mind, Voort dares contradict her: 'You're wrong.'

She shouts, knowing no one can hear, 'You were on my fire escape!'

She has to be careful, moving on the tiny point of high heels, balancing, women always have to balance, every second, or they get hurt in life. The snow tangles her hair and smears her makeup. It sticks to her eyelids, making vision heavy. In the parking lot, rows of cars are slowly being buried, becoming invisible, merging into an undulating urban surface of white.

Camilla finds the gap in the divider and totters onto the

bike path. On spring nights the place is alive with cyclists, roller bladers, book lovers on benches, reading Hammett and King and Morrison, and with sexy models and their photographers preparing spreads for *Glamour*, for *Vogue*. On spring nights the NYU film school students, aspiring directors and actors, shoot scenes down here, their four-minute-segment contest entries for film festivals in Telluride and Sundance. Win and get a job in Hollywood.

Brokers getting off from work, lovers carrying bag picnics, street people, tourists from Hamburg, Osaka, Oslo, Salt Lake City, Manila, Madrid, flock to the path when the weather is nice.

Camilla is alone now.

Maybe I should call Bainbridge.

The snow is accumulating so fast it is already three inches deep. Voort's turned even purgatory inside out. Purgatory is supposed to be hot, not frosty.

No. I always think better when I work on the boathouse. I can handle this myself.

She can't go back to work, can't stand going into the studio with all those people. Those NBC nonstop gossips, looking concerned, eager for information, saying, 'What's the matter, Camilla? How's Voort?' Fuck them. She can't stand to be with other people. She's phoned the show and taken a few hours off. Hell, tomorrow's piece is in the can anyway, and the network only owes her about fifteen thousand days of vacation time, and the place should be able to totter along without her for a few measly hours.

If it can't, too bad.

Camilla makes it across the path, feels her way, in the driving storm, along the one-story-high brick wall of the boathouse to the corrugated iron fence sealing off the pier it occupies. She finds the lock and, rummaging in her purse, pulls out her key chain, which has on it, besides the keys to Voort's apartment and half the locked rooms on the sixth floor of NBC, the way past the big Medico lock securing this fence.

On summer nights here, she likes to take the kayak out, dragging it to the ladder, climbing down after it, working up a sweat in the Hudson, before the sun goes down.

On the pier now, she locks the gate behind her and feels her way to the front door of the boathouse. She unlocks another Medico and pulls the door aside.

Inside, the wind sounds louder, but at least she can't feel it anymore. It's freezing in here, the cold coming in waves off the concrete floor, down from the conical, corrugated tin roof, through the cracked, thirty-year-old walls of knobby pine, which she's been insulating with fiberglass, on and off, section by section, since August, with Voort's help.

Camilla switches on half a dozen big electric space heaters, strategically scattered in the one big room. It'll take fifteen minutes before the place begins to warm a little.

The kayaks gleam, glossy fiberglass in colors of lime, charcoal, turquoise, coral, in their berths against the east wall. There are supply closets, sawhorses for working on kayaks, a corkboard with scraps of handwritten paper offering boats for sale, a sign-up sheet for the winter clean-up Hudson River project.

Voort's voice says, in her mind, concerned, lying, working on her, *Camilla, if someone was on your fire escape, you have to find out who it is.*

Leave me alone.

But it doesn't work. He doesn't leave her alone. He's not getting out of her head. She can't stand it. She sees herself and Voort, in her mind, sliding a two-person Mad River kayak from its berth last summer, carrying it to the ladder out back, lowering it and climbing down to the small floating dock and then paddling, together, into the swifter, more dangerous current beyond the pier, into the deep-dredged channels where the cruise ships and garbage barges and tugs pass, on their way to or from Rotterdam, Wilmington, Antigua, Caracas.

In the supply closet she turns on another radiant space heater, and quickly strips off her wet clothing: raincoat, shoes, stockings. She puts on spare soft longjohns she stores here, of waffled lemon-colored cotton, then thick ski socks, paint-stained overalls, and a big Irish fisherman's sweater hopelessly stained with paint chips. On top of that she dons a spare parka and a pull-on hat of lime-green wool.

She fights off a vision of Voort and her, in this closet. She's wrapped her legs round Voort's hips. It's a fall night, warm, and no one else is around. He's slamming her into the coats hanging against the wall.

She takes a hammer and a roll of fiberglass sheeting into the main room. She'll work her problems out herself. She drags a stepladder to the west wall, where the insulating work is half finished, where sections of pink sheeting, covered by plastic, alternate with bare spots where wind hisses through slits in the weathered gray planks.

Camilla climbs to the top of the swaying ladder.

I will not think of Voort.

She unrolls a section of fiberglass, covers it over with plastic sheeting and hammers, hard, nailing insulation along a gap between two-by-fours. She finishes the first strip, cutting off an incoming stream of cold air.

See? A person can have an effect on things.

Except she doesn't stop hammering. The hammer keeps hitting the nail, then misses, rips the plastic sheeting, and the fiberglass tilts through the gash.

Fiberglass drops, a pink mass, onto the floor.

Camilla is crying.

I never cry. I will stop right now.

Voort. I never want to see you. I hate you. If you try to talk to me again, I'll kill you, bastard.

She climbs from the ladder, makes her way to the phone,

an old rotary dial model, caked with white blobs of dried paint. The hum of the dial moving beneath her finger is the sound of childhood.

'Hello? Dr Bainbridge? I'm embarrassed to be calling but . . . yes, it is an emergency, I guess. If you have time, if you don't mind, do you think it might be possible to see me, today, even right now?'

Bainbridge is in his brownstone office, thirty minutes before Camilla calls. He's upstairs, at his desk, by his computer. He doesn't remember how he got here from Central Park last night. He remembers Arthur killing the nurse, the body in the snow, the blood, the talk with Tillman, but after that, he can't remember anything. He doesn't recall changing into the clothes he's wearing, doesn't even remember going to sleep last night.

His headache is monumental.

Bainbridge glances at the mirror on the far wall, beside his bookshelf, his articles on love and rejection, on hate and broken hearts.

Dr Bainbridge gasps. He sees two people there.

One is himself, portly looking in old straight-leg, worn corduroys and a Canadian Air Force sweater. The other is a tall man, a man made of wood, a marionette, actually, of the Protector. It is a large version of the puppet that Dr Bainbridge's father used to play with, at the foot of the boy's bed, at bedtime, years ago; the marionette he would hold up while he said, *I will protect you.*

Now, in the mirror, Bainbridge sees the marionette holding both hands high, like a football player who's just scored a touchdown. The man does a jig, triumphant.

Bainbridge claps his hands, and the headache is gone abruptly. Bainbridge laughs with delight.

The marionette in the mirror wears a cape, and has a black mask like Batman. He says, in the father's old voice, 'I am the Protector! No one will hurt you when I am near! I have super powers!'

Bainbridge feels safe.

'If anyone even tries to hurt you,' the Wooden Man says, 'I will hit them on the head! I will punch them in the face! I will use my muscles and they will leave you alone!'

In the mirror, Bainbridge jumps up and down, happy. The Protector towers over him, benevolently, his wooden features exaggerated, mouth wide and hinged, eyes painted black, lashes an inch long. The elbows and knees squeak when the Stick Man moves, with powerful jerks of his wooden muscles.

'But now,' the Protector says, more seriously, sitting beside Bainbridge, on the edge of the desk, 'it is time for us to move away from here, to leave and go somewhere else again.'

'I don't want to. I'm in love,' Bainbridge says.

The Protector says, as if Bainbridge has not spoken, 'While you were asleep I took care of arrangements, like I always do. You'll have a new name, won't that be fun? It's Otis.'

'Otis?'

'You will have your very own gas station, in a little town called Lee, Massachusetts. You'll work on cars. You'll have a beautiful house. You'll go skiing and sledding in the winter. Don't worry about anything. You'll pack a suitcase. We'll walk out of this house. The money has been transferred. It's in your new bank, in Lee, in your new name, Otis. We'll go to the Port Authority bus station right now. We'll have dinner at a Howard Johnson's, you love that, on the road.'

Bainbridge shakes his head. 'I can't leave Camilla.'

The big marionette sighs. He can be fearful to other people, but to Bainbridge he is warm and caring. He says, gently, like a parent, 'You don't really know her. You only see her in your office. You can't really love someone you don't know. You'll get over her. You've never spent any real time with her.'

But Bainbridge shakes his head. 'I know in here,' he says,

touching his sweater over his heart with his index finger. 'I can tell from the way she looks at me. I'm lonely. I don't mind admitting it. Those plans you have are nice, but they don't mean anything if I'm alone.'

'You're not alone.'

'You're talking about you, but it's not the same.'

The Protector looks sad. 'Look, you have to get out of here. You've made mistakes. The police are looking for you, and there are clues. They will find you if you don't leave. I can protect you if we go *right now*.'

'They're not looking for me. They're looking for Tillman.'

'Oh God. Listen to me. You phoned them, and told them about Harris. If they find Harris, they'll get you.'

Bainbridge stubbornly crosses his arms.

The Wooden Man walks to the mirror. 'You never like this part, every time it comes up,' the man says. 'I don't mean to hurt you, but there are things I'm going to have to tell you. You never like hearing them. I always have to put you to sleep afterward, and years go by before I have to spell them out again.'

'I don't remember "things." '

The Wooden Man turns back, faces Bainbridge. 'Ian, when you became a psychologist, when you went to school and learned about people's minds, how they work, you started fighting me. I was always a friend to you, and I loved you, but you started resisting me. I control you. You don't control me.'

'What are you talking about, control?'

'I never should have let you become a psychologist. We had a system that worked, and you tried to change it. You tried to take over. It was unconscious. But in here,' the Protector says, tapping his wooden head, '*you knew* something wasn't right inside you. You didn't want me making our decisions anymore, after you fell in love. Is that fair? After all I've done for you, to try to make me go away?'

Bainbridge says, 'I don't know what you're talking about.' But he is starting to look frightened.

'I'm only saying this because if I don't hurt you a little now, you won't leave, won't save yourself,' the marionette says. 'I care for you, son, it's my job to help you, your parents never did. You were becoming more aware of the truth, who you are, what you've done. The headaches. You wouldn't let yourself remember, but you were trying. You brought those men back as "patients." Harris. Arthur. Eric. You had them meet each other. You encouraged them to get angry. Maybe you would have been able to integrate them, control them in the end. But why should I let you do that? Why should I show myself at your silly club, occupy that empty chair, let you see me when *you* want, let us all come together inside you so I lose control?'

'This is a riot. You're saying I'm some split personality? *I'm a psychologist!*'

'You want it in your own technical language? You're a dissociative personality. You fall asleep, go into a fugue state, when you have a trauma, and the trauma always happens when you fall in love and the woman doesn't reciprocate. You take on another identity. I come out and fix everything. You wake and remember nothing. It's been going on since you were a kid. You've studied cases like this. Look at you!'

'It's not true!'

'Then try to remember your mother. Remember her coming up the stairs to your room at night?'

Bainbridge's headache starts. 'Stop!'

'The door opening? How old are you? Five? She's sitting on the . . .'

His head is killing him. *'Stop it!'*

'. . . bed.'

'Stopstopstopstop!'

'See? You're not prepared to be on your own. And you don't have to. You don't need anyone else but me. Those women were never loyal to you like I am. They don't love you unconditionally, the way I do. I am the whisper in your head, in Harris's head, in Arthur's. It was me all along, pushing you, not Harris. He only does what I tell him. He's easier to get to do things because he's so angry to start with. I had to be extreme with you to get you to give up that club, to take me back, to leave Camilla, to leave New York.'

The puppet gets up and paces, stiffly, agitated.

'I had to remove any threats to me, and the threat is always a woman.'

Bainbridge is shaking.

In a small, frightened voice, almost the voice of a child, he says, 'You're telling me there's no club?'

'Finally. You see it.'

'You're saying I manufactured those men. That those men *never existed*?'

'Son, my boy, my friend, my ward, you know what split personalities are. You have the tools to understand it. Those "people" have been inside you, different sides of you, since you were a boy.'

'My head!'

The Puppet Man drives at him, drives the points home. 'The Banker, angry, wanting to hit back. The Mechanic, confused, a child. The Agent, brusk, insecure, a teenager. And me. The fourth one. The one who never shows up unless he's needed. The one who handles the transitions, protects each one from the other, controls who is in the light at that moment. But it got harder after you met Camilla. Love changed you. Once she's out of your life, we can go back to how things were before. You won't even remember this conversation.'

'No!'

'You won't remember moving to Massachusetts. It's beautiful, and the Banker will be gone, and—'

Bainbridge screams, 'You're saying *I killed those women!*'

The puppet puts a hand on Ian's shoulder. 'I warned you,

son. Every few years, when it's time to move on, we have these difficult conversations. You get in trouble. We come up with a new way of living. You feel better. It lasted nine years this time. I even thought I wasn't going to have to move you around anymore. But, Ian, do you know how hard it was for me to come this time? Camilla is really quite irritating, and face it, you have no chance of her ever liking you as a man, not a paid doctor. No woman will ever love you, because you are a dirty boy. A filthy boy—'

Bainbridge jerks to his feet, knocking the chair sideways. He's pressing his hands to his ears. His skull seems to be blowing apart. The spikes of pain shoot down his spine. He screams, 'It's not true!'

The marionette says, softly, '*You* are the Mechanic and the Literary Agent and the Doctor.'

'I'll find them!'

Bainbridge flees from his office, into the room where the Literary Agent should be asleep. No one is there. He runs into the bedrooms, calling, 'Harris! Eric!'

No one answers.

'Where are you hiding?' Bainbridge screeches.

'They were never here.'

'If they weren't, you aren't either!'

The puppet considers it. 'Actually, you have a point.'

In the mirror, Bainbridge turns, fat and old-looking in his worn clothes, crashing down the stairs, fighting off the strands of exposed wire that seem to reach for him, entangle him. He is almost at the front door, but suddenly the Puppet Man is blocking the door, wooden hands outstretched, as if to catch him.

'My poor friend.'

Bainbridge backs away, avoiding the fingers, turns and heads along the dark hallway and through the kitchen toward the double-locked, barred door in the back of the house. He's got the key in his hands.

Somehow, the Protector has managed to get around him, and blocks the door.

'Tillman and Arthur and Eric are gone. And soon you will be too. Let me help you, Otis. It'll just be me, Otis. And everything will be safe again, Otis.'

'*I won't go to sleep!*'

The doorbell rings.

Softly, the Puppet Man says, 'It's the police, son. Make your choice. You'll be too nervous to handle them. Give me back control.'

Bainbridge is squatting on the floor, in a corner, with his hands over his ears, the same way he used to back into a corner when Daddy and Mommy were fighting, when Mommy came upstairs, when Mommy told him: You are bad, you are filthy, women will hate you, the police will arrest you.

The Puppet Man leans over, cradles the weeping Psychologist in his arms. 'Ah, my poor hurt boy. My poor little man. All you have to do is relax.'

But Bainbridge says, 'What's the point of going anywhere without her!'

The bell rings again.

The Puppet Man blows out air, looks down the long hallway toward the front door. 'Haven't you figured it out yet? If you go to her, I'll hurt her. It's the only way to help you. You won't be strong enough to stop me.'

'You were never my friend.'

'Pshaw! You're just angry now. Besides, you'll be arrested if anything happens, not me. I'll go back inside. You'll take the pain.'

'I'm stronger than you,' Bainbridge says. 'And I'd never let you hurt her.'

The puppet smiles. 'Then there's no harm letting me take over now, is there?'

Bainbridge looks at the door again, terrified, and his eyes

glaze over, and a calm comes over him. He shudders, straightens. He holds himself with confidence, which makes him look, even in the old clothes, more dignified, less flabby.

The house is a mess.

The doctor runs his hands through his hair, walks to the front door.

When he opens it, two men are standing in the driving snow.

'Dr Bainbridge?'

'Yes?' the doctor says, in a friendly, curious tone.

'I'm Detective Voort. This is Detective Connor. We'd like to talk to you about a phone call someone made to the police a couple of days ago.'

Inside the house, a phone starts ringing.

Bainbridge says, 'You mean about Harris Tillman. Yes, I made that call.'

SEVENTEEN

'It's true. Harris Tillman used to be my patient,' Dr Bainbridge tells Voort and Mickie, in his consultation room. Voort occupies the fold-back 'stressless chair,' where Camilla probably lies during sessions, telling secrets, babbling about sex with Voort, their fights, her dancer lover. Mickie's pulled the wooden Windsor chair out from behind the doctor's desk and sits, arms over the back.

'*Used* to be your patient?'

'More tea?' Bainbridge asks with a maddeningly gentle nod toward the china pot of steaming herbal chamomile he has brought from the kitchen.

Mickie says, 'Do you have Tillman's address?'

'Only now do I understand why he never gave it to me.' Bainbridge shrugs. 'He paid cash. He was troubled. It's my duty, as a psychologist, to help people who are troubled, so I let the address ride.

'I'm afraid he's gone,' he says, and slurps tea from his I LOVE DOCTORS cup. 'He phoned me after I called you. I think he sensed what I'd done. I'm not,' he says sheepishly, 'good at hiding things.'

'When was this?'

'Right after. Two days ago. He said he was through here.'

235

Mickie shakes his head, meaning, I can't believe our luck. Voort's chair is slightly broken, so that anyone sitting on it has to recline, or keep from putting pressure on the back. He sits straight up. He's got to keep Camilla out of this. He has to ignore the rampant curiosity coursing through him. He's desperate to know what goes on in this room when she is here, spilling her guts to this hippie clone, with his frizzy hair, thick lenses that make his watery brown eyes bigger, patched Canadian Air Force sweater, looking like some city intellectual run off to pick peaches in Oregon. Bainbridge wears big furry felt sippers. His harmless, donnish air makes him seem older, seem like a man who has traded his masculinity for an air of sexless, almost matronly caring. There is also something vaguely familiar to Voort about him.

'If he's no longer a patient, you can show us his files.'

Bainbridge gives a small laugh, like a chess player admiring the clever yet ultimately non-threatening move of an opponent. 'It's not that simple.'

'Why?'

'You know. Doctor-patient privilege.'

Mickie spreads his hands. 'It's not exactly academic. He's murdered three people. How about some preventive medicine privilege? Want to bet, we don't catch him, he does it again?'

This bothers Bainbridge, he admits. The magnified eyes blink, slowly, look pained. 'Give me an hour, to consider. It's just that Tillman could call and want to come back. He's still a patient, in a way. Once a patient, always a patient, and once you have his records, I can't take them back.'

Voort studies him. Bainbridge does not really seem to appreciate the reality of the threat here, even though he tried to call the police. Voort has seen this attitude before. Bainbridge has trouble fully conceiving that someone he knows, actually speaks with, is capable of committing murder. Voort has often thought that the greatest ally of evil is an average person's inability to accept its existence.

But then Voort thinks there's also something more here, some mix of elements that doesn't fit. Is there something off about the doctor? Or is it just that Camilla's presence here throws off his usual instincts?

Bainbridge rises as the phone rings. 'Patient, probably. I'll get it in the other room,' he says, automatically guarding the caller's privacy.

He moves quickly for a sloppy-looking man, and makes sure to tightly slide the double door closed behind him when he leaves.

'Something's hinky,' Voort tells Mickey. 'You believe that shit about the address?'

'Who knows? He talks but doesn't say anything. You think he's protecting the guy? And those jerky movements. You think he has MS?'

'Doctors always think they know better than you,' Voort says, except he realizes he's referring to whatever shrink bullshit Bainbridge probably tells Camilla. Did Bainbridge advise her to leave him? he wonders.

Not to mention, the second Camilla learns he was here, the Chief of Detectives will get a call from NBC about the hang-up phone calls, the glove on her fire escape, the trip he took to the car service.

Camilla tells Voort, in his head: 'It'll be the end of your two-hundred-year family history as cops.'

The doctor will return any minute. Voort says, 'Quick. The desk.'

They move fast, a team, opening drawers, trying to mute the sound of squeaking wood. 'Gum. Just packs of Juicy Fruit,' Mickie says, looking in the top drawer.

In a side drawer, Voort finds a pile of glossy magazines. *New Psychologist*. And Bainbridge's name on the top one, as a contributing writer inside, beside a picture of a couch, and the issue's main headline, 'Sitting or Reclining? How to Get More Out from Your Patients in Less Time.'

'Listen to this,' he says, finding the article. ' "Love and Violence. Tracking Affection as It Turns to Hate." '

Voort reads out loud. ' "A patient, whom we will call A, works in finance, and has a history of rejection from women—" '

'Tillman!' Mickie says.

Voort keeps reading, ' "The patient experiences violent impulses. He can't stop thinking about it. Eventually, the pressure builds, and the patient finds himself dreaming of inflicting pain on a woman who hurt him . . . .'

'Jesus H. Christ.'

In the kitchen, Bainbridge leans into the phone, muting his voice, listening for a scraping sound the consultation room door would make if the detectives tried to follow him in here, if they tried to eavesdrop.

'Camilla.' His voice is gentle, but inside, the sound of her voice has thrown him off. 'Calm down.'

But it's impossible. She's raging, her lovely voice sending barbs of love into him even when she is in distress. She needs him, she says. She says Voort watched her from her fire escape last night. Voort followed her to a restaurant. Voort bullied her car service into telling him that a driver drops her at Bainbridge's every week.

'I need to have this conversation in person,' Camilla says. 'I'm sorry. Are you busy? I'll pay extra.'

Bainbridge lets the silence grow, and with it, her urgency. He's just about to tell her no, I can't see you, when he hears himself blurt, 'Of course.'

Goddamnit, Ian!

The Protector is furious over this resistance.

'Doctor? Are you there?'

She loves me, Bainbridge tells the Protector, in his head. *I wouldn't feel like this if there were no connection.*

'Doctor Bainbridge? Hello?'

There's no time to fight about it. The detectives could come in here any minute.

'Uh, sure I'll see you, Camilla. I was checking my calendar. But not here. It's funny, what you said about your car service. I hate to tell you, but Voort is in the house right now.'

'He's *there*?'

'He's a little scary. Voort's asking questions about you.'

Camilla whispers, 'I'll kill him!'

The doctor chuckles with seeming professional amusement. 'Well, not before we talk. I want to make sure you understand the consequences before you take on a New York City cop.'

'To hell with the consequences. *I can't believe him*! Put him on! What is he asking?'

'Oh, about what you say to me. What I advise. I'd never tell him,' he says, fighting off a surge of rage, happy to be driving *her* crazy for a change. 'Little things.'

'I'm calling the police. Now!'

He soothes her. 'I know how you feel, but if you don't mind your doctor – your friend, if I can call myself that, a little two cents from someone who cares – I'd advise you not to do anything until we talk. Tonight is fine, but the problem is, I don't think you should come here, with him around.'

'You think I'm going to stay away because of *him*?'

'Camilla, I have to confess, he makes me nervous, the way he was outside, watching the house.' He hears her sharp intake of breath. He tells himself, as he makes the story up, that whatever lies he tells only have to hold up for an hour. Until he gets out of here.

'He's a bit . . . excited,' he says, letting the worst connotations of the word sink in. 'I admit I'm not used to having people here who carry a . . . well, I know he'd never *use* it, but he keeps touching his, er . . .'

'His gun?'

'He keeps brushing it, unconsciously, I'm sure, with the

back of his hand. I'm sure it's nothing. They train police to control their emotions, don't they? But he's agitated. I'll tell you what. Let's meet somewhere else. I know it's unorthodox, not to come to the office. And I'm sorry about that, but—'

'No! Don't be sorry! Whatever you say!' She seems grateful for Bainbridge's time. 'I'm embarrassed he's subjecting you to this.'

He chuckles again, but makes it nervous, the sound of a man trying to convince someone else, unsuccessfully, he is unafraid. 'On this job, I see odder things than an old boyfriend. It's not the first time I've had to calm down an ex-lover.'

He sighs. 'But where do we meet? A restaurant is too public, and you need to rant a bit, it seems.'

'There's my apartment,' she offers.

'That's an idea.'

'No! He was there last night, on the fire escape. Can you believe it? The *fire escape*!'

'I don't think he'd do that two days in a row.'

'I didn't think he'd go to *you* either. I know! The boat-house!' she says. 'I'll pay double for this session. I'm humiliated that he's putting you through this.'

'He's the one who's acting up, not you.'

'Yeah, well, I chose him. You deserve double your fee.'

You see, Ian? She treats you like a servant. She doesn't love you.

Camilla gives him directions to the boathouse, by cab, by subway, or, if the road is closed, by foot. She says she'll be working there, alone. It's warm, she says, from space heaters, and as private as you can find in New York. She laughs. A terrorist could blow up a bomb in the boathouse on a night like this, and nobody would hear.

'I'll wait. I have plenty of work here,' she says. 'Are you sure you don't want me to call the police, to call him off?'

'I'm fine.'

'I can't believe Voort's doing this.'

He soothes her. The gun he bought is upstairs, with the new license, credit cards, bank book, bus ticket.

'Camilla, anyone can become very dangerous, given the right provocation.'

'What would I do without you?' Camilla says.

'Let's start over again,' Voort says when Bainbridge returns to the consultation room. 'There are a couple of things Detective Connor and I aren't clear about.'

Bainbridge, nodding, notices the blotter on the desk has been shifted a little. He'd hoped the detectives would move things around in his absence. It will make what he has to do now easier. Also, there are no records in this part of the house.

Voort says, softly, though a hard edge is apparent beneath, 'Why did you call the police in the first place?'

'I told you. Harris talked to me about Niana, and after she died, he didn't actually admit killing her, but he was so agitated I feared he might have.'

'So you called out of a . . . eh, vague suspicion?'

'More than vague. He nursed quite a hatred for her.'

'Then why did you hang up?'

The doctor looks uncomfortable. 'I thought maybe I could help him, get him to admit it, if he did it, I mean, and then I would go with him to the police.' Bainbridge shakes his head, as if sorry for the man. 'He's been betrayed by so many people in his life.'

'So he never admitted doing it.'

'If he had, believe me, I would have followed through.'

'Do you know what BHC means?' Mickie asks. 'Those initials, in relation to Tillman?'

'BHD?'

'Not D,' Mickie says, 'C.'

Bainbridge considers. 'I can't think of what that could mean,' he says. 'Hmmmm. No.'

Voort now reaches behind him, on the folding chair, and holds up the magazine. 'Your article,' he says. 'About a banker and a poet. It's Tillman you're writing about, right?'

Reluctantly, 'Ye-es.'

Mickie says, harshly, 'You know what happens to someone who shields a murderer? You know what aiding and abetting means?'

But Bainbridge just smiles gently. 'Is this where one of you acts friendly, and the other one acts angry? I've read about how you do this. Believe me, I haven't knowingly shielded anyone. I suspected. I didn't *know*. We *still* don't know, do we? He's just a suspect.'

'Doctor, stop playing around,' Voort says. 'The point is, if he's still your patient, if you have some idea of helping him, and telling us later, forget it. The law's clear on this. *It's not your option*. We've talked to you. You know the consequences. You're on tape. Now tell me, yes or no, are you *still seeing Tillman*?'

Bainbridge lowers his face, so the detectives cannot see his expression. His shoulders straighten. He breathes deeply. When he looks up, there is a slight shininess, a more direct intelligence in his face that was not there before. Almost a challenge.

'Maybe you're right, and this is over my head. You're very smart. Actually, he's due for a session, right in this room,' Bainbridge says, checking his watch, 'in two hours. He phoned to confirm the appointment, even in bad weather. I was going to ask him about the girl. The one in the park. I really was. I just can't believe he really did it. I just wanted, before I turned him in, to make sure.'

'That's better,' Mickie says.

'We'll wait in the house,' Voort says grimly, still feeling something wrong. 'With you.'

'No. Outside,' Bainbridge says. 'It would be better if I talked to him alone.'

'You'll be alone,' Mickie soothes. 'We'll be in the next room.'

Bainbridge shakes his head and rises, as if dismissing them, as if with his admission he has regained power in this room.

Is this what Camilla does here? Admit things?

'I'm sorry but I'd prefer you outside,' Bainbridge says, much more strongly. 'There are only two entrances to the house. Once Harris is in, he can't get out. You can watch the front from your car. Or wait in back or put a patrolman there if you'd like. But outside.'

'Any particular reason why you don't want us here?'

'Yes,' Bainbridge says, glancing at the magazine in Voort's hand. 'I don't want you going through my records upstairs when I can't watch you. It's clear, while I was on the phone, that you rifled my desk and took that magazine. Which, by the way, I don't believe you are legally permitted to do. I don't want to fight with you. I just want one more chance with my patient.'

Bainbridge softens his voice, sounds more reasonable, less combative. 'Detectives, do you want me on your side, if you have to arrest him, or do you want me making problems for you? You know, if there's a trial, I'll testify at some point. I like him. And no one has proven he's guilty yet. He's my patient. Can you understand that? Something about the benefit of doubt, you know?'

Voort can do nothing about it. He doesn't like it, but he's stuck. He decides to lie, knowing that the act he is about to threaten is illegal without a court order, but that the words themselves – the trick – is allowed under the law: 'Fine. But before we go, we're calling in, putting a monitor on your phone, in case you call him and ask him to stay away. Doctor, I don't trust you either. Right now, all I have is doubt.'

The snow is harder, thicker, piled seven or eight inches deep in places. Side streets are becoming impassable. Avenues are plowed, but only in the middle lanes, so the right and left ones are blocked.

It's thirty minutes later and the detectives sit in the Chevy, engine on, heat fitful, wipers going, lights off, as they watch Bainbridge's stoop.

Mickie's got the manila folder on the front seat between them, closed, the one Detective Quinlan gave them at One Police Plaza, the one with a rundown of all the tips Quinlan took today, relating to the Tillman case.

'You think Camilla tells that guy about your sex life?' Mickie says.

'No, I think she goes in, sits in that seat, pays him two hundred bucks an hour, and never opens her mouth.'

'Forget I said it.'

'Why is there something familiar about him?' Voort says. 'Like I talked to him another time?'

They straighten as Bainbridge's front door opens. A man's form fills the dark rectangle and the doctor emerges, in a sheepskin coat. He looks both ways, spots the police car.

He half sways, half limps down the stoop, as if hurt, toward the car.

He reaches Voort's side as Voort rolls down the window.

'If he says Tillman canceled, we're bringing him in,' Voort says out of the side of his mouth.

The doctor, leaning into the window, has regained his peaceful, Moonie appearance.

'I'm sorry about before. Please understand. I care for Harris. I'll cooperate with you if it turns out to be him. I promise.'

'Thanks,' Mickie says.

'I'm going to the Korean grocery for tissues. I'm out of tissues. I always keep tissues in the consultation room for, you know, if people start to cry.'

'I'll go with you,' Voort says.

The radio crackles to life. 'Car Eleven, it's Hazel. I got your information on Arthur Davis.'

Mickie reaches for the radio as Voort leaves the car. The cold is brutal. The snow stings, slapping him. He and Bainbridge lean into the wind, walking, cover their mouths against the wind with their hands. The sidewalk is shoveled in front of some brownstones, covered over in front of others. Nobody else is out on this block.

'Voort, you said your name was,' Bainbridge says as they walk.

'Yes.'

'She's a nice person. I hope things work out for you two,' Bainbridge says. 'I know you know about me.'

Surprised, Voort says, 'Thank you.' He feels wetness in the corner of one eye. It's the snow, he tells himself.

On the corner, the Korean grocery is open; it's always open. If a nuclear bomb went off, the Korean grocery on the corner would stay open. Bainbridge, humming, gathers items in the narrow, lone aisle; a tissue box, some triple expensive papayas, apples, bottles of seltzer. Toilet paper.

'The radio said stock up. Want anything?'

'No thanks.'

Bainbridge fills his arms with bulky paper towels, and adds two cans of Heinz baked beans.

One can falls and rolls in the aisle.

'I'll get a basket,' Voort says.

He walks down the aisle to the cash register, where the blue plastic shopping baskets are piled. As he leans to pick one up, he sees, in the circular mirror on the ceiling, that Bainbridge, in back, is running out the exit door by the ice cream freezers. He's not limping anymore.

'Shit!'

Voort collides with the owner, running toward the back, sending the angry woman into the salad bar that takes up most of the aisle. The floor is littered with the items Bainbridge had gathered, rolling, blocking Voort, who leaps over them or kicks them aside.

He races out the back door, into an empty alley.

He follows Bainbridge's footsteps in the snow, out the alley, to the curb, except there are a million footsteps on Lexington Avenue. And no Bainbridge. There's a single plowed lane in the middle of the street.

Voort looks around wildly. He sees a subway entrance to the right, fifteen feet away. And four or five cabs, down the block, lined, idle at a red light. Any one of them could have picked up Bainbridge.

Voort squints in all directions, but sees no one in a sheepskin coat.

He guesses, *the taxi*. He starts running, slipping, but the light turns green. Snow obscures the license plate of the last cab in the bunch, the only one he might have seen anyway. All five taxis outdistance Voort, disappearing into the wall of flakes, going, going gone.

He's phoning Harris!

By the time Voort gets back to the Chevy, Mickie is still on the radio, looking funny, looking upset even though he does not know what happened yet. The manila folder containing Quinlan's daily tips is open, and typed sheets are scattered all over the front seat.

'He ran off,' Voorts says. 'I went to get a basket and he ran out back. He's going to call Tillman and warn him.'

Mickie seems dazed. 'I don't think so.'

'You have a better idea?'

Mickie says, 'Davis's Social Security number turned out like Tillman's and Porter's. The last time he used it with ID was two days before Porter's went active.'

'So it's all the same guy. All three murders. Tillman.'

'Or whichever name he uses. But it's worse,' Mickie says, and laughs bitterly to himself, and shakes his head.

Mickie gathers up Detective Quinlan's tip sheets, which he'd been reading while Voort went to the store. He tells Voort about Mackie, the bar owner's story, about the man who rents Mackey's back room on Thursday, for a club. Who buys four dinners, but only one person shows up.

'Uh-oh.'

'Look at the sketch, Con Man.'

Voort glances at it and his heart sinks. He takes in the round, middle-aged face, the frizzy hair and thick-lensed glasses, the look of Moonie-like satisfaction on the charcoal sketch.

Mickey says the obvious. 'It's not his patient. It's *him*.'

'Then he's not coming back,' Voort says.

'We gotta get in that house. If he's not calling Tillman, *where's he going*?'

Voort grabs the cell phone.

They both know if they force their way in, without a warrant, any evidence they find will be discarded in court, thrown out. Voort needs a private line, not the police radio, for what he is about to do. There's no time to track down the Assistant D.A. in charge of this case.

'Directory assistance!'

He gets the number he needs, of a judge who, at this hour, will be home, hopefully, in Bayside, in Queens. A stern law and order judge, Hamish Kelly is usually friendly to police. Kelly announced on TV last week that he will be seeking a congressional seat, on the Republican ticket, in the fall.

'Judge Kelly here!'

'Sir, it's Detective Conrad Voort. Sorry to bother you at home.'

'No bother for you!' booms the judge, more like a politician, who knows the names of big donors in the city, than an appointed court official who can technically order around police. 'We were sitting down to dinner. Roast beef. Peas. Oughta come over some time and eat with us,' says Kelly.

Every politician in the city knows the story of Voort's $200,000 contribution to the new mayor's campaign.

Voort explains it is an emergency. He has identified the murderer in the Niana Embero case and needs a warrant to get into his house, this second, before the man hurts anyone else.

'Come by and we'll take care of it.'

Voort says no, there's no time to come by. He must get into the house right now. He asks Kelly to date the warrant today and put a time on it making it active immediately.

'Are you sure you know what you're doing?' Kelly says.

'Yes, sir. I do.'

'Because we've been asked to be extra careful on warrants, after that business in Staten Island two weeks ago. You know. Wrong house. Wrong guy.'

Voort doesn't like the way this is going. And he never likes to use the advantage his wealth gives him over municipal employees. But he says: 'Sir, I want to congratulate you on your announcement, about running for office.'

The offer and threat hang there. The judge says, 'What did you say, Conrad? I'm getting static on the line.'

Voort ignores the snow melting on his neck. He knows damn well there's no static, but he plays along, raises his voice. 'I heard you need to raise quite a war chest, against Gorman.'

'Damnit, this phone,' the judge says, clear as a bribe.

Silence. For a moment Voort thinks he overdid it.

Then the judge says, 'If you can hear me, if you think it's important to get into a house now, protect another victim, who am I to stop you? I'll call in the warrant.'

Voort, hanging up, hears Kelly's voice, tinny, disembodied, phony-friendly, six inches off. 'Come on by for dinner sometime! Mary makes a meat loaf you won't believe!'

Then Voort's running for Bainbridge's door.

EIGHTEEN

Mohammed Abdul Mohammed, legal refugee from Somalia, husband, father, cab driver for eight months, and thirty-two-year-old resident of Brooklyn Heights, steers his yellow Chevy Caprice cab through the Central Park Eighty-fifth Street crossover, relishing the challenge of driving in snow, and eyeing the crazy passenger in his backseat with amazement.

He is having the best night of his professional cab driver life, and the scene in the rearview mirror beats even the best movies.

First, there was the storm, which scared off other drivers, making New Yorkers desperate for rides, and no way would Mohammed pass up the opportunity to make real money, with his son's sixth birthday coming up. For the last three hours he's been cruising with his Off Duty sign on, stopping for people, telling them he's on his way home and allowing them to 'persuade' him to let them pay triple, even quadruple, the normal fare for rides.

Then there's the snow, a wonderful challenge. Mohammed, a superb driver and ex-militia fighter in Mogadishu, for the Aidid clan, loves the ice, the way the heavy car fishtails around corners, the narrow misses with buses. It gives excitement to an otherwise boring job.

And finally there's the passenger, who'd run up to his cab on Lexington and Ninety-third, jumped in and yelled, 'The Port Authority.'

Mohammed watches the man in the rearview mirror every chance he gets. He's never seen anything like the regular transformations taking place back there, never witnessed the kind of massive internal struggle that seems to be wrenching apart the white man on the backseat.

One minute he's lying down, moaning, holding his head, sick as an aneurysm victim being rushed to the hospital. Next minute his face is shiny with triumph. He's laughing, leaning forward against the plastic bulletproof barrier, as if urging the cab to go faster, to push through the heavy snow.

Mohammed risks another glance at a light, and the man is crying! Just sitting there, bawling, with tears rolling down his face.

The passenger says, talking to himself, 'I won't go unless I see her one last time!'

Women, Mohammed thinks. I should have known women were involved. Back in Mogadishu, where a man could have as many wives as he wants, Mohammed's uncle Hussein had married three. Hussein was a fearsome fighter who'd killed many enemies. But when it came to wives, Hussein had to buy them all houses. He had to sleep with them in a strict rotation, or they'd get mad. Hussein couldn't even take vacations because the wives would fight and make his life miserable over which one could go.

'Can't you drive any faster?' the passenger snaps.

Another rich upper East Sider who can't stand to be delayed.

'Sure, if you want to have an accident,' Mohammed says.

Nobody pushes Mohammed around.

The storm has turned the normally packed grid of Midtown into a maze. A stalled truck blocks Sixty-ninth, a big drift blocks Sixty-fourth. Mohammed gets stuck behind a plow, except the driver seems to be on a coffee break, or on strike, God forbid, although Mohammed has no complaints on the money end, since the passenger's already given him a hundred-dollar bill, the smallest denomination he had, for the ride.

Now he hears the passenger tell himself, in a different, deeper voice, 'And what will you tell her if you go to her? You just want to talk to her one last time? You're acting like a thirteen-year-old.'

A pause.

The passenger snorts. 'She doesn't love you, Ian. You'll throw away everything for a ten-minute conversation, and I won't let you! Go to sleep!'

Finally they reach Port Authority, the huge building running two blocks long, on Eighth Avenue. Buses leave from here to cross the whole United States. Passengers don't have to give a name to get a ticket. You just hand over money and get your Greyhound stub.

Mohammed's passenger opens the door but doesn't get out. He sits, half in, half out, glassy-eyed, as this month's recorded New York City Taxi Commission departure message blares, maddeningly:'Hey, man! Remember to take any articles you left with you! Have a nice day!'

The passenger slumps, then straightens.

'I changed my mind,' he says, in a softer voice, except he seems to be expending lots of effort to get the words out. 'I want to go somewhere else. You know the boathouse on Pier... P-Pier... on Pier Twenty-six?'

Mohammed is delighted. The boathouse is on the way home. But he makes himself look sad.

Wait till I tell the guys at the garage about this.

He says, 'I know it, but I live the other way. I told you,' he adds, remembering the man's wad of cash, 'that I could only give you one ride. It's dangerous to drive in the city tonight!'

* * *

'I'm not breaking into this house till the supervisor gets here,' the Emergency Services squad crew chief tells Voort, 'warrant or no warrant. I'm retiring in two weeks, and I ain't gonna fuck it up 'cause of you.'

'I told you, there's no time! He's stuck in the goddamn storm, *so open the door*!'

They argue on Bainbridge's steps, in the snow. The three-man squad, in blue parkas, stand with sledgehammers, while their chief goes nose-to-nose with Voort.

The chief says, 'Especially after that mix-up in Staten Island last week. *That* chief got suspended!'

Only after the supervising sergeant arrives five minutes later does the crew chief say, 'Do it, boys. Who lives here anyway? Windows barred! Five bolt locks. It's harder to get in here than an old lady's apartment.'

Four minutes later they're inside, rushing past the chief, who calls after them, 'You're welcome, assholes!' Bainbridge had mentioned 'my records upstairs,' so the detectives take the hallway steps two at a time.

The banister is so shaky it seems like it might break off any moment.

Despite the urgency, they halt at the top of the stairs, stunned.

'Holy shit,' Mickie says.

They're thinking the same thing. They have, over the years, rushed into transient hotels, crack houses, abandoned apartments with squatters living in them, and those places feel like this. The way they reek of ruin. The way they reflect not the lives of people who live in them, but the accumulated weight of the people who were there before. The way history seems more powerful than the present. The way the stains and watermarks and exposed wiring reveal the lack of any kind of interior life, any self-love, in the people inhabiting the space.

They separate. Voort takes the office, the only room that seems to have been worked on; Mickie takes the bedrooms. They are not looking for evidence now as much as clues to where Bainbridge went. Voort curses the way the man got away. He hates that they were in a room with him, a few feet away from him, and they let him just leave.

He hears Bainbridge's gentle, androgynous voice saying, all part of an act, a trick, 'Would you detectives like tea?'

In the office he rifles shelves, correspondence trays, the blotter, hoping to find a note, address, phone number, anything.

In the top right desk drawer he sees, heart sinking, an array of ID cards. Bainbridge's New York driver's license lies there, his Social Security card, charge cards, library card, membership card in the American Psychologists Association.

'He's changed again,' Voort says out loud. 'He's someone new now.'

He opens the next drawer and his heartbreat moves up, into his throat. He is looking, on top of a pile of manila folders, at two cardborard boxes of ammunition, .38 caliber bullets.

One of the boxes is half empty, and Voort does not find the gun.

'He took it. Shit.'

Mickie appears in the doorway, looking shaken, holding out something small and black in his hand. A tape recorder.

'I called Quinlan to get out an All Points on the sketch. But Conrad, you better hear this. It was in the bedroom. There are come stains all over the sheets. I think Bainbridge listens to this while he . . . uh, jerks off.'

From downstairs they hear the voices of other detectives arriving, spreading out, taking fingerprints, looking for evidence.

'I'll take care of them,' Mickie says. 'Give you a minute to yourself, with the tape.'

Voort switches it on when Mickie leaves, but even before he hears the voice on it, he has a premonition, from Mickie's expression, of whose voice will be there.

Sure enough, it's Camilla. 'His body is big, and hard . . .'

Voort pushes fast forward. '. . . One time, in a Jacuzzi in Montreal, when we were on vacation, Voort got ice in a bucket and . . .'

Voort groans.

He fast forwards again.

'. . . Trust Voort? What do you mean, do I trust him?'

Voort sags on the doctor's seat.

From downstairs he can hear Mickie's voice, low, and from the force of it, he knows that Mickie is filling in the other detectives.

Of all the damn doctors in the city, you had to choose this one.

He is filled with terror for Camilla.

He tells himself, *Bainbridge doesn't have time to hurt her. He's on the run.*

But it's no use. All Voort can think is: He killed three women. I have to know she's all right. I can't do anything else, work on this, look for him, until I warn her.

Voort makes it to the phone, punches in her extension at NBC. He has not called it for almost a month, and the simple act of doing so accentuates the gulf between them, which is still widening, in such a small amount of time.

At least a human voice answers.

'Camilla Ryan's line!'

He recognizes the voice. It belongs to another producer, a woman named Dorothea, one of Camilla's nosy and happily married friends.

'It's Conrad Voort. I have to speak to Camilla. It's important.'

Silence.

'Asshole. She told me what you did,' Dorothea says.

'Listen to me. I don't have time to explain things to you—'

'You were on her *fire escape*? What a pervert.'

Voort says, 'Put her on the phone.'

Silence.

'Dorothea, you may not believe this, but I was not on her fire escape, and the guy who *was* is looking for her. *Put her on the line.*'

'Don't talk to me in that tone,' says Dorothea.

'Look, just tell me if she's there.'

A snicker. 'Why, so you can stake out the lobby?'

'It's police business.'

'Oh, police business. Is that what it is?'

Voort fights off the urge to scream. She's on the verge of hanging up on him.

'Dorothea, if she's there, really there, take a message for her, and I'll hang up. Okay? If she's not there, she's in danger, do you hear? I'm serious. If she doesn't get this message, she could be hurt.'

'You're trying to scare me.'

'You're damn right about that.'

'I want you to know I am recording everything you say,' Dorothea says triumphantly. 'Your threat is on tape now.'

'Good.' Voort sighs. 'Then she's protected if I'm lying to you.' He puts his love, his fear for Camilla, into his voice. He realizes logic will never convince Dorothea. Maybe concern will.

'Please tell me if she's there.'

Silence.

'Dorothea!'

She says, doubtfully, 'If you're lying—'

'Look, you recorded me. If I screw up, the Chief of Detectives hears the tape, right?'

Silence. Then, 'She's not here.'

'Where is she?'

'Voort, she told me you'd probably call. She said not to

talk to you. She said if you asked questions, under no circumstances answer you. She's going to kill me for saying this much.'

She hangs up.

Shit.

Voort tries Camilla's beeper, hears the beep, wants to leave a message, but what can he say that she will believe, even remotely?

'Camilla, it's me. Whatever you think I did, even if you don't talk to me, stay away from Bainbridge. He's the one who was on your fire escape. I think he's the one who made the calls. He's dangerous. We're looking for him. He's—'

Beeeeeeep.

He tries her at home, and gets her cheery answering machine. 'I'm not *here* so please leave your *message*!'

He leaves the same message.

His fear for her is turning to panic.

He hears the other cops moving around the house, mounting stairs, opening kitchen cabinets, and knows they are dusting for fingerprints, hoping to find victims' clothing, or wigs, or a knife, bat, a list of incriminating phone numbers. Anything they can use.

Mickie appears in the doorway.

'Hazel called. She ran Bainbridge's Social Security number. It went active right after Tillman's stopped being used.'

'I can't find Camilla, Mickie.'

'Look,' Mickie soothes, 'he knows we're after him. He's running. He doesn't have time for her.'

But Mickie does not seem convinced.

Voort cries out, 'Her car service!'

'Great. They'll love hearing from you.'

Voort calls the car service.

He tells the smooth-sounding male operator that it's police business. He says he needs to know if they've given Camilla a ride this afternoon.

'Voort, you said your name was?'

'It's official business,' Voort says, which is exactly the lie he used to get information last time.

The operator replies, 'We gave no ride to her.'

'You said that pretty fast,' Voort says. 'Did you check your ride list first?'

'I'm sorry. I'm not supposed to talk to you,' the man says, and hangs up.

Voort tells Mickie, 'Gimme the keys!' He grabs his coat and runs down the stairs, Mickie trailing after him. As lead detectives on this case, one of them must remain at the house, to supervise the search for evidence.

'Take someone with you.'

'No, I'll look for him with her. You need everyone else here.'

Outside, the snow is still falling hard, and Voort has to waste time wiping the windshield with the sleeve of his coat or he won't be able to drive. The Chevy starts right up, though. He has the presence of mind to accelerate slowly, giving the rear wheels time to catch, and he half rolls, half slides into clogged, honking traffic, crawls to Lexington Avenue and turns downtown.

Voort turns on the siren. He puts the roof light on. Against the power of the storm, and the impediments it has created, there's hardly any room for traffic to get out of his way.

At least he doesn't have to stop for red lights.

Voort steers the Chevy up on the sidewalk, by Fortieth and Lex, to get around an accident. He bulls his way south, using the siren, to Twenty-first, turns left, and pulls in front of a half-buried hydrant in front of the car service, by Third Avenue. When he runs inside, in no mood for argument, the man behind the glass booth is not the one he talked to the other night. Other drivers, waiting for rides, or off duty, lounge on a wooden bench in the small, overheated, unadorned room.

She's fine. I just need to confirm it before I can do anything else.

He shoves the badge against the glass, like he did the other night, cursing the mistake he made by coming here then.

'I need to know if one of your drivers dropped off a certain passenger this afternoon.'

The man looks up, a dark, balding face that had been gazing down at a late edition *Daily News* financial pages.

'You're Voort, aren't you? You called.'

'Did one of your drivers pick up Camilla Ryan this afternoon, on the NBC account?'

'No one did.' But the operator's right arm slides left, away from the newspaper, to cover a clipboard on the desk, by a seltzer bottle.

Voort and the operator look at the covered clipboard.

'Let me in there,' Voort says.

'I was given strict instructions that any policeman can see the book any time, if he shows a warrant. Do you have a warrant? If you have a warrant, I will happily unlock the door.'

'Yes,' Voort lies.

'Show it to me.'

'There isn't time.'

'There is for me,' the man says. 'The other operator got fired for talking to you.'

'Open the fucking door,' Voort says.

Instead, reaching for the phone, the operator says, 'I'm calling the police!'

Behind him, the other drivers in the room start drifting away, not wanting to get involved, not wanting to risk a run-in with the police. Suddenly they remember they are hungry, or thirsty, or they need to buy a paper, or phone their wives from another room, or go home in the big storm.

The operator is calling 911. It's unbelievable.

Voort pulls out his gun.

He's not pointing it, though, just holding it at his side, aimed at the floor. The operator has frozen, on the phone, staring at the gun. Voort doesn't know what to do.

He puts the gun back in the holster.

'Just tell me where you took her,' Voort pleads. 'I love her, goddamn it. She could get hurt.'

But the operator is explaining to the police who answered, at 911, that Voort is threatening him.

'The boathouse,' says a voice behind Voort.

Voort whirls. A slight man, an Indian or Pakistani, is standing there in an oversize green parka, skinny, looking into Voort's eyes.

'You would not hurt her, would you? You said you loved her. It really is police business?'

'Yes. No. I'm not sure. But I wouldn't hurt her.'

The man repeats, clearly and slowly, as if for the benefit of the fuming operator behind the glass, 'I took her to the downtown boathouse, on Pier Twenty-six. A lovers' quarrel, yes? Men must stick together.'

The driver seems disgusted at the operator. 'Women turned him into a woman, like them,' he tells Voort. 'He's afraid of everything now, even to say a fact.'

'Was anyone else at the boathouse when she got there?'

The operator in the glass booth snorts and shakes his head. He shouts something at the driver, in another language, Hindi maybe, but whatever it is, it's an insult.

The driver yells back at the operator.

They're really going at it.

As for Voort, he is rushing out the door.

Outside, the Chevy starts up, reliable as always, but it gets stuck in traffic, crossing town, on Twenty-third.

The street is totally blocked, curb-to-curb, by honking cars. He tries another street. It's stalled. He's wasted eleven minutes in traffic.

Voort pulls the Chevy over, in front of a hydrant.

He calls the Homicide Unit on the radio. He tells the operator he has reason to believe the BHC killer may be at the boathouse, at Hubert and West on Pier 26. He doesn't care if it isn't true, if it's only his fear, only a premonition. He keeps remembering Camilla's voice on Bainbridge's tape.

'He's targeted her. Get someone there. She needs protection, now.'

For once, he hopes the hated *Daily News* is monitoring the police radio. He hopes all the journalists are listening. He hopes every police radio enthusiast within ten miles will head for the pier.

But the answering detective says, 'Ten-two, Detective,' which means, Drop whatever you're doing and come back to One Police Plaza, now.

'Didn't you hear what I said?'

'I heard you. Did you hear me? Ten-two. Addonizio's orders.'

'You don't understand,' Voort says, realizing Camilla's car service's complaint has reached the ears of the Chief of Detectives. Addonizio has the network on his ass screaming that one of his detectives pulled a gun on civilians.

'Voort, you there?'

'Just send people to the pier, okay?'

Slipping, Voort gets out of the car, locks it, leaves it in front of the hydrant. He knows that the squad cars, at least any moving in this storm, will be looking for him now. He knows if they find him, they've been ordered to bring him back, to accept no arguments. A New York City detective is never, ever, supposed to draw a gun without a good reason. And if a detective *does* draw a gun, it's unwise to do it over an argument with NBC News.

Hell, who needs to be a policeman anyway? I'll go work on the family tugboat.

It is two miles to the boathouse, he estimates, through

drifts and across the West Side Highway.

Traffic is stopped. Horns are blaring. It seems, in the storm, like the cars will never move again.

Voort starts to run.

NINETEEN

'More champagne,' says Marla Voort, Conrad's cousin, balancing on the deck of the tugboat *Admiral*, holding out an antique silver tray of fluted glasses of Bollinger's to Voort and Camilla, beside the front rail.

It's their second date, and he has taken her to the 300th annual family reunion of the New York Voorts, held, as always, on the water, in the Hudson, north of the Verrazano Narrows. A cold autumn day, clear and cloudless. Voort's wearing Levi cords, deck shoes, and a brown flight jacket against the chill. Camilla's in an Armani fitted jacket of black wool, a cashmere sweater beneath. Her tight jeans tuck into soft leather boots, and her long hair is down, glowing in the dusk sun.

'Big family,' she says, enjoying the laughing, boisterous celebrants; Voorts from all over New York City and the Hudson Valley, swarming over the decks, sipping wine in the pilothouse, the kids playing tag, the adults dancing to live country music from a four-person band called The Dutchmen, all Voorts, from Croton, where they play in a well-known weekend act.

Marla sips champagne. 'Nat Voort, our first cousin, owns the tugboat, out of Staten Island. Hendrik, from the Hudson

Valley crew, brought those gigantic pumpkin pies, roast turkeys and hams, autumn corn, apple cider, hot black breads. Everybody brings something.'

'What did you bring, Marla?' Camilla says.

'We own a liquor store in Soho.'

'Voort, what did you contribute?'

'Him? He brought you, and he never brings a date,' Marla says. 'And the rest of the time,' she winks, 'he fixes parking tickets. He solves legal snafus. He saves our kids from life and death situations. He must have told you about—'

'Marla,' Voort warns as he gazes at the Statue of Liberty.

'You didn't tell her? Why not?'

A banner, made by the Greenwich Village Voorts, and hung with bunting over the railings, says, THREE CENTURIES OF VOORTS. And it seems to Camilla that every passing tug, barge, and cruise ship acknowledges the family with blasts of their horns.

'For God's sake,' Marla says,'this is no time to be shy, cousin. She'll fall in love with you when she hears.'

Voort says, 'Camilla, do you know that there was a Voort on Henry Hudson's ship, when he first sailed into New York Harbor? He was the cabin boy.'

'You can be so exasperating,' Marla sniffs, but gives up. She's darker than Voort, robust, with braided jet-black hair to her shoulders, large hips, broad shoulders, and vaguely Asian, almond-shaped eyes from a Mohegan ancestor who married a fur-trapper Voort when the French and British vied for control of North American colonies, in 1703.

'I can see, though, cousin,' Marla says, 'why you've been smiling so much lately.'

Camilla feels welcome here, like a member. It's been a long time since she wanted to be accepted by someone else's family. She savors the Bollinger's, the food, the harbor at its best.

She asks, 'Doesn't he usually smile?' She has not slept

with Voort yet, and her hand, on his bicep, feels hard muscle beneath the soft leather. It excites her.

'Oh, he never smiles,' Marla says, downing another glass instead of circulating. 'He beats children. He gets into fistfights. He follows women down streets, scaring them. Anything good I told you about him is a lie. Happy now, Conrad?'

'Sure, give her the ugly truth. And give me another glass before you leave.'

'Thank you to you too. And by the way, our intrepid captain, Nat, asked me to tell you two to check out Cabin 102. Key's above the door. He says there's a treat down there for you, Connie.'

'Is it ticking?'

The tug heads north, past Governor's Island, as Voort tells her history. Past the Battery, the old Dutch fort at the southern tip of Manhattan, where Voorts manned the cannons and fired blunderbusses against Iroquois, to the forested north, now the Wall Street area, and British men-of-war, in the harbor, to the south. Past the World Financial Center and West Side Highway, where Voorts chopped down oaks with hand axes, built thatch-roofed houses, planted gardens with peas, tomatoes, potatoes from Europe. Past the Palisades, on the west, where Voorts smuggled silver from the old mines past the British, for the Revolutionary War effort.

'We took it through a church. The priest was a Voort.'

'We?' Camilla teases. 'You were there?'

'I'm older than I look. See the old pier there, where your kayak house is? During the Revolutionary War, the British dock was there, for their harbor patrol, against smugglers. Well, Voorts were smugglers. We rowed little boats, when it was foggy, past their ships.'

Camilla squeezes his arm and says, in a softer voice, 'Let's find that cabin Marla told you about.'

It turns out to be on the main deck, and it is the Captain's

Quarters, a small, cozy, portholed, V-shaped room with a queen-size bed, fresh linen, fresh flowers, a bucket of champagne, a silver tray of canapés, fruits, Dutch chocolates and cheeses.

Camilla breaks out laughing when she sees it.

'It's more like a country inn than a tugboat. Why do I feel like there's a conspiracy here?' she says.

Voort shakes is head. 'Said the fly to the spider. Check the stereo. Want to bet Sinatra's already on it? Five to one.'

Camilla stands on tiptoe, kisses him, and locks the door. 'We can't have all this preparation go to waste. By the way, what was that story Marla started to tell about, "saving children"?'

'You'll never get it out of me.'

Later, at the network, Camilla will look up Voort's name on the *New York Times* computerized News Service and find the article, from last year, headlined, COP SAVES NEPHEWS IN LIQUOR STORE HOSTAGE-TAKING. SHOOTS TWO.

Now, in the cabin, they fall onto the bed, kissing. Voort's hands are under her sweater, squeezing her breasts, pinching her nipples. She gasps. 'Harder!'

Camilla, undoing his belt buckle, hears the triumphant giggling of children, from out in the hall, or could it be the whole Voort clan, making a new acquisition?

Now it is five months later, such a small amount of time, yet such a great void of time, and Camilla sits on the boathouse floor, back against a corner, knees drawn up, sobbing.

She has never lost control like this. She cannot stop crying, cannot think, cannot stand. Her heart has left her. A hole has opened between rib cage and backbone, in the upper left quadrant of her body. Her organs, her tissues, have been torn out. And even though nothing fills the gap, she still feels something hurting, the way an amputee swears that a missing leg is there.

Camilla feels the physical pain of grief.

Why doesn't Bainbridge get here?

Outside, from the howling wind, she knows the storm has worsened. The tin roof twists, vibrates, rattles, pulls against its mooring. In cyclones, she knows, in footage that comes into the network from Asia, roofs are pulled off houses. People are sucked from their homes, to disappear into the black sky. In the boathouse, now, the electric light flickers. The kayaks gleam in their wooden berths, stored for the winter. The space heaters are arrayed in a glowing circle in the center of the room, around two folding chairs that face each other in a makeshift psychologist's consultation room.

Her doctor is coming to soothe her broken heart.

The buzzer breaks her reverie, calls her to the intercom, over which his voice shouts, 'It's crazy out here! Let me in!'

She envisions Ian, plump and teddy-bearish, wrapped against the snow, outside the chain-link fence. She buzzes her savior through the outer gate, and moments later unlocks the steel-coated wooden door, and he lumbers in out of the wind. She locks the door behind him.

'Traffic's blocked all the way down the West Side Highway,' Ian says. 'There are accidents all over the place. It's like Antarctica out there.'

'Thank you for coming.'

He embraces her. He is trembling, from the cold, she tells herself. He smells of wet wool, and unwashed hair. His upper arms are flabby, bulky but not muscular, not much power there, but they make her feel safe, like a friend has arrived.

'I have to admit, Voort frightened me,' he says, moving toward a space heater, holding his palms to the glow as if to a fire.

'I'll take care of him.' Already, in his presence, she is stronger.

'I didn't want to tell you before,' Ian says, 'and worry you, but he threatened me. He said I better stop seeing you.

He demanded to know if I was sleeping with you. He's not healthy, in his head.'

Bainbridge removes his coat and something bulky thuds against the floor through the right pocket. She wonders what weighs so much in there, makes such a loud, clunky thunk, like metal striking wood.

'Voort was shouting,' he says. 'He said he'd been watching me. He said – and I don't think he'd really do it, but he said – he'd "blow my head off." Those were his exact words. He should be in therapy.'

'Ian, we'll make sure he never threatens anyone again.'

The space heaters flicker with the bank of fluorescent lights above. The storm is battering Manhattan power lines.

Bainbridge eyes the lights, exhales, loud, calming himself. 'He reminds me of my patients,' he says. 'In a club, the Broken Hearts Club, I call it. Healthy-looking men on the outside, but twisted.'

'Club?'

'Group therapy, actually. Camilla, you would think these men were normal, if you met them; a banker, a mechanic, a literary agent. But they've been unable to recover from grief. I don't want to frighten you, but they've, well . . . hurt women. I do what I can to help.'

She envisions Voort, angry, and asks, in a small voice, 'Hurt women how?'

'We don't have to get into that. You've had a rough day. And I shouldn't discuss other patients. Let's talk about what happened to you.'

'I'll call the Chief of Detectives, now. He'll pull that bastard off the street by the six o'clock news.'

'No,' Ian says gently. 'You first. You're the important one. We can take care of Voort later. You first. Me later. Doctor's orders.'

'You're a good man, Ian. I even arranged the chairs, like your office.'

He grins. 'Better than home.'

'All I have is peppermint tea. That okay?'

'Fine.' Bainbridge takes in the kayaks, the windowless walls of wooden planking. 'We're sure isolated here,' he says.

Something in his words bring on the awkward moment, as they realize for the first time they are with each other outside his office. That they can exist, together, elsewhere besides East Ninety-third Street. He seems different in this environment, just as concerned, but without his chair, files, books, without his little black alarm clock counting down the minutes, he's more like an average person, a simple visitor come to chat.

She notes the tentative way he accepts tea, like a mere guest, notes the slight stoop of his shoulders, which makes him seem more frail. Voort must have given him quite a scare. There are real bones in there, she thinks, that can break. She sees spots of dandruff on his sweater, and his hands, taking the souvenir '86 Mets World Series mug from hers, tremble.

'From the cold,' he says, seating himself, leaning forward in what she thinks of as his attentive 'shrink' posture. 'Camilla, you sounded terrible on the phone. And after meeting your Voort, I understand why you're scared of him.'

They face each other inside the circle of glowing space heaters. The warmth travels up their legs, burns pleasantly, envelops them as she begins to tell him what happened tonight. How she went to Voort's office. How she was so sure she was in control of the confrontation, telling Voort off, and how, out of the blue, after she got to the boathouse, she started sobbing.

'I never had that kind of reaction before.'

'It scares you,' he says.

'You understand.'

'It makes you wonder if there's something wrong with

you, that you haven't been aware of until now, that you fear you hid from yourself.'

'Yes!'

'And your Voort—'

'He's not *my* Voort,' she says. 'Or *my* Kenny. My husband. All of them.'

'Men, you mean.'

'I never want a relationship again,' she says savagely. 'Never want a man to touch me. To hell with them, every one of them.'

She has the impression, from the way he shuts his eyes, that he's experienced a bolt of pain. Perhaps he twisted his ankle on the ice outside, or is getting the flu that's raging through the city. She is about to ask if he is all right when he says, more slowly, 'Not all men are like that.'

'Yeah, right.'

'Some men,' he says, 'special, loyal men, can be relied on all the time.'

'Got anyone in mind?'

'I'm not joking. Some men can love with all their heart.'

She sighs. 'You're too romantic, Ian. With that attitude, someone's going to break your heart, if they haven't already.'

'What's wrong with romance? You say it like it's a dirty word.'

'It's bullshit. It's for movies, for kids, for people who don't know any better. Not for adults.'

'You don't really mean that,' he says, as his right foot, crossed over the left, begins moving slowly up and down. His pupils seem smaller, his frown deeper. There is a new, unsettling element in his attitude, more direct, less benevolent.

Or is it that after the Voort episode, *everything* seems disturbing tonight, makes her doubt her basic instincts?

After all, he came here for me, took the time to do that, so what's bothering me about him?

'Who ever would have thought,' she says, pushing away

her questions, 'a month ago, things could degenerate so much? That crazy things would seem normal. Voort threatening you, actually threatening you with a gun.'

'Well, he did.'

From underneath the floor comes, *boom*!

He jumps. 'What's that?'

'Just a wave hitting the pier. I was talking about "normal." I guess after what he's done over the last couple of weeks, I actually believe he's sick enough to be dangerous.'

He does not seem to have heard her, does not nod, or respond in any way. He's withdrawn into himself. A lone dot of sweat has appeared on the right corner of his forehead.

'Ian? Are you all right?'

He reaches for his tea but pulls his hands back. His lips move but no sound comes out. Pressure seems to be building in him. And then she thinks she hears him say, in a barely audible voice, 'I love you.'

But he couldn't have said that. She tells herself that it is simply absurd that he could have said that. She leans forward to hear better.

'Ian, what did you say?'

'I said . . .' His face has gone shiny, become the face of a different man. More angular, more direct, less tolerant. His breathing has deepened, and he reminds her, the way he fixes his eyes on her, of her top investigative reporter, just before the man asks the question that signals a journalism kill about to begin.

But the look subsides as suddenly as it came on. 'I said I'm going away.'

It is not what she expected, and now she is off balance herself, now she is the one who feels panic. She has a vision of Bainbridge at an airport, boarding an airplane, carrying a suitcase. The plane is flying off. It terrifies her, the idea of his leaving. She's read about patients overreacting when their therapists depart for vacations, and always before thought the idea laughable. It is not laughable now.

She says, 'What do you mean, away? For how long?'

'I didn't want to tell you on the phone. Things can be difficult between a doctor and patient when a doctor even takes a little trip. And now I've been offered a job, a terrific opportunity, but it's out of New York,' he says. 'I'm going.'

'I thought you looked nervous, but I blamed it on Voort's visit.'

'I like the new job, but hate this part, telling patients I care about that I'm going. And I care about you,' he says, staring into her eyes. 'Very much.'

'When is this big move happening?' she gets out, trying for a light tone, but her anchor is slipping away. The whole day seems like one nonstop loss marathon.

'Tonight. It came up fast. But first we'll talk here a while. Hours, if you like.'

Her panic grows. What use is one lousy session, no matter how many hours it lasts, if he leaves?

'I thought the whole idea of therapy was that it takes a while,' she says. 'I feel like I'm twelve years old. I should be happy for you but I feel selfish. I don't like you going away.'

Nevertheless, she holds out her hand. 'Good luck.'

His fingers, on hers, seem to linger. 'It's not the end of the world, Camilla.'

'Everybody abandons everybody in the end,' she is surprised to hear herself say.

'That's not true,' he says, not letting go of her hand. 'Did you ever think that maybe *you're* the one who abandons people, people who love *you*? That *you* drive *them* away?'

'What are you talking about? Voort followed me, harassed me!'

He drops her hand. 'Oh. You're talking about Voort,' he says.

'Who else do you think we're talking about?'

'Well, you're right about *him*. There was such an extreme

element in him, it made me wonder how someone with a temper like that could be allowed to be a New York City detective. In fact, when he threatened me, it was worse than I told you. I worry that he may come after you. He needs therapy, Camilla. But . . . I care what happens,' he says, more strongly. 'I'll miss you, I really will.'

'I'll miss talking to you too.'

'You will?' he says, his mood swinging. He looks absurdly happy now, like an actual friend, not a man she pays money to, for sharing secrets, for intimate conversations she does not even have with the people she knows best.

And then she hears him say, 'If we both feel this way, perhaps it might be possible to see each other again.'

'If you're in another city? Ian, that's wishful thinking. We might as well get this over with, cold turkey. You'll refer me to another doctor, I suppose.'

He actually jerks, as if the suggestion shocked him. His whole body goes rigid, and when he puts his empty tea mug on the table, it rattles against the wooden top.

He says, sounding pained, 'Someone else?'

His hands, squeezing his knees, have gone white.

She says, 'I'm touched by how much you want to keep working with me, but be realistic. With my schedule, I can't keep seeing you professionally. I'm on call eighteen hours a day at the network. And if you're not in New York, what can we do? Unless you're returning to the city to hold office hours. *Are* you coming in for office hours?'

A single trickle of sweat glides down the right side of his face.

'Oh, professional,' he says, looking relieved, which puzzles her. 'You're right about the professional part. That would have to be terminated. We both knew,' he says, 'that the professional part would go when we reached our next big step.'

Camilla feels cold suddenly, despite the space heaters. The

room has gone dry, and a gust of wind tears at the roof again. He looks so eager.

She repeats, hoping she has no idea what he is talking about, and fearing that she does, 'Our next big step?'

She is a beautiful woman, and men have been coming on to her since she was twelve; in offices, in bars, on the street, on planes, in the subway. She does not want to believe that her doctor is doing it. She is suddenly aware of just how isolated the boathouse is. But she says, in a careful tone, 'Forgive me for asking, but this isn't an expression of personal interest on your part, is it?'

His knowing smile makes her cringe inside. He says, 'You can't be surprised that it's finally in the open. Would that be so bad?'

'Are you crazy? You're my shrink!'

His sweat is flowing freely now, down his forehead, into his eyes, utterly at odds with his calm expression. She has the sense that he is exerting massive control to try to keep himself looking easy. But whatever his expression, the face, when she considers it as a suitor's face, not a physician's, is repulsive; fleshy and moist, and his eyes are so big, behind those bottle-thick glasses, and his cheeks are puffy, swollen almost, too red from the storm, and his wet wool odor is stronger now, the smell of a mildewy blanket.

Seeing her response, he says, 'Camilla, do I disgust you that much, as a man?'

'You're not a man.'

He looks shocked.

'You're a doctor.'

He laughs and begins to stand up, but someone starts banging on the outside door. The sound echoes in the boathouse. Bainbridge freezes. Camilla thinks, The gate is locked outside, so how did someone reach the door?

'Who the hell is that?' she says. 'Didn't you lock the gate behind you?'

'I did.'

The banging increases in volume, Bainbridge, half standing, has frozen. He's staring at the sliding, locked door. 'It's him,' he says.

She rises too fast, steadies herself against the chair as dizziness hits her. 'You're being paranoid,' she says. 'You're saying he followed you? He would have shown up before this if he followed you. What do you think, he was standing around out there for the last twenty minutes?

'And anyway, you're telling me,' she adds, her fury replacing, for a moment, the grief that had been tearing at her, 'that your advice all along, things you asked me to do, was because you were interested in me?'

'My advice was professional.'

The banging stops.

'Oh. Professional! One professional pulls a gun and the other probes secrets to try to get me into the sack.'

The banging starts again. Between the thick door, the howling wind outside, the distance to the exit, the humming space heaters, and the conversation, she'd have to be right up against the door to hear a person shout out there.

'That's not fair,' he says, standing also, putting on his coat. He looks like a ten-year-old, with no defenses. 'Don't you like me even a little? A small part, that can grow?'

He adds, to himself almost, 'He *said* this would happen.'

'No, Ian, I don't like you that way, even a little. And what do you mean, *he* said? *Who* said?'

'Don't open the door,' he whispers as she moves toward it, away from the space heaters, into the colder air beyond.

She says, over her shoulder, 'Are you kidding? It's freezing out there.'

She hears the doctor's footsteps closing behind her, hears him say, in a completely different voice, smoother and more confident, so she even turns to look, 'Yes, you're right, of course. Let him in.'

She snaps, 'Do I need your permission to eat too?'

He's close enough so she can hear his labored breathing behind her, and smell his acrid sweat.

She is only peripherally aware that his right hand has disappeared into his coat pocket, the one with the heavy object in it, which clunked against the floor before.

'Who's there?' she calls at the door, more irritated than frightened, thinking that she will order Ian to leave when the door is open, thanking whoever is outside for showing up when he did.

Muffled by the steel, and the storm, comes the barely audible one-word answer.

'Voort!'

TWENTY

'Go away,' Camilla cries, feeling, from the other side of the door, Voort's urgency, his force and obsessiveness as she envisions him in the falling snow.

'Are you alone?' Voort calls. 'I promise, if you are, I'll leave.'

A lie, she knows, aghast that he has found her, that he tracked her here.

Bainbridge, only minutes ago, had said, *He accused us of sleeping together. He said he'd hurt me.*

Now the psychologist stands, terrified, behind her, right hand in the pocket of his overcoat, left index finger pressed to his lips.

He mouths, 'I'm not here.'

And Voort is trying to sound reasonable, to pitch his voice as if there is actually a rational explanation for his presence. 'Please! Camilla! Open the door!'

She has a flash of her mother telling her, years ago, 'You have to be careful with people. You have to know someone a very long time before you see all the sides to them, especially men.'

Voort says, in that same masculine tone she'd heard so many times, in her ear, in bed, 'Just tell me if you're alone! I'm worried about you.'

'I'm alone. Happy now? Go!'

'You're not alone. There are two sets of footprints out here, and one's a man's, and they're both going in, not out. And the shoe size looks like Bainbridge's.'

He knows my doctor's shoe size?

'How did you get past the fence?'

'I climbed it. Is he there? Is that why you can't talk? *Tell me if it's Bainbridge!*'

'Voort, if you haven't figured this out by now: who I'm with, who I talk to, where I go, is none of your business. Don't pretend you're worried because I'm obviously fine if I'm talking to you. You climbed the *fence?* That's trespassing! Normal people use the intercom.'

'You wouldn't talk to me if I did.'

'You got that right!'

Smiling despite herself, she glances back. Bainbridge is pulling something from his coat pocket, but before she sees what it is, Voort's voice draws her back.

'If you're with the dancer, I don't care. Or some new guy. None of my business. But Bainbridge is dangerous. *There's a warrant for his—*'

'I don't want to hear this anymore!'

Bainbridge comes right up beside her. She can feel him trembling.

Voort says, 'Open the door and I'll explain. Just for a second. I won't come in. I'll just talk. Is he listening? Is that it?'

'I'm calling 911!' Camilla cries. 'Now.'

Something big crashes against the door. She leaps back, envisioning Voort, a big, strong man, throwing himself against it.

He's crazy. The man who made love to her, slept with his arms around her, met her friends, the man who she actually considered living with, has turned into an animal.

And Ian as well, mooning after her, lying and twisting his 'advice' to serve his own needs.

Voort hits the door, again.

'Go ahead, break your goddamn shoulder!' she cries.

But the door is strong. It's a good door, with a bolt lock that cannot be picked, the kind police recommend. Voort, she realizes, will not get in. He can throw himself against the door all he wants. She's safe. Her breathing subsides. His assault grows less savage, the impacts weaker, and then there is silence outside. He's given up.

He's going away, she tells herself, seeing him in her mind trudging through the snow, toward the West Side Highway. But even as she thinks it she knows the image is as absurd as the notion of Voort giving up. More likely he's eyeing the walls, roof, power lines, trying to figure out another strategy to break in.

It is time, right now, to carry out her threat. Time to phone the police.

She turns toward the phone and hears two loud reports from outside, over the keening wind.

'Christ, Jesus Christ! He's shooting!' Bainbridge shouts.

They leap back, run from the door, crouched, scurrying toward the other side of the boathouse, keeping the pillars between them and the door. She hears another gunshot. She cannot believe this is happening. She reaches the phone, crouches behind a wooden pillar and presses the receiver to her ear and –

No dial tone.

The line is down outside. There are no underground lines on the pier.

Shit.

My cell phone. Where did I put it?

Another gunshot, but she realizes she's heard no sound of bullets impacting against the door. Voort is not firing at the door.

Then what *is* he shooting at?

She begins crawling toward the supply closet, where she

hopes she left the cell phone. She's cursing herself for waiting, for giving Voort a chance to leave on his own. For not having the killer instinct to go for Voort's jugular when she could have. Moving, palms on the cold floor, she glances at Bainbridge, who is pressed against the wall by the kayak berths, and she notes, at first only with the back of her mind, that there is something in Bainbridge's hand that was not there a moment ago.

A gun.

The pain grows huge in the pit of her stomach, rising into her throat.

Voort's firing has stopped. It is impossible, she tells herself, that Ian is armed too, but the gun in his hand is not disappearing, not turning into something else; like a glove seen at the wrong angle, or a black ashtray. Now he's wedged himself into one of the kayak berths, out of the line of fire, should Voort shoot into the boathouse.

She stares at the steel muzzle with sick fascination. The only gun she has ever seen, close up, until now, is Voort's, when he takes it off at night. He has a shoulder holster with a silvery buckle, a leather strap. She has accepted that firearm as part of Voort, but in Ian's white, smooth hand, a gun looks like a toy. It is impossible to associate Bainbridge with violence. He's a man of pipes, tea, books, theories.

Bainbridge says to her, in the huge silence, 'He said he'd hurt me.'

At that instant there's a hammering sound of something metallic, iron perhaps, an object and not a person, striking the door.

Bainbridge emits a low, long groan. He holds the gun toward the door, but does not fire. He's shaking too badly.

This time the sound of Voort's assault is too sharp, the point of impact too high to be Voort throwing himself against the door. She hears a loud tearing sound inside the door; screws weakening, or wood splintering.

She thinks, a sledgehammer.

Of course. That's where Voort disappeared to minutes ago. He was shooting at the lock on the toolshed outside, abutting the building.

Camilla hisses, 'Ian!'

She envisions the toolshed, and inside, its fire axe and sledgehammer, heavy tools for repairing the pier, roof, pilings. Voort would have known what was in the box. He's seen workmen loading it in the summer, when they were working on the dock.

His hammering echoes in the boathouse. But the door isn't breaking, isn't splintering, so it's not a sledgehammer, but it's *some* kind of tool, *something* he got out of that box.

Bainbridge says, in a low voice, 'I never shot a gun even once. I keep it for burglars. I took it because he scared me.'

Only a few minutes have passed. Camilla sees Bainbridge as if from far away. The funny thing is, at her job, she covers stories like this all the time. The man who went insane in Texas, the quiet stockbroker who killed his family with a shotgun. The woman who drove a car through the picture window of her boyfriend's home, just left work at a floral shop one day, got into her pickup, and pushed the accelerator to the floor. And yet now that it is happening to her, the kind of craziness she covers every day, when it touches her own life, it seems as unreal as the videos the technicians crack jokes about in the control room, safe from the violence, far away at NBC.

These things happen to other people.

Her haven, her beloved boathouse, has become a trap. Outside the front door is Voort, outside the back one is the river. The walls seem closer. The whole pier is shaking from the storm. Voort starts up again on the door, and she can see the top hinge wobble slightly, millimeter by millimeter, wresting itself from its frame.

What the hell is he doing to it?

There's no reasoning with Voort, but maybe, she tells herself, she can get to Ian.

'Put that away,' she says.

He does not seem to hear. Any second, he'll start firing.

'I'll call 911,' she offers. But she wants to laugh. She can't even remember where she left the damn cell phone, and what good is 911 anyway? Nine one one. The urban incantation. Magic words to dispel evil. But there is no time to call 911. The top hinge is almost off.

She thinks, I waited too long. I didn't want to hurt him.

She thinks, in the end, put to the test, I hesitated. Now the roads are blocked. The police won't reach us by the time the door goes down.

Her doctor and ex-lover have entered that primal realm, the core of rage-defining male existence, beyond law, reason, or feminine understanding, the aspect of men most terrifying to women, and certainly beyond her pathetic entreaties.

She tries one last time, begging, over the blows on the door, 'He'll kill you! He won medals for shooting!'

And then, as she watches, astounded, Ian seems to change. Lying in the berth, the fear leaves him abruptly. A calm settles onto his face. It is such a profound alteration that he seems like another person. It's more than a difference in posture or attitude. It's so pervasive that he emanates power, even attractiveness, so pervasive that his very clothing seems wrong for him.

Quite deliberately, his gun comes up, aims at the door. His shaking has stopped. She knows, without a doubt, that even before Voort breaches the door, Ian will shoot through it. This new, competent Ian will accurately aim and fire the gun.

Someone will be killed. Maybe all of us.

And with this realization, her terror lifts her to a plane where she sees that she has only herself to rely on; not Ian, not logic, not police, and certainly not fate.

A last chance before gunfire breaks out.

Camilla understands what she has to do.

'I'll get you out of here,' she calls to him, watching the clear, calm eyes swivel, fix on her, appraise her with almost a bizarre, chilling amusement. Wood is splintering in the doorjamb, by the middle hinge, fifteen feet away. She crosses the room to Ian, hoping Voort won't fire through the door. She pulls at Ian, trying to help him out of the berth.

'Voort won't know you were ever here. Listen to me! Put that thing down!'

His gaze follows her finger to the kayaks around them, small, light, excellent craft, one- and two-seaters, in their winter homes. And to the back door, leading to the river.

'We'll leave together,' she tells him, pulling at his sleeve. 'Help me get a boat down before Voort breaks in!'

Working the cat's-claw bar at the door, trying to smash and pry it open, Voort can't hear Camilla inside anymore. She won't answer him, won't even tell him to go away. He curses her under his breath. All she had to do was convince him that she was alone. All she had to do was open the damn door for one minute, and she couldn't even do that.

She's so stubborn. He hopes she really is phoning the police in there. He'd love a few squad cars to pull up, if they can get through the snow. But if Bainbridge is inside and hears sirens . . .

Voort shudders.

Bainbridge could be on the other side of the door right now, aiming his gun.

But Voort's fear for Camilla is greater than any fear he has ever known. He goes back to work.

Unable to convince her to open the door before, he'd groped his way through the storm to the toolshed, brushed off snow and, standing back, using his .38, managed to shoot off the combination lock after four direct hits. But instead of finding a sledgehammer inside, or fire axe, as he had expected, he'd seen that most of the big tools had been taken away for the winter. He'd rummaged among rusty screwdrivers and nails and old hammers, and come up with the cat's-claw bar, a kind of clawed iron crowbar normally used for removing embedded nails, but a tool that could be wedged and hammered into small spaces.

He'd shoved the tip of the bar between the door and doorjamb and started hammering, trying to loosen the lock, or splinter the door, or pry out the hinges. Anything.

Now, straining, pulling at the bar, he tries to shut out visions of Niana Embers in her apartment, sprawled amid her overturned furniture. He sees Karen Chambers on her dining room floor, in Brooklyn. He sees Greta Berger, in a black and white police photograph, propped beneath a tree, limbs all tangled, twisted on the ground in snowy Central Park, blood staining the white.

He cut his hand coming over the barbed wire fence, and wincing against the pain, he strains, pulling the bar. He's rewarded with the smallest groan of complaint inside the doorjamb. She's so stubborn. And the irony is, if she's in there with anyone besides Bainbridge, Voort's going to jail. It's way beyond a suspension from work now. There's breaking and entering, destruction of boathouse property. There's harassment pulling a gun at the car service, disobeying a direct commissioner's order to come downtown, discharging a firearm in a public area.

Two hundred years of Voort policemen, turning in their graves.

'Camilla!'

No answer.

He smashes the rusty hammer against the cat's-claw bar, trying to widen the opening between door and doorjamb. The door wobbles a little now. It may be giving, but he is not sure.

Voort leans into the bar. Despite the cold, sweat pours down his face from effort.

I made a mistake, but I can't stop.

I'm wrong. I'm fucked. But if I'm right, she could be dead.

Voort, straining, cannot get the photo of the dead nurse out of his mind.

'Hurry up,' Camilla whispers in the back of the boathouse. Her ears are ringing from the banging at the door, and the storm, boom of waves, the totality of sound – nature and human emotion – building in crescendo.

Bainbridge fumbles into the wet suit she's given him. With steady hands he zips it up.

It's like he's another person.

'We have a couple of minutes before he gets in,' she says, pulling her overalls over her wet suit. 'Remember, Ian, wear two pairs of socks. It'll be wet in the kayak. If you don't stay warm, your fingers cramp. You won't be able to grip the paddle.'

She pulls her jacket over the overalls and dons rubber shoes for the kayak, over thick wool socks.

He says, more curious than frightened, 'The boat won't tip?'

'We're not going to tip over if you watch yourself, and listen to instructions. But it's blowing hard. We're going to get wet no matter what.'

They pull a two-person kayak from its berth, and paddles, spray skirts, and two orange life jackets. When she unlocks the back door, snow sweeps in and she can see the back pier covered with undisturbed drifts, as no one has shoveled the accumulated mass in weeks. But visibility ends after ten feet.

'The only way he can get back here is through the boathouse,' she says. 'Once we're on the water, we're safe. So leave that gun here. I hate it.'

Is she mistaken, or does he actually issue a low chuckle?

Standing upright, his slouch gone, he's added inches to his frame, and with his shoulders back, he seems strong rather than pudgy. His voice is lower, smoother, and filled with a kind of superiority that, at any other time, would be irritating.

'If I won't need it, there's no reason for you to mind my taking it,' he says. 'Is there?'

'Two men. Two guns. You're a bunch of infants,' Camilla snaps as they heft the craft.

From the front door she hears a metallic tearing, like screws wrenched from wood and steel.

They carry the yellow kevlar and carbon fiber, ultralight model kayak out the back door, over the snow, to the side of the pier. They slide the kayak, easily, down a wooden ladder, to a floating dock ten feet down, which is surging in the angry water.

Camilla climbs down the ice-covered rungs.

'You think we can make it to Jersey?' Bainbridge says, gazing out into the thickly falling snow. 'It's a long way across.'

'Not Jersey. That's too dangerous. We row out past the breakwater, into the current. It'll sweep us south. All we have to do is keep control, stay close to shore, and three, four minutes later, bring it back in to the next pier. But if we miss that, we're in trouble.'

'I never kayaked before.' He doesn't sound nervous, though. Just curious.

'It's just balance. You can balance, can't you? Stay calm, and listen to what I tell you. Hypothermia can kill a person in three minutes. In the wet suits, if we tip over, we have a little more time than that, thirty minutes max before the future becomes a moot point. If we go over, release the spray skirt and slide out of the kayak.'

She turns, glances one last time at the boathouse, more at home with practical problems than psychological ones. 'After I get you to shore, I'm calling the police on him. And you, after what you said to me, I never want to see you again.'

Bainbridge stands up on the pier, gazing down at her. The muscles on his face seem to have arranged themselves into a new pattern, making his jaw tighter, his lips thinner. 'Don't worry,' he says.

'I promise,' he adds after a small pause. His movements, as he follows her down the ladder, have taken on a slightly jerky quality. 'After today, you won't see me again.'

Voort feels the door give, sees bits of wood splintering, makes out the white spruce doorjamb breaking apart beneath the green paint. The lock casing is loose. He throws his weight into the cat's-claw bar, straining.

The casing breaks and the door swings open.

Voort, gun out, enters. He's drenched with sweat.

'Camilla?'

No answer.

He pivots.

'Camilla!'

He takes in the silent boathouse. It makes absolutely no sense that no one seems to be here.

He hears nothing but wind, the rattling roof, and the broken swinging door behind him.

They're hiding.

'Bainbridge, if you touched her . . .' He trails off, realizes he's acting like an amateur. He remembers all those hostage seminars back at One Police Plaza, where he and Mickie had 'rescued' inflatable dummies, or giggling secretaries, or the Chief of Detective's nephew, who had volunteered to be a 'prisoner' that day. You weren't supposed to antagonize the kidnapper. You were supposed to soothe him, lull him. You were supposed to be his best buddy. It was bad strategy to threaten to blow his head off.

'Bainbridge, let's talk, okay?'

Advancing slowly into the room, Voort sees two folding

chairs in the center, surrounded by glowing space heaters. It's a loose approximation of the furniture arrangement in Bainbridge's consultation room.

'Dr Bainbridge, look, I know you have a lot of things to talk about. People who hurt you.'

They're hiding. Afraid of him. Or Bainbridge has her here, somewhere, gun pressed against her body. Voort strains to hear the sound of bodies shifting. Or of breathing. He looks for vapor trails rising from behind a kayak, worktable, or chair.

The kayaks lie in their berths, shiny, cold. Voort slides to the wall, praying that if he has to fire, he won't hit her.

He reaches the closet, pulls the door open, and moves inside.

Nothing.

'Doctor, you were pretty smart back at your house, the way you got away from me!'

He leaves the closet, and only then notices the back door, twenty feet off, barely open, half an inch, because the bottom of the door has wedged in the snow. Flakes blow in through the crack.

And now, opposite, he spots an empty berth in the kayak rack, with filled berths around it. His gaze moves to the life jacket pegs on the wall, where the wet suits and jackets normally hang. Two of the pegs are empty.

Christ, it's suicide to go out there today.

It's a trick, he thinks.

But if it is, where are they?

Voort spots a lone bullet beside the back door, dull and coppery on the floor, unspent, a .38 caliber, like the ones in Bainbridge's house.

There are no signs of struggle in here, no overturned chairs, or blood. Nothing out of place, even a little. And so far, the other times Bainbridge hurt people, the crime scenes were ripped apart. Blood was everywhere.

Maybe it was Camilla's idea to leave out back, to protect him. I really fucked everything up.

Voort hits the back door at a run, uses his shoulder, bursts out, pivoting. There's no one back here, but two pairs of footprints disappear toward the ladder to the floating dock.

He hurries back to the kayaks, chooses a one man racer, a light little Canadian model. It's less stable than the heavier two-person type, tougher to control in bad weather. It lacks the rudder the oceangoing kayaks have, which can make a big difference in a tough current. But if a kayaker is strong enough – and Voort is powerful – and skilled enough, which he hopes he is, he can coax more speed from the lighter craft.

Voort grabs a life jacket off a hook, and although he knows he should put on a wet suit in this cold, he simply has no time. The spray skirt he wriggles into – around his torso – will have to do.

Outside, as he lowers the kayak to the floating dock, the river swells and reaches for him and shoots an icy spray into his face.

Voort climbs into the kayak, balancing with one hand against the dock. He seals himself inside by stretching the spray skirt – a rubber membrane – around the lip.

He pushes off, into floating debris the storm has brought in; driftwood, beer cans, New York flotsam.

'Camilla!'

Spray hits his face, and already ice is forming on his eyelids. His gloves are wet. His joints are hurting. His coat and gun are soaked.

He paddles west, toward the end of the pier, fighting the current, angling toward the main part of the river, thinking, If this is the calm area, the more protected water, it must be hell in the channel.

Suddenly he hits the main river, and the kayak is swept sideways, south, viciously. He leans hard, left, trying to stay upright by using the paddle as rudder.

'Camillaaa!'

He's clear of the pier, sweeping into a fog bank, toward the Verrazano Narrows and the Atlantic, retracing, in a way, the route that the first Voort to ever reach New York took, on the sailing ship *Half Moon*, commanded by Captain Henry Hudson over three hundred years ago.

He cannot see the shore, or even lights on the buildings on the landfill, less than two hundred yards away.

If Camilla is smart, she's staying on this side of the river, not trying the crossing, to New Jersey.

He lets the current swing the kayak around, lets nature pick his choice. Now he is committed to this direction, paddling blind, assuming his risk. He puts all his power into it. In the swift water, the kayak leaps ahead, almost capsizes, caught in a surge. The water spins him into a big wake, from a ship out on the river. He manages to keep from going over.

If I chose wrong, I'll never see her again.

And even if he *is* following them, the best he can hope for, between Bainbridge and the weather, is a small chance of success.

Voort speeds south. Darkness is falling.

He prays, *Let me die, if she can live.*

TWENTY-ONE

British seaman Henry Hudson, working for the Dutch East India Company, first sailed into New York Harbor in 1609 and thought he'd reached paradise. Camilla had read his original journal in Voort's private library, after Voort bought it at a Christie's auction. Voort kept it locked in a glass case.

'After the rigors of the North Atlantic,' Hudson wrote, 'the river is blue, calm, and teems with shad, flounder, bass, and delicious fishes I have never seen before. The land is thickly forested with oak and maple. I've glimpsed black bear and deer on shore, and the interior is undoubtedly filled with other succulent creatures for our dining pleasure.'

But Hudson also wrote: 'The currents along the southern tip of the island are treacherous. Travellers should avoid trying to land small craft in this spot. Even experienced sailors have difficulty when their boats get caught in the whirlpools.'

Now, almost four hundred years later, Camilla knows the only part of the description still accurate is the warning. She and Bainbridge are caught in the kayak, sweeping south, fighting current, battling to stay afloat.

They've been carried past the pier at which she hoped to

land, and have plunged into a whiteout, a milky mist so thick it destroys any sense of direction. Up seems like down. Manhattan has disappeared, and Camilla can barely see even the garish orange life preserver on Bainbridge's back, only a few feet ahead.

She is in a capsule of white, trying to steer, hoping she will be able to land the kayak by memory. To their left, if she's correct, a hundred yards off, is a solid concrete retaining wall, sixteen feet high, blocking any landing from Tribeca to the old Dutch fort at the Battery. Get too close and they will be smashed. Stay offshore and they'll miss the only gap in the wall, the narrow entrance to the marina where the big yachts dock, in front of the World Trade Center.

If that happens, they will be swept past the island and into the deeper harbor, the realm of the big ships.

She controls her fear and says, calmly, 'Ian, follow through each stroke, like I told you.'

Actually, he's doing quite well under the circumstances, even battered by the storm and freezing water. He's controlling his fear, although his jerky movements cause his paddle to slap the water instead of stroking it, sending spray into her face. Unaccustomed to the confining kayak, Ian shifts too much in a swell, overcompensating and rocking the boat.

She tries to focus him. 'I'll steer. You just stroke it. We're almost,' she lies, 'ashore.'

But the truth is, the fog looks the same in all directions. The truth is, in minutes they might find themselves in the ferry lanes, invisible to the tugs and barges which could crush them with their hulls and propellers, without their crews ever even knowing a collision had taken place.

'Camillaaa!'

She jerks, almost drops the paddle, hearing Voort's voice, in the mist somewhere. He must have taken out another kayak, she thinks.

'Camilla, I didn't explain right before! You have to let me know where you are. He killed three—'

A boom of a ship's horn, out on the river, blocks out the rest of his words. Then, in the whiteout, his voice starts bouncing around again. She cannot tell how far away it is.

'For God's sake, Camilla! *He* made the phone calls to your apartment. *He* left the glove on your fire escape!'

She retorts under her breath, 'And how would he *get* the goddamn glove?'

Voort cries, sensing his ex-lover's thoughts, 'The glove. Right! How did he get the glove? *I know how crazy this sounds*! He's insane, some kind of . . . I don't know the word for him! He *changes*! Posture. Appearance. Voice. Better than an actor! He's a sick . . . he really believes he's different! We don't even know his real name! A totally different person! You've covered stories like this on TV!'

She thinks, slowing, Ian changes? She remembers the radical transformation – voice, posture, everything Voort is describing – that the psychologist had undergone, less than an hour ago. Remembers thinking he had turned into another person.

She paddles harder, and blocks the thoughts out.

But Voort, of course, is right about her network coverage of this sort of story. From her own show, on NBC, she knows the word for the syndrome he describes. *Multipersonality*. It always made a great story that got terrific audience ratings, but whether the stories were true was another matter. She flashes to a segment aired a year ago, on an Arizona rapist, Bobby Flannigan, declared innocent by reason of insanity because he was found in court to have eleven personalities. His lawyer claimed he was not responsible for his actions. Camilla had thought Flannigan a great actor, nothing more, but the jury believed him.

She remembers Clarissa, the most famous multipersonality, about whom a movie was made, a housewife who, under hypnosis, slipped in and out of a dozen personalities, none of which 'knew' the others. Camilla, the hard-edged producer, hadn't bought it at all.

Camilla, working in TV, knowing more about the world, accepted less of what she saw with her own eyes.

Now Voort is getting hoarse, but not letting up. 'He followed me into a bar. He even *talked* to me, and he was so different – voice, wig, contact lenses, different smell, different aftershave! We found corsets in his house! He was thinner! *I didn't realize it was the same guy when I met him later!*'

'Voort,' she snorts. 'Give me a break.'

Ian, in front of her, issues a soft, tsking noise. 'He's talking about himself, poor man. He's the one who has become a "different person." '

She paddles, paddles. The current is getting worse.

'Camilla, answer me!'

She wants to shut the men out, both of them.

Voort's disembodied voice drives at her from above, then behind, bouncing and echoing so at one point it even seems to be in front of them. She tries to turn the kayak toward shore. They must be close to the marina. But the river sweeps them faster, spins them sideways, and the air is shattered by the close-by boom of a horn.

'It's going to hit!' Bainbridge gasps.

'No. It's just a trick of sound. It's too shallow here for the barges to get in.'

But there's no way to know if the barge has strayed too close to shore.

Voort cries, 'Do you think I'm crazy enough to take a kayak out in this weather without a reason? He fell in love with you!'

'Ian, we have to turn it. Use the paddle on the left, gooooood . . .'

But the kayak is flung right, into a whirlpool. They tip dangerously and Ian cannot balance himself, his big body going the wrong way. She needs all her skill just to counter him, to lean hard, almost touching water, over the other side.

They shoot free of the whirlpool, in the crazy current. Free, but at the price of her sense of direction. She is unsure if they're facing Jersey or Manhattan, and which way is the nearer shore.

Voort has fallen silent. He's given up, she thinks, relieved.

But he's just changing tactics.

The voice starts up again.

'Tillman! Are you there?'

No response.

'You put on weight over the years. You were thin when you worked at that bank, had the beard. More hair. Ten years changes a guy! You looked nothing like the photo we got from the bank!'

She orders Bainbridge, 'Paddle!'

'Tillman, what I want to know is, when you change, I mean, into Eric Porter, do you even know it?'

Ian shakes his head. 'Ludicrous.'

Voort cries, 'Does the literary agent know about the mechanic? Does the mechanic know about the banker?'

And this time Camilla pauses. The pulse slows in her chest, and a sick feeling gathers in the pit of her stomach.

She whispers, 'Ian, those are the people you said were in your club.'

Ian doesn't turn around.

'A mechanic, an agent, a banker,' she says.

Ian keeps paddling, but his posture has become more rigid. 'Ian?'

And now she realizes that Voort's voice seems farther away, as if he is veering off.

Voort shouts, muffled, as if facing in the wrong direction, 'Tillman, that club, the Broken Hearts Club! Do you really believe those are different guys?'

Bainbridge's paddling stops. He turns. He's looking right into her eyes. His expression, this close, is clear through the milky fog, and she understands suddenly that Bainbridge is studying her to see if she believes Voort.

He's afraid.

'How did Voort know about the club?' she whispers to the doctor, trying to ignore the runaway slamming of her heart.

He pauses too long. He seems oblivious to the river. 'I'm afraid,' he says, 'that they must have broken into my file when I was talking on the phone with you.'

'They? Who's "they"?'

'Voort and that other detective.'

'You mean Mickie?' she says, startled. 'Mickie was with him? You didn't tell me that.'

'What difference does it make?'

But Camilla knows the huge difference it makes. She feels sweat pop out on her scalp, despite the cold. 'Tell me,' she says slowly, 'did Voort and Mickie *both* threaten you? Do they *both* need therapy? Are *both* of them making those hangup calls? What exactly are you saying?'

'That those cops stick together.'

'You're right,' she says, 'and Mickie would never let Voort end his career by doing the kind of things you're accusing him of, not if he was there. He's too good a friend. Mickie'd beat the shit out of Voort to stop him from doing something like that.'

Bainbridge transfers his paddle to his left hand, lays it over the bow. Ignoring the rocking kayak, he unclips the front of his life jacket, so he can slide his right hand into his parka pocket.

'Oh Christ,' Camilla says, looking at Bainbridge's gun coming up.

The mist is thinning. I can see more water now. If I can stay afloat, and keep us out here, in a few more minutes Voort may be able to see us.

296

Bainbridge nods toward the fog, as if indicating Voort out there. 'He doesn't understand anything. But he's right that Ian thought he loved you.'

'But you're Ian.'

'We won't get into that,' he says. 'You're thinking that he'll be able to see us in a few more minutes.' Ian shakes his head. 'The fog is thinning. Just get me to shore, and I'll leave. I promise. I won't hurt you.'

Voort's voice cries, even farther away, 'You called the tip line, Bainbridge! You want to get caught!'

Ian tells her, in the same low, coaxing tone, 'I give my word, Camilla, as the Protector. I always tell the truth.'

Camilla can hardly breathe. 'Protector?'

'Ian's gone. He won't hurt anyone anymore. I'm in control, and I know you can get us ashore. You've told Ian enough times how you love these kayaks, how you excel at paddling them. *Shore.*'

'I don't know which way,' she says, stalling.

But Bainbridge points left, and north slightly, and says, 'That way.' Following his finger, she sees, with a sinking feeling, the blinking red and green lights atop the World Trade Center, before the fog closes in again.

'And I've been paying you to listen to *my* problems?' Camilla says.

When she doesn't move, he cautions, 'Don't make the Protector angry.'

She has to decide. She has less than five seconds, she sees, from their position, to make up her mind and swing west before the current takes them too far.

Camilla shouts, 'Voort, he has a gun!'

Bainbridge extends it, aims at her chest. 'Last chance.'

'You won't use it,' she says with confidence she does not feel. 'If I fall, we capsize, we both freeze, or drown. I wouldn't want to test the life jackets in this current.'

But Bainbridge just smiles and shakes his head.

'I'm wood,' he says. 'I float.'

Camilla looks into the shiny, mad face and screams. 'Voort! *We're here*!'

She sees the spurt of flame before feeling the impact. There's a punching sensation in her right shoulder, whipping her backward, snapping her head back as she hears the roar.

The paddle flies from her hands and she's tilting. The kayak is going over. Ian's not coordinated enough to counter the weight problem, nor does he seem to care.

The dark water rushes at her, and then she is under. She kicks free of the kayak, the first safety drill every kayaker learns. She's weighted by her clothes, buoyed by the life jacket. But the current has locked her under the surface, she's weightless, she's being flung around. She cannot breathe, and the detached journalist part of her mind, the perpetual observer thinks, clinically, *so this is what it's like to be shot, to be drowning*.

I hope Voort will reach shore.

And I hope he'll forgive me.

For a fraction of an instant she even thinks, What a great story this'll make on the six o'clock news.

But now she needs air. The pressure begins in the bottom of her throat, as a pulse in her lungs instead of her heart, as a throbbing in her head. She fights to keep from sucking in saltwater. The current spins her upside down. So cold, and she exhales the last of the air in her chest. Bubbles rising. She flails, trying to swim upward, unsure, in the dark, exactly which way that is.

But then she is pushed to the surface, without being aware that she was even rising. She gulps freezing air. I *won't suffocate*. But the pain from being shot is in her shoulder, spreading down her neck, her spine. The mist is gone. The current has swept her free of it. She will be able to see the harbor as it kills her with hypothermia. The whiteout hangs behind her, in a solid mass. She does not see the kayak, or

Ian, who must have been swept under also, or any boats at all. She is aware of the distant Christmas-tree-like green and red lights atop the World Trade Center, and of the semi-circular glow from the Statue of Liberty's crown, pretty, closer than she would have thought, maybe a mile off.

We're way past the marina, in the main harbor.

The numbness grows in her feet, her hands. Voort's voice has disappeared. He's back in the mist. At least the cold is a blessing. She feels her extremities shutting down. Her shoulder is going numb. In moments she'll lose power to move, see, and then feel, and finally to even think.

What a mess I made.

Camilla floats, only peripherally aware that out of the mist has floated a long piece of wood, a log, or piece of driftwood, except she realizes, with the small functioning part of her brain, that the prow of a kayak has pulled alongside.

'Camilla,' she hears Voort say. 'Thank God!'

'You died for me,' she says.

He's reaching for her.

'Don't be dramatic. We can still try for Governor's Island,' he says, trying to keep the fear for her from his voice.

He's shaking with cold. He's not wearing a wet suit, and he's soaked.

'Ian's gone,' she says, meaning swept away, in the current. 'He . . . shot me.'

But there's no more point to talking. She doesn't have the energy. She tells herself she should try to help get herself on the kayak, but her arms aren't moving.

And besides, his kayak is tilting, going over . . .

He's capsizing it on purpose, putting himself into the harbor, so he can try to get her in the boat.

'No . . .'

Voort's in the water, gripping her and trying to right the kayak, trying, as the cold reaches into his joints, to push her, help her into the half-flooded compartment. Teeth chattering, he says, 'Try to hold on to it, we'll d-d-drift.'

Drift. What a lovely word. What a perfect sensation. To float. To feel pain diminishing, seeping from her, passing out of her nerve endings into some dulled, drugged state. They will die together. They will be found, floating, after the storm, in the harbor, with the pieces of timber and garbage and old condoms around them. They will be nibbled by fishes. They will drift into the marshes on the Jersey shore, or along Staten Island.

She wants to tell him how sorry she is. She forces herself to turn to him, not that she can speak anymore, not that she has the slightest control over sound.

And Bainbridge pops to the surface two feet behind him.

Voort forces out, 'If we can make Governor's I-Island, there'll be a d-doctor.'

Bainbridge is looking directly into Camilla's eyes, over Voort's shoulder. He seems oblivious to the cold. His face is as shiny as the surface of the ocean. His smile is as white as the quarter moon.

He has grasped the situation immediately, but then again, madmen adapt quickly to mad situations. His gun is coming up, out of the water, almost in slow motion, and she wants to warn Voort.

But her voice will not come out.

Click.

Too wet to fire.

Voort turns at the noise as Bainbridge brings the gun down, but it misses Voort's head, deflects off the shoulder. It has not been a night for human accuracy. The two men tangle, clawing at each other, as they all sweep south in the current.

Voort, groaning with pain, sinks.

And Bainbridge tells Camilla, the shock of cold in his voice, 'I told you I float.'

He starts swimming toward her.

He says, 'You broke Ian's heart.'

And suddenly something pulls him down.

Camilla is only three feet away, half-frozen, and draped over Voort's half-flooded kayak. The men surface, together, locked in combat. She can do nothing. She's barely aware of the struggle. Her legs trail in the water. The river cruelly maintains the distance between the kayak and Voort; close enough to see each other, too far away to touch.

They are in the sea-lanes now, freed from the mist, and Camilla sees, through the lessening snowfall and in the winter night, the glistening lights of the Verrazano Bridge, which mark the entrance to the Atlantic Ocean.

Sleep. Close your eyes.

Lovely sleep.

Minutes before, Voort had turned in the water in time to see Bainbridge's fist coming down at him, but too late to stop it. Something heavy struck his shoulder. There was a snapping noise inside, a bolt of pain, and the current swept him into a whirlpool. He went down.

In the dark he bumped against something, *Bainbridge's legs*. He grabbed them and pulled the man down. And then they were tumbling under the water, clawing at each other, rolling, and they broke the surface, gulping air, Bainbridge's face, swollen and shiny, inches from his own.

Bainbridge trying to hit him again with the butt of the gun.

Now Voort must concentrate. His shoulder is burning, and he's lost feeling in his fingers. Bainbridge wears a wet suit, so he's warmer, he has more control of his body. Voort has only his sodden clothes and the life jacket. Normally, in a fight, he could take the doctor in a minute. Bainbridge is older, fatter, flabbier, and he's lost his glasses. But he has dexterity in his fingers and hands, and he's filled with adrenaline, the power of the mad. He grips Voort's wounded shoulder and claws at Voort's eyes with his other hand.

Bainbridge gasps, 'She . . . loves . . . you . . . not me.'

Then water fills his mouth as they tumble, half afloat, in and out of whirlpools and eddies in the driving current. Voort needs all his effort to keep the stabbing fingers from his eyes. He hears the horn of a barge, too loud, too close and then the deep growl of an engine. The prow of the ship slides toward them, out of the mist, its crew safe and oblivious in the pilothouse, blind to three tiny figures in the water ahead.

'You will . . . not hurt . . . Ian,' Bainbridge says as Voort uses all his strength to reach up and pull the hand off his shoulder.

The barge misses them, passing only feet away, but its swell lifts and pushes them up and under again. Voort spits water from his mouth. He's at the end of his strength. He can't even see Bainbridge's face anymore under the water, just the doctor's flapping life jacket, and *Bainbridge's life jacket is open*, Voort realizes.

The doctor must have unfastened it to reach his gun.

Voort brings his knee up in the water, into the rubber wet suit protecting Bainbridge's crotch, but the water makes him too slow, and the rubber shields the doctor from impact.

Voort cannot bend his fingers anymore. He pushes up, kicks hard, and manages to produce one last surge of motion, driving himself out of the water enough so his right hand comes free. It is half-frozen into a flat wedge, and remembering all those defense classes, he drives the outside of his hand into the doctor's exposed throat.

Instantly, the hands at his face drop away. Bainbridge's eyes bulge and he claws at his own throat. Voort hits him again. Bainbridge rolls in the water; they're caught by a surge of current, and as Bainbridge flails, his open life jacket slips free over his left shoulder, trailing. The doctor seems to realize only now that if he loses the other sleeve of the jacket he will go under all the way.

He forces out, half choking, '*I will not let you hurt Ian*!'

Voort hits him on the bridge of the nose, watches a dark splash of liquid erupt from his mouth. Bainbridge gags, uses both hands to pull at his face.

'*You must not hurt Ian!*'

But Voort rolls in the water, reaches down and hooks his hand under the shoulder hole of Bainbridge's life jacket, which is still attached to the doctor. He kicks at Bainbridge, pushing the body away and at the same time drawing the life jacket closer. It slips off Bainbridge's shoulder, leaving Voort with two life jackets.

Bainbridge flails and goes down.

The current divides now. Voort is in an eddy, near the kayak, floating in a circle as Bainbridge pops to the surface, in swifter current, though he's only a few feet away. Accelerating, the drowning man begins to be swept off.

Bainbridge cries, 'Help me!'

Then, in another voice, a higher, younger voice, the voice of another man, Voort hears the doctor cry, 'Greta! I love you!'

He is getting farther away.

'Karen!'

And the voice keeps changing. Now it is low, throaty, the voice of the man Voort met in the Chinese restaurant. And Voort realizes that, drowning, Bainbridge is trying to save himself by switching worlds again, switching lives again, with the other members of his club, the Broken Hearts Club, one last meeting, one last call to order in the river, as each personality understands, horrified, what is happening.

'Niana! I need you!'

And finally, from the dark, a gagging sound, as if he is used up, and there comes a last lingering cry, a boy's voice,

high-pitched, the sound of a scared ten-year-old, in the dark,
a plea to break a parent's heart.

'Mommeeee~'

The sound cuts off.

There is nothing after that.

For Voort, drifting, there is no more pain now. He bumps
against something, realizes it is the kayak. Camilla's eyes are
closed. He can see a pulse in her throat. It is better that she
has lost consciousness. Why suffer? He half pulls himself
onto the back of the kayak. He reaches for her, lays his
sopping glove on the back of her parka, as if to soothe her, as
if to say, 'It will all be all right.'

But it will not be all right. They are dying together, nudged
by the Hudson toward the Statue of Liberty, which looks
four times as huge from the surface of the sea. From all
around him he hears sounds of the harbor. The horn of a
barge. The motor of a tugboat. A bullhorn somewhere, as he
looks up, a brightness on his eyelids, into a bright, silver
moon.

He thinks, as the pain in his shoulder begins to subside, as
the cold reaches into the recesses of his body, shutting off his
nerve endings, anesthetizing him for the end: Well, at least I
won't be fired by the department. And at least I got him. He
won't hurt anyone else.

The bullhorn is crying, 'Con Man! We followed the
shooting! Con Man!'

Voort opens his eyes, blinded.

It's not the moon, but a spotlight.

How? he thinks. Who?

Mickie?

TWENTY-TWO

Eight days later Detective Second Grade Conrad Voort, suspended from the New York City Police Department, rises late in his four-million-dollar, Thirteenth Street town house, wraps himself in a big terry-cloth robe, and makes his way barefoot down to his enormous Dutch kitchen on the ground floor.

The morning *Wall Street Journal*, *Times*, and late edition *Post* are on the Dutch table. The oven is on warm, and he takes out freshly made plates of blueberry wheat pancakes, country sausages, scrambled eggs, and pours a hot mug of hazelnut coffee.

The Hudson Valley Voorts are in town for the weekend, using the second floor guest room. Sarah Voort always leaves him enormous breakfasts before she goes out to shop.

Humming, Voort scans the *Journal*, checking the Uruguay fund Mickie got him to invest in last month, then runs through the other papers, especially the small articles, searching for any mention of Bainbridge. One headline reads, MYSTERY SHRINK. WHO WAS HE? Another, OUTCRY OVER SUSPENDED HERO. A third says, COPS TO CITY: BAINBRIDGE SWEPT TO SEA!

Voort puts the dirty dishes in the dishwasher, takes a long

hot shower, and is dressing when the phone rings.

'Conrad! Billy Roth!' says the mellow, eager-to-please voice of the mayor's chief of staff. 'How's the hero, big guy?'

'Fine.'

'Feeling better?'

'All better, Billy.'

'Hey, about the suspension, Hizzoner just wants you to know, its just for a week or two, make the liberals happy, then reinstate you. I mean, considering that you never pulled the gun all the way out of your holster,' Billy says slowly – letting Voort know the way the story will be 'adjusted' – 'and considering how things turned out, nobody's making an issue.'

'Sure. I never pulled it out.'

'A little paid vacation, right?'

'Never hurts.'

'El Supremo was wondering if you felt like coming to breakfast at Gracie next Wednesday. You'll be reinstated by then, and there are a few guys, very nice guys we think you'll want to meet.'

'What's this going to cost me?'

'It's not a fund-raiser!'

'With you, Billy? No such thing.'

'I'm hurt, Voort. Whaddaya, not trust us? It's a law and order thing. Cranston, Melnick, Richards,' Billy says, naming some big money donors, real estate types who are tough on law and order issues, and probably angry over Voort's suspension. 'El Supremo wants to show 'em he's behind you all the way.'

'Billy, do me a favor. At least get some real food this time, not croissants and jelly.'

It's a sunny day outside. Voort puts on his dark brown cords, cordovan loafers, and a forest-green sweater of Scottish cashmere, which he picked up on a golfing vacation at St. Andrews last year. He takes the L.L. Bean zip-up jacket and emerges on the town house steps, into the sunlight. The day is dazzling, cold and beautiful. The block smells of wood fires.

Voort walks crosstown to NYU Medical Center. He takes the elevator to the fifth floor, Camilla's floor. When he enters her room, she's awake, propped up, talking to Kenny, who's looking fit and muscular in his tight jeans and blue turtleneck. There are fresh roses in a vase by her bedside. The dancer is talking low and gently to her, sitting beside the bed, and he gets up when he sees Voort and shakes his hand.

'Hell, Voort,' Kenny says with real emotion. 'Thank you for saving her. I guess I always knew it wouldn't be me, with her, in the end. I hope you have better luck than I did.'

'Thanks. How you feeling this morning, Cam?' Voort says as Kenny waves goodbye, a sad flip of his hand as he goes out the door.

'Fine.' Her cell phone is ringing, with calls from the office. They call her fifty times a day, even in the hospital. There's a problem with a show from Atlanta. Something about buying satellite time. Camilla snaps, into the phone, 'If they won't play ball, have Tucker cancel the fucking thing.'

Voort grins. She must be feeling better if she's back to talking like a stevedore.

'I was a little out of it when you tried to explain this to me Friday,' she tells him, 'but what I still can't figure out, and the newspapers don't really say, is how Mickie found us out there.'

Voort pulls up a chair next to Camilla, close enough to smell, over the odors of alcohol and Lysol, her perfume, her essence.

'He did it by leaving Bainbridge's house, which he technically wasn't supposed to do. He handed off the scene. See, when your car service called the department, complaining about me, he heard the order go out for me to return to headquarters. He knew I was heading for the boathouse, and he knew Bainbridge had targeted you.

'Mickie likes you, Camilla. He didn't want to take a chance on any kind of delay with our guys reaching the boathouse. So he called in a favor, reached a friend in the harbor section, drove crosstown, met a police launch at Seventy-ninth Street. He knew traffic was blocked, and he took the launch downtown.'

Camilla nods. 'And when he landed at the boathouse, it was empty.'

'Right. he finds the door open. The kayaks are gone. He sees the bullet on the floor. He figures I've gone after you, on the water.'

Camilla says, 'But how did he know which way to go?'

Voort shrugs. 'The police launch guys followed the current. Everything in the river was going in the same direction. Then they heard the gunshots. By then the mist had lifted and they saw us.'

'Pretty good partner,' Camilla says. 'That Mickie.'

'Loyal,' Voort says, looking into her eyes.

'Reliable,' she says, embarrassed.

'One hundred percent.'

They just gaze at each other. The room faces east, toward the East River, and over the bed he can see the spires of the Queensboro Bridge, and steam rising off the flat, green surface of the water. He sees Roosevelt Island, and the tram carrying passengers into the city. He sees a helicopter coming in from Kennedy Airport, toward the riverside landing pad. He hears her say, 'I'm sorry, Voort.'

'I know.'

'I guess I always knew Kenny had nothing to do with why I stopped being with you. The problem's me, Voort, plain old me. I'm not seeing him anymore, but I would be doing things for the wrong reasons if I went back to you now. I need time, alone, to figure things out.'

Voort says. 'It's all right.'

'Really?' She looks at him keenly, and says, with sad acceptance, 'But you're not waiting around.'

'Camilla, I fell in love with you. Whatever I do, it's not a strategy. It's just how I feel inside.'

She smiles. 'No cake and eating it too, huh?'

Voort leans down, kisses her on her forehead, which is still a little too warm. She is running a slight fever.

'Take care of yourself,' he says. 'Who can tell what will happen?'

Downstairs, Voort leaves the hospital and walks west, along Thirty-second Street.

There's no rush, no hurry. He'll take the Jaguar upstate this afternoon, for some skiing. One of the Voorts owns a lodge north of Albany, and always keeps a room for the family. He'll stay over the weekend, swap stories, eat well, and be back by Monday, when he has a feeling he'll be back at work.

Voort reaches Seventh Avenue and turns south, strolling into Greenwich Village. He stops at a florist and picks out a bunch of winter tulips. He has them wrapped, in crisp new paper, and takes them down to Sheridan Square.

The bank at West Fourth Street is busy when he enters, with a long line of customers waiting at the teller's window. Voort makes his way to the Customers Help counter and can see, behind that, in the rear of the bank, the manager, typing at her computer terminal.

Shari looks up and sees him. She has the nicest walk, he remembers, watching her approach. Today she's wearing another tailored business suit, gray with beige pinstripes, and dark blue high heels.

'I was so happy,' she says, eyeing the flowers, 'when I heard on the news you were all right.'

Something moves inside him. It isn't love, but it's alive, and it's not grief.

Voort holds out the flowers.

'To be honest, I have a way to go before I get over her,' he says, 'but if your offer is still open, how about that cup of coffee now?'

Cat and Mouse

James Patterson

Psychopath Gary Soneji is back – filled with hatred and obsessed with gaining revenge on detective Alex Cross. Soneji seems determined to go down in a blaze of glory and he wants Alex Cross to be there. Will this be the final showdown?

Two powerful and exciting thrillers packed into one, with the electrifying page-turning quality that is the hallmark of James Patterson's writing, CAT AND MOUSE is the most original and audacious of the internationally bestselling Alex Cross novels.

'Patterson's action-packed story keeps the pages flicking by' *The Sunday Times*

'Patterson, among the best novelists of crime stories ever, has reached his pinnacle' *USA Today*

'Packed with white-knuckle twists' *Daily Mail*

'Patterson has a way with plot twists that freshens the material and keeps the adrenalin level high' *Publishing News*

0 7472 5788 4

The Mercy Rule

John Lescroart

An old man suffering from the implacable advance of Alzheimer's is found dead, an empty morphine vial by his side: obviously suicide. Or did someone – a loving son, perhaps – help him die? Who would blame him?

But Graham Russo insists he had nothing to do with his father's death. A claim that, as more and more incriminating evidence come to light, even his lawyer, Dismas Hardy, finds increasingly hard to believe. But despite his unease about his engaging but unreliable client, Hardy knows there is no way he can abandon Russo when the politicians turn him into the pawn at the heart of the media issue of the year . . .

'The courtroom drama king' *Independent*

'High-class . . . first-rate' *Sunday Telegraph*

0 7472 5458 3

If you enjoyed this book here is a selection of other bestselling titles from Headline

CAT AND MOUSE	James Patterson	£5.99	☐
CLOSER	Kit Craig	£5.99	☐
WITHOUT PREJUDICE	Nicola Williams	£5.99	☐
CLOSE QUARTERS	Jeff Gulvin	£5.99	☐
INHERITANCE	Keith Baker	£5.99	☐
SERPENT'S TOOTH	Faye Kellerman	£5.99	☐
UNDONE	Michael Kimball	£5.99	☐
GUILT	John Lescroart	£5.99	☐
A DESPERATE SILENCE	Sarah Lovett	£5.99	☐
THE LIST	Steve Martini	£5.99	☐
FOOLPROOF	Dianne Pugh	£5.99	☐
DUE DILIGENCE	Grant Sutherland	£5.99	☐

Headline books are available at your local bookshop or newsagent. Alternatively, books can be ordered direct from the publisher. Just tick the titles you want and fill in the form below. Prices and availability subject to change without notice.

Buy four books from the selection above and get free postage and packaging and delivery within 48 hours. Just send a cheque or postal order made payable to Bookpoint Ltd to the value of the total cover price of the four books. Alternatively, if you wish to buy fewer than four books the following postage and packaging applies:

UK and BFPO £4.30 for one book; £6.30 for two books; £8.30 for three books.

Overseas and Eire: £4.80 for one book; £7.10 for 2 or 3 books (surface mail).

Please enclose a cheque or postal order made payable to *Bookpoint Limited*, and send to: Headline Publishing Ltd, 39 Milton Park, Abingdon, OXON OX14 4TD, UK.
Email Address: orders@bookpoint.co.uk

If you would prefer to pay by credit card, our call team would be delighted to take your order by telephone. Our direct line is 01235 400 414 (lines open 9.00 am–6.00 pm Monday to Saturday 24 hour message answering service). Alternatively you can send a fax on 01235 400 454.

Name ....

Address ....

....

....

If you would prefer to pay by credit card, please complete:
Please debit my Visa/Access/Diner's Card/American Express (delete as applicable) card number:

Signature .... Expiry Date..............